Balance

THE AMPED SERIES: BOOK ONE

M.J. Woods

This book is intended for a mature audience.

Balance
The Amped Series: Book One

Copyright ©2016 M.J. Woods

Cover design by M.J. Woods Books
Cover photo licensed by iStock ©piranka

www.mjwoodsbooks.com

First published by Dog Ear Publishing
4011 Vincennes Road
Indianapolis, IN 46268
www.dogearpublishing.net

ISBN 978-1-4575-5174-1

This is a work of fiction. Names, characters, places and incidents either are the product of the author's imagination or are used fictitiously, and any resemblance to actual persons, living or dead, businss establishments, events or locales is entirely coincidental. The publisher does not have any control over and does not assume any responsibility for author or third party websites or their content.

Printed in the United States of America

for my husband, for making so many dreams come true

thank you for living a love story with me

Acknowledgements

Saying "thank you" on one page of this book seems inadequate. This story would never have seen the light of day without the encouragement, love and support from the following beautiful souls.

To my editor extraordinaire, Cheryl Meany: Thank you for loving this work, for making it better, and for allowing me to realize I created something worth reading. "This is a thing!" I love you, woman!

To my first readers: Sharon, Christine, Lynn, Danielle, Jill, Claire, Nikki, Paula, Taylor, Erika, Sue G., Ashley, Cheryl, Kelly, Allyson, Melissa, Susan A., Barb, Mary & Sharon. The excitement you ladies have shared with me and with each other for these characters is contagious. Thank you for loving and investing in my "people" as much as I do.

To my parents, for their unyielding love and support, with a special thank you to my dad for giving me the gift of knowledge about the legal field for over twenty years. I would not be successful in anything without my two crazy-amazing parents to guide me. Loving you both, always.

To my children, someday you will (hopefully) understand why Mama got lost in her stories and asked for your patience when she needed to turn them into a book. Thank you for being patient, for being proud, and for giving me the time to create. You are polite and cool little ladies, and I can't wait to return the favor someday as I sit back and watch you follow your own dreams, whatever they may be.

To my best friend, my sister-by-choice, my "person", who is as much family to me as my family is: Jill, I love you most. (I said it here in a published work of fiction, so I win!)

To my family near and far (including my two brothers who have always looked out for their little sister like it was their job), I'm not me without each and every one of you. I'm so thankful to have a huge family to fall back on in this life. Thank you for your words of encouragement throughout this crazy ride!

Lastly to my husband, whom I have loved since before there was text messaging. You have encouraged me in everything I've ever done, no matter how crazy the idea. You helped me bring ideas from my brain to the page including one undeniably *hot* cover design. Thank you, babe. Laughing with you will always be my favorite thing to do.

Grazie.

~ M.J. Woods

1

Aidan

Summer 1989

In the room I share with my brother I pack my red backpack, the one with the broken zipper that mom put a safety pin on. I stuff in the peanut butter sandwich I made yesterday when no one was looking. I take three cookies that I hid in my dresser drawer, the ones Aunt Emma bakes at her farm and brings to us.

Every Friday night before Mom goes to work, Aunt Emma visits. We go to sleep listening to the sound of them talking and laughing or sometimes crying.

On Saturday mornings, we are alone. Mom has been at the hospital all night taking care of the sick people.

But Father is here today.

And he is angry.

I have not seen him in three sleeps. I keep track with chalk marks on the wood floor underneath my mattress.

Always three sleeps, and then he is back.

He is shouting that there is no bourbon. He is out of cigarettes. Mom is not here to cook anything.

"That bitch is never here to put food on the fucking table," he hollers. "No food and no fucking smokes and no goddamn booze."

He is mad.

Not grouchy mad, like Mom sometimes is.

The Scary Mad.

I do not want to stay here.

I think about Aunt Emma and Uncle Eli's farm to keep me not scared.

That is my favorite place to be. They have chickens and cows, and there are so many places to run and play and hide. Sometimes in spring I get to feed the new calves. That's the best. They have an old brown dog too. He loves to lick our hands after we eat cookies.

If the farm was close I would go there, but it is too far for my legs.

I can walk by the lake and follow the shoreline down to the fishing shack.

Because I don't want to be here.

Mom always says she does not know how I walk so far. She says it's a good mile. The first time I went there by myself she was mad.

Not mad like Father gets, but I got a good talking to that day.

Then one day she changed her mind. I can go there whenever I want now.

Especially when Father is the Scary Mad.

"As long as you're careful," she said.

"Don't end up with a fishhook in your eye," she said.

I will fish when I get there like I always do. Maybe I will catch some perch to cook so Father is not angry anymore.

First I have to wait until he falls asleep. I can sneak away then, right through the front door. I stay put, waiting to hear him stop yelling. He will sit in the chair soon. When he snores, it is safe.

Thaddeus is hiding under his bed with the flashlight Mom gave him, hugging his scruffy brown teddy.

I wish he would throw that teddy away. It is so old and dirty and embarrassing. He should grow up already. But Mom says he needs it.

Thaddeus can't come with me because Mom says no. Even if he wanted to, his legs could not carry him all the way like mine can. He's too little.

I peek under Thad's bed. He has the nice bed, the one with the mattress high off the floor. My bed is on the floor in the corner of our room.

My brother lays on his belly looking through a book, looking at the pictures.

He is only three. He can't read.

Mom says I could read when I was three. But Thad is different.

Not different because I am the big brother. And not *bad* different. Just different than me.

I hear the loud snoring through the crack in the door. It sounds like a big bear is sleeping in the living room. I put my backpack on my shoulder and whisper to Thad not to come out until Mom gets home.

She will be home soon, I remind him. She is always home in the morning on Saturdays.

I sneak past Father while he sleeps in the big chair, the one that Mom likes to sit in when he is gone. It's the only one big enough for Thad and me to sit next to her while she reads us stories.

I open the screen door and hope that it will not squeak, but it does.

Father does not wake up.

I trip over his big boots on the porch outside the door, and I crash to the floor.

"Boy!"

No.

"Boy! Is that you?"

No. Please no.

"Where you off to, boy?"

I hear him get up and come for me.

No. No. No.

The door squeaks again when he opens it.

"What you got there?" He stands over me in his bare feet and torn pants. His shirt is off.

It's hot today.

He smells like he always does.

Like sweat and smoke and beer.

I can see the tattoos on his arms. He has big arms, lots of muscles. The scariest picture is on his shoulder. A skull with red eyes.

I am lying on the porch floor.

He snatches my backpack out from under me.

He unzips it fast.

He is so mad.

He dumps it upside down and the food falls to the floor.

"You think you can hold out on your ole' man, boy? These are Emma's cookies." He puts a whole one in his mouth and smiles.

The scary smile.

No. No. No.

"Damn good, ain't they, boy?" He still has the scary look. "Best thing Eli did was marry your mama's sister. That woman knows her place."

I keep quiet, but he gets mad some more.

"I'll show you what you get for hoardin' food in my house." He is yelling in his scary voice. "That's my mouth you're stealing from, you little shit. You need a lesson 'bout respect."

He disappears into the house with the sandwich and the rest of the cookies.

I can get away if I hurry.

Maybe taking the food away was my lesson.

Maybe I am safe.

I look up the dirt driveway, thinking about where to go.

But the screen door squeaks again.

I did not hurry fast enough.

Father stands over me.

He takes off his belt.

No. No. No.

I don't get up. I don't run. It will be worse if I run now.

A man does not back down.

A man does not run.

A man takes it.

That's what Father always says.

He folds the belt in half and snaps it together. The crack makes me jump.

"What? You scared, boy?"

"No." My voice does not work very good.

"No what?"

"No, Father."

"Ain't no boy of mine gonna be a scared little shit. Now get up and be a man!"

I scramble to get to my feet, but I'm not fast enough for him. He yanks me by the shirt and drags me.

My sneakers skid across the planks of the floor. He is so strong.

He lets go and I face the wooden bench on the porch, the white one with the peeling paint. Mom makes us sit there to wait for church so we don't get dirty.

I lean my hands on the bench to take my punishment.

I shut my eyes tight as he pulls up my shirt.

I think about church and the beautiful sound of the choir.

I think about feeding the cows.

I think about Aunt Emma pulling cookies out of her great big white oven at the farmhouse.

And I count.

Thwack!

One.

Thwack!

Two.

I don't know how many I will get to. Sometimes I only get to five. Sometimes all the way to twenty.

Thwack!

Three.

I will not cry.

I can hear movement in the house.

No, Thad. Stay in the house.

I hope he can hear my mind.

Stay in there, Thad.

Do. Not. Come. Out.

I open one eye and look up. Thad is standing inside at the screen door. I see his teddy through the window. The sun shines on the brown fuzz.

"Father?"

No. No. No.

Do not interrupt. Go away, Thad! Go away!

I want to scream, but nothing comes out.

I do not feel the belt anymore. I only feel the sting on my back.

I turn around and Father is gone. He is nowhere.

I look through the screen door, through the window.

Thad is gone too.

I run as fast as I can over the rocky driveway, up the dirt path that leads away from our cabin and all the other cabins along this side of Mirror Lake, all the way up to the road.

Something seems different.

I am bigger than before, stronger.

The trees that line the dirt road seem smaller, the uphill path is just an incline.

I make it to the end, to a clearing beyond the trees, and then to the main road. The pavement is so hot it is releasing steam.

Thaddeus is in the road.

He is bigger too – but he is lying in the road next to his Lotus. The brand new one I bought for him when he turned twenty.

But I bought that in California. This is New York.

And it's all ruined now.

The grill is smashed in. The windshield has a gaping hole in it. Shattered glass is everywhere.

My brother isn't moving.

Something dark lies next to him.

I run to him, screaming for him, looking down at his body.

It doesn't look like my brother.

There is no life in his soft eyes.

The grin he always has is absent.

There is blood everywhere.

On his clothes, on his head.

In a pool next to him on the pavement.

Thaddeus!

I wake up screaming my dead brother's name.

Again.

This is the third time this week.

For a moment I'm thankful the recollections of childhood in my nightmares are actually the *less* violent ones.

I'm grateful the dream about the accident is the same as always, except for the setting.

This I can deal with.

Perception is everything.

But the sheets beneath me cost more than a half year's rent in that foul, dilapidated cabin I dreamt of and they are drenched with sweat.

This will not do. I cannot leave my housekeeper to deal with this.

I rub my hands over my face, trying to settle myself into reality, rising to strip the bed.

I'm in the present.

It's May.

May 2016.

Sunday.

I can launder the sheets before Mrs. Schmidt comes in tomorrow.

They need it anyway, after last night's inescapable bar-fly-fuck.

Fuck up, more like.

I groan aloud at my lack of discipline brought about by the stress of the last several days. I was not in my right mind.

It was a slip.

I drank one too many and lost control.

And I never lose control.

Not anymore.

Rhonda or Rachel (or whatever her name was) did not constitute some ideal fantasy lover, some celestial goddess that I just had to have. She was not the end-all, be-all woman of my dreams.

I know better than to think such a creature exists.

Truthfully, she hadn't even been a great lay.

She was pretty, sure. Blonde and cute with firm tits (thankfully real), and she was an insatiable flirt. She had a nice smile. Her navel flaunted a piercing between where her tank top ended and the waistband of her (short) shorts began.

She had fallen all over me, like women always do. Before I could even open my mouth to ask for a drink, I got the batting eyelashes, the stare-down like she would much rather devour me than listen to anything I had to say.

Like I've never been given that look before, honey.

She was just like the rest, happily unaware that appearances don't mean shit when you carry internal scars like mine.

Normally this attention would be enough to turn me in the opposite direction, fleeing the scene like a wanted criminal. I'm long past consuming the attention of every woman that passes by me giving me that look.

I wasn't looking for some inflation to my ego.

But then she sang karaoke from behind the bar while she waited on customers. She didn't sing well, really. Just that she was brave enough to do it had me taking notice.

Music always helped me take notice.

And the song she chose – "You're So Vain" by Carly Simon.

Unexpected and clever choice. She directed it at me, though we'd never even met.

I sipped a whiskey, then another, let her chat me up. I answered questions like where am I from and what am I doing in a place like this.

It was a change of pace for me. No one ever asked me that in California. Everyone knew who I was there, and I didn't frequent places 'like this'.

Renee (or was it Rita?) didn't seem like a complete dolt, but she didn't come across as intellectual either. There were no supremely interesting conversations to be had with this one.

She admitted she wasn't especially good at being a college student. Her Stanton University classes were done for the year. Bartending would pay the rent, which was news to me. When I was at Cal Tech as an undergrad over ten years ago, bartenders were typically male.

Chalk one up for feminism, I guess.

As a barmaid she could afford to pay for a summer of freedom before her senior year and escape going home to mommy and daddy in…where was it again?

Oh yeah. Pennsylvania.

Last night with Robin was an exception to my learned distaste for the chase. (That was it, *Robin*.)

Between the stress of my past and present colliding, the eventual one-too-many shots she poured, and my new surroundings (where I can blend in semi-unnoticed), she piqued my interest enough that I entertained her flirtations.

It didn't hurt her cause that she was the antithesis of Stella Ireland.

They were nothing alike.

Yeah, this one had that in spades.

Blonde, not raven haired. Sweet, not a sociopathic bitch.

And she didn't seem the type to wield her influence – whether that influence be feminine wiles or some other, more powerful form – to manipulate a man. To twist him into doing whatever the fuck she wanted him to do on her whim, only for the sake of her entertainment.

Yes. The "anti-Stella" was exactly the girl I needed in that moment.

I use the thought to resolve that it wasn't so bad, what I did last night.

When her early shift waiting on weary businessmen at The Wall ended, I brought the lady back here. I got off, she got off (not in that order because I am, first and foremost, a gentleman), and she got the consolation prize of a ride home in the Lincoln with Byron.

After spending hours in a dark barroom in this small city in Central New York with men twice her age, she had to rate the evening I'd given her in the top five of her most memorable.

My man Byron took her home at midnight. No walk of shame for my never-to-be-seen-again woman of the evening. She deserved better for her willingness to participate in my distraction and agree to my terms.

She definitely wasn't a law student at the University. She was too young and before coming up (or coming at all), she signed the non-disclosure after barely glancing through it.

I saw her eyes bug out once she realized just who it was she was agreeing to spend the night with, mumbling something about thinking I looked familiar. But then she handed over her phone to Byron, as required. She let me do whatever I wanted to her, and though it was nothing out of the ordinary – no bondage or sadomasochism, for Chrissakes – she thoroughly enjoyed it. I had her screaming in less than twenty minutes and multiple times after that.

Just like the long parade of women that had come before Stella.

My techniques have never failed to disappoint the opposite sex, at least not since I'd schooled myself. A man can only go so far on instincts and libido. I'd done my research over the years, learned what women liked and didn't. Figured out that none of them were the same, yet all of them were same – they all needed to be convinced to get out of their own way (or more importantly, out of their own heads) to enjoy themselves.

The hidden key to every one of them was different, the teeth of each carved in a diverse intricacy to unlock a different door.

Yet they all possessed that hidden key.

And once you got through the door, there it was waiting for you. That sacred place, glowing brighter than a bare bulb in a black room.

A place above all, superior to Heaven or Earth. Worth Herculean efforts to unlock.

In that moment when a woman unravels enough to let you in and completely open herself to you, she is at your mercy in every sense of the word.

I found it one of the most exquisite sights to behold.

I'd experimented with enough women, not discriminating in any particular way.

I never had a type.

Before Stella, I was careful about the women I chose, but not in the sense of her background or specific appearance. Not because of the size of her ass or whether her hair was blonde or red, whether her skin was the color of melted caramel or dotted with enough freckles to make a constellation if you connected them in ink.

Variety had always been a well-stocked spice in my sex life.

Until I got tired of the one-hundred-percent-predictable outcome that variety led to.

At least in part, the reason I had been able to prove myself so capable with women was the result of my experience with varied, glorious specimens of them throughout my twenties.

But eventually it just got old, always leading to some sort of complication.

If a woman of the hour turned into a woman of the month (or longer), it would turn out she was after my money or my connections, or she had a hang up of some sort that would change my perception of her from appealing to repulsive.

Or even more terrifying, she'd want full-blown intimacy.

Why wouldn't I let her in? Why didn't I want her company longer than a few hours at a time?

Didn't I want a commitment sooner or later? A family someday? I wasn't getting any younger (now chasing down thirty-five as my next milestone birthday).

I really shouldn't lose sight of that, one girl had said.

Fuck no and there's the door. Thanks anyway, Princess.

All of this hassle was precisely why I thought Stella Ireland would have been my emancipator from a life of same-old, same-old.

I could concentrate on my business dealings and my philanthropic endeavor that would take everything I had to birth it into this world.

As it turned out, I was unmistakably (and possibly irrevocably) wrong.

Since figuring out just how wrong, I put an end to my arrangement with Stella and finally got my shit together to come back to New York to do what I had been planning for years. Last night had been my first return to that same-old, same-old parade.

Just as I remembered, it wasn't satisfying beyond provisional entertainment.

With Robin I wrapped it, like I always do, as much as I hated doing it. I never trust the words "I'm on the pill". *Ever.* That may be true, but I have no idea if you're *clean*, darling.

You don't get the privilege of the real feel.

After I'd pleasured her to the point of fever pitch until she could take no more, I politely saw her out. Home she went, without so much as a 'Hey stud, can I get your number?' (though she did hint that her next shift at The Wall would be Tuesday). Not noteworthy to me, as I'd never step foot in that pub again.

She left before one day turned into the next, with enough time for me to sleep off one too many.

And before the dreaming began.

My nightmares have been hindering my rest since I returned to New York. I've been in the city of Stanton for almost a month.

I sleep less here, dream more.

Maybe coming back here was a mistake.

Coward.

I shudder, hearing the bastard's voice in my head.

Fuck you. I do not run. You're the coward.

I head for my closet intending to deposit the sheets into a clothes hamper, but I don't have one yet. The rest of the household items I requested won't be delivered until tomorrow when Mrs. Schmidt will be here to set everything up the way I like it. Only the major furnishings are here now.

My suits were ordered from Manhattan and arrived when I did. The cedar shelving was just added to yesterday with clothing for a spring warm up.

I need clothes for all seasons here with Central New York weather being so fucking unpredictable. I'm not used to it after being in California so long.

Everything in my loft is still fresh and new. I inhale, letting the smells ground me, pushing away my recall of the scent of stale tobacco and cheap beer from my nightmares.

Construction here only finished two months ago, and it took four weeks more to get the details just right. The work for the HVAC updates was a bitch in this old relic of a building (though the historical charm was a draw for me), and even without the hoops the city had me jumping through for the required permits, this alone put the project behind schedule. I was on a first-name basis with the electrician. Painters came back three times to fix mistakes.

I supervised everything from the West Coast, which made for a challenge. After two years of construction (and once I showed up on-site), a never-ending punch-list had been completed with greater speed and, at my insistence, to perfection.

Now the real work could begin.

I toss the sheets on the floor and head for the bathroom to do the necessary, then splash some cold water on my face. I catch a glimpse of my eyes in the mirror. They are tired, yet steely enough to cut through the reflection. The blue irises shake me alert. I pound a fist to my chest in an effort to push me past the edge of emotion and full on into action.

Suck it up, Pierce.

It's five a.m.

Sunday or not, I'm late.

I dress in shorts and a t-shirt and throw on my running shoes. I grab my phone off the charger at my bedside and find some driving music to motivate me during my usual eight miles through the city streets where I run and run and run.

In the dark, in a city where no one knows me, I run.

"Wake Me Up" by Avicii blares in my ears.

I pass by bums asleep under the bus stop canopy or look up at the occasional window lit by an early riser.

But no one sees me.

I run not to escape, but to chase down demons, using the darkness to see myself.

To bring me back to the surface.

To obliterate haunting memories and remember who the fuck I am.

I am Aidan Michael Pierce.

And I am no fucking coward.

2

Alexis

January 2015

My husband is dead.

It's a frigid Monday in January. I'm wishing I could stay home, sheltered in my bed, but I have to get up.

The dog needs to be let out. I have to work because law school loans don't pay themselves off.

And, oh by the way, that shit accrues astronomical interest.

I hate that the rat race is my only current link to sanity. Start work at seven and come home ten hours later, driving in the dark on every commute. My life seems like a trip through a black hole set on repeat. Maybe somewhere in there, I'd eat. I could actually get behind that idea right now.

Wait. I'm hungry?!

It's a relished thought, since I've spent my first month as a young widow eating infrequently and sleeping soundly even less.

Ben's death was news on local radio and television stations for the first week after I lost him. He was a reporter for Stanton City Channel Eight, and viewers numbering in the thousands watched him on their flat screens daily.

Every sign-off ended with Ben's beautiful smile and his anchor-worthy voice announcing that he was broadcasting live from various locations. He was just starting out there, but he had been chosen to sit behind the desk as soon as the current anchor retired.

Losing him has been a shock to his colleagues and to the people of Mirror Lake where we live.

And to me.

"I'm sorry, Mrs. Clayton," the doctor had said. "We did all we could. It was just too late."

His words sounded rehearsed, but he didn't owe me any informality. He didn't know me, which would have been clear to anyone that did.

I don't go by "Mrs. Clayton".

Ever.

It didn't occur to me to ask the doctor to use my maiden name, as I usually did when meeting someone. The words that hung over me like a dark cloud were "too late".

At four o'clock in the afternoon on the day before Christmas Eve, I sat on the edge of a plastic chair at St. Luke's Hospital when I should have been at work.

My feet were restless, knees bouncing in anticipation of that conversation. I remember looking down at the orthopedic shoes peeking out from Dr. Newman's blue scrubs.

But I was not sobbing or screaming in protest.

Just staring.

I did not look the part of a freshly made widow overcome by grief. I didn't bawl like an actress in an emergency room drama.

Ben was gone. I knew it was true, but I just couldn't react the right way. There wasn't much to do or say about it. Husbands die. Shit happens.

Now, a month after Ben's death, my head is still stuck in that moment.

I should have cried or said something profound. Anything to let Dr. Newman or anyone standing within earshot know, without question, that I was devastated.

No one told me that my initial reaction was wrong, but I can't shake that it didn't *feel* right. If I could just fix that moment, maybe I could be okay. Or at least better.

Our little town was a flurry of mourners for a solid week after Christmas. Some flocked to our door with casseroles and condolences. Canadian folks who grew up with Benjamin Clayton crossed the border, making the hour-and-a-half trek to our Central New York suburb to pay their respects. They meandered around the community like tourists, taking selfies on the local ski slopes or at the diner having an American breakfast.

They spoke softly when they talked to me, as if I was suddenly too delicate to hear loud conversation. Sometimes I felt a hand on my shoulder or someone holding my hand in theirs while they babbled on. I couldn't seem to look anyone in the eye.

People who knew him from work or college (and always knew him as *my* Ben) came for the funeral.

"I'm so sorry," they said. "It will take time, but you will get through this. You'll be okay." Or my least favorite, "You're so young, you will overcome this. You've got your whole life ahead of you!"

Their words made them feel better, regardless of how inconsequential they might be for me. I let them go on, nod, act polite.

I know how to put on a façade better than any of them.

Their future is not a big question mark. Their twenty-eight year-old husband is not buried after his body gave up on him far too early. He had his whole life ahead of him too. Just a short month ago he was young and ambitious, just like me.

Nothing is *okay*, I think when I see these people. My husband is dead and this lake community is an over-priced housing development built on a glorified swamp.

Life is a big bag of *suck*.

Ben's parents and sister went back to Ontario the week after he died. They volunteered to help with anything I might need. His sister Pam even offered to stay an extra few days, but I declined. I was glad to get our house back to myself.

Wait. *Our* house? *My* house? I don't know how to refer to it anymore. It's just me and the damn dog.

Dr. Newman called on Friday to report that the autopsy results had come in. A clot in the brain, he said. Ben likely felt no pain. He was gone before he knew anything was happening.

"Nothing we could have foreseen, Mrs. Clayton. Sometimes our bodies just don't serve us as we'd like," he said.

I still didn't correct him, telling him to call me Alexis Greene. What was the point? It was case-closed for him. Put that little manila folder away, Doc. Nothing more to do here.

Ben died playing racquetball at the Stanton City Gym, and I'm glad that it didn't happen in our home.

How cold is that?

I shudder at my abrasiveness. Or maybe it's the January chill, seeping in from the banks of snow outside.

You're just pissed. Suck it up, buttercup.

Surely I'll need to start seeing a shrink.

I need to get rid of the inner monologue I can't seem to turn off.

I need to get through this jumbled mess of feelings.

I need to keep myself from driving to Channel Eight to give a certain curvy blonde reporter a roundhouse kick to her jaw.

At Ben's funeral, Melanie Adams had feigned ignorance that Ben even *had* a wife. She was a notorious flirt with a gazillion watt smile and she had been directing it (along with her other body parts) at Ben since he'd started reporting for Channel Eight.

However naïve she believed me to be, I knew a girl like her would certainly have taken note of Ben's wedding band. Not to mention we'd met at the television station before where he had introduced me as his wife. *Twice.*

Yet that was behind me. No reason to care about some woman that might want to lay claim to Ben. I'd never felt the need to be jealous about Ben and other women, but more importantly he no longer breathed the same air we did. Her flirtations and intentions were moot.

I'm capable of suppressing my impulse to kick Melanie Adams in the teeth, but I still feel the urge to talk to someone. Sort through my fog. Figure out what to do next.

I fear walking out my front door for lack of direction, wondering what people will say about Ben Clayton's widow and what she might do.

Will she fall apart? How will she carry on?

When it comes to confidantes, few people come to mind. It doesn't help my cause that two of them are dead.

My father, Albert Greene, died three years ago. Even a visit to his gravesite for my usual one-sided chat doesn't seem therapeutic enough.

The other person would have been my husband of six years. After meeting him my freshman year of college, I found a best friend in Ben. He was my go-to for everything. Without him, I wouldn't have made it through the grief of my dad's passing. Graduating law school last spring, passing the State Bar Exam – all of it would have been an unattainable goal without him.

Hell, even getting dressed was easier with him at my side.

What would I do now? I had no secrets to keep anymore and no one to keep them with. Nothing and no one to guard against.

I could keep on the same. I could work my boring job in Falcon Lake. The firm of Martin & Reynolds had big fish to reel in, and I could go on forever as an underling, riding the coattails of the named partners and their high-paying clientele.

I could keep living in a vanilla house on a quiet street in the same little town I grew up in.

Alone.

Or I could just give up.

Unplug the alarm clock. Let my cell phone battery die. Eliminate contact with the outside world altogether and stay in bed. Stop worrying about working or shaving or showering or eating.

Stop everything.

Just *stop*.

What did it matter when either scenario left me alone?

It doesn't. Just stay here, under the covers, and shut the world out.

I catch a glimpse of future me.

Grossly overweight, a doe-eyed girl with tangled brown hair looking a complete wreck. She would need to grease the doorways just so she could pass through them, except that she can't free herself from the mountains of empty gelato containers and piles of collection notices that surround her in the first place.

I shudder again, goosebumps rising on my skin.

There is only one person I can talk to about Ben openly and about the fact that I might be totally and completely losing it.

I get up and pad downstairs to the kitchen in my unflattering night-gown and slippers, Huck the Bernese Mountain dog lumbering along at my heels. It's only seven a.m. but I reach for a bag of cookies and fire up my coffee maker.

I haven't added fifty pounds to my usual one-thirty-five just yet, but I promise myself I'll eat better tomorrow.

Tomorrow, there will be no dessert for breakfast.

I take my cell off the charger and scroll through the contacts.

No, not my half-sister Jill. We're not that close. She was here for the funeral and left the next day muttering about her too-busy life with her part-time catering business and full-time mommy-hood somewhere in the Arizona desert.

It's not our mother's number I'm scrolling to find either. The one in my contact list probably doesn't even work anymore. I can't remember where she landed last or whom she had landed under.

Marco in Florida? Johnny in Vegas?

Who cares? Moving on.

I find my only option, the last entry of the list. I press Charlie Young and wait with a mouthful of cookie as the phone dials. He's probably sleeping in his tiny apartment some three and a half odd hours south in Manhattan. I expect to get voicemail as I roll my eyes at my pathetic self, sinking to the floor on my ever-growing ass.

He answers immediately, his voice full of concern.

"Lex? You okay?"

"Yes, Charlie. I…" Suddenly I feel like a complete whimp.

Why are you bothering this poor guy?

"Lex. Please. What is it? What can I do?" He thinks I'm in trouble, and now I can add guilt to the jumble of feelings. My mental to-do list grows as I add 'call shrink'.

"I'm okay, really. I'm sorry to bother you. It's just…I need to, you know, talk to someone, I guess."

There's a brief pause. "Girl, you know I'm coming. Call in to work. Get a shower and fire up Netflix. I'm coming."

Tears roll as I feel something ease inside me.

Exhaustion remains, sadness raw and real.

But I am also lighter, saved.

Charlie is coming.

"I trust you already got the gelato," he says. I can hear the smile in his voice.

"Check," I say through tears.

"I'll be there soon, noon at the latest," he promises.

I thank him and disconnect, sobbing and hugging the dog while he licks crumbs off my lap.

I thank my angels – my dad and Ben. I thank God. And my lucky stars. And what-the-fuck-ever applies for this guy who is coming to my rescue when I just can't do it alone.

Thank heaven for Charlie.

May 2016

I'm down by the lake, and I can hear the birds singing themselves sense-less, waking the neighborhood. It's just past dawn. I've decided to go for a swim off the community dock, even though it's only May.

May 2016, I think.

The water feels warm as I dive in. I come up for air, standing in shoulder deep water, my feet dug into the sandy bottom.

Something is missing.

Ben?

No.

Well, yes.

Ben is not with me, but this time I know that already. Know it as fact. He's been gone well over a year now.

Something else is missing. I swirl my hands through the murky water as I stare at the opposite shoreline about a half mile away. I feel my thighs, my stomach, and then my exposed breasts. There's no fabric between them and the flow of the water.

Where the hell is my bikini top?

I turn to charge for the dock and run, most literally, into my heavenly new neighbor, Jackson Dean.

"I'm so sorry. I…my suit…" I trail off. Suddenly I forget why the hell I care that I'm half naked in front of this six foot wall of tan, lean muscle that stands very, very close to me.

And now it seems like this is exactly what I'm here for.

He says nothing, grabs me at the nape of my neck with his right hand. It's a strong grip but his hand is soft. He skims my hip and reaches around my back with the other hand. My pulse quickens, my breathing is halted and full of something.

I think it's desire or maybe even lust.

I don't recognize it.

But I am completely overtaken.

He's closed the inches of distance between us. I'm in his arms now and his lips are all over me, from my closed eyelids to my naked shoulders.

Our tongues finally meet. He wants it too. His hands are on me, fondling beneath the water.

I open my eyes and look past him at the mist rising off the lake, then close my eyes again, tighter now. He lifts my legs, wrapping them around his waist.

Whoa! I'm without bottoms too?

But he is wearing trunks. It seems unfair.

I feel his hand reach around my backside, and his fingers find a thrilling place I had forgotten existed. His clothing be damned. We've found another way.

I'm writhing now, heading straight for the end of a tunnel, toward my goal of satiation. I'm going to get there this time.

Sweet climax is close, so close.

I'm distracted by pain. It's excruciating.

But I was so close!

It's my neck that aches. I'm losing the moment.

I struggle to get back to a very real dream.

Back to the fabulous fingers of Mr. Dean.

But I can't ignore the pain anymore.

I'm startled awake and realize the agony in my neck is the only real thing about my almost-wet-dream.

At six a.m., I'm sitting in my front porch swing all slumped to one side. My feet are curled beneath me, my head kinked in a tense hold against my shoulder.

My three-bedroom house is still dark in the shadows behind me, save the light over the kitchen stove and the digital blue read out on my coffee maker.

This is per my usual lately. Every morning in May on the quiet street in Central New York where I live, even if it rains.

As with several other mornings the last few weeks, I've been in a complete daze as I sit and sip my coffee, then inevitably fall asleep fantasizing about another woman's husband.

I'm out here under the pretense of watching the sun rise, which happens to occur over my neighbor's house.

Not over my northerly neighbor's house, which belongs to Mr. Dingham. He's an ancient man, describing himself as older than dirt. I'd agree and add that he has all the charm of a bee sting.

The sun doesn't rise from the direction of the Parkers' house either. The house at the crown of the cul-de-sac has a white picket fence and direct access to the lake. The Parkers shop for whole foods on the weekends and drive a fleet of hybrid vehicles.

Instead, the sun comes up directly across the street, over what used to be the Allens' house and now belongs to the Deans. They closed on the large contemporary three weeks ago. Their eight-year-old daughter Emma will have the summer to acquaint herself with Mirror Lake before starting at a new school.

This is the kind of dirt the local grapevine lives to pass on, especially to me as I'm always the last to know.

But this time I already had the dirt.

I was the Allens' lawyer when they sold their house and took off to re-tire in Florida. The memory of the closing and meeting Mr. Jackson Dean swam (semi-unwelcome) through my head ever since.

It was a shock to my system, feeling like this. My dreams screamed as much.

Maybe these urges are rampant because I haven't met his wife yet. She was delayed at their home in North Carolina, packing and staying behind with their daughter.

It must be easier to stop fantasizing about a married man after you've met his wife.

Still, it was no wonder I wasn't rational. I could not resist a Southern gentleman that also happened to be a dirty-blond haired and quite exemplary version of the male form.

Once I'd met his wife, I'd stop fantasizing about these crazy chance encounters. I was sure of it.

I'm derailed from thoughts of my fantasy affair by Mrs. Parker. She's power-walking by my mailbox. Huck barks his fool head off by way of alarm, which is likely what woke me up.

The *woof* of a one hundred pound Bernese Mountain dog might have scared a stranger, but the residents of Peaceful Drive know Huck is a gentle giant. Mrs. Parker is unfazed as she struts by. I'm irritated at her perky stride, her presence causing me to abandon my dream moments too soon.

I wave anyway as she zooms by, elbows flailing. Her fluorescent yellow earbuds match her runner's vest. She waves back shouting a too-loud hello. Huck stretches and lumbers across the wide plank floor, leaning into me for some love as Berners tend to do. My cell rings through the open window behind me.

I can think of only one or two people who would call me at the crack of dawn.

I head into my study, the dog following. The display on my smart phone confirms my hunch.

It's my saving grace.

My friend, my assistant, and sometimes fashion advisor, Charlie.

Anyone with a pulse can tell he's gay as soon as they speak to him, which I love that he makes no apologies for. With smooth skin the color of a mocha latte and a body that's a gorgeous hybrid of pro-athlete and male model, Charlie has gay men (and some determined, clueless women) fawning over him wherever he goes.

He looks like he could knock you over just by bumping into you, but his stature is deceiving. He is the most laid-back guy I know. Faced with conflict, Charlie would always be the first to take the high road.

His brown eyes are beautiful, sincere, and able to throw a glance to cut through bullshit when required. At times, he can be too smart for his own good.

And I consider myself lucky to have him in my life, even when he calls me far too fucking early.

"Yeah, Charlie. Morning," I say. I don't hide irritation behind my words. This call is not coming in without necessity. Something for my multi-thousand-dollar deal has probably come undone at the last minute. "Is it the Myers deal? What's happened?"

"No, we're clear there," he says, immediately relieving me. I know he's nervous about today too. "It's just a minor thing. Leeds to Halstead sale. I've just been over the docs and there's a signature missing."

"That closing is happening at nine-thirty." The ounce of patience I have vanishes. "What the hell, Charlie? I thought he signed with Claudia yesterday." I'm practically shouting now. But I know what's happened, and I'm shouting at the wrong person.

Charlie is explaining away Claudia's oversight hurriedly with random excuses. I'm irked that he's championing the blonde nineteen-year-old ditz that is my receptionist.

But I'm only half listening, as out my office windows I glimpse a shirt-less Jackson Dean taking out the trash.

Shit! It's Friday. Trash day.

"All right, Charlie. I get it. Let's forget the how and why of Claudia's latest screw up. We just need to get the missing signature from Leeds before nine a.m. Call him on his cell. He should be at the diner. Meet him there and get it taken care of. And Charlie?"

"Yes?" He's tentative, waiting for the other shoe to drop.

"I'm going to fire her ass. Soon."

"No. Please, Lex. I'll talk to her. She needs us. Let's give her one more chance."

I'm silent. Half of me is indifferent to Charlie's plea, the other half too distracted by Jackson Dean. I ogle him sauntering back to the garage to fetch his recycling. He's sporting only cut-off jeans and a tan.

Yowsah.

"Whatever," I finally mutter. "See you at the office in an hour." I disconnect and sigh. Mr. Dean has retreated into his house.

So much for naughty neighbors, I think to myself.

And I mean me. I'm the naughty one.

I'm appalled at myself.

My annoying subconscious signs the controls back over to rational Ms. Alexis M. Greene, attorney and sometimes grieving widow.

The trash is out. The dog is confined to his quarters in the cool, finished basement (complete with his own couch and tv).

Upstairs, I discard my too-big, black yoga pants and matching tank top in the hamper, congratulating myself for losing the twenty pounds I gained when Ben died. I couldn't tally the number of mindless hours I'd spent on the treadmill for the last few winter months.

I shower, contemplating the indecent thoughts that have been plaguing me lately.

I've been a widow for less than two years. I shouldn't be craving another man, should I? Especially not a man that belongs to someone else.

Shouldn't I still be wearing black and sulking about? Lighting candles in a church, praying for my deceased husband? It shouldn't matter that I never went to church for any reason, save the occasional wedding or funeral. Or that my marriage to Ben Clayton was one of varied conveniences and quite the unique arrangement.

It shouldn't matter that we didn't share a bed, or a child, or even a bathroom. It should only matter that I was committed to him, in sickness and health, for as long as we both *should have* lived.

I turn in front of the mirror in my small walk-in closet, wondering what other people might think to look at me.

Five foot seven, dressed in a black pantsuit, I look older than my twenty-nine years. Maybe it's the bags under my eyes that aren't yet doused in concealer. Or my stuffy looking suit, that is also slightly oversized now. I look like a spinster, a crazy cat lady that might do your taxes on evenings and weekends.

Or a schoolmarm.

I'm not sure which is worse.

My brown hair is pin straight and in need of a cut. I whip it up into a plastic clip, and it almost resembles a bun to complete the schoolmarm look. Oh well. I prefer hair out of my face while I work.

I'm surveying all of my sensible shoes, which my Grandma Alice always told me I could never have too many of. Sensuous thoughts of Mr. Dean creep back in, all muscles and tan and…*yowsah*.

I swap the sensible pumps in my hand for a pair of black high *high* heels that Charlie helped me pick out. I've never worn them more than the few minutes in the store, just to see if I could walk in them without heading to the floor ass-over-tea-kettle. I'd passed that test, but I felt too conspicuous in them, too 'hey-everyone-look-at-my-slut-shoes'.

So in the closet they remained.

Until now.

I ditch the suit for a black pencil skirt that falls just above my knee and keep the white button-down shirt. The shorter sleeves will be welcome on this warmer-than-usual May day. A couple buttons have somehow come undone at the top, showing off just a peek of the girls. I slip into the heels and turn around to look in the mirror, surprised at my own reflection.

This is the best I've looked in months. Except for the careless hair, the outfit is a win.

In my head I'm apologizing to my grandmother, to my father, to Ben as I put on make-up.

Guilt is taking over, as sensible has always been expected of me. Conservative might as well replace my given middle name.

And this outfit is more sophisticated sex kitten than drowning-in-sorrow professional widow.

"Sorry, everyone," I mutter, as if apologizing to ghosts out loud will be more sincere. "But I'm landing the deal of the century today. And *I* am not dead yet."

3

Aidan

By Friday, I am better rested. Even more than that, I'm driven. Focused.

Everything in the loft is in place. Byron is on call as usual for whatever I need. My personal assistant Samira arrives today, along with the rest of the staff I've assigned for my new endeavor. I had IT in Wednesday to finish outfitting the office downstairs with computers and required security. I could have done it myself ten times faster, but I had to delegate and maintain hope the firm I hired is not incompetent.

I have limited patience for the workings of this smaller city. Nothing seems to happen here quite as efficiently as I'm used to, but I push that aside. Too much is riding on the launch of Pierce Philanthropy Group, on what I have in mind for Mirror Lake. My attention needs to be on the bigger details.

This morning I will return to the small lake town where I lived as a boy. I have to meet with the town's supervisor to discuss the details about what I'm proposing.

I will see my uncle – my deceased Aunt Emma's husband, Eli Myers – for the first time in twenty-five years.

Then I'm heading the thirty miles back north to Stanton to attend a lunch meeting with the Lake County Bar Association at the Sheridan Hotel.

I need to get the legal community on board for this. They will be an asset and help me spread the message on to the law students of the community when I'm ready for that. There are two law schools within Lake County and if anyone can help my cause, it will be the students and professionals in this field.

I'd rather be propelling all this from behind the scenes, but I can do the public speaking thing in my sleep. Address the crowd, make them laugh, show them my strengths, ask for what I want, then get it.

I always get it.

After all, what I'm proposing is mutually beneficial. I might have assets that rival royalty or bigoted billionaires that want to take over the world, but I'm *not* an asshole.

I'm for the greater good. Always for the greater good.

Of course after this meeting, and the one I had with the Mayor of the City of Stanton last week, my anonymity around here will be disappearing. The local press will show up at the meeting today as I've asked them to and word will get out.

It's certainly easier to blend in here than in L.A., but Manhattan is a short flight away on the jet if I really need to escape the resulting attention.

In L.A. the Pierce name is prominent, but it's more than that. The quality of the air, the quality of the people there (and the sheer amount of them) seem to be incompatible with the depths of me.

I can still blend in for a while here or in the small suburbs outlying the city. The upstanding people here keep to themselves. They're salt of the earth. Honest. Hard-working.

Just like my mother.

My nightmares play in my mind on recall, but I snap myself back to present. In reality, they have subsided in the last few days.

I know going back to Mirror Lake might be a trigger, so I've asked Samira to add a meeting with Dr. Mason to my calendar for seven o'clock tonight. I'll be the last session of his day in California, via Skype.

I hope that will be enough to set me back on course with what I'm doing here in the first place.

Slay the demons I started fighting the day I left.

Strengthen the roots of the community I came from, as I've wanted to do since I sold my first company twelve years ago.

My first brainchild, my first sacrifice in the name of the greater good.

I can only hope.

Eli Myers looks nothing like I remember.

  Standing up straight the man would be as tall as I am. But his posture is stooped even as he sits. His face is weather-beaten. A lifetime of hard work has rendered him a slighter man. He appears far more aged than he might otherwise have been in the twenty-five years since I saw him last.

His hair is grayed to silver, poking out from beneath his green John Deere hat in wiry tufts. Yet his eyes are still kind. Even though his expression holds no smile, his sincerity and good character are palpable.

We sit at his kitchen table with two mugs of lukewarm coffee discussing what I first proposed to him by phone three months ago. As much as I've tried to ignore our surroundings in a struggle to keep my memories at bay, I can't help but take in the details of one of the few places I felt safe as a child.

Aunt Emma's antique white oven has been replaced by a smaller, modern one. Otherwise, the room feels the same as it did when I was a boy. Same oak cabinets in the large kitchen, same linoleum floors underfoot. Same window overlooking the fields, though the window seems much smaller now than it did then.

Even the yellow, rotary dial wall phone is unmoved, affixed to the side of the cupboard that once held my aunt's favorite tea.

"I'm sure thankful for you to think of me, Mr. Pierce," Eli says.

I feel out of place sitting across from him in my suit. He wears jeans and a t-shirt that was likely white once, however briefly. I would have dressed down to make him (or hell, to make both of us) more comfortable, but I have to get back to Stanton for the luncheon in less than an hour.

"Please, call me Aidan," I say.

"Sure, son, sure," he says. "Listen, I know what yer offerin' is good money. I believe in what you wanna do here. But, like I told ya, I'm already tangled up in this mess with this company. I can't put a year's worth of my lawyer's hard work down the toilet just for a big pile of dollars I can't spend in the rest of my lifetime."

This is not the way I expected this conversation to go. He's right; I've offered him more cash than he'll ever live to spend. But my intentions for buying him out are noble. I thought a man of his character would easily be swayed by my good intentions more than the money.

"I understand, Mr. Myers." I don't know what else to call him. Calling him Uncle Eli would seem odd after years without contact, yet I want him to know I respect him. "Would you like to know more about the project? I've just come from meeting with the town supervisor. Mr. Aberdeen assures me the town is behind this one hundred percent. And it's going to mean so much more for Mirror Lake. Investments in the school and upgrading amenities for the whole town."

He doesn't answer. He just looks at me, as though he's trying to size me up. Meanwhile, I can't get a read on him like I can with most people.

What does he want? More money?

"I understand the project. You want to build a community center here, take care of the growin' number of young hooligans we got in Mirror Lake and in the city."

"Yes, well, that's part of it. I also hoped you could use the money, too. I know it's been years, Mr. Myers, but…" I hesitate, hoping my sincerity is being conveyed. "We are still family. Even if not by blood."

"I appreciate that, boy," he says. "I really do. But what happens here in Mirror Lake, and in the city – shit, son. It's everywhere. Ya can't escape it. They got all kinds of drugs now, running 'em up from New York. Hell, makin' some of it in their own backyards."

I know he's referring to the crystal meth epidemic that's plaguing the city's outlying towns where kids are drawn to the shit like moths to a hot light bulb. "I know, Mr. Myers. That's exactly what I want to prevent. I would like to use the center as a way for kids to learn, before their choices become a lifetime of regrets or a death sentence. Get them out of the city gangs or out of the backyard trailers they're using to cook meth. Give them options. Solid, worthwhile options."

"So much worse than when yer father was runnin' the streets," he goes on, almost ignoring my spiel. "He had shit for brains, but these drugs now…they make them kids do crazy things. They'd make babies and sell them off for a high if they had to. I'm not sure I see how yer project is gonna make a dent in all that nonsense."

"It's a complicated endeavor, Mr. Myers. I'll give you that. But I've been working up to this for years. This is a long-term plan that has countless hours and research invested. By me. A plan that can now finally come to fruition. A plan that needs a place to call home."

He sighs then leans back in his chair, considering me again.

"I don't know. I'm sure proud of ya, of what ya accomplished. Yer mom did a smart thing, leavin' here. How is she?"

"She's fine, thank you. She sends her regards."

Now I'm lying. My mother is fully aware of my plans, she understands them. But she has her own demons here, and she had no intention of acknowledging the husband of her dead sister when I told her I had to involve him. Keep the past in the past, she said.

I let her, for her own sake – but she knew better than to prevent me from facing mine.

"Well that's good. I really ought to think about this some more. My lawyer, she's put so much behind this deal. She's just starting out, but her dad was a lawyer too. Did you know Al Greene? He was a great man."

"No, I don't believe I did."

But I do know all about the deal my uncle has been blindly led to.

He has no idea how abysmal this proposed sale to Renewable Energy is, what a shit storm it would be for him and this community if it happened. I'm not ready to be the bearer of that bad news. I can sense how he operates. If I present myself as the better option by revealing the bad guys, he might deny me just to keep his dignity and to prove to himself that he wasn't about to make a mistake unknowingly.

"Great, great man," Eli goes on. "Died 'bout four years back. His daughter rebuilt his firm. She's a beauty, that one. And smart, too. She lost her husband just over a year ago. She's done right by me, makes sure those big wigs at Renewable Energy know I'm not gonna just *give* my land away. I'd hate to go back on my word with her and with those folks. The company could develop some pretty nice homes around here."

"Mr. Myers," I start.

I may have to let the cat out of the bag sooner than I wanted to.

"Eli," he insists.

"I assume you know, Eli, that over the years my family has garnered a lot of wealth. That I've more than duplicated that wealth with my own career."

"Yeah," he says. He takes a sip of his coffee, then removes his hat long enough to run a hand through his hair before he replaces the cap firmly on his head. "I do, sure. So?"

Good. The money does not impress him. That's the angle I want.

"With that wealth comes certain capabilities and knowledge. Ways to investigate things that some people don't have access to. Now, I am prepared to offer you more money than we first talked about, but I also have information. Information that I'm willing to give you for free." I pause to add weight to my words. "Information that might be of importance to you personally."

"Important," he bristles. "Important how?"

"Important in the sense that if you had this information, the same knowledge that I have, you might not want Renewable Energy to so much as step foot on your land, never mind sell them your entire farm. At *any* price."

"Huh," he says simply. I can tell he's trying to determine if I'm blowing smoke up his ass.

"Eli, please hear me out. If you don't want to sell to me, I'll walk out that door today for the last time and never look back. I'll find another way for the Center, another place for it. But I'm telling you right now, as someone whose only fond memories of childhood come from sitting in this very spot, you don't want to sell to those bastards. If you knew the truth, you'd sooner shoot them as look at them."

He looks at me with burning curiosity. I'm earning his trust, but he wants to know more.

Time to lay my cards out.

"I will tell you why you might not want to go through with this deal. In detail. And whatever you decide, there will be no hard feelings. But you shouldn't make this decision before you know the facts. *All* the facts."

An hour later I'm sitting in the back of my Lincoln, using my tablet to type out details to Samira and my attorney in Manhattan about the beginnings of the proposed deal with Eli Myers.

I'd left the farm feeling hopeful, knowing I'd taken a step further in my own goals. But I also knew I saved Myers from himself and from the ambitions of some inexperienced attorney that led him down this path to near catastrophe.

And, in doing so, we'd reached an agreement.

I think.

He wants to break the news to his lawyer later today. He had a meeting scheduled with her to sign the purchase contracts. Thank fuck that won't happen now. He hadn't even signed a letter of intent with them, so that part – cutting ties with R.E.E. – should be easy.

He gave me his word that as soon as I left he would call his contact at R.E.E. directly to tell him he wouldn't be signing.

I'm not sure how Eli's attorney will react, knowing after my conversation with him that she's put a year's worth of work into this. But that's irrelevant to me. She can close this deal with me, if Myers accepts, and bring in a bigger legal fee given the increased sale price.

Or she can get the fuck out of the way and find some other client to poorly advise.

I set a reminder on my tablet to look into her firm as soon as possible, so I know what I'm facing. Myers will need his own attorney for this, and if his current one is truly incapable, I'll have to do more research to find another disinterested party to represent him.

It won't be as simple as picking a name from a local attorney roster. It will have to be someone he'll trust, someone he'll have an instant rapport with. My uncle is clearly set in his ways.

But I will be sure he has someone with experience that he can count on.

With or without his current attorney though, it's looking more and more like my years (and years) of hard work will finally allow me to be of service to someone – to a county full of someones – that really need it.

I'm on a high thinking about it, practically erect from the excitement as I finish typing the email and close my tablet.

Samira is in a limo parked ahead of Byron and me with two of my trusted security agents – Ivan and Curtis. They are intimidating to look at and will bring just enough authority to the room of lawyers I'll be addressing (and to anyone from R.E.E. should they be watching). Of course Samira, with her striking Swedish looks, will be a welcome distraction for the gentlemen. The attorneys in the Bar Association are predominately males over forty.

The press is already inside, the meeting scheduled to start in ten minutes.

My phone pings with a notification. It's Samira, texting to tell me they're ready for us. I exit the car and she and the guys fall in behind me as we head for the meeting that I hope will change many lives for the better.

Including mine.

4

Alexis

It's a thirty minute drive to my office in Stanton City. I'm not listening to my usual morning news. It's Friday, and it's too gorgeous out. Seventy-five degrees already at eight-fifteen and blue skies are broken only by a few whispy clouds.

I've got Train cranked in my new convertible, wishing I had time to drive back roads with the top down. I sold Ben's Cadillac to Charlie and used a little of his life insurance money to treat myself. I know Ben would love that Charlie was driving his pride and joy now and that I'd treated myself to something fun.

Of course, sensible me kept my old SUV stowed away in the garage because how else would I get around this snow globe in January?

The sight of farmland dotted with housing developments fades as I drive north on the highway. Well-manicured lawns and homes filled with non-smoking All-American families give way to low-income housing with backyards the size of postage stamps. The residents inside are likely perfecting their defrauding of the government.

As I drive, I should be contemplating the near million-dollar deal that I've been nursing with Eli Myers since I opened my practice a year ago.

Myers is a farmer in my hometown of Mirror Lake and an old client of my dad's. He is as smart and wealthy as any lawyer in Stanton, and he works three times as hard. He retained me as his attorney to negotiate the sale of his farmland to a company in Pennsylvania.

We would be signing contracts today after almost a year of negotiations on terms, which I know contributed to my first gray hair. I've prayed that the favorable publicity for my fledgling firm and a hefty fee at the end of it all will be worth the stress and effort.

But instead of concentrating on this, I'm wrapped up in my dream from this morning.

I can pinpoint why this is happening, knowing I haven't had sex since… *when?* Jeez, it's not even calculable at eighty miles an hour.

Flip off the daydreaming switch, Alexis!

I shake off my thoughts and force myself into work mode as I cruise off the highway exit.

I park in the lot behind my one-story office building and head through the back door to our small break room, which hasn't changed much since my Dad owned the building in the eighties. White and gray linoleum tiles on the floor, walls of dark wood cabinets topped with stained laminate from years of use. Lighting is fluorescent and ugly. An old refrigerator sits in one corner.

The newest thing in the room is a single cup coffee brewer, a gift from Charlie when I opened for business.

I had the building remodeled when I bought it back out of nostalgia, wanting to start my firm in the same building my dad had practiced in until he died. The money was put into the street façade and the visible interior space in the hopes of attracting more appealing clientele. Besides me, only my current staff of two see this eyesore.

Charlie has a bottled water and breakfast bar waiting for me. His blue shirt is neatly pressed and tucked into snug-fitting black pants. His shoes are as shiny and polished as his bald head and his tie is a retro Jerry Garcia. It's on point with his bright personality. Just about anyone would swoon.

"Nice skirt, Lex! Heading out this evening?" He grins slyly as he grabs his coffee mug off the counter.

I'd forgotten my recently awakened libido picked out my outfit. His eyes travel to my shoes.

"O-M-G, girl! The stilettos!" He's practically yelling. I give him a look that says tone down your inner girl, and he lowers his voice. "We picked those out last spring. What's made you wear them now?"

"To answer your question, no I am not going out tonight, Charlie." I change the subject. "Leeds all taken care of?"

"Absolutely. The file is on your desk. I got to interrupt his breakfast of corned beef hash, thank you *so* much for that," he says grimacing.

"Well, if we'd gotten rid of Claudia…" I say, my sing-song voice trailing off.

"Nice try, Lex. I ain't bitin'. So what is it, then?"

"What?" I'm heading for my office ahead of him, cracking open the water he handed me. It's already humid. "Did you turn on the A/C? Gonna be a hot one today."

"Quit dodging my question, Lex. The shoes. Why are you wearing the fuck-me shoes?" Then he gasps as though he's figured it out. "Do you have a date tonight?"

"No, sir. And I was going for more of a come-hither look, but I guess fuck-me works too. Let's drop it, okay?"

I'm waiting for my computer to come to life and it purrs away as I flip through the Leeds file. I'm getting uncomfortable now about my choice of footwear. These shoes might as well light up and sing "I'm horny". I'm trying to recall if I have an extra pair of flats in the back room.

"Have it your way, girl. But I know you. Something's up. Or someone." He grins at his perverted play on words. "And by the way, you are rockin' them. Don't you *dare* take them off."

I smile, more in polite fashion than in agreement. "See to Claudia please, Charlie. Or I will."

That closes the subject, sending him off to the reception desk to reprimand his pet and leaving me to get down to business.

I've finished with Mr. Leeds' closing and two other appointments by quarter after eleven.

I'm lost in thought about how this room has changed since my father last sat here behind the same grand mahogany desk. I kept his tattered leather chair. It looks odd in the newly remodeled surroundings, but it keeps his memory close.

The dark hardwood floors, fresh beige paint and black wood furnishings were picked out by Charlie's decorator friend Ariana. I love what she did, but everything kept out of nostalgia were pieces I'd insisted on.

I have one window in my office. It faces the brick wall of the neighboring building, so I've turned the desk to face the door to the hallway instead. The window is now framed by an upholstered sage green cornice with matching drapes.

Black and white photos my father had of the Stanton City Courthouse line the wall across from me, beyond the leather club chairs in front of my desk. In the year I've had my office open, I'm surprised at the number of clients that have sat across from me here.

I wonder what Dad would think of the new surroundings. It feels like a lifetime since I lost him, but it was just four years ago. It was the first real heartache I'd ever experienced.

That was before Ben died, before I accomplished my dream of becoming a lawyer and followed in Dad's footsteps.

He'd often spoken to me about the old days in this office, in the years I'd spent working with him on breaks from my state college courses or while I attended law school here in Stanton.

The funniest recollections were of how things used to get done.

Carbon copies, heavy law books, tape recorders and typewriters.

The old IBM typewriter he used is on display in a glass case in my waiting room. I can't imagine how much longer it must have taken him to get anything accomplished. But, then again, I've got Claudia to hinder my progress.

I send Charlie some voice files for the preparation of Mrs. Loomis' will. As they zoom invisibly down the hall to his office, my phone buzzes with a text from him.

> Don't forget the County Bar Association lunch
> meeting today. Noon at the Sheridan Hotel.

Damn.

Not another boring luncheon.

The same attorneys I've known for years as my Dad's cronies will be in attendance, all sitting around talking politics and weather, eating dried out club sandwiches and sipping bland coffee. I never look forward to these.

But I'm one of the newest members. Networking is essential. I have to go.

I text back.

> *Why wasn't this in my calendar?*

I know it's because of Claudia. Strike three!

Charlie writes back immediately.

> *My fault. SORRY! BTW, it should be an*
> *interesting meeting today.*

> *Why's that?*

> *Aidan Michael Pierce is coming to speak to*
> *the Bar. He's AH-MAZING!*

Aidan Michael Pierce. The name rings a bell, but I can't think of why.

> *I'll go to the stupid meeting, but I'm going*
> *against my will. Thanks for the reminder. And*
> *fire Claudia.*

> *Very funny, Lex. P.S. Here's a picture of the*
> *hunk speaking at the 'stupid' meeting.*

The picture comes through a second later, a screenshot of one of those glossy magazines that has more ads for muscle cars and beer than written articles. Aidan Pierce is the sole subject on the cover.

Or I should say, *gracing* the cover.

Holy hell.

The photo quality isn't original – Charlie no doubt pulled it from somewhere on the internet – but it's certainly good enough.

It was taken from far enough away that his whole physique fits into the frame.

He's in a pair of dark pants that are clearly tailored to fit, but the only thing adorning his skillfully muscled upper body is a black bow tie.

And he's barefoot.

Yum.

His hair is mussed but styled, though it's hard to tell just what color it is from the picture. He's staring into the lens with an intense gaze, underneath a headline that reads *The Ivy League's Sexiest Bachelors*. I note the date on the cover and see the photo is more than a few years old.

Aidan Pierce is obviously one of those beautifully made men. He's the type you can't help but admire, wondering if he stepped out of a box that way.

Even in the grainy picture the guy looks like he could melt your panties with that laser stare of precision and maybe the word "hello".

I can't recall much beyond the fact that he's a business tycoon of some sort that spends most of his time in California mingling among the rich and famous.

I text Charlie back.

Meh, big deal. Sounds like a snooze-a-thon
either way.

I'm sure this much is true, but admit to myself that at least the view might keep me awake today.

I leave the office on foot and stop off for a salad at the café around the corner. I won't eat the unappealing food at the luncheon, and I don't need my stomach rumbling for the entire room to hear when I meet with Myers later.

I pop some gum after my meal and pick up my phone to check email realizing it's noon already. I'll definitely be late walking another block to the hotel in these heels.

I can see the Channel Eight van parked close to the hotel's front entrance as I arrive. A beat up Chevy truck is parked behind the van, and I know it belongs to a reporter for the Mirror Lake Chronicle. I don't know why reporters would be here, but there are usually several events occurring at the hotel simultaneously. I'm sure it's not for our customarily boring monthly meeting.

I arrive less than fifteen minutes late and seek out my friend Gloria Stearns. She's a forty-something attorney with curly red hair and green eyes. She's the only other woman in the room that, like me, has been at this job of lawyering under five years. She waited to finish law school until her twin daughters were grown and we've been confidants since I left Martin & Reynolds to open my office while she stayed on there.

"What kept you?" she whispers. "I've been suffering here alone for twenty minutes! O'Hara cornered me twice before he went up there!"

I stifle a giggle and apologize, taking a seat next to her at a round table with a few other attorneys.

Attorney Steven O'Hara is the rotund sixty-year-old current President of the Bar Association. He's at the podium droning on about changes to the Attorney for the Child program and the accomplishments of our guest speaker. We're seated towards the front of the large room that doubles as a ballroom, depending on the need.

In conversation, O'Hara's jokes about women border on offensive, but we secretly find them corny and amusing. Gloria and I are used to the boys' club mentality around here, often commiserating about the misogynist mentality of a declining breed.

My friend faces front with her back to me, pretending to listen intently to O'Hara who is so short we can barely see him. It's then I see that Channel Eight has a crew *here*. Several small-town reporters from local newspapers are also seated at a table in front of the podium, sipping water and coffee and listening intently.

What's the big deal?

Apparently I've missed something noteworthy while living under a rock with the Myers file.

I catch something about our guest's philanthropic efforts of late and how he's donated some of his gazillions of dollars to community projects around New York and California.

But my concentration is hampered by my now infuriating dream from this morning as it runs through my mind and I entirely miss what O'Hara goes on about the next few minutes.

Thunderous applause erupts and the crowd is on its feet. I rise with no trouble on my stilettos, wishing my hair would behave as well as my feet have managed today in my fuck-me shoes. A few strands have come loose, escaping my clip and hanging slightly curled around my face from the humidity. They are an annoyance and I blow out a breath to move them aside as I pop my gum. Gloria turns around and gives me a wink.

"I'll take two of those on a platter, eh?" she whispers to me. "And he's got millions too!"

I don't know what she's talking about. I can't see through to the podium with her standing in front of me.

Whatever the fuss is about, this guy has gotten our local press to bite. I can't imagine why. So far it's just another boring lecture at the County Bar Association meeting.

O'Hara stops talking and, without warning, a new voice comes through the microphone, vibrating through the speakers. It's captivating with obvious experience addressing a crowd. The disembodied sound is melodic, dripping with charm and poise, yet all he's done is thank the audience, asking them to please sit.

Everyone does, except for me.

I'm intrigued and have to get a look. I feign like I'm looking for someone as Gloria sits down and Aidan Michael Pierce comes into full view.

Dang. Wow. And holy fuck.

I think I might fall over.

So that's what all the fuss is about.

He's much taller than O'Hara, easily over six foot. He is dressed in a crisp, gray suit and pressed white shirt, two undone buttons revealing bronzed skin from just the right amount of sun. He's got a tough guy stubble going on that contradicts his expensive clothes and suave demeanor but it's not grungy.

It's sexy as hell.

His caramel brown hair has a rough-around-the-edges cut. His eyes are the same pearlescent blue as my convertible and they are quite piercing indeed.

Everything about him is unforgettable.

In the moment I recall what little I know about him from tabloids and television, my brain finally putting the story with the man.

He would have been just another rich brat, a millionaire's son born to aristocrats Reginald and Veronica Pierce. Instead, he started his own company after graduating from Cal Tech. He later sold the company to a much larger one to make his *first* few million (all before completing graduate school at Yale, of course).

Investments and side-projects he had a hand in were reported in the news here and there, especially when those earned him his first billion by age twenty-nine.

I think that was a few years ago.

He recently stopped dating someone according to *The Online Buzz*. Stella Something-or-other. I think he broke it off with the socialite or maybe he was the dumpee.

I just remember the picture of her with her father on the cover of *The Tattler* that Charlie pointed out to me in the supermarket a few weeks ago.

She looked like a stick figure, but with boobs and long jet black hair. Her tanned cleavage was accented by large, gaudy jewelry. I think she owned a boutique in L.A., or maybe Miami, but I remember it reported that her father owns a lot of high-end real estate in L.A. and Manhattan.

The headline of that article had reported that Aidan Pierce fled L.A. for the East Coast after his relationship with the California native ended badly.

Beyond this, I know nothing about the eye candy seducing my ears, his voice amplified by the microphone. But for the first time in three weeks, I forget about my hot new neighbor.

This guy is in a class by himself, far too worthy to be a lowly human.

At least by now I'm subconsciously drooling over single men, not married ones.

Progress!

I consider lifting my phone out to snap a picture for Charlie, recalling how excited he'd been over this guy until I realize *why* those eyes seem so intense.

He's still talking without missing a beat, but his eyes aren't on the crowd ahead of him. His gaze is trained to his left.

He's staring right at me.

I feel like I'm in college again, on the receiving end of a professor's 'you-interrupted-my-lecture-and-must-be-scolded' glare. I sit, look away, and nod in the direction of another lawyer across the room, pretending we have acknowledged each other. In reality, my colleague is paying no attention to me whatsoever and is engrossed in what our guest is saying.

I believe I've deflected Pierce's gaze, but it's short lived.

I can feel his eyes on me again as I pop my gum and blow hair away from my face. Damn humidity. I pretend to be occupied as I scroll through my phone until Gloria reaches behind her chair and squeezes my knee.

Crap. Even she's noticed the unwanted attention I'm trying to deflect.

Screw this.

Somehow (maybe just by my choice of outrageous footwear today), I'm emboldened. I straighten my posture and look up at the podium, squaring my eyes with his in a manner of defiance. I'm about to be entranced by his stare, but before I can be defeated, he turns back to the rest of the audience, seemingly satisfied.

He just wanted you to pay attention, Greene!

Now I feel stupid.

I scold myself, stealing looks around the room as our guest finishes his presentation. The few women in the room are swooning, waitresses included.

I roll my eyes and sip some water. It is unbelievable the effect this guy has. Even the men seem enthralled. If Charlie were here, he would have moved his seat to the press table just to gawk at him.

Right there I vow not to lose *my* wits because of this man.

Nope, not this girl.

Despite his mussed, I-want-it-to-look-this-way hair and intoxicating voice.

Despite his striking features and mesmerizing persona.

This playboy will *not* have this girl melting into a puddle.

I'm so above it.

The crowd chuckles as a whole, and then they are clapping and on their feet again. I mentally shake myself at the shoulders and then applaud too, only out of courtesy of course. Attorney O'Hara steps back to the podium after a handshake with Aidan Pierce. I figure the guy's going to make his exit, but he doesn't leave as O'Hara steps back to the microphone.

Instead he takes a couple of steps back and relaxes into a patient stance. He has a small entourage around him. Two even taller men who look like linebackers in suits flank him, and there's a blonde about my size standing off to his right with a tablet in hand.

She is beautiful. I couldn't pinpoint her age, but she's a studious looking woman (probably Nordic) with hair pulled taught into a sturdy bun. Rectangular, black framed glasses rest on her button nose. She's wearing a fitted ivory dress and matching low heels. She taps away on the tablet as O'Hara talks to us again.

"Now then, ladies and gentlemen," he begins. "I think it's time to select the three people for the committee, for uh…" O'Hara fumbles with some pieces of paper, knocking into the microphone. It sends out a squeal, but he sets it upright, shuffling with his papers as he continues. "…for Mr. Pierce's new project. I open the floor for nominations."

Committee? What project?

Gloria raises her hand and O'Hara calls on her. I can't believe she's volunteering to spend her spare time on some project that this guy is spearheading rather than with her family. She's always complaining about too many hours at the office away from the twins and her husband Harold. A ten minute lecture and even a devoted family woman has fallen under his spell and ditched her family obligations.

"I nominate Attorney Alexis Greene to head up the committee," she says.

I can't see the look on her face because she has her back to me, so I don't know if she's serious or amused. But it sounds like she's smiling.

I want to kick her. Hard.

Before I can object, the nomination is seconded by one of my father's old colleagues, David Buckingham.

No. No, not me!

Now the whole room is staring at me.

Including him.

Attorney O'Hara asks me to stay standing while everyone else is free to take their seats. I open my mouth to express my hesitation, to blurt an excuse not to accept…something! All I can do is take a breath, blowing my wayward hair out of my face.

"No objections then?" It seems like he waits only seconds. "Good. Ms. Greene will head up the committee as a liaison to Mr. Pierce. Now, we'll need a fundraising chairperson as well and another attorney for the uh, red tape end of things." O'Hara chuckles at his own words. "Any other necessary positions can be decided on at a later time."

I'm perfectly still, in shock. I mutter a thank you for the Bar's confidence in me and take my seat again as someone nominates Jade McCall as the head of fundraising. She is in her fifties and her husband is the top plastic surgeon in the area so she has the best connections for the job of raising funds for whatever this project is. I dread having to spend any amount of time with her. No doubt she will have her husband tidy her up with a new procedure just to come to a meeting with the undeniably gorgeous Mr. Pierce.

The third committee person (who nominated himself) will be Attorney Allen Richardson. He's an up-and-coming young lawyer and is new to Stanton City. He's currently building his private office, splitting time between his general practice and criminal assignments by the Court to get some experience locally. Rumor has it he is a good attorney, but he's still earning his place around here.

I don't even know what the hell this committee is supposed to do. I will have to pull Gloria aside when the meeting adjourns and ask her. Right after I kick her.

Finally, the attention of the room is drawn away from me and the other committee persons as the meeting adjourns and lunch is served. I'm sure I'm crimson with embarrassment.

I watch Pierce tap away at his phone, then he shakes hands once again with Attorney O'Hara, leaning in to say something. O'Hara seems to give him a reassuring expression, saying something in response, then they're both smiling as they part company.

I pull out my phone, intending to text Charlie. I feel one pair of eyes still on me try as I might to ignore the stare.

I look up. I know they belong to him.

The man with the piercing blue eyes, charismatic smile and entourage of bad asses ready to take on this city and Mirror Lake, like some sort of superhero ready to do good.

Though exactly what good he's here to do, I have no idea.

Must pay better attention.

He sends his charming smirk across the sea of lunching lawyers right to me.

Then as quickly as he came and upended the room, he and his entourage are gone.

Since I've already eaten and I am so ticked at Gloria I could care less if she eats, I've pulled her away from her crappy lunch to pow wow in the ladies' room. I keep my voice low but have already checked that we are alone.

"Why in the hell did you volunteer me?"

I try hard to hide the fact that the idea of being in close proximity to Aidan Pierce excites me, makes me almost giddy. How lame am I?

"Oh please, Lex," she chastises. "What better have you got to do? Besides, Mister Mega Bucks isn't the sorriest thing you could be staring at on Tuesday nights."

"That's not the point, Gloria. How he looks doesn't matter. It isn't like he came here to be admired. He means business." I'm leaning up against the counter, exasperated. "And this guy is so out of my realm of possibilities in this life. I know I was blessed with brains and not drop dead looks, and I've made my way being smarter than most men I'm in a room with. This guy is, he's just dangerous. I can sense it."

"Quit dogging yourself. You are the most beautiful young woman in this room."

I look around with sarcasm as Gloria's kind words echo in an empty four-stall bathroom.

"You know what I mean," she scolds. "You are gorgeous, inside and out. And maybe you need a little danger in your life. You've always played it safe and that hasn't gotten you any further ahead in your social life. Or your career." She gestures to my feet. "Your head is screaming at you to take a risk. Just look at those shoes you picked today."

I look down and curse them aloud.

"Lex," she says with hands on my shoulders. "You're ready for something more."

I want to believe her, but I'm still miffed. And petrified of stepping out of my comfort zone.

"I'm doing just fine with what Dad left behind and building on it at a pretty good pace. And with what Ben set up, I'm comfortable. I don't need to mingle with Mister Mega Bucks to validate my status or to look for a hand up." Now I'm standing next to her, pretending to look intently in the mirror and hopeful that she accepts my next question as nonchalant. "And what the hell is this project even about?"

Gloria has turned to the mirror too. She applies fire engine red lipstick and blots it with a tissue. "Oh, so maybe you were admiring the hunk in a suit and not really paying attention?"

She acts inquisitive but she knows the answer. I have to look elsewhere before my face turns red. The bozo-sized coffee I consumed earlier forces me to head for a stall, and I'm grateful I can hide my embarrassment. I listen to her as I do the necessary.

"Well, apparently Mr. Pierce is investing around here. He's going to build and run a center for at-risk youth in the community. Can you believe that? A good heart and all that cash too. Too bad I already married my knight in shining armor."

I emerge to wash my hands, chuckling at the image of Harry with middle-age spread forced into a clinking metal suit, his receding hairline covered by a medieval silver helmet.

"Well, I'm skeptical of your blanket statement of what a saint this guy is. I'm not sure why he would choose Mirror Lake," I say. "What's the connection? What's in it for him?"

"I don't know, but I think he has a small headquarters here in Stanton for his business or something. I read in the tabloids that he ran back here after his girlfriend dumped him." She pulls a comb and a mini can of hairspray from her purse. "He didn't offer much detail about that. He joked about how he liked his privacy when he thanked the reporters for being here."

The reporters. I had forgotten about them.

Shit, will I be on the news? I don't know if they were filming anything, like O'Hara appointing me to head the committee. I groan internally. I hope not.

"Well thanks for nothing," I tell her. "Now I have to spend Tuesday nights with this guy, not to mention Plastic Surgery Barbie out there who'll be heading up fundraising. What do we need funds for anyway? This guy could finance a trip to Mars if he wanted. He doesn't need handouts from our insignificant population."

"Apparently, *according his speech*," she says pointedly at me, "he feels some community fundraising and involvement will bring positive publicity to the project. You know, awareness about the plight of these youth who don't have it so good. And it will help the community feel like it's their project too. I don't think he expects to have to raise a whole lot."

Now I groan out loud to express my lack of appreciation. I mean, kudos for having a cause, I guess. But what an assignment Gloria's gotten me into.

"Well good for him," I pout. "But I really don't need this hassle. And Gloria," I continue with sarcasm, "no one says 'hunk' these days."

I'm still ticked, so I don't share the fact that Charlie, a gay man who is the epitome of cool, used that very word to describe Pierce not an hour ago.

"Oh?" she smiles. "What would you call him then?" She leans back from the mirror, an obnoxious amount of hairspray hanging in the air trying to find its way to her red curls.

"Sex personified," I say.

"Indeed, Lex," she mutters at the mirror, finally satisfied with her immovable hair. "Indeed."

When we return from the restroom, the wait staff has cleared lunch and is serving dessert and more horrid coffee. I can see O'Hara motioning to me from across the room. He's standing alongside a few reporters and the camera crew for Channel Eight.

Oh *fuck* my luck today.

Melanie Adams is adjusting her pink suit and preparing herself in front of the camera. The lights pointed at her cast a glow around her blonde mane, which rivals the immobility of Gloria's.

Shit. Shit. Shit.

I head in their direction, plotting my revenge on Gloria for getting me into this as I go.

"Melanie, how are you?" I interrupt her primping and she shakes my hand, smiling at me.

"Hi, Eliza." Her tone drips with false sympathy. "How are you doing?"

This bitch is unbelievable. She knows my name. I have no doubt she is doing this on purpose.

"It's Alexis, actually." I glare at her, then turn my attention to O'Hara. "What can I do for you, Steve?"

"I've promised Ms. Adams a quick interview, if that's okay, Alexis? Shouldn't take long."

"Yes," Melanie says. "I understand you will be the liaison between the Bar Association and Mr. Pierce on his new project." Her attention is focused across the room in an attempt to ignore me.

"I guess so." I don't hide my lack of enthusiasm.

"You're going to be great, Alexis," O'Hara says. "I'm so glad Gloria spoke out to recommend you. If you'll excuse me, I'll be right back."

He leaves us, and I'm not sure I can believe I have to stand here and do this alone with someone I loathe.

Melanie turns to me. "Oh, don't worry," she says with false reassurance. "We're not going to be live. I can have it edited if needed."

I manage a smile back.

"And I'm sorry we couldn't have had more notice for you," she adds. "I can see you weren't planning to be on camera today."

This is typical Melanie.

Thankfully, I neatened my outfit and hair in the bathroom and dabbed some fresh concealer under my eyes. I wasn't willing to borrow the bright red lipstick from Gloria, though she offered. I probably look underwhelming next to Melanie, but I know at least I'm presentable and pick my head up.

I refuse to let this woman get the better of me.

At least my shoes won't be seen on the air.

Melanie gets into position next to me and the cameraman confirms he's ready. She turns on her stupid tv smile that makes me want to punch her, just as I see someone pacing towards us.

It's Aidan Pierce.

By the time the little red light is on, Melanie is still smiling, but stands more like a deer caught in the headlights of a tractor trailer than a put-together reporter. She stares at the unbelievably handsome man now two feet in front of us, awestruck.

I can smell his scent, a mix of masculine wood-scented soap (oak maybe?) and cologne of some sort. No doubt expensive. It smells edible. This time he's minus his entourage and he looks a bit more relaxed, almost as though he's being entertained.

I can hear Melanie's voice next to me. Somehow she's peeled her eyes off of him long enough to be professional. She asks if I think I'm cut out for this new appointment by the Bar Assocation.

I can see him from the corner of my eye. His arms are folded across his chest as he taps his fingers on his arms expectantly. He seems almost annoyed, like he wants to step forward and take over.

Oh *hell* no. I will not let that happen. I can do this. It's important to get this right. He can't think I'm vulnerable. Or weak. Or incompetent.

I've got to put Melanie in her place.

I turn on my own fake Hollywood smile.

"I'm quite certain I'm cut out for this. I intend to take the project very seriously. It is a worthy cause that Mr. Pierce is undertaking, but the project presents a lot of challenges, a lot of work. I hope my experience in the legal field will come of some use in his endeavor."

"Yes, ma'am, I'm sure it will."

Did she seriously just call me *'ma'am'* on camera? In front of *him*?

Pierce doesn't seem to notice. I can see a change in his posture again, an interest in what I'm saying and how I'm handling this. It doesn't seem like he's paying the slightest attention to Melanie.

"And what can we expect you to contribute to this project?" Melanie says, her smile fixed in place as she speaks. She's trying a bit too hard to impress Pierce, coming off like a rabid animal baring fangs.

Feeling his gaze on me, I'm thrown off for a moment, unsure of how to answer. Damn it! Why didn't I pay closer attention to what he said up there?

Ben's reporter voice invades my brain, sending me instructions seemingly from beyond.

Go for the generic answer. It's a sure fire out.

"As I said, my legal experience should serve the project well. I learned a great deal from my father about commercial real estate transactions. I will be honored to use the knowledge learned from him and hope that my experience will assist Mr. Pierce and the rest of the committee."

"And how are you holding up now, a year and a half after your husband's death?"

My eyes shoot daggers at Melanie. She puts the microphone down, unable to go on. From my glare her demeanor has been turned upside down from over-eager cheese-bomb to shrinking violet.

"Uh, er…we can cut that part out, Alexis. Cut, Hans. That's enough."

I turn back to see what Pierce has made of this, but he's gone again. I spot him a few paces away in the lobby, talking on his cell.

I politely thank Melanie and leave her, passing by Pierce as I make my way towards the bank of revolving doors at the exit.

His scent fills me up as I pass by and I'm smiling.

Just at the *smell* of him I'm smiling. What the hell? I force myself to keep moving when my cell buzzes.

I stop walking to search my bag and a muscular frame bumps into me from behind.

My phone has stopped sounding off, but now I'm buzzing. Somewhere deep I'm humming as much as I was in my dream this morning.

I take a step forward, then turn around and look up.

Right into those indigo eyes.

Lord, have mercy on me.

"Miss Greene," he says. "It's a pleasure." He extends his hand.

The anticipation of touching him is so intense, or at least in my mind it is. As I shake his hand, I'm wrestling with the way my body responds to him.

It's just a handshake for God's sake. I can't fathom why I'm reacting like this.

"Mr. Pierce," I say back. *What the fuck else can I say?* I'm speechless, feet glued to the floor.

His right hand is soft, not a laborer's hand at all. Neatly manicured, yet very strong. My hand is swallowed up by his. I have to ignore the tingling that's radiating up my arm as I grip firmly and let go, honoring my rule never to give a limp handshake to a man.

I decide to take it a step further, wanting some sort of assertion. I can only come up with one.

"I must correct you, though. It's actually *Ms.* Greene."

He is still looking me in the eye, still very close. I put space between us, wishing we were not in the middle of a public place. People are passing by, some hurried, but some gawking. I try to ignore them.

Why do I want him to be closer?

"I'm, uh...I'm..." *Undersexed? Lonely? Exhausted?* "I'm married."

This guy is trouble. Something in his eyes tells me intensity radiates through his entire life, not only in the carnal magnetism he exudes. He's got something to hide and it probably isn't something benign.

"I believe I heard something like that, although I didn't notice a wedding ring. I thought you were a recent widow, Ms. Greene," he says, laying emphasis on the *Ms.* He's eyeing me, trying to figure me out. I can see it. I've done it myself to countless others.

"Yes, well, you heard correctly as Ms. Adams pointed out on camera." I'm shocked that my voice is not failing me, making me stutter or stop altogether. "Is there something I can do for you at this moment? It's my understanding our committee will be meeting here on Tuesdays, and I've got to get back to my office to prepare for a four o'clock."

"Not here. At my office. 250 Harrison Street. And just you."

My confusion must be visible, and he continues in explanation.

"I have asked Mr. O'Hara to have the committee meet here on Thursdays at noon, but you will be the only attorney working directly with me Tuesday evenings at seven. Does that suit you?"

"If that is what you require to see your project through."

And what if it doesn't suit me?

Somehow I know that is not an option. This guy gets what he wants every time, even if he might go into a situation presuming too much. I've failed myself and fallen into the trap, unable to object at his insistence. I'm one of those Stepford wives being controlled by some mysterious male enigma when normally I'd object and break the mold, insisting on doing things my own way.

"Is that all?" I ask.

He pulls out a thin, silver case from his breast pocket and takes out a business card. I can see it has his initials engraved on it and the intricate pattern of a symbol of some sort. He hands me a card, his eyes never leaving mine. He tilts his head when I pocket the card without looking at it.

He's uncertain how to read me.

Good!

Exactly what I was going for. I high-five myself in my own head, excited and proud that I have not rolled over with my legs in the air like most women must do when he looks their way or talks to them. Everyday words suddenly seem plump with passion when they come from his lips, like nothing I've ever heard.

"Might you have a business card as well? In the event that my staff needs to contact you it would be helpful." He smiles as though I'm amusing him again. His teeth are flawless and straight.

My head is clearly up my ass. Of course he needs to know how to reach me.

I pull a card out of my purse and hand it over, wishing I had gone with a flashier design like Charlie had suggested. Instead the card is simple. It's black print on white stock with my name, office address, e-mail and phone number. It's understated, but classic. Like me, I guess.

He does not look at my card either. Instead he takes a step forward and closes the gap between us again. His scent is inebriating, knocking off my functioning brain cells one at a time like tin cans shot off a fence with a pellet gun.

"That is all, Ms. Greene," he says, pocketing the card and dismissing me.

He looks down at me, eyes softened and damn if it doesn't make me melt. I wonder if he can see through my I'm-a-big-girl-that-can-handle-the-likes-of-you façade. His expression gives nothing away.

"Except to say," he finally says in a near whisper, "that I very much look forward to seeing you on Tuesday." His gaze shifts down my legs, halting at my feet. "Until then." He says it right in the vicinity of my ear. He backs up, a devilish grin forming as he turns to go.

I stand, dumbfounded in the glass fronted lobby, watching him make his way to a fancy black car parked at the curb. An older man with a salt-and-pepper beard opens the door for him. I peg him to be in his mid-fifties and his name is probably Jeeves or something like that. Pierce gets in, disappearing into the darkness of the backseat. In contrast, the afternoon sun is bright. I put on my sunglasses as I exit the building, watching him pull away.

The temperature must be eighty-five by now. I'm left on the sidewalk, breathless and hot not from the sun, but just from encountering him.

5

Aidan

I'm back at the loft, stripping to rid myself of my suit in haste after returning from the luncheon.

I'm standing in my briefs in my bedroom, unsure what course of action to take.

I need to run a few miles or do something to blow off steam.

It's too hot to run outside in this afternoon humidity. The home gym I have in mind for the fourth floor of the building is still in the planning stages, so working out here isn't an option. I don't feel like going to the city gym either. I have no desire to be around other people right now.

Except maybe the tempting *Ms.* Alexis Greene. I could definitely be around her at the moment.

Around her, above her, inside her.

Any of those options would be welcome.

Meeting her was the unexpected highlight of my day. My uncle was right, Ms. Greene was certainly beautiful (possibly the understatement of the century and all future centuries) and seemingly smart.

Her looks were arresting, though it was obvious she had no awareness of this fact.

None whatsoever.

She was not demure or meek by any means. In fact, quite the contrary.

Her feminine allure was palpable.

Yet she wasn't full of that arrogant, haughty style of grace I'd become accustomed to while living on the West Coast, or even traipsing Manhattan when I was a graduate student at Yale just looking to escape for a weekend.

Those women were gorgeous, sure, but they were fully aware they had looks that could stop a clock. They were so used to flaunting their attributes for personal gain that it had the adverse effect.

It actually made them considerably unattractive, at least to me.

Especially after having bedded so many of them.

Admittedly there was something about Alexis Greene, even beyond her looks. Whatever that intangible was, it was something that (apparently) I could not shake because I'm standing here with a raging hard-on and no sufficient way to relieve it.

At least none that involve her.

She was confident yet seemingly humble, accommodating but not a pushover you could command and get away with it. She had backbone, that was for certain. I'd seen it when that ditz of a reporter tried to interview her (and failed miserably). There was a fire in her eyes and in her entire being when she shut Melanie Adams down with nothing more than a pointed glance.

I witnessed raw power from her in that moment, saw it come through like a force of nature. It was a major turn on, even though she appeared oblivious to her own capabilities.

She was one of those rarities. I'd heard of the breed, the stunning variation of woman that a man might live a lifetime without coming across.

The fantastical unicorn that anyone could describe from myth or lore, yet no one has ever seen.

Not in reality.

She had a mess of upturned hair, some of the soft walnut strands misbehaving to hang around her face as I'd stared her down for not paying attention during my speech. I could barely keep my words flowing properly as I watched her, my eyes following the rogue strands of hair that blew away with each breath she released in an attempt to tame them.

Her lips were glossed and full, meeting each other firmly when she chewed her gum at me. Those lips were taunting me to abandon the podium and lick them, bite them, kiss them without mercy.

And once I'd gotten close to her, it was undeniable that I craved a chance to kiss her.

She had not given my business card a second glance when I gave it to her. She just tucked it away, as though she couldn't possibly care any less that there was a tangible, mind-blowing chemistry circling us when we stood next to each other.

Could it be she really didn't feel that?

She hadn't swooned at all, not like most women do, even when I flat out ignore them – which usually made them more persistent.

But then her eyes.

I recall their intensity and how they reminded me of my own. Hers didn't reveal a depth of darkness or unhealed wounds like I saw in the mirror, but they were just as guarded – and an amazing shade of cerulean I'd not seen in any other woman's. They were captivating to a fault; an incentive capable of launching men to fight wars to lay claim to her, just for the right to get lost in them if even for a moment.

If I read her solely by her eyes, they were certainly telling a different story.

No, she hadn't swooned. But she definitely looked at me with a hunger I was familiar with, albeit in a more controlled form. She was reserved and conservative, careful. But for a split second I had seen invitation, that look a woman gives when she wants to take you to the nearest secret place and devour you.

Then the flicker had vanished, and she was in control enough to shun the likes of me with purpose, even if she was affected by giving me the once over.

My only gratification in our fleeting encounter today was being allowed to study her prior to touching her, drinking her in while she was unaware. It had been beyond arousing.

Those striking eyes were perfectly set and framed with thick, dark lashes. Her skin was tanned from the early spring sun, at least for being from New York, though she'd probably be pasty in comparison to Stella's over-bronzed complexion. I couldn't pinpoint her nationality. She was a bit too fair to be Italian, yet too golden to be Irish.

I concluded that she was just a beautifully melded creature.

An all-American girl that would probably look as hot climbing the mountains of Lake County in hiking boots as she did cutting you to the quick with just a glare and wearing a tiny skirt and heels.

In other words, she was a myth.

She was probably a raging bitch. Or an alcoholic. Or crazy.

Of course I'm a guy, so it didn't go unnoticed that she had ample tits peeking up from beneath the teasing, unbuttoned-just-enough collar of her white blouse. Her legs were smooth and lean, stretching soberly from the hem of her short skirt a *long* way down. The added height from her heels brought her eyes almost even with mine, so she was probably about five-seven. I'd looked those stems over enough times while she was giving that interview to memorize them, the whole time wishing I could get as good a look at her backside for later recollections too.

And those fucking shoes alone were worthy of worship. Her inappropriate footwear stood out in that sea of ultra-conformist lawyers all dressed in their frumpy business attire. Her legs punctuated with those heels were enough to make a man bow at an altar and ask forgiveness for sinning, just for imagining her wrapped around him wearing nothing but those heels and a pleasured smile.

Amen and hallelujah.

Fuck.

Still hard.

For a minute, I think about heading to The Wall to see if Robin is working. But I immediately banish the thought.

Get a grip, Pierce.

I'd had to work myself up to getting this interested in Robin the first time.

The likes of her will not satisfy this urge. It would be like craving a filet of the finest red meat and trying to satisfy it with a glass of tepid water.

But I need to get rid of this pent-up need somehow.

I'm pumped from my meeting with my uncle, from the possibility that this is all going to come together exactly how I'd hoped from day one.

And, now admitting it freely to myself, I'm more than hot and bothered from meeting Alexis.

It's unusual for me. I'm typically in better control of my thoughts than this. I'd literally traveled the globe in search of ways to use my mind to its fullest potential for fuck's sake.

It took work to control whims and urges, to prevent addictions and avoid the clichéd noise of the world that attempts to distract me from potential greatness.

For some random woman to affect me this way was definitely unfamiliar, but there's no denying my reaction at the thought of her.

I decide the best course of action is to shower. First, so I can take care of my sexual frustration and second, to get a fresh start for the afternoon. I've got calls to make, and I need to be sure I'm ready to Skype with Dr. Mason later too.

Downstairs in my office I can also see if the background check I asked Byron to run on the stunning Ms. Greene is available yet.

While waiting for Attorney O'Hara to wrap up the bar meeting I'd sent Byron an email, asking him to get as complete a history as possible on her.

O'Hara had seemed thrilled about her appointment when we spoke, even offering his unsolicited opinion about her integrity and what an asset she would be. But I need to see for myself.

Her appointment as my go-to in all this was a stroke of luck I hadn't seen coming.

I suppose I owe thanks to some higher power or maybe just to her colleague (one Mrs. Gloria Stearns, if memory serves) for offering her up to me without even having to ask.

If I'm going to trust her to head up this committee, I need to know everything about her though. Especially if she's going to handle the land sale for my uncle.

I'd requested background checks on the other two lawyers for the committee as well, but with her I need to dig deeper. Find out whether her naivety is considerable.

It could be possible it stopped at a lack of knowledge about R.E.E.'s well-disguised objectives. But I had to be sure it was not sheer stupidity that caused her to steer my uncle towards a path that would have destroyed both of them in the process.

She didn't seem that ignorant.

But I had to be sure.

As I'm lathering up in the shower, I realize there might be a third scenario.

What if she neglected to share with Myers the details about R.E.E. intentionally? What if she was coming at this from their angle, an inside player to guarantee their acquisition of the farm?

It could be just as possible that R.E.E. is (or was) guaranteeing her some sort of safety net. Her career in Stanton would end quickly once people here got wise to what was really going on.

Maybe R.E.E. had offered to compensate her for that.

Shit.

This does present a challenge.

Any one of these circumstances might be too detrimental to my cause to allow her to be a part of this project in any capacity.

I decide to give her the benefit of the doubt, at least until I read up on her and meet with her Tuesday. By then, she'll be aware that the deal she helped my uncle negotiate with R.E.E. isn't going to make it out of the gate.

I can always cut ties with her on Tuesday if it turns out our interests are not aligned.

Idly I wonder if she knows yet that her year-long negotiations are now moot.

Maybe I should call her, explain what I'm doing here, why I'm doing it at all. It's not my intention to shoot anyone's plans all to hell. My intentions are well meaning.

The greater good. Always.

I backpedal in my head. It's too soon to call. I'm not yet informed enough about the lovely Alexis Greene. I don't have confirmation that my uncle went through with his promises, so it's possible she doesn't know about her deal falling apart anyway, or at least not that it has anything to do with me.

I have no way to know what she will do with that information when she does find out. It's likely I won't be her favorite person on the planet.

I try to disregard my persistent hard-on as I finish my shower, but it's not working.

Beyond the center, the land deal, my years of planning an endeavor that needs to be meticulously calculated, I'd like nothing more than to have *Mizz* Greene spread eagle in my bed as soon as humanly possible.

I imagine her doing exactly that as the steam closes in on me and I get myself off, coming just from the thought of her, hopeful the visions of her opening herself up to me will turn into reality soon enough.

Maybe, against all odds, the capture of an elusive unicorn is imminent.

6

Alexis

I've been back at my desk for what seems like an eternity, but it's only three o'clock. I fill Charlie in on the gossip resulting from the bar meeting and he is awestruck. I never did get to snap a picture, so immediately we scour the internet for recent photos of Aidan Pierce.

Hundreds come up. Some recent but most are from a few years ago. There is nothing that dates back further than his college years (Cal Tech and Yale, as I'd already learned from his Ivy League Bachelor cover).

Well la-dee dah.

Mr. Pierce is also Mr. Smarty Pants. His brain is probably as impressive to examine as the rest of him.

And speaking of the rest of him, Charlie and I have spent the better part of an hour looking through all the photos we could find, practically needing bibs to catch the drool.

Finally, I put Charlie back to task in the conference room preparing the table with copies of the Myers sale agreements that Attorney Whitmore sent up yesterday.

It's likely my client will want to go through the contract line by line, even though we've already discussed each contingency, sometimes until my voice was hoarse or I had a migraine the size of Texas.

Renewable Energy's lead attorney, Mark Whitmore, was a partner in a Pennsylvania law firm, and he'd expressed similar frustrations on occasion. Mark and I had developed a rapport after working on this for the last year.

Too often we had to press for our clients to hammer out important details rather than waste billable hours on their tangents to haggle over things that weren't critical to either one of them.

I'm beyond grateful that this day is finally here.

Charlie pops his head in my office.

"All set. I'm going to head back to my desk and get started on those files you sent earlier. And I had a talk with Claudia. I think you'll be impressed with her turnaround."

I roll my eyes at him. "We'll see," I say. And he's gone.

I peek out both of my office doors, the one to the hallway and the one to the conference room. Seeing no one, I close them both. I fire up a search engine and again look up Aidan Michael Pierce, but this time I'm not searching for images.

I'm searching for information.

I'm not having much luck finding anything other than articles about the sale of his first business several years ago and some about his accomplishments while in college. He'd won varied academic competitions, and during his two-year stint with the swim team at Cal Tech he'd led them to a championship.

Everything else I've stumbled on amounts to nothing more than random photos circulated a thousand times online or seen in glossy magazines.

In them, he's either at a professional sporting event or various charitable events with his parents or Stella Ireland, the stick figure with boobs.

These pictures of her are far more flattering than others I'd seen in the supermarket, and I can see why he might have picked her for a girlfriend. She is model-pretty, or at least all made up she is, and she comes from money too.

A match made in heaven.

The Tattler photo was less flattering, but it was snapped as she and her father were exiting a restaurant in L.A., likely not expecting (or at least not intending) to be photographed.

But nothing with her dates back further than two years ago, and there are no recent pictures of them together.

So what else has this guy been up to since he made his money and subsequently parted ways with the horrendously tan and big-breasted Ms. Ireland?

Partying and gambling his nights away in Vegas?

Tanning himself on the best beaches all over the globe?

In the few minutes I observed him that doesn't seem to suit him. In person, he is outwardly ambitious and purposeful. I doubt he is the laze-about-and-do-nothing type. It was obvious from my reading that he was well traveled. From what I could glean from his academic history alone, this guy is a fucking go-getter.

The lack of older information is mysterious but not unusual. The internet was non-existent in his youth. Just fifteen years ago it wasn't as all-encompassing as it is now where celebrity gossip is reported on a twenty-four-hour news cycle opposite the weather report.

He can pay any sum of money for anything he wants, which likely includes controlling the media to some extent. From what I've read, anyone interviewing him says he's likeable but reserved about himself.

He talks about what he wants to talk about and nothing more. There are no unauthorized pieces that try to expose him for any oddities.

If he wants any aspect of his life to stay out of the public eye, whether it involves personal matters or business transactions, it's a done deal.

Likewise when he wants the media's attention, he can get it.

Like today.

I wonder if news of this community project will go national and say a prayer right there that it does not.

At four-thirty, my client has not shown up to sign contracts in acceptance of the biggest real estate deal of my infant career.

No one from Renewable Energy Enterprises has called or emailed asking why I haven't sent the signed contracts yet. I know that will be coming if I don't have signatures to them by five o'clock tonight.

Mark Whitmore wouldn't let this go the weekend without giving me grief that we were at an impasse on this deal yet again.

I've been pacing like a caged animal for the last fifteen minutes. The phone hasn't rung since before four, and the silence is provoking panic within me. I've been too nervous to reach out to my client.

Where the fuck is Eli Myers?

Charlie made me drink some water and tried to get me to sit down. He sent Claudia home an hour early in an attempt to make me feel better.

"What the hell?" I question to the air, finally breaking the quiet. "Where is he? What the fuck is happening?" I pick my cell up off the reception desk to scroll through it for the tenth time to see if I missed a call, which would be impossible since I've turned the volume to maximum and have been hovering over it the whole time.

The office phone rings and I jump. Charlie lays a reassuring hand on my shoulder, then moves to answer the phone.

"Greene Law Office. May I help you?" He waits a moment. "Yes, oh thank goodness Mr. Myers. We were starting to worry. Yes, she's free. I'll put you through."

I point in the direction of my office and head there to take the call, leaving Charlie out front as I close my office doors.

"Mr. Myers, is everything all right? I had our meeting calendared for four o'clock today." I'm fuming thinking this is yet another one of Claudia's mistakes. I will fire her immediately if she has screwed this up and maybe stop by her apartment and choke her too.

"Oh yeah. Everything is fine. I was just out in the field and I remembered I should have called ya this mornin'. I apologize."

"It's no problem, Mr. Myers," I assure him. I'm used to his procrastination. This is a big deal, and I'm willing to hold my breath and wait for his answer, wait for this tiresome undertaking to bear fruit no matter the delay.

It's already been so many months of headaches, I can't even count the number of ibuprofen I've gone through. I'm searching my desk drawer for some as I listen to him go on.

"Well, I guess I won't be needin' to come in today after all," he says.

"Yes, I've gathered that much. Did you speak with someone from Renewable Energy?" I grab the bottle of water off my desk and slip down a couple of pills.

"Well, yeah, I did. This mornin'. Again I'm sorry. I know yer time is valuable. I'll still pay ya for an hour today. I shoulda called sooner."

I'm starting to get anxious. This is not how our conversations normally go. It's usually about whatever new objections Myers has thought up in his head while in the field, or in the barn, or in the john. Who knows? But this time he's not getting into anything specific.

"As your attorney I must advise you that direct contact with the company could result in an outcome you may not actually want, Mr. Myers. Is there something else we need to negotiate? I thought we were ready to sign."

Patience, I cajole myself. Patience. No one wants a hot-headed woman as their attorney.

"I was, I was. But it's just…well, can I get sued for not signing? Is there anything legal that says I hafta sign this contract?"

Holy shit. Why is he asking me this?

"Well, technically no. You have not signed a letter of intent with R.E.E., nor have they signed one with you. Everything to this point has been just negotiations. There is no expressed intent in writing, no meeting of the minds until the contract is signed." I hold back my anger and continue. "Why do you ask?"

"Oh, good Alexis. That's good. I guess what I mean to say is that I can't sign with Renewable Energy. I won't be selling to them."

My stomach lurches and I throw a hand to my mouth. Somehow I will myself not to throw up.

The bright red balloon over my baby career, the one holding my ambitions as a new attorney, bursts into a thousand pieces and lands all around me.

My hopes to at least keep up with the competition as a small fish in a pond of sharks, hopes that I'd eventually soar into the air with a dream career, one I can honor my father with – all of those hopes are gone in this moment.

Tears are welling. I can't believe my shitty luck today.

"I, I'm sorry to hear that," I stammer.

Don't lose it! Put on your big girl panties!

"Please send me your bill for what ya put in, ya know, for your time so far," Myers says.

Ha! You bet your ass. And it won't be anywhere near covered by the five grand you retained me with, either.

"Of course. I think we have a few disbursements too, but nothing excessive."

"Well I'll pay it, whatever it is. And I'll be seekin' your advice soon on a new deal, if yer not too busy."

Is he kidding? Of course I'm not busy. Not anymore!

"Sure, whatever you need, Mr. Myers. Do you need to make an appointment now? I can put you back to Charlie."

The words come out absent-mindedly. I don't even care what he needs. It's probably something insignificant, like reviewing a lease or looking over yet another proposal he received to sell more equipment while downsizing the farm.

"No, not yet," he says. "Probably next week. I hafta call back. Got more work to do before the sun sets. Please say sorry to Mr. Whitmore for me. I know you both worked real hard."

No shit.

"Yes, I'll do that, Mr. Myers."

"Your dad would be real proud. You're a good lawyer. I promise to be in touch in a few days when I'm ready to talk again."

I muster a goodbye and he disconnects.

I sit, head-down in folded arms resting on Dad's desk as my tears freely flow, and I mourn my first huge loss as a lawyer.

It's finally Friday night, thank my fucking stars. This day has chewed me up and spit me out. My cheeks are stained from crying, but my head finally stopped pounding after a third ibuprofen.

I'm in jean shorts and a tank top, trying to relax on my back deck. Charlie is with me, manning the grill. His polo shirt and blue shorts are covered up with a bright red apron that belonged to Ben. It reads "Kiss The Cook...And Bring Him A Beer!" He looks so handsome even with the ridiculous accessory.

My wine glass has been refilled hourly, and I've got a nice buzz going. Jimmy Buffett is singing about sailing in the background.

"Really, Lex. Don't sweat it. He said he had something new to work on, right?"

"Yeah, I guess. I just feel so defeated, like I've spent the last year spinning my wheels. This was my first big fish. I thought I was reeling it in, all the while it was wiggling away from me. I just can't figure out why. Whitmore won't return my calls."

I tried to call the buyer's lawyer when my sobbing subsided, but got his voicemail. I left messages on his cell and at his office, apologizing profusely and saying that I didn't have much information to go on but that he was free to call me over the weekend. I'd refrained from emailing him, but that didn't stop me from checking the app on my phone every ten minutes to see if he'd sent one to me.

"Ours is not to reason why, babe. Let's just forget about it tonight. You need a break."

He flips a steak and flames flare up. It smells delicious. Huck is lying at Charlie's feet, his nose sniffing the smoke coming off the grill.

My two gentle giants.

I don't want to know what would I do without either of them.

"You're right. Enough with this pity party. Let's finish this bottle of Merlot and crash on the couch after our meal." I make a move to head for the kitchen and retrieve baked potatoes from the oven.

"You up for a movie?" I call out through the open window. "I'm not keeping you from Carter, am I?"

Carter is Charlie's sometimes-partner, who enters and exits like a weather front in Charlie's life. Right now, they are on-again though. They would likely have had plans for tonight.

"Nope. I'm meeting him out tomorrow night at The Rainforest for dancing. You should totally come out!"

Huck comes through the back door first, Charlie following with the platter of meat and grilled veggies.

"No thanks," I say. "I'd rather wallow in my troubles than try to out-dance your ass."

"Have it your way," he concedes. "And I'll even let you pick the flick tonight. *Pretty Woman? Steel Magnolias?* We can wallow together in the sadness that is Julia Roberts."

"How about *Iron Man?*" I ask. "The first one."

"Ooo, Robert Downey Jr. Excellent call. Done and done," he says, plating the meat at the counter where I've set our places. He takes a seat at one of the wooden stools. "Mmm, mmm, mmm," he says in appreciation. "I love meat!"

He chuckles to himself, and I laugh at another one of his perverse word plays, happy to have anything to laugh about at the end of this crap day.

7

Aidan

By Friday evening, my muscles are tense and my temper is easily brought to the surface by the slightest irritation. I'm on the verge of needing another shower or some raw physical exertion just to calm me down.

I've heard nothing from my uncle since I left him this morning, and no one can tell me what the hell is going on – not Byron or Samira, not our team in Manhattan. No one has been able to confirm whether Eli Myers did what he said he would do, and it's too risky (and too pushy) for me to call him now and directly ask.

Pushing my agenda would definitely not sit well with him, no matter how much he agreed with it.

I've snapped at Samira multiple times and made her stay an hour past her usual departure time of five o'clock to help Byron facilitate the full background check on Ms. Greene. We'd finally dug up everything there was, but still nothing from any of our contacts about Myers.

At six o'clock, I apologized for my shitty attitude to both of them. I sent Byron home to the smaller of my two lake houses in Falcon Lake where his home base has been whenever he's here. He would keep working our contacts from there on the Myers' side of things.

I sent Samira home with an extra five hundred bucks in cash to blow as she saw fit on the way. In fact, those were my specific instructions to her.

"Spend this before you get to your hotel."

I told her to buy something frivolous and fun, to make up for my ending her day so terribly.

She was grateful, as she always was. Above all, she was professional about the whole *Aidan-is-being-an-unreasonable-asshole* situation. She was always professional, which was precisely why I insisted she try living in the city of Stanton before deciding to depart my employ.

Just give it a chance, I had told her. I would set her up to work with a colleague in New York City or L.A. if she really didn't like it after a month.

She never flirted with me, never tried to use her looks to get her way or make advances. Perhaps it was her Nordic heritage, but her persona bordered on cold, which I found a great attribute in this circumstance. I could appreciate her beauty, of course – but I was not attracted to her at all. And she knew that I was a line not to be crossed if she was going to excel at her job – and keep it.

The token gift of cash was the least I could do before sending her back to her extended-stay hotel. She didn't complain about the accommodations. The property wasn't the finest hotel in the city, and nowhere near as luxurious as a place I would lease for her in Manhattan if we were there.

Still, it was the finest suite in the hotel, with all the amenities to sustain herself for the trial month – full kitchen, laundry facilities, two bedrooms, two bathrooms – anything she might need for herself or any visitors she might have. It would be enough until she figured out whether she was going to stay on here.

If I was forced, finding her replacement wouldn't be too daunting. Samira was capable, of course – and trustworthy. But I had a small pool of candidates to pick from that I'd vetted over the years. The handful of people that would drop everything at a moment's notice to become my personal assistant were former colleagues or classmates from college. Each one could step into Samira's role here in New York swiftly, with equal skill and the same degree of trust.

No one I had in mind would need more than a week of training at Samira's side to fine tune the complexities of the position. Whomever I selected could jump right in, but I am not comfortable with change – I hope Samira will stay.

I haven't told her as much and my attitude on nights like tonight certainly make it no bargain for her. But at least I'd praised her when she helped Byron get over the last hurdle to obtain Alexis Greene's medical history.

That had to be done discreetly (and slightly illegally) but we'd managed it without leaving a trace, without harm.

I avoided all conversation and external distractions while I waited for what I wanted. All distractions except for work, that is.

I ignored my mother's call to my cell that came in after five o'clock. I'd call her later or tomorrow when I had more news. She didn't want to dig up the past anyway. She probably just wanted to know I was all right.

I ignored the growing kink in my neck from hovering over my laptop for hours straight, plowing through a series of reports that I needed to catch up on.

Under normal circumstances, I would have been intrigued to get through the additional marketing research for a product one of my college buddies had begun to develop last year, after a solid five years of the idea rattling around in his head. Investing in the new tech for music streaming was a sure thing. It would likely fast track to become mainstream, even if he ended up selling it to a competitor so they could improve it and corner the market.

Instead, I felt an anxious determination to know every detail about her. I found myself rereading the same sentence of my man Oates' report three times, before pulling myself away to pace the room as Byron and Samira worked.

Thankfully, Greene's connection to Eli Myers and her appointment today by the Bar Association provided enough circumstance to warrant my anxiety in the eyes of my employees. Byron and Samira have not batted an eye at my request to find out *everything* about her or at my frustration each time we hit a dead end. Neither of them exhibited concern when I cursed under my breath with clenched jaw, moving restlessly between their side of the floor to mine to knock back a shot of whiskey in my private office.

Now, after six-thirty in the evening, I have quite the collection of material to read through about the mythical creature I'd met today.

Just as soon as I finish meeting with my shrink.

I'm aware that my impulsive need to learn more about her is likely a result of lust, as opposed to some noble desire to protect my philanthropy or myself. Images of the enchanting Mizz Greene have been tormenting me.

I've imagined her naked in every single one.

I fire up the seventy-inch flat screen at the end of the room, using the remote to pull up the menu for video conferencing. I push thoughts of her aside. I don't need my doctor to see me with a hard on as soon as I answer his call.

I take a seat on the sofa that faces the large screen, bringing Greene's file with me. It's an inch thick, but I can start to get through it while I wait for Doc Mason to call.

I glance through her academic transcripts from high school to law school, more impressed with each passing milestone. She graduated from a state university about an hour's drive away in 2011 with a Bachelor's Degree and a 3.9 grade point average. She'd majored in English with a minor in Music where my sources report she met the man that would become her boyfriend before her sophomore year of college and, later, her husband.

She went on to graduate Cum Laude from Stanton University College of Law in the spring of 2014.

I find the address of her law firm (literally two blocks from where I sit at this moment) and the address where she lives.

She owns her own home in Mirror Lake, on the opposite side of the lake from where I spent my first seven years of life. The deed is in both her name and her deceased husband's name, but as she told me face-to-face, she went by her maiden name.

Alexis Marie Greene.

Her husband was Benjamin Clayton. He died in December 2014.

Her list of accomplishments as a lawyer is slight, but she's only been at it two years. With that taken into account, she's well on her way to an exemplary career. She is a member in good standing of both Lake County and the state Bar Associations, as would be expected.

But she also obtained her real estate license after undergraduate study (why I don't know, but nevertheless it's there in black and white), and she is still licensed in that capacity.

She sat on several boards and committees from the time she was in law school, but not all of these were law related.

While she sat on some local boards as a student observer for a semester here or there (as with the county's Board of Realtors), she had varied volunteering pursuits, all of which appeared (at least on paper) to have the common thread of rectifying the plight of local men and women that were struggling with something.

Addiction. Disease. Illiteracy.

She volunteered at one philanthropic organization per year throughout her law school career, from Alcoholics Anonymous to the Children's Hospital to volunteering as a tutor for the local adult literacy program during her final year.

On paper, it appeared that Ms. Greene was not only smart and capable, but she actually gave a shit about more than herself.

And drop-dead looks too?

Yup. She's a fucking unicorn all right.

Before I can read on, the screen above me bleeps with my incoming conference call.

In that moment I decide not to bring up Alexis Greene.

And I'm definitely not going to bring up the girl from last week.

Robin, right?

Right.

No need to mention that momentary lapse in judgment.

I will talk to Doc Mason about the nightmares and what I can do to control them and talk through whatever I decide to be of importance in the moment.

On task and in daylight hours I'm fine, the memories buried deep enough that they do not surface. So far, it has been in the dark of night and in solitude that those demons rise up.

I will answer questions about how it's going, being back here. And what do I think the trigger for the nightmares is, what do I think they mean…blah, blah, blah.

But I'm not talking about my fucking feelings, guy.

You want to analyze it? Break it down like a football play with x's and o's? Discuss the least number of moves needed to put the demons in checkmate?

Good. Fine. I can do that.

But feelings? And do I want to sleep with my mother and do I want to kill my biological father and all that psychobabble bullshit?

No fucking way. And Doc knows better than to come at me with that.

I'm not naïve. I have knowledge and respect for the depths of this arena – the benefits, the contradictions, the enlightenment. From philosophy to psychology to psychiatry, I've learned. I'm no expert, but I'm wise to the teachings, having studied it some as a grad student, and even beyond that for as long as it piqued my interest.

Yes, therapy can be helpful or I wouldn't waste my time on it. And, yes, it can help us learn about ourselves, about where our guilt or idiosyncrasies stem from or (in my case) aid in dealing with the fact that we can't pass by an accident scene without physically becoming ill on the spot.

I'd come through that phase, better capable of dealing with my own demons.

All of them have name tags.

They've all met, been introduced to each other at the Class of 2008 "Aidan Is A Fucked Up Mess" reunion.

And oh what a party.

Once they all got together, it was the culmination of every bad thing within me finally getting the air needed to fuel a fire capable of overtaking me.

But after that…

After that, they were thoroughly suffocated by yours truly. Beaten to bloody by my hands and, eventually, with the help of my allies like Doc Mason.

I'd beaten them down the best ways I knew how.

With drive. With work. With exercise.

Passion and pride in all things, including sexual greatness (which is still – hands down – my favorite pursuit).

Those demons were bound with chains and devoid of oxygen, thrown into the depths of ocean in my imagination, locked in a weighted steel trunk.

Where they will fucking stay.

All I need to know is how to keep them there, while I'm getting acclimated here, getting my bearings in new surroundings that were once a home to me (however dark that home was).

I had taken Doc's advice about making my office and home base in the city as opposed to Mirror Lake. He thought it would be best and, after thinking on it myself, it was an obvious solution. I didn't need to prove myself by living in the small town that had made me a survivor.

Just coming here at all, taking on what I had in mind to open The Mirror Lake Center – it was enough.

It was more prudent to be in the city anyway, where there were as many amenities available as I needed and enough distance from my boyhood home that I could (hopefully) keep an even keel.

I'd been back to the Myers' farm today and, so far, that had evoked happy memories. But living in that area day-to-day?

That would have been a different story.

Doc and I open with talk about the weather changes and how things are going with the project before we delve into the nitty gritty.

The entire time I'm talking, I'm in just a pleasant mood.

My uncle is going to do what he said, if I listen to my gut. As I'm talking about it to the good doctor I can hear my instincts telling me I've panicked all afternoon for nothing.

I have research to engross myself in about exactly who Alexis Greene is.

Mystical Unicorn? Or just a disguised thoroughbred horse whitewashed and accessorized to perfection?

Just as soon as Doc finishes counseling me about how to put my nightmares into check, that will be the newest addendum to my list of goals.

8

Alexis

My weekend passes with a combination of rest and productivity as I try to keep from dwelling on the Myers fiasco.

Saturday it's near eighty-five again, and I am thankful for the central air in the house when I come in from mowing the yard.

By the afternoon, I've dropped off my dry cleaning and retrieved Huck from his appointment at Life's Ruff Doggie Day Spa in the center of town. He looks regal now, all clipped and trimmed to perfection with a fresh red bandana around his neck.

I spend Saturday evening with Chinese take-out, checking e-mails and surfing the web. I don't turn up anything new on Mr. Pierce.

I have not turned on the television since Charlie left the night before, hoping I missed seeing my interview with Melanie air on Channel Eight. Curiosity leads me to search the station website, but there is nothing there.

My thoughts are interrupted by a call from Gloria. We've texted back and forth about my lost deal since yesterday. We touch briefly on that, but she's calling to remind me her husband Harry's band has a gig next Saturday at O'Reilly's Bar in Falcon Lake. I love Harry's band, a mix of talented middle-aged guys that are crazy good musicians. They get together to do these gigs for fun when they are not at their day jobs or enjoying retirement.

Maybe I'll come, I tell her. She thinks we should do our rendition of The Indigo Girls' song that we worked on over the winter. It's been awhile since we rehearsed with the band, but I know we wouldn't really need it to get through it.

Music seems to be in my blood, just like the law.

My father introduced me to everything from the Big Band era to Led Zeppelin and, much as I hate to admit it, one of my mother's best qualities is the ability to captivate people when she sings, even with only the radio to accompany her.

I'm sensitive about music since I lost Ben. It was one of the things we both loved. We'd been to concerts all over the state, the East Coast and Canada. He loved seeing live local bands like Harry's. At home, I'd sing along while he played the guitar which he was damn good at.

Gloria makes me promise to think about going to the gig later in the week. She invites me to come over tomorrow too. Sunday is family day at her house, which always includes a big meal and a motley crew of friends, including Harry's buddy, Frank.

Frank is a great guy – an electrician from town – but he's a little sweet on me. Harry's been trying to encourage us to go out for a month now, but there are not even enough sparks there to light a match.

"Thanks Gloria, but I'll pass. I have some more stuff to do around here and I'd like to just relax tomorrow. Maybe lay out in the sun with a good book."

"How boring, Lex. Are you absolutely sure? The girls miss you."

Her teenage daughters are smart and beautiful, and I always enjoy chatting with them about celebrity gossip or boy crushes or tough teachers.

"Give them a squeeze for me and tell them I'll be over soon. Maybe next weekend."

"Have it your way," she says. "But don't wallow!"

I swear I won't and we disconnect.

Sunday, I putter around the house, knowing the woman I hired to help keep up on things around here isn't due in until Wednesday. As a reward, I sunbathe with a trashy romance novel on the deck and by night I'm relaxed and almost over the Myers deal.

I'm starting to see a bright side.

I'll still be compensated for my billable hours and maybe Myers' new case is an even bigger fish – if it's not just some document review he needs me for.

I can also get some favorable press from being Pierce's go-to for his community center project.

I've scanned the paper but still see no reports about Friday's meeting or Pierce's big announcement. I wonder if he's put a gag order on the local press.

Or maybe they're holding it as a story for tomorrow. There's always a lot of crime to report on over the weekend, especially when it's hot. People go even more *loco* in Stanton when it's hot. Shootings, theft, drug arrests, alcohol-related accidents. Maybe Pierce decided Monday would be a better day to share his pet project with the world, after the craziness of the weekend passed.

I'm hopeful this whole thing will not take too long. How long would it take to plan and complete a project like that anyway? Throw up a building, put out a sign, and fill the place with experienced staff for the kids that need help. No biggie.

Yeah, right.

I know with all the red tape the county will throw at us, it will not be that simple. No amount of money can buy off the planning committees, the environmental people that have to approve. The list is endless. I'm sure Pierce has a plan, but how close to fruition it is, I'm unaware. Maybe he's already done all this legwork.

Maybe I should call him, get him talking about it. Or himself.

What the hell? Where did that thought come from? I send it away. That isn't in my job description, as far as I know. Let him tell me what he wants me to do. I'm not that interested in pursuing him.

Er…it. The project.

I'm on a mission to stop thinking about the Billion Dollar Man and head for the kitchen. Huck and I are contemplating our dinner in front of the open refrigerator doors when my phone rings.

Charlie is checking up on me.

I'm fine, I tell him. He recounts his Saturday night to me – drinks, flirting with some bartender, and dancing with Carter. They had another fight, but took a cab home together. He knows I hate the thought of anyone drinking and driving.

He doesn't go into detail beyond that though. This is what we do. I love to hear all about Charlie, but I don't need to know about how he and Carter made up. The topic of sex isn't comfortable for me, especially considering I'm not having any.

I thank him for checking in and disconnect, ending up in my study staring out at the street.

A few kids are playing baseball in the yard across from me, and Mrs. Parker is riding past on her bike with her daughter Sophie.

And here comes Mr. Jackson Dean to take my mind off of Pierce, off of everything. There's still been no sign of Mrs. Dean or their daughter.

Jackson is jogging by in the evening's lazy heat, shirtless and shiny with perspiration. He's in green shorts that rise and fall, rise and fall with each forward motion to reveal his tanned, muscular thighs.

I bet he could crack walnuts with those things.

His skin is glistening in the sun. He probably doesn't smell very good, not like Pierce. But who cares at this distance? He's still a lovely distraction.

He's gone all too soon and I pass by Ben's old room before I head up the stairs just wishing for my bed, damn the early hour. The dog must have bumped the door open. I always keep this room closed off.

The room had been a den when we moved in. We had borrowed money to put a small addition onto the back of the house, turning the room into a bedroom by adding a large closet and a bathroom. I haven't been in there in months.

I can still smell his familiar scent. Gucci cologne and fresh linens.

I should really think about donating his things, but it's been too painful to even go in there. I close the door and head upstairs, Huck lumbering along behind me.

I feel sad again, and this time I couldn't give a shit about work or handsome neighbors, about failed real estate deals or working as a liaison to an attractive, wealthy man.

I'm just plain heartbroken from missing my best friend.

Monday I'm determined to get a fresh start. I'm up early, getting in a quick run on the treadmill. Huck's business is done and I'm showered and dressed by seven. I'm wearing black dress pants and a silk tank top in hot pink. I throw on a black business jacket to even out the loudness of the top.

I leave the fuck-me shoes in the closet and go with a lower pair of black heels today.

Early bird gets the worm! The words echo in my head in my dad's voice. I climb into the convertible to head for the city. It's too hot to have the top down, so it's windows up and A/C cranked.

I'm in my office by eight, coffee and a well-deserved pastry from the café fueling me. My computer blares highly motivating classic rock tunes. I'm thankful one wall is lined with volume after volume of the Laws of New York dating back to the late 1800's, which I inherited from my dad. It makes for great insulation, keeping the sound from reaching Reception.

Charlie comes in by quarter to nine in a regular Monday mood, ready to work but happy as usual. He says Claudia is out front, but I wouldn't know whether she was in the office or at home updating her social media accounts. I've been rocking out in my own little world, getting through a pile of work I've been putting off.

"Do you think we ought to talk about the Myers thing?" He eyes me hesitantly.

"No, I do not," I say firmly. "I'm fine, really." I smile at him, and the change in his posture is visible. He's relieved. "I would like us to talk some more about that marketing strategy you came up with using Dad's old contacts," I continue. "But preferably the young-old contacts, not the ones that actually *are* old. Or dead. You know how I shy away from estate work."

He laughs at my corny joke. This is better, I think. I hadn't realized how tense I was, how much we all had been, about Mr. Myers' sale. I'm almost thankful he's on the back burner now.

By five o'clock, I'm looking forward to a leisurely glass of wine when I get home and maybe a bubble bath. The weather is forecasted to turn cooler tonight. A front is expected to bring more seasonable May weather.

That's the way it is smack in the center of New York State. If you don't like what it's doing outside, wait five minutes and it'll change. It's a way of life here.

My cell is ringing as Claudia knocks on my office door. I know Charlie is otherwise occupied in his office, working on the marketing plan we went over earlier. I call to her that it's open, then hold my hand up gesturing that I'll be just a minute as I answer the call. I can see from the display that it's Ben's mother and our conversations are always short. She's calling from her home in Canada.

"Hello, Mrs. Clayton. How are you?"

I'm trying to listen to her, yet I can't help but notice what Claudia has come in here for. She's holding the newspaper from this morning which I have yet to see today. I motion to her to hand me the paper and leave. She smiles, lays the paper folded on my desk and exits.

I catch Mrs. Clayton say something about Ben. What did she say? I think I heard her say birthday.

Of course.

Ben's birthday is in June. Or was in June? My heart aches at the thought.

My poor Ben.

"So would you like to come up?" she concludes.

"I would love to, Mrs. Clayton. You are gathering on the weekend, you say?"

"Yes, in two weeks. The weekend after your American Memorial holiday. Can you make it?" She pauses in a wistful sigh. "George and I have been so lonely since Pamela went to school. She's home from University, and we'd love to have you both here."

Ben's sister Pam is such a beautiful soul. I do miss hearing about what she's up to. She hasn't texted me in a few weeks, our chats becoming more infrequent as the months passed.

"I promise I'll try. I will let you know in a few days if I can make it for sure. Okay?"

"You bet, dear. And if I don't hear from you by next Friday I'll phone you back. Take care of yourself, eh?"

Oh how I've missed those Canadian eccentricities of speech.

"Very good, Mrs. Clayton. I'll speak with you soon."

I hang up and unfold the paper. Claudia has left a note stuck to it that says, "Congratulations! You made page one!"

Typical Claudia. She's completely oblivious. Her excitement does not echo my sentiment at all.

A large picture of Aidan Pierce graces the front page. In it, he is dressed in the suit he wore on Friday. He's not smiling, but somehow he still looks approachable, friendly even.

And astoundingly hot.

Panty-melting, orgasm-inducing *hot*.

There's also a photo of me being interviewed by Melanie. I'm thankful the picture isn't very big. The caption reads *Alexis Greene, Esq. will be heading up the Community Center Project Committee for Mr. Aidan Pierce.*

The newspaper article has only a brief reference to me and my acceptance of the position based upon motion of Gloria Stearns, and a few quotes from Attorney Steven O'Hara about his fondness of the project and gratitude to Mr. Pierce for choosing our county for his grand gesture, for recognizing that our community needs this.

Then I get to the meat of the article.

Aidan Pierce is indeed no stranger to our area. He has had ties to the City of Stanton and the community of Mirror Lake since his youth. He intends to purchase real estate in Mirror Lake for the center, a non-profit organization that will be designed to assist at-risk youth. Eli Myers has declined to confirm, but this reporter has learned from unnamed sources that a large parcel of land owned by Mr. Myers is the sought after spot for Mr. Pierce's new project.

I'm stunned by the revelation.

Fuck. Me.

The pinprick to my baby business balloon, the cause of death for my lost (near million dollar) career-catapulting real estate deal with Eli Myers is none other than one Aidan Michael Pierce.

Sonnovabitch.

9

Aidan

I've spent the entire weekend dividing my time in half.

Half the time I'm in a state of constant motion, pushing myself physically.

The other half has been spent pushing my brain as a student of the perplexing Ms. Alexis Greene.

I've gone running each morning and afternoon, splitting my usual eight miles into four each time knowing I'd need the exertion twice a day to tame my physical response to the subject matter I'm studying.

Byron has convinced the owner of the city gym a block over to allow me to use his facility for a brief time after his normal business hours end. Any night between nine and eleven the place is mine alone. This will be sufficient until my home gym is out of the planning stages and completed on the fourth floor. At the city gym I can lift weights, swim, use any equipment I'd like or run the indoor track without dealing with the public.

All of that comes at a cost of course. But it's worth every cent.

My reading about Alexis has been interesting, and I was surprised to learn she has a skeleton of her own tucked away in a figurative closet.

Yet, I have not uncovered anything to disparage her place in my mind as the rare breed of woman I'd predicted.

The kind of woman I'd never come across before.

Her medical history reveals nothing of consequence. She's healthy and has maintained regular exams with her doctors (a general practitioner and a GYN) throughout her adult life. She has a prescription for birth control pills.

She met with a therapist beginning a few months after her husband's death and regularly for a year, but it appears that stopped a few months ago.

I admire that she took the initiative to deal with her grief head-on and with professional help. She was stronger than I had been in my grief. Apparently, she didn't need to sabotage herself with a downward, out of control spiral before seeking help.

The cause of her husband's death was natural from what I've uncovered – but it was a sudden loss, clearly unexpected – and definitely something worthy of time in therapy.

Her birth date is September 29, 1989.

She's a Libra.

How appropriate.

The sign of balance and harmony with a symbol of the scales, as interpreted from The Scales of Justice held by the Greek personification of divine law and custom, Themis.

That seemed to suit her perfectly.

Someone whose strengths would lie in her ability to cooperate and remain diplomatic in any situation, to be a problem solver. Who else would make a better lawyer?

She also fit the astrological profile of having that unique haze of harmony around her, the kind that would naturally draw others in.

I realized I was certainly fitting into that category.

I was drawn to her.

I hadn't been able to put her out of my mind completely since I'd shaken her hand.

I never give astrology a significant amount of weight when it comes to sizing someone up, but I always found it an added layer of insight.

I used a combination of tools to chip away at someone's façade to get to the bottom of who they really were if I truly needed to know.

Some were easier to crack than others but the tool kit was always the same.

Knowledge.

Psychology.

Philosophy.

Logic.

All necessary, of course.

But a bit of mysticism never hurt and instinct had to be a considered factor.

I've never been of the camp that insists the world is black and white, all practical and nothing more, like so many of my intellectual peers.

The human condition is so much more and so influential to that practical world, even if some might not admit it.

As much as I knew fact, I'd learned just as much about the other end of the spectrum. I valued balance in everything, took solace in countering the metaphysical with the tangible and sensible.

Ms. Greene certainly had that coming out of her pores.

Balance.

A contradiction between conservative and just the opposite, as much as she didn't realize it. I could see that wildfire lying dormant underneath, like when she'd handled that reporter.

She had a drive to succeed, as evidenced by her stellar academic history and the ambition to reopen her father's law firm.

According to a newspaper article from a year ago, she chose to start her practice in tribute to her deceased father in the same building he once owned. Her practical ambitions are balanced with sentiment and seemingly absent of any ego-driven motivations.

When I meet with her Tuesday, I intend to push her on it just enough to see if I'm right.

In the meantime, Byron came through with my uncle's status.

Eli called R.E.E. to back out of the sale just as he promised he would.

I am not aware if Ms. Greene knows this yet (or whether she knows it has anything to do with me), but I presume not. She has my card, and I would not put it past her to contact me directly the minute she finds out.

Sunday afternoon I make time to review the background reports on the other two attorneys.

Jade McCall is the wife of prominent plastic surgeon Sawyer McCall. I'm aware of the name. Some of the women I've met in L.A. have crossed the country to consult with him.

Mrs. McCall has been an attorney since the late nineties and has a successful career locally in matrimonial and estate law.

She also has a history of running around on her husband according to my sources, but publicly her marriage was intact. If I can keep Greene running point on the committee, I'll likely not have to see McCall much, if ever. Dr. and Mrs. McCall have a list of prominent colleagues and friends in Lake County that will hopefully contribute to my cause. She is an asset and not a liability at this point.

The other attorney could prove to be a problem, however. Allen Richardson has fewer connections here locally, no experience in real estate acquisition needing town, county, and environmental approvals (the area of my project he'd volunteered for), and he has a lot of connections downstate close to R.E.E.'s headquarters.

It also appears he had some connection to Jade McCall, but I haven't uncovered what yet. I find no evidence that they were sleeping together, but I have not ruled it out.

I've insisted that Byron dig deeper on him so that we don't miss anything that might cause scandal or conflict for the whole project.

More importantly, I have to be sure that Richardson doesn't have an agenda of his own.

His education was sufficient, though his background was meager, coming from low income parents that resided in Pennsylvania. Beyond this, instinct told me to proceed with caution.

I've eliminated the possibility of Ms. Greene's interview to air on Channel Eight tonight. Melanie Adams had not done an acceptable job, a fact which I made sure to point out to her boss, in addition to the fact that she had crossed a professional line when she probed about Greene's dead husband on camera.

I contacted the newspaper, making certain they could feature an article tomorrow with the details I'd prefer be released. An anonymous source will be quoted in the article.

At that point, I have no doubt shit will certainly hit the fan.

After my workout at the gym Sunday night, I head back to the loft and shower, again contemplating the overwhelming Ms. Greene and relieving myself of the thoughts of her the only way I can. My release comes with a shudder as the scalding water cascades over me, my cock in my hand.

The anticipation of meeting her here on Tuesday is greater than the Christmas morning I'd woken up with my first million in the bank.

I'll be one floor below, talking about my goals and ambitions and probably having to spell out for her exactly what a tidal wave she was unknowingly about to drown in, all the time wondering if I'll ever have her right here where I stand, naked and wet.

And mine.

By ten a.m. Monday morning, I'm pacing my private office a floor below my loft on Harrison Street envisioning what to do about the situation at hand.

The newspaper has placed the story about my endeavor on the front page. Alexis is featured in a very flattering picture, but it's a small inset within the article. The larger picture is of me, the bulk of the article focused on the Center.

That's fine. Great, actually. My project is getting press.

What is frustrating, however, is that she hasn't contacted me.

No emails or calls berating me for sending a year's worth of her hard work sailing off a proverbial cliff to certain doom.

Is it possible she's even more balanced than I thought? Callous, even?

If that had been me, there's no doubt I'd be chasing down my adversary asking why, asking what could possibly be worth sabotaging someone in such a way.

And if she could see her way clear to do that, to track me down and let me have it, at least I could explain myself.

I'm realizing I may never be given the chance. She might be too angry to confront me, or worse, she may not give a damn at all. And if the latter was the case, I'd no doubt lose respect for her.

After the way she'd commanded that scene with the reporter, I could not fathom that was a rare display, that she wasn't full of that fire in all that she did especially when it came to something as consuming as a deal she'd spent a year negotiating for Eli Myers.

Could it be she hadn't seen the article yet? Between the local radio broadcasts commenting about it and the paper itself, I don't know how could she have avoided it.

My thoughts are interrupted by an incoming call on my cell.

It's my mother.

"Good morning," I answer.

"Aidan! There you are. I've left three messages and you haven't called back. Are you really *that* busy?" She sounds overly relieved to talk to me, leaving me feeling like an asshole for neglecting her when she reached out.

"I'm fine, Mom. I'm sorry, I've just been trying to catch up with things this weekend and get the Center off the ground with the locals. How are things there?"

"Oh fine, fine. We're off to London tomorrow but just for a week. The Leonards' son is getting married this weekend."

"Great. Tell Niall congratulations for me."

"I certainly will." She pauses. "Have you been doing well since you've been in Stanton?"

"I'm fine. Really." *Except for the nightmares.*

"You know how I worry about you."

I sigh. This much I know. And I've learned it's better to keep quiet because she'll worry no matter what.

"I'm so proud of you, Aidan. I just don't want you to sacrifice how far you've come. If you decide it's too much, please reach out to us. Dad and I are only a call away. We can always…"

I cut her off before she can get emotional. We've covered this. Several times.

I love my mother, but she can be overly cautious when it comes to me. With good reason perhaps, given my track record – but I never want to be the cause of her concern.

"I'm fine. I've met with Eli Myers and it went well. He's decided to sell to me. The planning stages are moving along. I've got the Town Supervisor on board. It's full steam ahead."

She's quiet for a minute, likely lost in her own memories of her sister's husband.

"So," she pauses again, "you went back to the farm then?"

"I did."

"How – how was he?"

"Aged, but doing fine. He asked about you."

"He did?" She sounds genuinely shocked.

"He did."

"And what did you say?"

"I just told him you sent your regards and left it at that."

"Oh," she sighs aloud. "Did you…remember anything, going back there?"

"Just being at the farm. It hasn't changed much. It's unreal. Of course the town has grown up some. But the farmhouse itself was very familiar."

"I don't know why you're doing this. It can't be easy for you."

"I am handling it. I Skyped with Doc Mason Friday night. He assures me I'm not experiencing anything of concern since I've been here."

"Good, good," she says. "Wait – what are you experiencing?"

Shit. I don't reply. I hear her suck in a breath as though she has figured something out.

"Your night terrors. They're back?"

Vivid memories flood me of her coming into my room, shaking me awake, trying to stop my screaming. I remember hearing my own voice howling as I'd finally snap out of it.

The dreams happened often at certain points in my life.

First when we moved to California and I was only eight, then many years later after losing Thaddeus. It was months before I got back to any semblance of normalcy, but Mom was there through it all until I was coping on my own. She'd had her own grief to deal with, losing a son – but she was always more concerned with me.

"I can handle it, Mom. It's okay. They haven't been that bad."

"Aidan. Please. You don't have to do this. There is so much you can do from here. Whatever it is you want to do, your Dad and I can match your funds. Really put a dent in the problems there. But it doesn't require you to be there."

"I appreciate that, but this is where I'm meant to be now. And really, I am fine. It's only happened a couple of times." This is not the complete truth, but I have to put her mind at ease in any way I can. I hear her resigning some three thousand miles away. She knows how stubborn I am when I set my mind to something.

"All right, Aidan. It's your call. Obviously, you've been an adult long enough to make this choice. But please don't sacrifice your health."

"Deal," I say. "I have to get going. I've got people waiting on me." This is the truth. Byron and Samira are outside my office door waiting for me to let them in. We were due to meet five minutes ago.

"Okay, hon. I'll call you the minute we get back from London."

"Thanks. I appreciate the call. Love to Dad."

She says her farewell wistfully, and I disconnect more determined than ever.

The only thing that will make her anxiety go away, the only thing that can justify my actions and how they will affect Ms. Greene, and the only possible outcome I will accept is the success of this center.

The Center's success meant the course of thousands of young lives here would be changed for the better.

In this place that failed my mother so miserably in the faraway past, I will make certain that in the future it doesn't happen that way again.

I'm still restless Monday afternoon, hearing nothing from *Ms.* Greene. My determination is dwindling into exhaustion. My nightmares have not come back since talking to Doc Mason, but my sleep has been showing an unhealthy pattern of only coming a few hours at a time with an hour (or longer) break in between.

I need to rest easy and early tonight.

At five o'clock, I dismiss my staff of six from their cubicles and ask Byron to stay in the city tonight. He has an efficiency apartment available nearby in the instances that I prefer him to be here rather than a half an hour's drive away in Falcon Lake. I need him to be on-call tonight in case more research is required before I meet with the tantalizing Ms. Greene tomorrow.

There's a storm predicted for later on but right now the evening is beautiful. Upstairs, I head to my walk-in closet and replace my business attire with jeans and a t-shirt. I grab my motorcycle helmet, deciding to take a ride to an out of the way Italian joint a few miles outside the city.

The drive is short but just the jaunt I needed to clear my head. The fresh air whizzes by me as all of my concentration is on the ride, the thrum of the bike, the highway noise, the tactical maneuvers between traffic to get where I need to be.

All of it allows me to turn off my nagging thoughts, if only for ten minutes.

I park and head into Antonio's. It's a mom and pop establishment I found my first week here. The restaurant would have been here as far back as when my mom worked in Stanton, having opened in the late forties, the business being handed down from generation to generation.

The menu likely hadn't changed much. Everything was authentic and homemade from the sauce to the pasta.

The smell of baking bread hits me as I enter, making my mouth water. It's early (only five-thirty) and there are only two other sets of patrons in the small dining room to my right. I'd guess them all to be an average age of seventy-five.

I take one of the stools at the small bar, rather than intruding for a table to my right where the other two couples are.

A woman approaches me from behind the bar. She's in her forties and, judging by her dark hair and olive complexion, I've pegged her as a granddaughter of one of the immigrants that started this business over sixty years ago.

"What can I get you, Mr. Pierce?" I've been here twice now and she's waited on me both times. I don't know her name. She's all business, having done this for a number of years. She is always seemingly unimpressed by me. I know this is one reason why I like this place so much, but the food trumps even this fact. It's the best I've had since I've been here.

I order the specialties of the house for both my drink and meal – an old-fashioned with top shelf rye and the lasagna.

"Coming right up," she says.

She relays my drink order to the bartender. He's a large, tall man with hair as white as his tailored suit coat. I learned my first time here that he's hard of hearing, but he was always friendly. The only thing I've ever seen him do is make drinks. He doesn't cash people out, and he doesn't wait tables. I'm certain he is an older member of the family that just does this because he loves it, and it gives him reason to get up each day. He sets my drink down as the waitress departs for the kitchen to place my order.

I nod by way of thanks and again look around to take in the place, which is likely as unchanged as the menu since its inception in the forties.

The few booths in the dining area are tuck-and-roll tan vinyl. The chairs are silver metal with red vinyl seats. There are pictures of the owners and their family gracing every wall.

The room is adorned with red, green and white ambient light above a continuous shelf that runs below the ceiling. It's decorated with cutouts of various shapes – trees and Italian landmarks like the Colosseum and the Roman Forum. Glenn Miller and His Orchestra play softly through the old-timey speakers in the corners of the room.

The place emanates nostalgia. Old-school charm. Simpler times. Even the cash register is a relic, though it's there only for show now. It's probably as old as the bartender.

A woman approaches from behind me, from the corner of the dining area where she had been sitting with her husband. I could hear them speaking Italian from their corner booth. She's barely over five foot with graying hair, dark features, and a plump figure. She stands on tiptoe to peer through the pass through window between the bar and the kitchen, waving to the waitress as she catches sight of her.

The waitress comes out from the kitchen and the two of them converse in Italian as the elderly woman waits to be cashed out.

The waitress's name is Angelica, I learn. They talk about how bad the storm is going to be later, neither having any idea that I speak fluent Italian.

"Sento che la tempesta sta per venire rapidamente e furiosamente," I start.

I hear the storm is going to come quickly and furiously.

They both stop talking and turn to look at me.

"Voi Signore dovrebbe essere molto attenti sempre a casa," I finish.

You ladies should be careful getting home.

"Ah sì, signore. Sì." The older woman says. "How do you learn the Italian so well?"

"Ho imparato da solo i migliori insegnanti. E ho vissuto a Roma per un tempo."

I learned from only the best teachers. And I lived in Rome for a time.

"Ah sì, sì. Roma. Una bella città. E tu sei un uomo bellissimo," she says.

Yes, Rome. A beautiful city. And you are a beautiful man.

"Grazie," I say.

"Se non fossi così vecchio Faccio i bambini con questo," This she directs at Angelica as she lets out a hearty laugh.

If I was not so old, I make babies with this one.

That has me full on smiling.

"You have a wife?" she asks me.

"No, ma'am. I do not."

"Ah, see Angelica?" she says. "You should marry this man."

"Stop, Mrs. Romano," she scolds. "You know I'm engaged to David."

Mrs. Romano bristles. "Bah!" she says. She turns her attention to me. "He's no good for her. He's in a band. Out all the time. She needs you."

She directs her next statement to Angelica. "Un bel uomo che parla la vostra lingua."

A beautiful man that speaks your language.

I smile again as Angelica looks at me pointedly. "I'm sorry," she says. "One too many Old-Fashioneds for Mrs. Romano tonight."

I chuckle and put up a hand as if to say no, it's fine. She's a charming old world woman. I'm not put off in the slightest.

Mr. Romano pipes up from the corner of the room, asking what is taking so long. Mrs. Romano tells him she's coming right over.

"Good night, Mrs. Romano," I tell her. "È stato un piacere conoscerti."

It was a pleasure to meet you.

"Sì," she says. "Sì." She leans up to where I sit on the stool and air kisses both cheeks. "Ciao, beautiful man. You find yourself a nice woman. A good woman," she says, "and you make the babies with her."

She is certainly full of character. Old-fashioned and adorable.

But right now all I can think about is the beautiful woman that I want to find me.

How is Alexis Greene not lighting up my phone right now? How is she not feeling any inclination to reach out to me?

I finish my drink and contemplate what I can do to facilitate a conversation with her.

And more importantly, how I'm going to get her to understand that the deal I pulled out from under her was not in her best interests anyway. That my intentions are good and honorable.

That I want to fuck her mercilessly.

Ah, but no.

I'll definitely leave out that last bit.

No mixing business with pleasure.

I've never crossed that line, and I don't intend to start now.

But what if she won't keep our meeting tomorrow? What if she read that newspaper article and was so livid she fled to Canada?

I'm being irrational on that one, but I can't help it. My mind reels.

My lasagna arrives (which looks as amazing as it smells) and an idea comes to mind. I pull out my phone and send an email to Byron while my food cools to a temperature that won't sear the inside of my mouth.

If Alexis Greene isn't going to come to me, I may need to go to her.

She could be thinking a thousand things right now, and it leaves me supremely unsettled not to know exactly what those thoughts are.

Though I can't pinpoint why, my obsessive need to know wins.

I have to find out where she is and confront her.

As soon as possible.

10

Alexis

By seven p.m., I've shared the article with Charlie and dragged him to the Little Italy section of the city. We've each finished a plate of the Monday night pasta special at Piccolini's.

Dean Martin serenades in the background and we've nearly reached the bottom of our second bottle of wine. I paid no attention to what kind of wine it was when Charlie ordered it. I don't care. It's red and wet and taking the sting out of my wounds.

"Can't fuckin' believe it," Charlie says, shaking his head as he pushes his plate away. "It's not fuckin' believable."

I just nod. I haven't found words yet.

"You worked so hard, Lex. Then poof! Mr. Money Bags comes in and upends it all on his philanthropic whim. I don't care if he is sex on sticks. He's a selfish a-hole."

I can't help but laugh at that.

"We both worked hard, Charlie. And it's not even that." I think about how smug Pierce had been when we met. He must have known I was involved in the Myers sale.

I'm flat out pissed again and feeling riled despite the calming effects of the wine. "This whole scenario playing out makes me look like an idiot that doesn't know what's going on right under her nose. Not only in my own town but with my own client for hell's sake!"

"I know that's how you feel. But that's just your perception, Lex."

I huff in non-agreement, but he continues.

"Look, no one really knows the depth of our work for Myers, except us and Whitmore. And he can't discuss it either with client confidentiality. The public will just see it as you helping out on a charitable project for a good cause." Charlie tops his wine glass off and sets the empty bottle on the table. "If you still do it," he adds.

A new wave of nausea washes over me. It does not mix well with anger.

"I hadn't even thought about that." I take a sip of wine and push my plate away. "What happens when Whitmore finds out that I'm some lackey for Pierce on his community center set smack dab in the middle of land his client was set to buy? He'll think I'm either an idiot, an opportunist, or worse – that I sabotaged his client's deal. I could get in serious trouble for this."

"We both know that is not how it went. He would never think any of those things about you. It's just a coincidence. No one would believe you put your heart and soul into this for a year just to be working with Pierce on the sly."

I consider what he's saying but can't believe how this is all unfolding. *Why me?*

"I told you I shouldn't have gone to that meeting Friday," I mutter at him. "Maybe I need to call him, get myself off this project. I think it's the best move," I say.

I'm secretly wishing it weren't the case, saddened by the thought that I'll never again get to take in the sight of him up close if I make that call. But I know I'm right.

The waiter brings my receipt and credit card and leaves after clearing the table. I put my card away, and Charlie tries to hand me a twenty.

"No," I insist. "This is on me, especially after today." I shoo Charlie's gesture away. "I'll get paid for the hours on Myers so far. The least I can do for all your hard work is buy you dinner."

"Thanks, Lex," he says. "Next one's on me."

"Never mind that," I say, dismissing him. "Let's go get drinks somewhere. You know anyplace?"

"There's Sitting Bull next door," he says, smiling coyly.

"That's a gay, er…gentleman's bar, right?" I'm smiling too.

Charlie's laughing, his eyes twinkling from the wine and my ridiculous attempt at being politically correct. "It is, but they also allow pretty girls in on occasion," he says, taking my arm.

I give him a sideways glance and prop my sunglasses on my head as we make our way to the street. The sun is about to set and the cold front they've predicted will probably be through soon, judging by the warm breeze that's now a stiff wind.

"Whatever. I just want to get shitfaced and take a cab home."

"What about Huck?"

"I'll text Mrs. Parker. She'll have her daughter walk him for me. He ate this morning."

"Alright then, honey. Let's do this."

Moments later, we're standing at the bar's entrance. I'm looking over Charlie's muscular frame, all handsome even in his business attire. He's left his tie back at the office and undone the top button on his blue silk shirt to reveal just enough skin, enticing everyone within thirty feet of him.

We show our licenses to the bouncer and Charlie pays for our covers. Thankfully, the music is still a bit quiet and we don't have to shout at each other. It's only eight-thirty.

"Heads up, Lex," he says to me before we even make it past the front door. "It'll probably be busy for a weeknight. Their *Mount Up Monday* promo for the mechanical bull starts at ten and shots are on special for two bucks."

Oh boy.

I look around at the darkened barroom, lit only by purple fluorescent lights and glow-in-the-dark bracelets worn by the wait staff. The guys are all young and well-built, wearing black bull rider's pants and nothing above their waists but a red silk bow tie. Even if I don't fit in, at least the view is pleasing.

There's an average sized dance floor and the DJ is gearing up for the night, going through files on his laptop. The mechanical bull is in the back near a second bar area and the restrooms.

We grab stools at the bar near the entrance, and Charlie asks me what I'd like.

"I'll have a White Russian."

"I knew one of those once," he says with a wink. He orders a beer and my drink and sets money on the bar. While we wait, I text Mrs. Parker who assures me that Sophie will take Huck for a walk before she turns in for the night.

By the time the cheap shots start, I've only nursed one drink and my goal of getting drunk is some ways away. The pasta in my belly has soaked up the wine and I'm feeling sleepy. We've moved to a small table at the back of the bar, in view of the dance floor and the bull riding. Only a few timid souls have stepped up to ride or dance, but the crowd is starting to build and outside there's a line to get in.

"I'm not feeling this," I say, sliding my near empty drink across the table.

A very attractive waiter passes by and Charlie grabs his arm. He's about my height, but he has a slightly better tan, a lot more muscles, and spiky blond hair. I can tell he's about to object to being pawed, but when he sees Charlie he smiles and leans in close.

"What can I do for you, sir?" A name tag pinned to his belt loop advertises that his name is The Matador.

I can't tell what Charlie orders. The music is cranked then, the bass line drowning them out.

The waiter leaves and Charlie just smiles at me.

Uh oh.

B y eleven, sensible Alexis Greene is M.I.A.

Undersexed Lex isn't here either though. It is a gay bar, after all.

I'm feeling glad to just be alive and feeling no pain either. Charlie's bought us at least three rounds of shots. I lost track because every time The Matador comes by Charlie stops him for something, unless we're on the dance floor.

Usually I'm feeling too reserved to be out here, but it isn't like I'm trying to land a date. I'm just losing myself in the music, letting go. It feels unlike me. I haven't been on a dance floor since law school. Even then I suffered through it for the bachelorette party of the one girlfriend I had who has since gotten pregnant and moved to Manhattan with her rich husband.

Tonight the dancing feels amazing.

I'm insistent that I must look ridiculous in my low heels and business attire, but Charlie's removed my jacket, telling me I'm one sexy bitch as he reveals my pink silk tank top.

"Of course no one here will take you home," he grins, shouting over the music. "But you're still hot!"

Try as he might though, Charlie cannot get me on the bull. At that, I drew the line. I can tell he's contemplating it. He's watched just about every guy that's made an attempt from our spot on the dance floor.

He's left me to my own devices a few times and I'm drawn in by one attractive guy, then feel one moving in time behind me. The guys are flirty and fun but so much different than a straight guy that's trying to separate you from your clothes when the song is over.

I pull my sunglasses over my eyes and throw my head back, taking in the heat of the lights. I'm in my own little groove dancing to a Sia song. I can't think of the name of it. I can't think at all, really. My head is swimming from the liquor, bathing in the bass-driven music.

Dance partner number two tells me what hot moves I've got and nicknames me Hollywood. I laugh, throw the sunglasses back on top of my head and wink at him as I leave the floor in search of Charlie. The DJ has selected a slow song and the dance floor clears out, save a few couples.

I can't find my friend back at the table and there's a large crowd around the bull riding area. It occurs to me that I have to pee, but something else seems more pressing in my recently liberated state.

I have to call Aidan Pierce and quit his project before it starts.

I pull his business card out of my purse and run my thumb over the glossy print. The card is classy, professional. I put it away without even looking at it but now realize it's understated in the same way mine is.

The symbol I saw on the silver holder he pulled from his pocket is on here too, but it has no meaning to me. His phone number is beneath his name and title.

I head for the restroom and dial the number, but don't program it in. What's the point? I'm calling to put an end to this guy's influence in my life.

I never want to hear his name again.

The door to the ladies' room closes behind me, blocking out the music and the cheers of the crowd. The only sounds I can hear are my heavy breathing and him talking on the other end with that captivating voice. My breath catches in my throat until I realize it's only his voicemail greeting.

Shit! Do I leave a message?

No dumbass, it's after ten at night. The guy is a genius billionaire, he's probably sleeping.

Not that he needs any beauty rest.

I panic and hang up just as the beep finishes.

Moments later my phone is put away, thank goodness, and I'm steadying myself in a stall doing what I should have done in the first place – pee and get the hell out of here. Maybe I'll head back to the dance floor.

I stand at the sink a minute after washing, finally feeling my heartbeat slow down after that ridiculous test of bravery.

Aidan Fucking Pierce. What the hell was I thinking?

I'm looking for myself in the mirror, but all I can see is some tousle haired, visibly drunk woman with a surprisingly unwrinkled silk top. My jacket is somewhere. Where? Yes, back at the table. I'm grateful that the flush caused by alcohol is keeping my sleeveless arms warm. I may even need another shot.

I reach for a breath mint from my purse and return my sunglasses to it. I take a mental survey before I exit. Do I need to throw up? Am I queasy? Do I have the spins? No, no and no. Headache? Not yet. I squirt myself with a bit of flowery body spray from the array of product on the counter. Good to go.

As I exit the bathroom I'm actually feeling a little hungry. I'm considering asking Charlie if we can hit the diner up the street before I head home when I see the crowd still gathered around the bull. They're ogling and cheering for someone.

I make my way through in time to see Charlie up on the mechanical threat, holding his own. I smile proudly, shouting in encouragement and watching him dazzle everyone as he dominates the beast.

My smile has turned into laughter as the bull comes to a stop and he's still on, roaring with dominance and circling his arm in the air like he's got a lasso. I'm clutching my stomach from laughing so hard as he makes his way off the bull and over to me. He picks me up and spins me around in celebration, then sets me down as a few guys come over to congratulate him (and hit on him, I'm sure). He's the only one who's stayed on that long.

I roll my eyes and head back for the table still laughing, looking to collect my jacket.

Carter is sitting where I had been earlier, looking none too thrilled and sipping a martini. He is wearing jeans, sandals, and a grey t-shirt with a washed-out logo on it. His black hair is gelled to crispy perfection and he appears freshly showered.

He's handsome, even when he looks angry.

"Carter!" I exclaim, acting a little overjoyed to see him. He gives me a smile, but he's clearly ticked at Charlie's new little fan club. We hug and I pick up my jacket. After the pleasantries I'm out of here before World War Three starts.

"How are you, Lex? You look great," he says, sitting back down. I stay standing.

"Thanks. I'm doing all right. It's been a rough couple of days at the office, so Charlie thought he'd take me out. Get my mind off things."

I don't bother to go into detail, as Carter doesn't pay much attention to our work. Usually he's all about himself or all about sex. There isn't much else left to discuss except the weather.

"So, is it raining yet?"

He looks beyond me at the small crowd finally dispersing around Charlie.

His reply is a curt "no".

Charlie makes his way back to me and rests a hand on my shoulder as he addresses his on-again, off-again lover.

"Hey," he says.

"Hey yourself," Carter replies coldly.

I can feel the chill radiate between them. *Time to go!*

"Thanks for taking me out, Charlie. It was much needed. I'm going to call a cab and head out." I give him a hug and a peck on the cheek. "Play nice," I whisper. "I'll see you in the morning."

I say goodbye to Carter and give him a half wave. I hate how possessive he is of Charlie, when half the time he could care less about what's going on in Charlie's life.

It's none of your business! No one asked you!

I shout back in my own head. *That's precisely why I'm leaving!*

I leave the lovers to quarrel or make up or whatever the hell they feel like doing as I step outside into the night.

11

Aidan

Byron hasn't tracked Ms. Greene's whereabouts just yet, and I've got some time to kill.

I take a long drive after dinner, favoring back country roads instead of the highway. The landscape is jaw-dropping to me, so different than anywhere else I've lived. Hills are dotted with trees turning bright green. The roads wind through them smooth and even with elevation changes every few miles. I love the solitude I find on the drive. No one is in front of me or behind me. It's just me and the bike.

Lake County is aptly named. There are more lakes than I can count, each one of them its own unique appeal. I head south, past Mirror Lake and through Raeford on my way to one of my most recent property acquisitions.

This one is in Falcon Lake, which is a bit larger and a tourist attraction at the town's center. The affluent are more prominent here than in other areas of the county.

Byron stays at the second of my two properties here, but this one – this one is for me.

The massive log A-frame sits on a few acres, which made it one of the rarities here. Lake properties were sold at a premium, even here in rural New York, and typically with small lots. Water frontage increased sale prices and hiked taxes from expensive to outrageous for most people.

I'd bought the home from a successful car dealer that had dealerships all over the state. He decided to retire and head for a warmer climate.

His abandonment was my gain.

He'd only had it built two years ago, furnishing it with high-end everything from the logs themselves to the imported finishes throughout the house.

So far I haven't even had time to turn on the power, but that doesn't prevent me from riding up the steep driveway now. I climb the steps to the wrap around porch. I sit in the swing that's hewn from the same cedar logs as the house and take in the view of the lake far below. The shoreline is across the road, accented with a boathouse and a sprawling lawn that must have been an expensive investment for the prior owner.

Before I can take a breath and relax, my cell rings with a call from Byron.

"Yeah?" I answer. Longer than a moment's peace would have been nice.

"I found her."

By ten o'clock, I'm back at the loft.

I'm sitting on the couch in my office ignoring news on the television only because I'm not sure what else to do.

Byron has tracked Ms. Greene's cell phone to a bar across town in the Little Italy section of the city. With our combined resources, that part was fairly easy.

The difficult part is that it's a gay bar.

One that boasts it's the home of a mechanical bull.

In other words, completely outside my comfort zone.

What she'd be doing there, I have no idea. Nevertheless, that's where she is.

As much as I want to confront her, ask her why she's not letting me have it for wrecking the Myers sale to R.E.E., I can't bring myself to go there and find her.

I put Byron on call to keep track of her whereabouts for the evening from his apartment nearby.

I'm restless, wanting to go out for a run but too full from my indulgence at Antonio's to make it a reality. Instead I head upstairs to shower, shave, and re-dress in fresh jeans and t-shirt. I sweat through everything after my ride in the muggy evening heat, anyway.

I head for my desk in the home office of the loft and check email, figuring I'll respond to a few before turning in. I have several from Lionel Grey, my trusted right hand man in L.A. I address each one quickly, but one sent only moments ago catches my attention. The subject line is R.E.E. and the content of the message is one sentence asking me to call him at my earliest convenience.

Jesus, Lionel. He could have just called me. Since moving out here, he'd been treating me like a delicate situation. He never wanted to disturb me or inadvertently wake me given the time difference.

During our last conversation, I reprimanded him – which I'd never had to do before. I had no qualms doing it, despite the fact he had twenty years on me and more experience in business than I did. He needed reminding that I was to be kept informed of everything that was going on out there in my absence, nevermind what the fuck time it was here or that I was here to face something I'd long since buried.

I dial his cell.

"Sir."

"What's going on with R.E.E.?"

"I believe they are aware that your negotiations for the Myers farm have prevented their purchase."

"Not surprising. We knew they'd figure it out sooner rather than later. It's been reported here already." Though Myers' land being my target was only speculation, it would not be far reaching for them to put it together. "Is there more?"

He hesitates, "I...I'm not sure this is information you should have, sir. We need to keep you insulated. You need to have the ability to plausibly deny..."

"Lionel. Fucking tell me."

"I believe they have a leak within their organization."

"How do we know this?"

"I got a call from a reporter for the *L.A. Times*. Says he's working on a story about your purchase of Myers' land and the Center."

"When did this call come in?"

"About three hours ago."

Jesus Christ.

This should have been brought to my attention long before now. "Who's the reporter?"

"Gene Dobbs."

Shit. This guy had connections all over the country. Over his thirty year career he'd broken stories about everything from corruption in Washington to Wall Street fraud and people took him seriously. If he was digging into R.E.E., he'd soon find out what I already knew, especially if he had an inside source.

"What the fuck? I should have had this information hours ago."

"I apologize, sir. But he says he has an inside source at R.E.E. He won't name the source. I don't think it's a good idea for you to get too close. Let me handle it."

I'm speaking through clenched teeth, trying not to rage out on him. This is completely unacceptable. "I need to be aware of these kinds of developments immediately, Lionel, or it's going to cost you your job. Is that clear?"

"Yes, sir."

"Find out what he knows. And tell him I'm not giving any interviews."

"If we promise him one down the road, it might keep him at bay long enough to find out who the leak is."

"No. It will just feed his suspicions."

"Your call, sir. Should I get Mr. Floros on board to find out what information Dobbs has?"

Dimitri Floros is a genius, the best hacker I'd ever known – a completely unassuming one, given the lifestyle he now lived. He was also the best friend my brother ever had. For that reason alone, I don't want him dragged into this.

"No. We'll have to find another way."

"That being said, sir, I'm more concerned that the source might be discovered by the company. If that happens, he or she might be eliminated."

"That's a valid concern."

"Given their history, I'd say it's more than valid." Lionel and I had uncovered a few employees and associates of R.E.E.'s affiliates had mysterious circumstances surrounding the end of their careers, and in the case of one unfortunate soul, his life had come to an abrupt and suspicious end.

"Do you think Ireland has anything to do with this?" Stella's father had allowed me to use his Manhattan connections a year ago to investigate the company when I'd learned they were looking to buy land around here.

Of course I was balls deep in owing him now because of that favor but that couldn't be helped. In the meantime, I had to know if he was trying to sabotage my whole endeavor from behind the curtain.

"Likely not, but I haven't been able to rule it out yet."

"Find out for sure. Immediately."

"Yes, sir."

"And I expect to be updated to the minute on what's happening."

"Of course."

I disconnect, twice as restless as before. I'm on my feet, pacing around the loft, playing out the possible scenarios here.

If R.E.E. was exposed too soon, it could hinder my progress here.

And Ms. Greene could be facing career-ending consequences before I could prevent it.

An hour later I'm back downstairs in my private office, reviewing everything I had at my disposal about R.E.E. to see if I've missed anything.

But nothing is presenting itself.

Lionel calls to tell me he's deflected Dobbs, at least for now. He's also ruled out that John Ireland has anything to do with the reporter's digging. I don't know how he ruled it out, but it doesn't matter. To some degree, I have to grant Lionel his insistence to insulate me from his methods.

The best place for me is bed, but I'm still on edge. I'm on the couch in front of the giant flat screen, flipping through news stations. My cell phone rings on my desk at the other end of the room. I'd forgotten I left it there.

I figure it's Byron calling to tell me Alexis is leaving the bar.

Then again, he would just send me a text.

I head for my desk in a hurry and grab my phone in time to read the caller's name on the display.

Alexis Greene.

I'd programmed her contact information into my phone in anticipation of our working together as soon as tomorrow. Before I can answer, voicemail picks up the call.

Goddammit.

I scroll back to the missed call screen. She left no voicemail.

I check my watch.

Quarter after eleven.

Why is she out late on a work night? Is this a habitual thing with her?

I did crush the biggest deal of her young law career today. Maybe that had her out tying one on, drowning her sorrows.

I call Byron.

"Is Alexis still at the gay bar?"

"Yes, sir."

"You'll need to get over there and tail her. Discreetly. But make sure she does not drive home if she's been drinking."

"Very good. I will."

I disconnect. I could drive down there myself and take her home. I could take the Corvette out.

Except Byron told me the wipers were in need of repair after the car came out of storage and the rainstorm they'd predicted would be closing in soon.

I pull up the radar on my phone and, sure enough, the storm is moving in from the west at a pretty good clip.

Byron has the Lincoln so that only left me with the Ducati. Out of the question with the impending storm.

I hadn't been planning on going out tonight. I've wasted ten minutes contemplating all of this. I'll just call her back. Maybe she wants to discuss tomorrow's meeting.

Or shout obscenities at me for tanking a multi-thousand-dollar deal for her client.

I press the call back button on the phone and wait in breathless anticipation.

She doesn't answer. Her voicemail picks up.

God, her voice. It's so sexy. She is polite and professional with her word choice but it's the way she speaks them.

Her New York twist on the words, the way she says her own name. Damn.

I head to the bathroom and take a leak, then wash and literally slap myself in the face.

I exit the bathroom and call Byron back.

"Change of plans," I say. "Come get me first."

12

Alexis

As I leave Sitting Bull, the bass still booms reaching outside and rattling the small windows of the club. A few patrons stand in a roped off area in front of the building smoking cigarettes and sipping drinks.

The air is oppressive. I can hear thunder in the distance as the atmosphere signals that quite a storm is brewing. The few trees that line the city street have upturned leaves. The wind has settled some but is persistent.

I'm thankful to be wearing pants and not a skirt that might blow up to give people around me quite a show.

There are no cabs to be found. I'm up only a block from the bar contemplating a visit to Cliff's, the hole in the wall diner I considered going to with Charlie. Instead, I opt for the establishment across the street from it called Mac's, a cigar and whiskey bar that's been in the same downtown spot since the sixties.

I climb the few steps up to the entrance of the bar. The scene here is old-school and little has changed since the MacIntyre family opened the place. Same scuffed wood floors, same red leather bar stools, and the same stained oriental rugs strewn about the hardwood in a haphazard way. The bar is directly in front of me along the wall. A mirror reflects off the various whiskeys and other spirits.

The music is quieter, all soothing jazz and no thumping bass. My head is thankful as I sink into one of the small but comfy velvet chairs, running my thumbs along the ornate wood carvings on the arms. I'm in a cozy seating area that faces the street, my back to the vastness of the open barroom behind me. There are a few regulars at the bar to my right.

Smoking isn't allowed by law anymore, but the stale scent of smoke from years ago still clings to the surfaces around me.

I feel like I'm in the library of a stately old manor. College kids normally dominate this place, but most of the students have finished for the semester. Besides the four people at the bar, there's only one young couple playing pool behind me at the back of the room. I'm glad for the lack of a crowd. I'm feeling a shitty mood coming on and I'm drunk. I don't much feel like socializing.

My chair faces the street and I'm staring through the large front window in a daze when I'm approached by a friendly blonde waiter named Chip asking me if I'd like anything. His presence is opposite my mood. I can't believe he's old enough to work, let alone work in a bar. I order a whiskey on the rocks as a nightcap and pull my phone out of my purse when he leaves me.

I move to the edge of my seat when I see one missed call.

From him.

I recognize the number from having dialed it earlier.

Shit!

Is there a voicemail?

I scroll through the menu on the phone to see, but there is nothing. Just the missed call. I can't decide if I'm relieved or disappointed that I didn't talk to him.

Or that he didn't leave me a message in that sexy voice of his.

He probably just tried to call back and see who it was.

That means he'd have heard my voicemail greeting, then he'd know for sure it was me.

Or he could have just matched the number up with your business card, stupid.

I'm about to get up, cancel my nightcap and bolt back to Sitting Bull with Charlie when I see a familiar face through the window. He's walking from the curb towards the bar, looking for something, then stops smack in front of the window when he sees me. He's a few paces away on the sidewalk, only the glass between us.

I recognize the silver-gray beard, the black suit, and the distinguished look.

It's Jeeves.

I never realized how intimidating he was when I saw him at the Sheridan the other day. Tonight he looks like he could kick the shit out of anyone. He's taller and sturdier than I remember, and I wouldn't mess with him even if I had some sort of heavyweight title. There is no sign of the rest of the entourage.

Maybe Jeeves lives around here.

Yeah, and he's standing outside of this bar why?

I'm afraid to know the answer. He's probably been sent here to keep stupid women like me from hanging up on his employer.

He's made his way in, but instead of coming over to me as I anticipate, he heads for the bar. He sits at a stool, then calls the bartender over.

I'm so relieved I can feel myself let out a breath, my muscles relaxing involuntarily. He's paid me no attention whatsoever.

Jeeves has his back turned, and I get ready to make a move for the exit. In my haste, I bump into Chip. He nearly loses his tray but swiftly steers around me and sets the drink down.

"You aren't leaving, are you ma'am?"

Jeeves turns to look at us and I put my head down. I turn on my heel to head for the bookshelves on the opposite wall behind Chip.

"No," I say quietly. "I was just looking for something to read while I waited."

"Great, help yourself," he says, grinning. "Would you like to run a tab?"

"*No.*" I practically shout.

Control, I think. Stay in control!

"I mean, I have cash. How much?"

"Six fifty, please."

I hand him eight bucks and wave him off. He heads for the back of the bar as I scan the shelves. A collection of English poetry catches my eye, and I pluck it from its dusty home and return to my seat. I bury my head in the pages that I'm too nervous to actually read and try to hear the conversation that Jeeves is having with the bartender. Even without thumping bass, I can't hear what they are saying. He mutters something in a low voice, then a glass hits the wooden bar top.

I take a chance and look to my right. He's ordered a glass of water by the looks and the bartender is nowhere to be seen. Jeeves still has his back to me.

I'm feeling very lightheaded and not in a good way like when I was dancing earlier. I can hear some loud discussion in the very back of the bar, probably in an office.

A moment later, a short, thin man with a graying comb over comes out front. He looks to be about the same age as Jeeves, but aged and disheveled, wearied by a life of labor. He's wearing a gray t-shirt with the bar's logo and tan pants stained with fryer grease. I assume he is an owner of some sort, probably a MacIntyre either by blood or marriage.

He and Jeeves have a brief conversation and Jeeves gets up to leave. I bury my head back in the book which is opened to *It Is The Hour* by Lord Byron. I sigh. It's one of my favorites, full of passion with all its words about lonely ears whispered in, lovers, and night winds.

None of which await me here.

I set the book on the table next to me, about to hightail it out of there when Jeeves gives me a 'stay' hand signal. He pulls his phone from his breast pocket, taps away at it, then turns his attention back to me.

Out of fear I choose to obey and retake my seat. He nods at me as I sit back down, then he moves to the exit.

I can hear MacIntyre talking to the couple in the back. The bartender returns up front asking the few people seated to leave, saying he's closing up. No one complains, behaving as though this happens all the time. Instead the patrons mutter about the incoming storm and make their way out, including the couple from the pool table behind me. They stroll past holding hands as they make their way down the steps and onto the sidewalk below. Jeeves nods at them from his post on the sidewalk as they cross the street, heading in the direction of the diner.

I'm waiting to be asked to leave too, but no one has come near me.

I'm not sure whether to stay put and be scared or run away and be petrified. This is an Irish bar, but everything unfolding around me is feeling very *Godfather*. As MacIntyre approaches me, I stand up making sure not to have my back to the front door.

"Joseph MacIntyre, ma'am," he nods as he approaches. "Please, sit and relax" he says kindly, laying one hand on my shoulder.

I stay standing.

Since being interrupted by the bartender, MacIntyre's demeanor has softened.

"If there's anything you need, you let me know. I'll be in my office out back. G'night, ma'am."

And he leaves me.

It's just me and the bartender in the room. We look at each other a moment and he shrugs, turning his attention back to the television above his head.

I sit in my seat tentatively, on edge in both the figurative and literal sense. I'm not sure what the hell is going on. I sip down the rest of my drink.

Jeeves is still standing outside in front of the bar. I can see just his head and shoulders through the window, since it's a few steps down to street level. The sign flashing Mac's in pink neon lights up the back of him.

Then I smell it.

That clean, masculine scent that speeds up my pulse and takes over all my senses.

But it comes from behind me, from the direction of the pool table where a moment ago I'm certain there was no one.

"Whiskey, neat," he says in the direction of the bartender.

I hear the drink being poured, liquid as smooth as the voice of Aidan Pierce that echoes in my ears.

"Can I have your drink refreshed?" he asks from behind my chair.

"No," I reply curtly, leaning back. I cross my arms over my chest like a petulant child.

Who the fuck does this guy think he is? First he screws up my deal with Myers, now he's taking over bars I happen to be in like he's some sort of mob boss? And how did he know where to find me?

Told you this guy has issues. You should run.

I'm stubborn. I do not heed my own inner monologue, instead staying put.

"Fine then," he says, his tone nearly as pissy as mine.

I hear him move away and turn to watch. His back is to me as he takes his drink off the bar. He must give a powerful look to the bartender because the guy remotes the television off and leaves us in a hurry.

Crap.

My adversary comes back to where I'm seated, landing in one of the velvet chairs across from me, the window to the street at his back. The chair is dwarfed beneath him.

He takes a long, slow sip from his drink and sets it on the table to his left.

I'm not sure what to do and mull over some options.

Sprint for the door?

No, Jeeves would surely tackle me.

Run out the back?

No, that would worry old Mr. MacIntyre.

I decide to stay in my seat, but change my position to that of the upper hand. Posture straightened, tail to the rear, hands folded in my lap. I cross my legs at the ankle.

The best defense is offense, I hear in my dad's tenor voice.

The alcohol has me feeling brave enough to try the strategy.

Norah Jones is crooning "Sunrise" in the background, but then as I look at Aidan Pierce all I can hear in my head is the soundtrack from *Magic Mike*.

Foreigner, Ginuwine, Big and Rich. Their songs are playing through my mind's imaginary stage, picturing Pierce greased up and accepting dollar bills.

Where the hell did that come from?

I want to burst into laughter.

Perhaps I'm beyond drunk after all. I decide to keep my mouth shut as long as possible but keep my steadfast posture. Somehow I manage not to smile at my silly thoughts.

"So, you called?" he says, leaning back. He's trying to play it cool but he's failing at it because his knees are practically touching his chin in the petite chair.

I'm smiling now. I can't help it. I need to change tactics if I'm going to win this battle, show him that I mean business.

He can sense my amusement and gets up, wandering over to the bookshelf where my selected book has left a hole. He looks at the book on the table next to me.

"English poetry? I never would have thought you a romantic."

"I'm not," I throw back at him.

Why does he have to look so amazing?

He's leaning up against the bookshelf, casual in jeans and flip flops and a tight-fitting, plain white tee. His leather belt looks expensive, and I know the watch must have set him back a couple grand or more.

He's standing there all relaxed and sexy and looking amused again, like he had nothing better to do than to come here and get a kick out of silly, drunken me.

"I was just about to leave. I'm meeting up with my friend Charlie."

"Well I don't mean to keep you, Mizz Greene," he says, again emphasizing the Ms. just as he did a few days ago. "But I will remind you that you called me."

"I… yes, well that was a mistake. I mean…"

I'm interrupted by a loud crack of thunder as the storm closes in. Lightning flashes through the window.

I'm suddenly concerned for Jeeves.

"You should tell him to come inside," I say, standing and motioning to the sidewalk.

His eyes don't leave mine.

"He's fine."

He moves towards me, picking up his drink as he does. I'm noticing that dressed down, his physique is far more apparent than it was in Friday's suit. It's probably worth standing in line for hours to see that body naked. And now that body is right in front of me, close enough that I can smell his aftershave.

Aftershave!

His face is clean shaven, his strong jawline exposed. No more sexy stubble like he had when we met. He looks even younger, his perfect complexion revealed. I want to run my fingers down his cheek, test just how close he managed to get.

Must be the alcohol doing the thinking.

Nope.

It's Undersexed Lex.

I definitely don't need any help from the likes of her, especially now.

I'm facing him, my eyes coming to the vicinity of his shoulders. I tip my head back so I can look right into those cobalt eyes, then I close my own and inhale. No one should be allowed to smell this good. I'm trying to program his scent to memory so I can recreate it, bottle it, and keep it all to myself.

Instead of mastering his scent, I become increasingly dizzy.

"I don't like calls after ten, Ms. Greene." He's speaking firmly but in a whisper, melting my eardrums. "That's my time to think at the end of a busy day. What was so important?" My eyes snap open. He's looking at me intently, waiting for a profound answer.

"I need to quit your project," I blurt.

"I see. And why is that?" His back is to the window. There's another flash of lightning beyond his shoulder. I wince, then count in my head.

One one-thousand, two one-thousand, three one-thousand.

Crack!

Thunder erupts again, even louder this time. We're in the thick of it now. I expect the skies to release a downpour at any moment, but Jeeves has not moved.

"I'm, it's just…"

I can't get the words out. I want to. I want to tell this guy off and that he can shove it. But my head is fuzzier with each passing moment that I stand so close to him.

I'm worried about the man standing out there all alone in what might be the storm of the century.

And I'm so conflicted by the one that's in front of me.

Once again, he's too close to me yet not close enough.

"I'm waiting for an answer," he says softly.

His tone changes as another moment passes in silence.

"I do not like to be kept waiting." He seems irritated.

Fury builds in me at his switch to arrogance and frustration. How dare he? My anger fights against intoxication and, finally, I find my voice.

"Your answer, Mr. Pierce, is that I am not going to work with you on this project, nor will I ever work with you on any project, no matter how noble. In one fell swoop, you have ruined a year's worth of my hard work and that of my staff, not to mention what that work would have meant for my firm and my father's legacy had the deal closed."

It doesn't matter that I'm only referring to half of my staff, right? Claudia wouldn't know what the Myers file was if it fell on her.

He takes a step back, seemingly wounded. But he responds in the same irritated tone as though he's explaining his grand plans to a child.

"I'm fully aware of the implications my project has on your firm. This is something that I planned to discuss with you, whether or not you were appointed through the Bar Association. The fact that you were nominated as my contact just saved me a step in reaching out to you of my own accord."

Now I'm completely confused. What the hell is he talking about? How could he know anything about me?

Might as well just ask.

"How do you know anything about me, Mr. Pierthe?"

Fuck, fuck, fuck! Did I just lisp his name?

There goes all my credibility, swan diving out the window into the street below.

He raises a brow at me.

"This is probably not a conversation we should have now or in this setting, don't you agree? Our first meeting tomorrow night would be more appropriate."

My head goes blank as the next flash of lightning illuminates the entire barroom, and I sway a bit too much. He pulls me close, catching me just as the thunder booms again, after only *one-one-thousand.*

Shit that's close!

Did I say that out loud? I'm not sure, but I'm trying to steady myself on my feet and doing a terrible job of it.

I break free and manage the steps down to the entrance, but I'm still finding it hard to stay upright on my own. I'm proud to have made it this far but it doesn't help my balance that I've ended up here. It's very dark.

"Stay where you are," he commands. His voice is loud, even from several feet away.

I'm standing on the last step before the entrance to the street, leaning on a metal railing for support. I hear him yell to MacIntyre and then he's behind me with that sexy scent of his.

"I'll see you get home, Ms. Greene."

He states it as fact, right in the vicinity of my ear.

Gawd, that voice.

I just want to lean back into him and ask him to say more. Anything. Recite the alphabet. Read the maximum occupancy sign over our heads. I don't care what. I'll just relax and enjoy it.

"Home is thirty miles away. Thanks anyhow," I muster. "Just call me a cab."

So I can throw up in the back of it and pass out.

I have never been a heavy drinker, and it's very clear to me why in this moment. I hate losing myself to anything that causes me to abandon control.

He takes the last step down the darkened stairway and stands next to me, his arm around my waist, essentially holding me up. He shoves open the door and nods at Jeeves. I also nod to him, with what I'm sure is a doofy smile plastered on my face. I can't help it. I'm so thankful the good man will get out of the storm now.

Jeeves heads for the car parked at the curb, but before he opens the door I notice that (miraculously) he is not wet.

I look up to the sky in disbelief.

I guess it hasn't actually started raining yet.

In that moment the heavens open up, the oppressive air dissipating as a torrential rain is upon us. The two of us are standing under an awning, but Jeeves is getting drenched. He opens the front passenger door to retrieve an umbrella.

The last thing I'm conscious for is being thrown over the shoulder of Aidan Pierce, hoping like hell I won't lose my pasta primavera all over his backside as he carries me to the car where Jeeves awaits.

13

Alexis

I blink fast as I wake, having no idea what time it is. The sun seems to have risen without me. I can feel it warming my face.

My sight is failing me, so I keep my eyes closed and feel around for something familiar while hoping I've somehow been deposited in my bed at home.

A goose down duvet covers me. Underneath me are sheets so soft and comfortable that the thread count is probably in the thousands.

And now I'm certain I don't know where the fuck I am.

I bolt upright, throwing off the duvet and rubbing my eyes. I can see some, but it's blurry. I realize I'm not wearing the clothes I had on when I left Mac's. Instead I'm stripped to my underwear, which are thankfully out of sight underneath a large t-shirt that says Yale University.

Ivy League. Impressive!

My all girl tribe of subconscious sluts is awake before me this morning, already having its imaginary pot of coffee.

Shut up! Definitely not the focus of this situation!

My head hurts just trying to quiet my mind.

I'm panicked at the thought that the Billion Dollar Man may have seen me like this, put me to bed like this. My legs aren't exactly shaved smooth and alcohol breath is not very becoming. Of course by now it's downright putrid, even though I had refrained from vomiting.

I think.

I wrack my pounding brain but the last thing I can remember is being thrown over his shoulder and carried to the backseat of his car in a downpour.

I'm in the oversized bed alone, looking around a well-appointed room I don't know where. I thank the heavens that at least I'm alone.

As my eyes come into better focus, I notice a note on the pillow, on the untouched side of the bed. White linen paper folded tent style reads Ms. Alexis Greene in handwritten print on the front. Like Alice in her Wonderland, I can't resist. I snatch it up and flip it open. The inside message is also handwritten in the neatest printing I've ever seen.

Ms. Greene,

You have a newly scheduled 10:00 meeting with Mr. Myers at your office. I insist you keep it. New attire is in the closet for you to save you a trip home. I understand you have a dog and he has been taken care of as well, until you return home this evening.

Please help yourself to the facilities prior to your departure. Anything you need should be there for you.

Kind regards,
Aidan Pierce

Kind regards?

Is that what you say to someone you kidnapped and took home while she could not move under her own power?

The bedside clock says 8:12. My phone lies next to it. I grab it and scroll through the recent history. One missed call from Charlie an hour ago and three texts from last night.

Did you make it home?

Are you still with Mr. Money Bags?

Are you okay??? Call me bitch!

I scratch my head about the second one. Why would he think to ask that? I see that text came in at about midnight. I'm about to call him back when the bell of my phone calendar dings.

Meeting with Eli Myers
10:00 a.m.
What the hell?

I know I did not put that in there. Pierce must have done it.

Now he's looking through my phone? Putting shit in my calendar? This guy is infuriating.

A fuzzy memory returns of lazing in the backseat of the car, seeing him with my phone in one hand and my key ring in the other.

I scramble out of bed and search for my clothes, but they're nowhere to be found. My purse is lying on one of the chairs by the huge picture window that I assume faces the street. The room is set up sort of like a hotel suite with a large armoire opposite the bed, probably housing a television. In front of the window are two Queen Anne chairs with pretty rose-pink flowered upholstery flanking a matching cherry table.

The room is far too large to be a hotel room though.

I don't have time to contemplate how I ended up here, or why I'm wearing one of his shirts, or why he's now making appointments for me and putting them in my calendar.

In less than two hours I'm meeting my one big-fish of a client. I have to bring my A-game.

I'm staggering a bit as I head for the closet. I'm trying to overcome my fantastic headcahe to look at this outfit Pierce has been oh too kind to assign to me.

There's a knock at the bedroom door just as I walk by it, and I jump.

"Ms. Greene?" a female voice asks.

Is it a girlfriend? A maid? I have no idea.

"Yes?"

"It's Mrs. Schmidt, dear. I'm Mr. Pierce's housekeeper. May I come in? I have something for you."

Whew! Not a girlfriend. And she sounds older, grandmotherly even.

"Yes," I squeak out. My voice is a little hoarse from shouting over club music with Charlie. "But I'm not dressed. I, er – I'm not sure where my clothes have gone."

The door opens slowly and a kind-faced, plump woman with her silvery white hair in a bun enters carrying a tray.

"Breakfast, Ms. Greene. At Mr. Pierce's request."

A glass of orange juice, a plate of toast, fresh berries and eggs are arranged beautifully on the silver tray. There's even a small crystal pitcher of ice water, two pills, and a spray of lilacs in a short pink vase. The whole thing is lovely.

"Thank you," I manage. The realness of my surroundings sink in and I have no more words.

I'm half dressed in the home of a millionaire. Billionaire? I don't even know.

And what room is this anyway? His? A guest suite? Furnishings are beautiful but few. The sleigh bed I've just climbed out of is far too large to be designated to a guest, though it could accommodate the first string of a baseball team. I can see an ensuite bathroom entrance next to what I can only assume is a room-sized closet.

"I hope Mr. Pierce's t-shirt was satisfactory. I had to improvise."

She moves past me and sets the tray on the table over by the window. As I look out I can see we are definitely not at street level.

"Oh, it's fine thank you." Should I ask? Yes, I have to. I cannot wonder this all day. "Did you, uh…put me into it? The t-shirt?"

What if he did?

"Yes, ma'am. I'm afraid I did. But it was no trouble at all."

It wasn't him, thank God.

My feeling of embarrassment lingers anyway.

"I'm so sorry, Mrs. Schmidt. I don't normally, I mean, I never…"

I don't know how to go on because really I can't remember just what it is I *never* did last night.

"What ma'am, been tipsy? A little too much liquor at the end of a rough day?"

I sigh, hanging my head, cringing as I look up. She beams at me, placing a plump hand on my arm.

"Yes, dear. Me either."

She winks at me and I warm to this sweet, understanding woman on the spot. She hands me another note.

"Here, dear. A note from Mr. Pierce. Now, there's a dress in the closet for you, your shoes and a new set of underthings, which should be in your size. I've sent your things to be laundered and delivered to your home address. Peaceful Drive in Mirror Lake, is it?"

I nod. She's a domestic goddess and a sweetheart. If I had the money, I'd steal her away and employ her myself. She makes my Marta look as incompetent as Claudia.

"Please help yourself to a shower after your breakfast. I understand you have a meeting at ten so do be swift. Your car is in the lot out back."

"Thank you. Please call me Alexis."

"Of course, dear. You have a good day."

She's about to close the door and I think of one more thing.

"Oh wait," I plead. "My dog? Mr. Pierce said that he's been taken care of?"

"Yes, ma'am. Mr. Pierce had Byron use your keys to tend to him. He has some experience with animals. I believe he walked him and left him in his quarters in the basement. Your dog is quite the handsome animal, I understand."

I don't know who the hell Byron is, but I hope he's not dangerous since he's now had access to my keys and been in my house unsupervised. My only comfort is that Huck would not let anyone past the front door if he didn't want to.

"His name is Huck. Please thank Byron for me."

She nods and smiles as she exits, leaving me to it.

Before eating a bite, I down two glasses of water and the ibuprofen from the tray. My appetite is subpar, which stinks. The meal in front of me looks delicious.

The ceilings in this room are loft height, but done in a trey style with what looks like Venetian plaster. In other words, expensive. I look out the window and realize I must be about three floors up.

I recognize the city block below. There's a menswear shop across the street with residential apartments above it. I'm only two blocks from my office.

I know from our initial meeting at the Sheridan that his office is on this street, but prior to that I had no idea the likes of Aidan Pierce owned property so close to my office. Below me at street level, the building houses a cell phone store and an insurance agency.

I've never paid much attention to the second through fourth floors of this building, but there were some renovations started a year or two ago.

It's nothing out of the ordinary here. The downtown buildings are always turning over, being renovated, abandoned, or reclaimed again.

I recall the second note and pick it up from the tray where I'd dropped it. This one is blank on the outside save an *A-M-P* monogram, but it has the same perfect handwritten print on the inside. I'm tempted to be charmed at the chivalry of a handwritten note in this day and age.

Ms. Greene,

You've no time to waste. Get moving. Please note the 4:00 meeting in your calendar as well. And thank you for the entertainment last night. I quite enjoyed it.

Kind regards,
Aidan Pierce

Entertainment? Oh Lord. My head is still foggy and throbbing and it prevents me from remembering anything.

Probably a good thing.

I check my calendar again, seeing a meeting with Aidan Pierce at four o'clock at his office on 250 Harrison Street. Apparently, he will not wait until seven tonight as he'd originally suggested.

It's now 8:30. I pick at the berries, take two bites of toast and head for the shower. Great job, Mrs. Schmidt, but I could have used some coffee. Like two pots.

I'm in the bathroom soaping up and shampooing, taking in my surroundings. There are no masculine items anywhere. The shower surround, double vanities and floor tiles are bright Carrera marble. Every surface is immaculate. The towels match the accent color in a soft pink and they feel as soft as the sheets.

I dry my hair with the built-in appliance on the wall, then notice my prayers have been answered. A travel toothbrush and paste have been left for me. I look around at the very feminine room as I brush, wondering who in Pierce's life would spend time here. I can't see him being comfortable in this room.

I open a pair of double doors to an enormous closet which is empty except the items put there for me. The room seems vast without anything to grace the oodles of cedar shelves and velvet hangers. If I spoke out loud, I'm sure it would echo.

The undergarments selected for me are obviously new, even though the tags have been removed. They look expensive and I read the branding. *Zora's Closet*, Black Label. *Whoa!* Unattainably expensive for someone of my meager salary. I'm not used to anything so fancy, but they fit perfectly and are a pretty shade of blue.

The lilac dress hanging in front of me looks to be just as flattering. It's sleeveless but business-worthy. There's a black thread detail around the conservative neckline and a skinny black belt across the middle, both of which complement my shoes from the night before. I slip it on, zip up the side and fasten the belt.

Thankfully, I look much better than I feel.

I gather up my phone and purse, shoving my dirty unmentionables inside.

There's a coffee shop two storefronts down. I'm on a mission by the time I emerge from the bedroom. Jeeves is at the end of the short hall, seemingly waiting for me.

"Ms. Greene." He nods. "I'll see you to your car, ma'am."

"No, that isn't necessary."

"I have my instructions."

Apparently this isn't up for discussion.

I follow as my heels click and clack across the mahogany floors on our way out. We pass by an office on the left, then make a right down another short hall. An open floor plan living room and kitchen are to my left, an intimate yet formal dining room to my right. The hallway separates the two spaces and leads to the foyer. All of the rooms have loft height ceilings, but there isn't an industrial feel to the space. There are no exposed mechanicals. Beams are covered in what looks like reclaimed wood.

The space is simple but clean and comfortable. Not too modern for my taste.

Like it matters if I like it.

My inner crazy tribe is enjoying my walk of shame while eating brunch, stuffing their faces with croissants and sipping mimosas.

Above us in the foyer there's a domed skylight encased in a metal grid. Jeeves and I are bathed in daylight waiting for the elevator, the sun washing over white marble floors beneath our feet.

A round black table is the only furniture in the massive foyer, the polished wood reflecting some lilacs that peek out from a crystal vase.

There is still no sign of Pierce. I take the opportunity to prod, but start out friendly.

"I'm sorry, I didn't get your name." I smile at Jeeves. I should learn it before I accidentally call him that out loud, which I don't think he'd appreciate. He's just as intimidating as the night before. I don't have any desire to tick him off.

"Byron, ma'am. You may call me Byron."

Byron! So he's the one that took care of Huck.

"Did you find my dog well?" I ask, concerned. "I have never left him unattended before."

"Yes. He's fine. He had a walk and some food at six this morning. I followed Mr. Pierce's instructions which he obtained from your friend."

My friend?

I'm visibly confused.

"Your friend Charlie gave him instructions, ma'am."

So that's why my phone isn't ringing off the hook this morning. He knows I'm here. He'll get the wrong idea for sure.

"I see. Well, thank you. So Huck's in the basement now?"

"Yes, ma'am. A fine animal, he is."

"Yes. He likes the basement. It's nice and cool down there. And he loves to stretch out on the couch." I don't know why I feel the need to explain anything to this stranger. I guess I just don't want him to think I'm an irresposible dog owner. Huck was more spoiled than any canine I knew.

"Yes, ma'am."

"So, is this Mr. Pierce's permanent home?" I try to sound as if I don't really care, looking around like I'm bored.

"I am not at liberty to say." He's so serious. This may be tougher than I thought.

"Can you tell me if his office is in this building? I have to meet him at four this afternoon."

"Yes, ma'am. Take the elevator to the second floor." He's staring straight ahead.

"You can call me Alexis, Byron." I turn my head to address him, this time serious myself. He does not flinch. "Enough with the ma'am."

"Very well," is all he says. And the elevator pings in front of us, ready to take us down to reality three floors below.

B y nine-thirty, I've retrieved my coffee and driven my car the short distance to the office. The weather has turned back to the typical late May pattern, the high predicted in the low seventies. It's only sixty now, and I'm chilled in the sleeveless dress that was chosen for me.

My head only pounds when I turn it too fast or look in the direction of the sunlight so that's an improvement. And I've managed to beat Charlie here. I can't tell if Claudia is here yet since she walks from her apartment near campus.

I enter through the back door and all the lights are on. Claudia is grooving in place as she makes herself a cup of coffee, her blonde hair tied up in a high ponytail. She's wearing peep-toe sandals and a bright yellow sundress with huge white and pink flowers all over it, which are partially covered by a white fuzzy cardigan. There's pop music piping into her ear buds and radiating into the break room.

I motion to her to take out the ear buds and she does so, smiling.

"Turn that crap off."

Whoops. Apparently I'm in a shitty mood.

Her smile fades, her expression contrasting her cheery dress. She hurriedly shuts off her iPod and puts creamer back in the refrigerator.

"I'm sorry, Alexis."

"No, it's fine," I say, softening. It isn't her fault I'm hung over. "You should be out front though, Claudia. Someone could walk into Reception and there is no one to greet them."

"Yes, I'm on it," she says smiling again. And she's off.

I head straight for my office and close both doors. I start up my machine, check my e-mail and scroll through a few voice messages from the system at work. Most of them are nuisance calls, but there's one from Charlie.

"Lex, OH-EM-GEE. Are you still with Aidan Pierce? I can't get you on your cell. I'll be in by ten. It's eight-thirty and I have to sweat out the alcohol and get some breakfast before I come in. See you soon."

He's lucky we're friends and that I can sympathize with a hangover this morning.

Moments later he's knocking on my office door.

"Lex? You decent?"

"Come," I say flatly.

He waltzes in, his typical fine self. He's refreshed and smiling wearing casual beige pants and a blue Tattersall shirt. I know both are his favorite – Ralph Lauren. He's tie-less today.

"So…" he begins, "what the fuck?"

"It isn't what you think, Charlie."

"Well then I'm sooo sorry for you," he teases. "What the hell happened? One minute you tell me you're getting a cab home and two hours later I'm getting a call from Aidan fricken' Pierce! He's all *Ms. Greene is unable to meet up with you.*" He's changed his tone to imitation, drawing a laugh from me at his impersonation. "And then he says he has you in the back of his car."

"I think I, uh…passed out."

He gives me a look that says "no shit".

"Look, it's really not that complicated. I was going to go to Cliff's, but decided on a nightcap at Mac's instead. There were no cabs hanging around yet. He showed up in stealth mode, made the owner go to the back office, and made the few people in there leave before he came in."

Charlie is seated in one of the club chairs in front of my desk, motionless and more attentive than I've ever seen him.

"Next thing I know I'm trying to tell him I'm not going to work on his project and he asks why. I can't remember much after that. I blacked out. I think it started storming right about then."

"I know, that was crazy. Thank God someone was there to rescue you. I told him about Huck, I figured he'd take you home to your place."

"No, he has a guy to take care of anything he wants. Byron, his name is. So I guess he went home and walked Huck this morning, and fed him."

"A girl could get used to being catered to like that, no?" He's beaming, like I've hit some sort of lottery.

"Look, Charlie. I'm very confused about last night. Pierce is very attractive, we can agree on that." I neglect to mention that attractive doesn't even begin to cover it.

Or that standing in his proximity (or just the scent of him) makes me crazy-horny enough to hump a lamppost.

"Uh huh," is all he says.

"What?"

"You think he's way more than attractive, Lex."

Oh shitballs. Am I that transparent?

"What I think is that he's presumptuous and demanding."

"No way," he says. "You're totally crushing on him."

"Am not," I spout.

"Ladies and gentleman," he says with a booming voice like he's Bob freaking Barker. "Please welcome our next contestant on *Who Wants to Bang A Billionaire*! Miss Alexis Greene!" He hoots and applauds for me and I hurl my pen at him.

"Shut up, Chuck. Your last name isn't Woolery."

He's rolling with laughter. I roll my eyes at him, but I can't help my smile.

"Listen," I say, attempting to steer the conversation back to business. "It's an off-limits topic of conversation today. Okay?"

"Okay," he says, catching a breath. "You're the boss, Boss."

"Besides," I reluctantly admit. "We have Eli Myers coming in here in ten minutes, and I have no idea why."

"What? Get the *hell* out. Did he call you last night or something?"

"No. I have no idea when he decided to come in. I... it was in my calendar this morning when I woke up."

"Girl, the billion dollar question is just where *did* you wake up? In his bed?"

"No. In a guest room. I didn't even see him this morning. But he did leave a note."

Before Charlie can pry any more, Claudia buzzes me on the intercom. "Mr. Myers to see you, Ms. Greene."

"Just a moment, Claudia. Charlie will come out and see him back to the conference room." I disconnect.

"Show time," I say. "Do not keep him waiting."

I sit back in my chair and take a moment to catch my breath, wondering what the hell I'm about to find out about my client and his connection to the very influential Aidan Pierce.

14

Aidan

Tuesday at seven a.m. I'm in my office, scarcely able to think.

Alexis Greene is sleeping a floor above me in my guest room.

I'd carried her slender frame upstairs last night in the elevator, wishing she would wake up and be as aroused as I was just looking at her.

She didn't.

I'd laid her in the bed, brushing her hair back away from her face, still hoping she would wake.

But she had definitely overdone it. She was out cold. I briefly agonized over her irresponsibility, still wondering if she made a habit of this sort of thing.

I knew her mother was affected by the disease of alcoholism. Could it be she was too?

Nothing in her background indicated she had any issues with alcohol or with drugs of any kind.

Like you've never gotten fucked up beyond the point of consciousness.

I shake my head at my own reprimand.

Between her ending up involved in my project and unraveling her deal with Myers, I'd just turned her entire professional world upside down. I hoped her carelessness was nothing more than a result of that stress.

I had to call Mrs. Schmidt to come over and take care of her after I deposited her in the bed for two reasons.

First, I didn't want her thinking I'd undressed her without her permission. When I eventually *did* undress her, I wanted her to be intensely, provocatively, and unmistakably aware of it.

Second, I want to savor that moment when it finally comes. (I know it will.) Taking her clothes off in the state she was in last night would have been like peeking at presents before Christmas, unwrapping them only to have to rewrap them and act elated and surprised later.

I didn't want to spoil the sheer joy of unwrapping her for the first time.

Mrs. Schmidt came over from her nearby home and put Alexis to sleep comfortably. She never woke (so Mrs. Schmidt told me), and she was sleeping quite comfortably in one of my old Yale t-shirts. In the meantime, I woke Samira up at midnight and asked her to call the owner of the boutiques nearby to arrange for an outfit (business attire and lingerie) to be selected and delivered by eight a.m. this morning. Samira had risen to the task (as she always did) and everything was delivered ten minutes ago – an hour ahead of my deadline.

Mrs. Schmidt helped me obtain the required sizes from Alexis's discarded laundry. I further requested that she prepare breakfast for the sleeping beauty, and I left Alexis a note that (presumptively) outlined the result of the call I'm about to make to my uncle.

I use my office phone to dial him. He answers on the first ring.

"Mm 'ello."

I picture him standing in the kitchen, speaking into the old yellow phone on the wall.

"Mr. Myers," I say. "This is Aidan Pierce."

"Good mornin' Mr. Pierce. And a fine one it is. What can I do for you?"

"I'm sorry to bother you, Eli." My gut tells me it's better to change to a tone of informality. "I understand your deal with R.E.E. is not moving forward as we had discussed."

"That's right. I'd a guessed you knew that, seein' as how I had a call from the paper."

"Yes. I hope that wasn't too much bother."

"Nah, I just said I wouldn't talk 'bout it and they left me the hell alone."

"I'm calling to ask, Eli, if you're ready to meet with Ms. Greene about how we might proceed. Are you comfortable with selling to me to use your land for the Center?"

He pauses a minute.

This could go either way.

"Well boy, I'm thinkin' I am. I can't say how thankful I am that you kept my lawyer and me from making one big mistake with those bastards."

"I only made you aware of the facts," I say. "The decision was all yours. And still is. I don't intend to push you into my agenda, Eli. But if you will entertain my proposal, I believe Ms. Greene can see you as early as this morning so that you can relay to her our intentions. I can have my attorney draft up an official offer for you by the end of the week so you can review it with her."

"I'd talk to her today, sure. And I'm in no hurry. End of the week would be fine to see your offer. What time today?"

"Does ten work for you?" The calendar on her phone had indicated she was open at that time. Perhaps that had been crossing a line, but I had done it for her benefit. She would see that. She had to.

"It does. I have a couple more chores and I'd like to get cleaned up before I head downtown."

"Great. I'll let her know. I would ask one more thing of you, if you agree."

"What's that?"

"I would prefer to keep our familial relationship between us, at least for the time being."

"Well I'm not so sure I'd like to lie 'bout that. Why shouldn't she know I'm sellin' to my own nephew?"

"The fact that you're my uncle is not public knowledge, at least not yet. No one has put two and two together. I don't want you consumed with more calls from reporters." I go on further, with my more pressing concern. "I'd also like to disclose this information to her myself, when the time is right. She will be working with me on this. The local attorney's association appointed her to head up our committee for the project. So long as you don't find that in conflict with her representing you, of course."

"No, I don't have a problem with that. She's an upstanding young woman. Cut from the same cloth as her dad."

"Good. She and I will be in close contact throughout the coming months, so I'd like to tell her myself."

Very close, with any luck.

"Oh. I see. Aright, well – that makes sense I guess. An' I certainly don't need my phone ringing off the wall with calls from those damn reporters."

"Agreed," I conclude. "So Ms. Greene will see you at ten. And I'll personally see the contract delivered to her this week."

"Okay, Aidan. Thanks for the call."

"No, thank you, Eli. I am looking forward to this project more than you know."

Am I ever.

B yron reports back to me at nine a.m. that Ms. Greene has left for her office. He gives me the run down about his trip to her home, describing where it is and the basics about it – three bedrooms, two baths, quiet cul-de-sac in Mirror Lake. He tells me all about her dog, which does not surprise me in the slightest.

Byron would associate with a loyal canine before a human any day.

While he's talking all I can think about is what her bedroom looks like, what her bathroom shower looks like. (Any rooms she might be lying down or lathering up in to pleasure herself.)

I know how amazing she looks sleeping in my guest room and my thoughts effortlessly segue beyond that. I imagine her naked underneath me in my own bed, her flawless skin writhing on my soft sheets as I make her come.

I blow out a breath. *Shit.* It feels hot in here, even though the storm that came through last night cooled things off over ten degrees.

Byron heads back to his desk and, thankfully, I'm left alone.

Never in my life have I been affected by a woman like this. Not to this degree. And definitely not by someone that likely would rather see me swinging by a noose for the way I've screwed up her life, personally and professionally.

I'm on the brink of panic that she's so pissed she won't take the meeting with Myers, but even more anxious wondering if she will show up to meet me.

What the fuck is wrong with you, Pierce?

Sure, that would leave me to start from square one finding a new attorney for my uncle but that isn't a concern in the least. My fear is driven by the thought I wouldn't have the privilege of laying eyes on her again, if she chose to classify me as an enemy.

The thought makes me jittery. I get up and pace my office, then head to the kitchenette for a bottle of cold water.

I converted the whole second floor into office space, dividing it in half down the center. On the street side are workstations for six of my employees, including Samira and Byron, and on the side where I currently pace is my private office. This side faces the rear of the building and is complete with an elaborate conference area and small kitchen.

I also had a living area with a gas fireplace put in at the opposite end of the room, where I can sit back and relax on the sofa when I need to think. I'd sat there just a few days ago to conference with Doc Mason on the large flat screen.

But there's no way I can sit right now.

I head back to my desk and buzz Byron's intercom.

"Sir?"

"Can you find out if Ms. Greene intends to meet me today?"

"I believe she does, sir. When I escorted her to her car she asked if your office was in the building. She said she had to meet you at four this afternoon."

My posture relaxes in relief, enough so it would raise questions about what the hell had me so worked up in the first place. I'm thankful no one is in here with me. The room is separated from my employees by a floor to ceiling wall.

I regain control and start breathing normally.

She's coming.

"Very good. Thank you. How are we on the Ireland front?"

"Still working on it, sir."

"Keep me updated. I do not need this hassle now. She needs to be kept in check. Put Ivan on it if you have to."

"Consider it done, sir."

I disconnect.

Rumor has it that Stella's behavior since I'd left California was on the downward spiral. My people on the West Coast confirmed and had then caught her in (and removed her from) some shady situations for the last two weeks. Drugs, celebrity gossip bullshit, parties and club life where she was in way over her head.

That wasn't the lifestyle she had ever preferred. She was too naïve to handle it.

She was shallow, yes. Manipulative and immature, sure. But she was not a party girl. She could barely handle getting drunk. She was too vain to deal with resulting hangovers and the way they lessened her appearance. She'd also been too disgusted at the thought she might end up throwing up in private or, even worse, in public.

If she didn't get her shit together soon, there was no doubt in my mind her father would be getting involved.

And that was absolutely the last thing I needed.

John Ireland was a powerful man, not to mention the most arrogant, short-sighted, asshole-mother-fucker I'd ever seen do business. If he blamed her troubles on me (which he undoubtedly would, because he always did), there would be a storm of epic proportions coming my way.

And he would be the eye of it.

I buzz Byron again, considering another angle.

"Sir."

"Track down Alanna Rossi please."

"Very well, sir."

"She should be in New York now, unless her staff says she hasn't yet left Miami. Relay that it's urgent."

"Yes, sir."

If I can't get to Stella myself, her mother might be able to talk some sense into her delusional head. They were not close, it was true. Never like a mother and daughter should be. Alanna had stayed out of her daughter's life intentionally for as long as John Ireland wanted her to (which had been for most of Stella's life).

But this was different.

This was the first time Stella had been allowed to make all the wrong choices as a semi-responsible adult or, more to the point, an adult with a prominent name – one that her father would not allow to be tarnished with negative attention.

I will call her mother and ask her to intervene, if necessary.

Anything that will keep me from having to go back there and deal with her daughter in person is worth pursuing.

My place is here now. That much I'm sure of and too fucking bad if Stella can't see that.

I had to put myself on offense when it came to Stella and her father. Offense was a picnic under green trees against the Irelands, a relaxing afternoon in a warm summer wind.

The alternative was defending myself against them, which would not be a run of the mill hurricane warning I'd have to board up my metaphorical windows to prepare for. On defense, with the Irelands after me, it would be more like a tornado on the most destructive end of the Fujita scale, a greed-driven violence powerful enough to propel objects that might literally kill me.

At ten-thirty in the morning I'm at my desk, reading through the reports I'd tried to get through yesterday but couldn't.

Samira buzzes my intercom.

"There's a call for you on line two," she says. "It's Eli Myers."

I dismiss her and pick up the line.

"Eli? What can I do for you?" *Shit*. Did she cancel their meeting after all?

"Oh nothin', nothin'. I just wanted to let ya know that I met with my lawyer."

Thank God.

His voice sounds crackly, distant. Is he on a cell phone? I never would have pictured that.

"Great," I say. "And you feel it went well?"

"I think so. She agrees to go ahead with me. We'll do your deal."

"That's great news, Eli. I think you'll be happy with the outcome."

"Just be sure your lawyers put in there that the barns remain with the farmhouse. That and about twenty five acres is all I want. And a'course any of the extra farm equipment that I won't need, I get to sell."

We have never discussed this in depth, but I had intended to carve out even more land for him to keep. There's over two hundred acres and I don't need all of it by a long shot.

"That's absolutely fine, Eli. I will be sure it's written that way. What would you like to do with the tenant house?" The secondary farmhouse was intended for farmhands, but Eli's operations had downsized dramatically since Aunt Emma passed a few years ago. I knew he rented it out, but it wasn't worth much. It was old and in need of repair, and only had a few bedrooms. It sat about three quarters of a mile down the road from the main farmhouse.

"That's up to you. Got a good tenant in there now, but if you want the place…well I'd already told them they'd have to move because of R.E.E. Just need to give them some notice. They're a good Christian family. I don't want them homeless without a place to go. I met 'em through church. Hawthorne is their last name."

"Of course. We can keep them on, if you'd like. It's out of the way of where our operation will be so I could let you keep the tenant house if you'd like it for the income." This would be less hassle for me too. I thoroughly disliked being a landlord. Property owner, sure. But I had no interest in having residential tenants.

"That'd be good, I think. And I told Alexis the part about continuing the farm but donatin' some of what I produce. She was surprised by that. But she didn't say I shouldn't."

"It will be a worthy cause you're contributing to, Eli." I'm certainly not shocked that she doubted my charitable ambitions. In her mind I was a rich bastard throwing my weight around and annihilating her ambitions in my wake.

"Thanks, son. I'm gonna head home, if I can figure out how to turn off this phone. I look forward to doin' business."

"As do I." I say goodbye and end the call. I will definitely see plenty of Ms. Greene, whether she likes it or not.

15

Alexis

Eli Myers sits at the conference table in the library, surrounded by old law books that I've never read. The setting contradicts him as he sits there, hands folded on the table, wearing old dungarees and a short sleeve button-down shirt that's the same shade of blue as his jeans.

This is his conservative ensemble, I know. He isn't wearing his field boots today which are typically caked in manure. Claudia hates having to vacuum up after his departure, always complaining about the smell.

It's never bothered me in the slightest.

"Mr. Myers," I say as he stands to greet me. We shake and he takes his seat again. Myers' round face is darkened from years of farming under the sun through all seasons. He's a tall man, though his posture is stooped from age and labor. He is visibly uncomfortable trying to right himself in one of the upholstered chairs on wheels. I take a seat in my executive chair, the only one at the table with any essence of power. I have found I sometimes need it to keep my backbone. Today is no exception.

"So, what can I do for you? I understand from Mr. Pierce that you wanted to see me today."

"Yes, he thought it best to get things going." His mood seems serious, but apprehensive. I'm not certain but can only assume he's concerned about my reaction to whatever he's about to tell me.

"I see. And what things are we about to get going? You'll have to forgive me as I was in the dark about your abandonment of the deal with

Renewable Energy Enterprises until you called me late on Friday, and I only have the speculation of the Stanton Times as to why that might be." I can't hide my irritable tone, but he is unfazed.

"The paper got something right for once. I do intend to sell to Mr. Pierce."

"Okay, that is certainly your right. But may I ask why you have so willingly changed your allegiance to him as a buyer after all the work that went into hammering out the Renewable Energy deal?"

"That's personal, and I can't talk about it just now. But he has offered me a bit more money too."

Of course he has.

"How much more?"

"Well, all told the sellin' price is a million and a half. And I will be able to keep some land to farm. Keep, mind you. Not just lease back from him."

Idly I smooth out the purple dress under the table, the one Aidan Pierce bought me. I'm mentally picking up my jaw which in my mind has just hit my lap. My knee won't stop shaking. I have to press my hands to my lap to make it stop.

"Understood. And what are the conditions to this deal?"

"There are none. Only that he be allowed to put the community center on the Hudson Street side of the property and my access to the house and acreage can't interfere with that."

Well that seems…reasonable. Could it be that Pierce really does have only good intentions? For someone of his wealth and power, it doesn't seem likely.

"Oh, and there's one more thing," Myers adds.

Ha! Here it comes.

"Whatever crops I grow, I gotta give half away. Some to the new community center and some to the city shelter kitchens. And I've agreed to let the youth of the community come for field trips to learn about the operation."

What the hell?

Where is the ulterior motive?

"And that's it?"

"Yes, ma'am, that's it. His lawyer's gonna draw somethin' up for us."

I'm just staring at him blankly.

"With those terms and if it looks okay by you, I'll sign."

"Well then, I guess we'll wait to see the proposed agreement and go from there," I say.

"Thank you," he says, letting out a sigh of relief. "I hope you can forgive an old man for not tellin' you the way things changed with the other buyer right away. I didn't mean to be dishonest. I told Mr. Pierce I wasn't goin' a step further without talkin' to you."

"It's fine, Mr. Myers. I appreciate your confidence in me, even if I had to be left out of your initial discussion."

He smiles and nods. He's clearly happy that I've stuck by him.

"I hope you know, however, that you can always trust me with this kind of thing *while* it's happening," I continue. "There's no reason to withhold information from me. I will always have your best interests in mind when I advise you. It's your land to do with as you please. I hope the offer comes in as promised."

He seems joyous now that he's let the cat out of the bag and I haven't flipped my lid. And money or not, the goal is always happy clients.

My fee will be higher than on the Renewable Energy deal, but I know I'll give Myers a break. I've always had a soft spot for him. He'd been one of my dad's first clients as they were about the same age. I was like my dad in this way. I couldn't count the number of times he lowered his earned pay just because it was the neighborly thing to do.

I admit to myself that my pride was hurt when he changed his course of action without telling me. But I'd never let anyone take advantage of him.

The positive press opportunity is still there in this scenario too. Hopefully that will bring in more business.

I still need to quit the Bar Association's appointment for Pierce though. It could appear a conflict of interest if I don't and it will keep Pierce at arm's length – exactly where I need him – if I do.

I shake Myers' hand and walk him out, making small talk about the weather and the work he has ahead of him for the season. I'm still cautious of the whole matter but I'm smiling and trying to match his mood.

I'm hopeful that my luck has turned around, yet in my depths I'm still apprehensive.

Because luck was not due the credit here, you idiot.

Unless luck also happened to go by the name of Aidan Pierce.

O ver lunch in my office, I break my earlier set rule to remove Pierce as a topic of conversation and tell Charlie all about this morning – the notes, and Mrs. Schmidt, and the dress I'm wearing.

I even mention the *Zora's Closet* unmentionables. He's jealous of my good fortune but I correct his perception. I feel more like a trapped animal than a fortunate, rescued one.

I change the subject and ask him about Carter.

They argued after I left (of course), made up (again) and danced the night away before going home. Apparently Charlie was in the bathroom at Sitting Bull when he got the call from Pierce. He was able to field questions, get him my address (which apparently he told Charlie he already had), and relay to him what to do with the dog.

Why did Pierce already know where I lived?

I have to remember to ask.

A s four p.m. approaches, my head is no longer pounding and I'm feeling ready for this meeting with the guy that's furnished my clothing today.

Charlie and Claudia will keep the office open until five as usual. I could walk to Pierce's office, but it's too chilly. I make my way around the one-way streets and park my car where I found it this morning, in the lot adjacent to 250 Harrison Street.

I have a game plan that is quite simple.

First, get the name of his attorney so we can negotiate the Myers deal. Second, quit the Bar appointment as lead for the community center project. Anyone else would be just as capable and, this way, I won't have to see him again until we sit down to close the Myers sale.

My third goal is to pay him back for my outfit, sending the clear message that I don't need his gifts or charity, and make damn certain he knows last night was not typical behavior for me.

Conservative, capable Alexis Greene is ready to lay down the law, and she's ten minutes early.

I walk around to the front of the building and look up. I've never noticed the beauty of it before. The blinkety-blink of the cell store's neon signs contrast the simple window decal for the insurance agency, but both distract from the architecture.

The building is only partially faced in its original red brick and what remains of it has been cleaned up and repaired. New mirrored glass graces the windows, taking up most of the street façade. The look doesn't much resemble the original construction of the thirties.

The second floor shows no indications of what lies within, though I know from Byron that's where Pierce's office is.

Only from waking up there this morning do I know that the third floor makes up the residence but the building is four stories tall. I have no idea what the top floor is home to.

I enter the small lobby and hear both storefronts on either side of me humming with work, wrapping up a regular Tuesday behind closed glass doors.

The lobby is trimmed in gold fixtures adorning carved cherry paneling. Tile underfoot is clean but well-worn. The black and white checkerboard pattern is more typical of the building's original era. I love that someone chose to keep it this way. This unexpected, nostalgic reminder of long ago is completely unlike the exterior.

I get into the small, very old elevator and press two.

It's just as quiet now as when I rode down with Byron this morning. I'm far more nervous this time, probably due to the overwhelming sense that I'm heading into the lion's den rather than escaping it.

The doors open, revealing a sign that reads PIERCE PHILAN-THROPY GROUP in three-dimensional letters. The wall behind the bold, black lettering is done in a silvery patterned wallpaper. There's a sleek reception desk but no one is manning it.

156 · M.J. WOODS

To the left is a long hallway. To the right, the corridor continues a short distance to a closed steel door.

I catch the increasingly familiar scent coming from the long hall to my left.

I can't move.

He comes seemingly from nowhere to greet me.

He can stop traffic as usual, but this time he's dressed in a different way. Business casual, I guess. A brown belt accents his tan pants. They fit so well I've snapped a mental picture.

The sleeves are rolled up on his blue chambray shirt (which fits as well as the pants). His forearms are strong and tanned, the left wrist dressed with the same expensive watch as last night. He's also sockless in a pair of dark loafers.

My horny girl tribe subconscious is busy fanning themselves to prevent a dead faint.

"Ms. Greene," he says, his voice smooth as ever. "Please come this way."

He doesn't come to the elevator, instead turning to head back in the direction he came from. I follow in the wake of his scent, feeling like a tether is pulling me.

A doorway at the end of the hall leads into a large office, a bank of workstations separated by modern black-and-glass cubicle walls. There are six in all and they overlook the street. Not a soul is in here.

I wonder if that's odd, being that it's just four o'clock in the afternoon. Did he send employees out because of our meeting or do they always leave this early? Then again, maybe no one works here at all on a regular basis.

We move through the room towards the back of the building, headed for a doorway in the far right corner. I realize then that the cubicle side takes up only half of the space. A stark white floor-to- ceiling wall separates the two halves.

We walk through a massive wooden door into a very large room, which is apparently Pierce's office. It's private, completely closed off from the work station side of the second floor.

"Can I get you anything? Something to drink maybe?"

I nod, giving myself permission to accept that much. "A glass of water would be fine."

He makes his way to a kitchenette off to the far right and I have a moment to take in my surroundings. I'm not sure where to sit, there are so many options.

The room feels professionally decorated. It's also functional, with designated areas for working alone or with a team of people.

Through windows to my left, I can see where my car is parked at the side of the building. Windows straight ahead reveal another parking area behind the building with twenty or so designated parking spaces. There are two cars parked there and something covered with a black cover – likely a motorcycle – but I can't make out any details from where I stand.

To my immediate right, there is a conference area with an array of audio-visual equipment including a projector. It's mounted to a sculptured recess in the ceiling and faces the wall that divides the office from the cubicles next door. The mammoth projector screen comes down in front of an elegant cherry-wood paneled wall. The conference table seats ten and is made of the same wood, polished to a shine.

Beyond the kitchenette is a living area with a leather couch. It faces a wall mounted gas fireplace. The giant flat screen television hovering above is mounted to a peacock blue wall. All of the floors are wide-planked hardwood, but there's a fuzzy white rug in front of the couch that softens the space.

It's all I can do not to beeline for the couch and take a nap, suddenly exhausted from the night before and the whirlwind of a day I've had.

And all causes of my exhaustion are the direct result of the man standing in the room with me.

Pierce is putting ice in a glass, pouring me some water. He's gotten nothing for himself.

Directly in front of me, facing the vastness of the space, is his desk. It's also polished cherry and neat as a pin. The only things on it are a laptop and a desk phone. There are no trinkets, no photographs. Not even any papers, notes, or pens.

Two dark wood chairs sit in front of the desk, backs to the room. I take a seat in one. The chair is surprisingly comfortable for being made of wood, probably some expensive ergonomic design.

"So, we meet again Ms. Greene," he says, taking a seat behind his desk and passing me the glass of water. "How did your meeting with Mr. Myers go this morning?"

I'm not sure whether I'm disappointed or glad that he's all business, not referencing last night.

"Fine, thanks to you I suppose. When did you set that up?"

"Seven this morning. Caught him after barn chores and set the meeting time ahead of his lunch."

I never thought this man would have any knowledge about the schedule of a farmer.

"I understand you have representation and will be getting an agreement to us for our perusal."

"Yes, you should have something by Friday."

"Very good. And in the same vein, Mr. Pierce, I should not even be speaking with you, if you are represented in the matter by counsel."

"Then why are you here?" he asks plainly.

"To make sure you understand two things," I begin. Amazing how confident I can be when I've not indulged in umpteen shots of liquor. "First, I will not be able to work with you in the capacity that I was designated to by the Bar Association. And second, I do not need your charity."

"Charity?" He has that amused look again and damn if it doesn't fire me up.

"Yes, Mr. Pierce. Something I thought you were familiar with. Whisking me off in your car last night, the clothes this morning, the appointment set with Myers. All of it is unnecessary, presumptuous." I take a breath. "And quite frankly it's pissed me off."

His lips are set in a thin smile and he shakes his head as though he cannot believe me or my response to his over-reaching.

"I'd hardly call it 'whisking you off' in the condition you were in. And the two of us working together is not in any way a conflict to Mr. Myers or his interests in the real estate sale."

Suddenly I could care less about Myers and conflicts and anything else. I have to know what happened last night.

"How – er, why did you call Charlie last night?"

"You said you were on your way to meet him when I arrived at Mac's. Considering your state, I thought it best to deposit you in the nearest bed. I didn't want him to worry, so I found his number in your phone and let him know where I was taking you."

I had forgotten my little white lie about meeting back up with Charlie when in fact I had left him for the night.

A little white lie is sometimes necessary and never need be revealed, I can hear my mother say. She was usually referring to a denial to my father that she'd added liquor to her coffee, but I decide the same principle probably applies here.

"How very noble of you," I spout.

But I'm glad he told Charlie where I was. Why can't I seem to be grateful to this guy? I can sense he's losing patience with me or at least with my lack of appreciation. I imagine he is not used to consulting anyone about anything.

"I thought it was the practical thing to do, to call your friend. That's all. And thankfully Charlie told me about your dog or you probably would have had a mess on your hands this morning."

He's right. I should be grateful. But I can't just back down. I'll look like a pushover. At my lack of response, he continues.

"I don't customarily take women home with me, Ms. Greene. At least not one that I don't intend to be intimate with. I didn't have a playbook to consult." He gets up and comes around to the front of the desk, standing in front of me. He leans back, long legs crossed in front of him, arms folded under his chest. "Should I not have called him?"

"No. I mean, yes. It's fine that you did. He was concerned for me." *After he found out I was with you.* "But how did you know where I was in the first place?"

"Your phone call. I had Byron check it out, then went over when he confirmed he'd found you."

"So you were stalking me?"

"No, I don't think so. I think the definition of stalking would relate closer to what you did when you called and hung up on me."

"I did not hang up on you," I snap. "I hung up on your voicemail." *And your utterly sexy voice.* "People do it all the time."

"I suppose. Now, can we put last night behind us and concentrate on the Center? We have a lot to get through to prepare you for Thursday's meeting with your committee."

"The dress, though." I had almost forgotten. "I need to pay you back for this dress. I do not need you to buy me clothes. Or anything else."

"Fine. I think it was two-thousand and some change. Closer to twenty-five hundred if you add in the cost of what's under it."

I gulp. *Crap.*

"Would you like to write a check? Or do you carry that kind of cash?" He's smiling self-assuredly as he takes a seat back behind his desk, and I'm trying hard not to give him the satisfaction of a laugh.

"No, I...I guess I'll let it go. Just this one time." I'm failing miserably at this assertive thing when it comes to him. But I don't have an extra couple thousand laying around for a dress. "I should just return it to you," I mumble.

"I am certain you look far better in it than I would. Besides, the color suits you."

I blush, feeling embarrassed and silly. This guy is so out of my realm. He's got me. He's complimented me and spoiled me.

And he doesn't even know me.

I have nothing to add.

"Right then. Let's get on with this," he says, triumphant.

"No," I stop him. "I still do not think that's a good idea. Everyone involved peripherally, on the committee, in the Bar Association – they'll think you made sure it was me to handle this, to favor a deal with Myers."

"Your appointment happened organically at that meeting, did it not?"

I hesitate. He has a point. "Yes."

"And there are records to reflect that."

I nod.

He seems exasperated, standing again. He starts pacing back and forth, running a hand through his gorgeous hair.

"If we are to continue this conversation, I need two things. First, a drink."

He heads for the bar and pours some amber liquid from a decanter. He takes a sip, then sits in the chair next to me instead of returning to his chair behind the desk.

"And the second thing?" I'm feeling a bit more confident, since we are sitting face to face. It feels more like an equal playing field.

"I must insist we drop the formalities so I can be blunt with you," he sighs. "May I call you Alexis?"

"Fine."

He sets his glass down and continues.

"Do you have any idea the kind of deal Eli Myers was getting into with Renewable Energy Enterprises?"

"Of course," I say politely. Underneath this stupid dress, I'm fuming.

"Really. You are certain?"

Why does he keep second guessing me?

"I spent the better part of a year negotiating that deal, Mr. Pierce." I can't hold back my anger.

"Call me Aidan." He's calm as can be, even though I'm practically shouting at him.

"Well, *Aidan*," I snap. I reduce my volume slightly, but drip my own condescending tone. "I ate, slept and breathed that deal. Trying to help Myers make enough money to retire. Trying to help our town by adding new jobs to our community. People would have moved to Mirror Lake or somewhere nearby, stimulated our economy, worked in the offices Renewable Energy was going to put on that land at street level."

I'm ready to get louder again, standing up as I hit my point home.

"Not to mention the boost to the construction industry locally to build those offices and then develop the land surrounding it into housing tracts, each to be sold at about three hundred grand apiece."

I've made my point loud and clear, and I expect him to be put in his place or stunned by my confidence. Or hell, at least pissed that I'm shouting at him.

Instead he remains calm, but visibly annoyed. He leans back in his chair and stretches his arms, then clasps his hands behind his neck. He shakes his head and smiles as if to say, *oh you stupid girl*.

"You find this amusing?" I ask, still fuming.

"Not in the slightest, Alexis."

I'm about to move for the exit but as I do, he finally fights back.

"For the love of God, woman." His tone is sharp, angry – and then very loud. "*Sit. Down.*"

His command sends shivers up my spine.

Whoa. Mr. Pierce has a temper.

I'm completely taken aback. Sufficiently intimidated, I do as I'm told and retake my seat next to him, avoiding eye contact.

"You are a foolish, ambitious young woman, Alexis Greene." He continues, a little cooler now and not as loud or as scary. His change in demeanor gives me the courage to look at him. "One that was in way over her head without even realizing it. And I do not find that amusing."

He leans towards me, looks me right in the eye and goes on, without ever raising his voice.

"The fact that you are so adamant about being in this for a cause when all you sought was notoriety for your new firm and money for your pocket is laughable. And even worse, you were playing right into the devil's hands all the time."

Oh. He did not just say that.

"You don't know what the fuck you're talking about." I'm out of my chair again, all flailing arms, heart pounding, as angry as he was a moment ago.

How dare he accuse me of having no morals, which is essentially what he's done. Clearly he is the one that is misinformed. "R.E.E. had no ill intentions towards me, or Myers, or anyone else. They're a reputable company."

I'm so angry I seriously contemplate throwing something at him, but instead I keep going. I will not let his wealth or that charming veneer intimidate me. I spin around and face him. He's perfectly calm again, taking a sip of what I assume is whiskey. His eyes are fixed on me.

"For your information, I had no such concern about money, other than to get paid for hard work that I put in. I have done just fine on my own without anyone's help. The favorable publicity would have been a perk but I can assure you one thing, Aidan."

I move to him, grip the sides of his chair and lean in as close as I comfortably can without wanting to touch him.

"My only intent is to carry on the legacy my father left behind. He started this long before me with integrity and in a manner of service to our clients and community."

He's looking right into my eyes, and I hurry to finish my point.

Before those blue diamonds cut me to pieces.

Before the topic can bring me to tears, thinking about how I wished my father and I could have been in this together with Ben cheering us on.

"Eli Myers was Dad's client for thirty years, and I do not intend to let him be led astray or intimidated by anyone. *Especially you.*"

He leans forward and closes the gap between us to an inch. He's making my head spin.

"Good to hear it." He says it so softly, so calmly.

What the hell just happened?

"That is essentially what O'Hara indicated to me when I asked him about you, but I had to find out for myself. Well done, Greene." He leans back, as though he's suddenly satisfied.

"Oh, it's 'Greene' now?" Fuck I'm pissed. "What happened to Alexis?"

"It's Greene when I'm impressed with you, I suppose."

Why does that excite me?

"So what then, was this some sort of test of my morals? My intentions?" I'm nearly breathless.

"No, not really. More of a push to have you reveal what you would. I admit I had a curiosity whether my accusations may have been accurate, but it's clear to me that O'Hara was honest as you have been now." He's still sitting there with his satisfied smirk taking over his whole posture. "But if it had been a test, you'd have passed. May we get on with it now, Alexis?"

This guy is a piece of fucking work.

I've retaken my seat, not out of submission but out of sheer exhaustion. I can't fight him, but I still do not feel right about our working closely together. It's too heated. Too dangerous.

"I just don't think this is a good idea, Aidan. In case you didn't notice, you have insulted and angered me to a point beyond being rational. It would seem our working together would be ill-advised."

And I can't keep from touching you much longer.

I get up to go and make it as far as the closed door, but before my hand can turn the knob he's behind me, his arm stretched up over my head, his hand firmly holding the door closed.

"Do you know what Renewable Energy Enterprises is, Alexis? Do you know what they do?" If his lips were any closer, they'd be on my skin. His words fall right between my earlobe and my left shoulder.

He's essentially got me trapped between his body and the door. I can feel his breath on my neck. For some reason, it's not making me nervous for my safety.

It's turning me on.

I take a breath.

"Yes, I do. They're a fairly new company that deals in green energy alternatives." I have not turned around. I can't face him. I'll be too tempted to kiss him.

"That would be wrong," he says, again triumphant. He backs off, going to his desk to grab his empty glass. He heads for the decanter again. "They are not a new company at all," he continues from across the room. He brings his drink back and reseats himself in the chair next to mine, urging me to sit again. I do, out of mere curiosity.

"R.E.E. is actually an old company in disguise," he says, drawing a sip. I stare, waiting for him to finish. "A Trojan Horse, if you will."

I just look at him, bewildered. I have no idea what he's talking about.

"Ever heard of Waterman Oil and Gas?"

16

Aidan

My words just hang there in the air as if visible.

She is staring at me in disbelief, mouth agape. Blood has left her face.

I momentarily stop breathing until she finally speaks.

"I had no idea."

Mirror Lake spent every resource available in tandem with surrounding suburbs of Stanton to keep the oil and gas company from drilling here, from taking over. Ten years ago, the company sent some slick salesmen to sign people up for land leases, promising high payouts and little intrusions into the communities they were trolling. Farmers were promised even higher amounts and were paid bundles based on their high acreages.

I'd followed the story from afar, but I knew it well.

I was sure by her reaction. She was fully aware of the history too.

"I presume you know what that means, then."

"Yes," she says meekly.

"So you know that the oil and gas company's practices to mine the shale reserves were highly controversial and caused damage to water supplies in some towns they occupied in Pennsylvania?"

She nods.

"And you are aware that no drilling ever took place here thanks to everyone's campaign against it but that many of the leases were set to automatically renew because of inconspicuous language in the contracts?"

She nods again. She still looks pale, her shock having turned to recognition.

None of this is good news.

"And I suppose you're also aware that locals here were cost time and money, more than most people had, to get rid of the burden of the leases with Waterman Oil and Gas. That legislation was taken to state government. That people filed civil suits, held protests, sent the story to a national level. You're fully aware of all of this?"

She looks up at me, hurt and angry.

"Yes. I am fully aware."

She is such a smart girl. It isn't her fault she missed this. Waterman Oil and Gas no longer existed in its previous form and she would not have had the means to figure out they'd revamped their image in a further attempt to make a go at New York's resources.

I'm certain now she had no intentions of mixing my uncle up in all this. It was completely unintentional on her part.

I'm as relieved as the moment Byron told me she was coming here.

She has a heart. She is not in bed with those tycoons at R.E.E.

And she looks so stunning in the dress Samira chose. I suggested the color and the shade is amazing against her bronzed skin. The way her curves fill out every inch is beyond distracting.

I don't know how I kept myself from kissing her when she was leaning in to yell at me about her noble intentions and her father's legacy.

This girl has gumption.

And soul.

And fucking *amazing* blue eyes.

I still have her attention as I leave my desk and head for the couch. I remote the television on and surf for a music station. Frank Sinatra begins to croon about moonbeams and I gesture her over.

She gives me a questioning glance. "I'd never have pegged you a Sinatra fan."

"Well you were wrong. And it relaxes me. Do you have any objection?"

"Not at all. I love this song, actually. But I'd like something a little stronger to drink." She plops down on the opposite end of the couch, a space left between us.

"Like what?"

"Surprise me."

I get up and make her a rum and Coke. After last night I figure straight liquor is probably not a good idea.

"Don't you have something with liquor in it?"

I'm standing above her, the glass still in hand. "After last night that's the last thing you need."

She glares up at me. "I'm a big girl, thank you. I think I can make my own decisions."

"Really? Because you weren't concious when I asked you if you wanted me to take you home last night. Didn't seem like your best decision-making skills were at work then."

"I don't make a habit of the way I behaved last night. Considering you're partly to blame for the shitty day that turned into a night of poor choices, I'd say the least you could do is offer me a drink."

"There's rum in it."

"Oh," she resigns. I love it when I get one over on her. Something told me she didn't allow that to happen very often with anyone. Her expression when she's taken off guard is priceless, all pouty lips and humbled doe eyes. "I guess that'll do." She takes a couple of sips, sets the glass down on the coffee table in front of us and looks at me. "What other information do you have that I don't?"

I take a seat, leaning back into the sofa, an empty seat still between us. I'm arms folded but relaxed, my drink in hand. I close my eyes and speak, suddenly drowsy.

"Those people that you mentioned, that would have come from Pennsylvania? Right now three hundred workers are employed there. The company intended to downsize there and keep only about twenty-five workers on, then start out here with a smaller work force. After all of the upheaval their presence caused in that small town in Pennsylania, their intentions are to close up shop there and start the process all over again here. And they have no intention of correcting the mess they're leaving behind."

I pull a long sip from my glass and read her expression which conveys sheer interest.

"You do the math," I go on. "But I think it's pretty obvious that more jobs would have been lost than created. Not to mention the town's water supply that was damaged almost irreparably. It's practically a ghost town there now."

I continue while she remains silent. "The new housing development in Mirror Lake came with a cost. Each lot was to have a mandatory Oil and Gas Lease as a contingency without any compensation to the new lot owners. No guarantees were going to be in place for protection of the town's water supply or any other bodies of water or natural resources within a hundred miles."

"That's crazy. They'd never get away with that. And they represented to me they were all about green alternatives. Solar power and...."

I cut her off.

"Did they say that in writing?"

"To a degree. They sent Mr. Myers a proposal in the mail, but it was just about leasing the land for solar panels. He brought it to me and we declined their offer."

"And then?"

"And then their attorney contacted me and offered to buy the land outright. We began the negotiations. That was a year ago."

"Did you happen to notice the clause in the lease they first proposed about assignments?"

"Yes. That was one of the reasons I told him not to lease it to them. It gave them the right to assign the lease to any affiliate they chose."

I sit up and set down my drink, facing her. "Exactly."

"But this is a sale directly to R.E.E. I couldn't have predicted..."

I hold up a hand. "I know. They had all their bases covered. They intended to convey the land to yet another subsidiary, a new oil and gas company. The same affiliate they'd have leased to if Myers had agreed to that."

"So I saved him from one trap and sent him directly into another."

"In a manner of speaking."

"What did they plan to do with the land? Is there any truth to the housing development? To their desire to pursue solar power?"

"To the former, yes. To the latter, no."

She shakes her head in disbelief, visibly upset. I want to comfort her but decide against it.

"The oil and gas affiliate intended to set up a rig smack behind the homes on top of the hill – once those homes were already sold and occupied of course. They had to ensure those leases would stay in place without any further approvals required."

She gives me a look that says holy fuck. She's in shock once again.

As she should be.

"But couldn't our local government prevent this? I mean there's no drilling allowed by law in the entire state. R.E.E. – or whoever their fucking affiliate is – can't just come in and take over."

"You're right, as of now. But there are a lot of backroom deals going on – power shifts, politicians and influential people behind the scenes that want this to happen. There's no way to be sure the future doesn't hold some loophole that would let them in. I'm betting it's closer to possible than we realize, especially if they are still pursuing acreage in Mirror Lake under the mask of a shell company."

"Like the Myers Farm," she says, crestfallen.

"Exactly."

"How do you know all this?"

I turn to her and tilt my head. "Do you really need to ask?"

She thinks a moment. "I guess not. I get it. With your wealth you likely have any information you'd like at your disposal."

"Not any information," I emphasize.

Like how I can ever get you to let your guard down with me.

"Oh, yeah," she says in mocking. "Except maybe the daily schedule of the President? Or details about upcoming top secret NASA missions?"

She smiles at me and I can't help but laugh. Ms. Greene is witty. I like that.

I like her.

"The bottom line is the mess of ten years ago would have looked like a child's puzzle compared to the one the property owners in Mirror Lake would have faced with this. I don't know how much you know about hydro-fracking, but those that oppose it feel very strongly about keeping it out of their backyards."

"I know," she says. She seems tired. She rests back into the couch. "And yes, it's a hot button issue here. I avoid talking to clients about it, attempting to stay neutral. I know my limits and refer them to the right attorneys when I need to."

"I believe that's a battle any young attorney with a new practice would want to steer clear of."

Again she's speechless. She must know I've read the situation perfectly. She had no idea how deep a pile of shit she was headed for.

"You could not have known all of this, Alexis. Don't feel guilty. R.E.E. played you, played into your ambitions and your desirable position in the community with your father's reputable name making you an ideal mark. You are inexperienced yet affiliated with a name the entire town would trust. They used that to get the upper hand."

"I guess." She swallows hard. "And I guess I need to thank you." I can tell she means it, but she's reluctant to say it. "My career would have been over before it began when people around here found out what they'd have to face all because of me."

"There is no need to thank me. I have my own personal reasons for embarking on this project, which starts with acquiring Myers' farmland. I will not discuss those reasons with you, as they are irrelevant, but my point is I have my own agenda. I can assure you that it is a noble one, resulting in the Center as the highlight."

She's finally starting to relax, sipping her drink as I continue.

"I am no white knight intending to save you from yourself." I can't help my smirk. "It just so happens I accomplished that as a byproduct of my efforts."

"Well then. Round one to you, Aidan Pierce," she says, raising her glass to me and then to her lips. She empties the contents, the ice clinking in the glass as she sets it down.

God, I'd love to lick those lips.

I scold myself to stop that train of thought before it takes off with me in it.

Or with her underneath me right here on the couch.

"So it would be advisable for you to go forward as we originally planned, don't you think?" I say. "Myers will sign an agreement that he has no objection to you representing him and working with me on behalf of the Bar Association."

"I will have to review that document and would point out that as Myers' attorney I may require changes to it before he signs or dismiss it altogether."

I don't respond. Is she going to fight me on everything? God help me, she *is* a lawyer. Through and through.

"But I suppose," she goes on. "I suppose if it covers all the possible scenarios, I can go forward with this arrangement."

Finally. She's giving in.

Maybe I can win her over after all.

B y ten o'clock Alexis says her brain is hurting and I can't blame her. We finished our drinks hours ago and both switched to water, and we've eaten grilled chicken and vegetables that Mrs. Schmidt carried down to us for dinner.

We'd spent the evening in the conference area going over documents and slides. We scrolled through countless frames projected on the screen over the conference table. I've shown her some of the proposed plans for the Center, right down to the building's location and layout. I outlined how the programs and activities will work and what it will cost to run the whole thing.

She has interrupted with intelligent questions or offered ideas where I'd previously been blocked. Good, solid ideas. She truly does have an inquisitive but keen mind.

And the way her hair falls around her bare shoulders, the way she smiles at me, the way her eyes dance in anticipation when I'm getting excited about sharing my mission, about the good I want to do here – she is (almost) unbearably distracting.

Twice, I've had to divert my thoughts to keep from getting hard right in front of her.

Her job is going to be to keep the local committee on track. She will coordinate fundraising with Jade McCall and help Attorney Richardson with the town and county approvals (if his further background probing checks out). I want her to head up the law and justice program too. She'll need to reach out to local and state police authorities on that, as well as other attorneys, but she seemed happy to do so. Excited even.

Thankfully, we've been interrupted only twice. Once for me to field a call from Byron telling me that Ivan is in California on Stella Ireland duty for the foreseeable future. The other interruption was for her to make a call which, from what I could tell, was to ask a neighbor to walk the dog.

I have not revealed what personally motivates me in all of this, and she has been respectful enough not to pry. She did ask about whether I liked living here when I was a kid, but I deflected her question saying that I didn't remember it much. She let it go at that.

I walk her to the elevator. The building is silent around us.

I can't bring myself to push the call button. I don't want her to go.

"Do you have a few more minutes?" I ask.

She's totally thrown off.

"It's pretty late," she says.

"I'd like to show you something."

"And that would be?"

"I promise it's nothing crazy." I push the button to call the elevator and moments later it's lurching to a stop and opening for us. "Come," I say. She smiles a shy, silly smile, but she follows me anyway. I press four to take us up two floors.

"Where are we going?"

"You'll see," I say.

We get to the fourth floor, a floor above my loft. I guide her down the hall to a steel door and shove it open, revealing a set of short metal stairs that climb up to the roof.

She looks nervous. I smile and take her hand.

"Where the fuck are we going?"

I can't help but laugh. I love that she can be as crass as I can.

"Come on, it's all right," I coax. "I promise not to keep you long."

She follows me up the stairs. We reach the top where yet another metal door awaits us. This one opens out and I push it away.

I move through the door and down to the rooftop below, extending my hand to help her navigate down to me. The flat roof is covered in a rubber membrane, soft underfoot. More noticeable is the view, the city skyline stretching out before us, the twinkle of lights in the darkness impeded only by some of the building's mechanicals. I revel in watching her face light up as she takes it in.

"Wow." Her one word reaction is barely a whisper.

"This way," I say, moving farther towards the center of the building, around the huge skylight that lights up the foyer in the loft two floors below.

"Um, this might be a good time to mention my fear of heights," she mumbles.

"It's okay, we'll be away from the edge. And the sides come up pretty high. You'll be fine."

I bring her to the seating area where an array of plants and flowers surround us, all in bloom. A large wooden pergola with climbing vines defines the space. Her eyes seem to have forgotten the view, as she's fixed on the setting here. I can't blame her. The rooftop garden has been a month long work in progress, and the results are worth admiration.

"Why did you bring me up here?"

"I wanted to show it off, I guess – to someone other than Byron."

She gives me a quizzical look.

"He's the master gardener," I say by way of explanation.

"I never would have guessed that. Is there anything he can't do?"

"So far? No."

"Well, I guess you'll cross that bridge when you get to it."

I let go a short laugh and gesture for her to join me as I sit. I pull out a remote from a table next to me and illuminate some candles and rope lights that twinkle all around us.

She looks around, then looks at me sheepishly, as though she's come to a revelation.

"Look, I'm glad I could be a practice run for future attempts at wooing the opposite sex while you're in town, but I really should get going."

She thinks I'm trying to make this a date?

Shit.

I guess I can see how she'd think that.

Not good. I know she will scare easy.

"It's the only light up here," I insist. "I'm not pursuing you. There is something else I wanted to talk about."

When I pursued her, she'd damn well know it.

"And what is that?"

"I think you might be right about bowing out of the Center project."

She gives me a look of disbelief.

"May I ask why, after we've spent the last few hours hashing out the entire plan for it?"

"It could be dangerous."

And I can't fuck you if we work together.

"Okay, not what I was expecting," she utters, seemingly to herself.

"What reason were you thinking?"

"I, uh…"

I don't take my eyes off her. She looks so amazing in this light. That dress. The way her chestnut hair falls in soft waves. I can't help my crooked grin from forming as she stalls to answer.

"Well, for the reason I originally gave you," she claims. "It could be seen as an extraordinary conflict. Why do you think it's dangerous?"

"I've looked into Renewable Energy extensively. The players have a lot to lose. Mirror Lake was a last ditch effort to make a go of the latest shell company. A lot of people are going to lose a bundle without that purchase from Myers going through."

"That may be, but fair is fair. Myers is free to sell to whomever he wants. He's not bound to them."

"People behind the scenes don't always play fair. In fact they've built a reputation of quite the opposite. They've been known to resort to certain tactics to protect their interests."

"Such as?"

"Intimidation. Fraud." I pause. "Homicide."

She swallows hard. She looks unsure as to whether I'm telling the truth, but at the same time a bit nauseous.

"Come on," she says. "Really?"

"I'd just feel better if," I stop for a minute. I want to forewarn her, but I don't want her to be petrified. I'd never let anything happen to her.

Whoa. Where'd that thought come from?

I move past it.

"I would prefer someone else take the position. Most likely a man."

She doesn't hesitate in her answer.

"No."

And apparently her answer is firm. I'm surprised at her defiance, reacting like a stubborn child.

"Excuse me, did you say no?"

"I will not back out because of danger, and especially not on the pretense that a big, strong man is better suited to face any sort of threat than I am. I'm not about to abandon my best client either. Knowledge about how you will handle things for the Center is a piece of the puzzle in making sure my guy gets what he needs."

I shake my head. *Women.*

"I can't fathom anyone actually bothering with Mirror Lake, anyway. It would be far easier to start over somewhere else, maybe even in another state." She hasn't convinced me, but I'm quiet, listening while she goes on. "I don't need you to rescue or save me, remember?"

"Throwing my words back at me – especially taken out of context – that's dirty pool, Alexis."

She moves to the edge of her seat and speaks again, her words gentler this time.

"That may be, but I'm staying on. And I believe in your project, Aidan. Didn't you just spend an evening convincing me of it?"

Apparently she won't be dissuaded. I bow my head in my hands, defeated. When I look up, I give her as serious an expression as she's likely ever seen from me.

"Have it your way, Greene. But if you stay on, there are three irrevocable conditions."

She leans back, crossing her legs, folding her arms, waiting for my demands. The way she crosses those stems makes my cock twitch. I have to take a breath before I can go on.

"First, you can have no further contact with R.E.E."

"That shouldn't be a problem. I haven't even heard from their attorney after things fell apart Friday. He hasn't returned any of my calls or emails."

"Really. That's interesting. You'll need to forward me his contact information. And you are not to contact him again."

"Um, pardon me? I don't think this arrangement is going to work if you think you can tell me who I can and cannot speak to."

"This is non-negotiable, Alexis. No contact with R.E.E. or their lawyers, and if they contact you, you tell me immediately. You need to trust me."

"I'll concede on this point," she sighs, "but only because I have no reason to contact him now anyway. " She changes her tone to sarcastic. "What are the other two conditions?"

I'm aggravated that she doesn't realize the severity of the situation, but I go on anyway.

"If there is ever any danger, real or even sensed by either of us, we follow my game plan to address the threat, no matter what it is. And if I take you off the project or out of the loop, you comply."

She nods.

Good. I internally sigh with relief.

"The third condition…"

She interrupts me, putting up her hand.

"Sorry, Mr. Pierce, but that's already three things."

"Wait. What?"

"I'll agree to those three conditions. One, I don't contact R.E.E. or Mark Whitmore. Two, I follow your rules if any danger – real or implied – presents itself. And three, if you take me off the project, I stay off."

I consider her a moment. Damn she's good. She actually has a point.

Yet she has no idea what my third (or apparently, my fourth) condition was.

"Fine," I say, my coy smile returning. "If you insist."

"What was the other rule you intended to impose on me?"

"No, no Alexis. You don't need protecting. By all means, let's leave rule *four* out."

She looks at me, pleading. I stand, remote the battery lights off and gesture to the roof exit. I head in that direction without looking back.

"If it saves me from danger, perhaps I should hear it," she says at my back.

I keep walking and she follows. We enter the stair tower and I close and lock the roof entrance.

"It just might have, Greene. But since you've taken it off the table, I guess you'll just have to take your chances."

I sprint down the steps through the dim stairwell as she tries to catch up to me. My heart is pounding loud in my ears as we reach the door below and head for the elevator. It's exciting, having her chase after me. I know she can't stop herself from wondering what I've left out.

I take a few deep breaths and center myself. She's winded too, but apparently the jaunt down the stairs didn't consume her at all. If anything she looks more beautiful, her chest rising and falling fast.

"Byron will greet you in the lobby and see you get to your car safely."

"Thank you, I appreciate it." Her breathing has evened, thankfully. Seeing her winded had too much effect on me.

"Unless you think you might be feeling faint again," I tease.

She laughs softly. It's a beautiful sound that echoes in the open hall, like a melody in an empty church on a Monday morning.

"No thank you, Aidan. I have my own cold bed to go home to. I will not be needing your guest suite this evening."

I smile back at her, genuinely amused.

Why do I want her to stay so badly?

"And where has your staff been all this time?" she asks as we wait for the elevator.

"They leave at five customarily," I say, looking down at my feet. I don't want her to know I'd cleared the room before she came here, unsure what might happen.

Would we have a yelling match? Would we just have a regular business meeting?

Or would I slip her dress off her and take her in the middle of the conference table?

As it turned out, only the first two events came to fruition.

And I was beginning to regret that the third had not.

I run my hands through my hair, as I've done all night in her presence either out of excitement or frustration. This woman just has me riled.

She gets my attention by speaking in the direction I'm looking, down at my feet.

"But I arrived just before four," she says, resurrecting the topic. "No one was here then, Aidan. And no one was leaving, either."

I look up at her with a guilty expression, grinning ear to ear. I can't help it. She's got me. "Yes, well…I may have anticipated that our conversation would be heated and told them to take off a bit early."

"Did you, now?"

I take a few steps closer to her, inhaling her, wanting to kiss her.

The elevator chimes.

"I did," I manage, still unable to contain my smile.

Damn!

I don't want her to leave.

"And what is this rule number four we've omitted?"

I knew she would ask again. I wait a beat, then confess.

"That I never get involved with someone I work with. On a sexual level."

The elevator pings, doors opening just as the words leave my mouth and move through the air towards her.

"Good night, Mr. Pierce," she says, stepping backwards into the elevator.

She flushes pink from her ears to her neck. She is enticing me again, her breath quickened, her lips parted.

I can't help myself. I'm staring her down.

As the doors close I whisper, but loud enough that she can hear every syllable.

"As requested Greene, that rule is off the table."

17

Alexis

I'm lying in bed, wondering if I've been dreaming again. But I open an eye and realize it was no dream. I actually did spend the evening with Aidan Pierce.

A smile comes easily as I think about him when we parted ways at the elevator.

His hair scruffy from the rooftop breeze, from running his hands through it throughout the night. His prevalent and sexy five o'clock shadow. His strong forearms, the softness of his hand as he had helped me down to the roof.

The way he looked at me when he said aloud that he was changing the rules of his own game as the elevator doors closed.

And how engaging he had been as he talked about the Center. He was a brilliant man following a passion.

A man I couldn't seem to get enough of.

I was in awe of him and of my desire not to leave his presence as the elevator doors closed.

My alarm blares in objection that I have not yet risen and I slam down on the off button.

I didn't arrive home until eleven the night before. I'm sure I'm still dopey with adrenaline after last night.

I spent the half hour ride home talking excitedly to Charlie as I drove. I told him about Aidan's elaborate office, the new project, and that our evening included drinks and dinner. He insisted it was a date, but then agreed with me that would be a big fat no after I told him about the Eli Myers developments.

I gave him the gist about the mess Aidan got me out of but kept details limited. It's better if he can plausibly deny that he knows anything, if he's ever asked.

I laid awake for an hour after getting home, unable to sleep. Yet, I don't feel tired now.

I shower and dress quickly, long before Huck wakes up which is unusual. He was happy to have his human mama home, his enthusiasm apparent when I entered last night and he practically knocked me down in forgiveness of my absence the night before.

Now he's content, snoring loudly on the floor at the foot of the bed.

My cleaning woman Marta is due in today. I know her results won't come close to Aidan's Mrs. Schmidt, but I'm not wealthy beyond my wildest dreams, able to afford someone so capable full time.

At least every two weeks I don't have to scrub toilets, mop the kitchen floor, or prep meals that hold up in the depths of my freezer. She does it all. And I won't be set back more than the usual hundred and fifty bucks. The gracious, gray-haired woman will spend the whole day at the house and keep Huck company too.

This Wednesday morning is another chilly one, more spring like. I've opted for hot coffee on my way in. It's six-thirty and traffic on the highway is just picking up.

I'm excited about the Myers deal again and about Aidan's project.

You're excited about being in close proximity to a remarkable God.

My undersexed alter-ego is back, also rising at dawn. I didn't take time to lengthen my shower this morning and shut her up, so I locked the horny bitch away, stowed on a mental closet shelf along with slut stilettos and too-short skirts.

Apparently she's broken free, but at least I escaped the house without her influencing my outfit.

I'm full on conservative today in navy pants, a white blouse and short spiked heels. I'm having lunch with Gloria at the Lake County Country Club so something a bit more lawyerly is appropriate.

The only skin I have showing is a hint of cleavage exposed by my slightly low-cut neckline.

I refuse to acknowledge that I did so in case I run into Aidan.

No one is at the office when I arrive. I make notes for Eli Myers' new sale, things I want to be sure are in the new contract. Then I'm on the computer, trolling websites for more information about Aidan.

I don't feel I can lurk about the internet for information about him unless I am completely alone.

Thankfully, no one is due in for another hour.

I research his philanthropy, trying to find out why he is so enamored with this cause for the youth of Mirror Lake and the City of Stanton.

I come up with zip, beyond some articles reporting sizable donations to organizations that uplift traumatized youth.

I pull up the tax roll for all properties in Lake County. The only thing I can find under Pierce Philanthropy Group is the building at 250 Harrison Street. Under Aidan's name there are four more properties though. They all indicate 250 Harrison as the billing address.

Two are residential properties in nearby Falcon Lake where I used to work at Martin and Reynolds. That area is more of a tourist hot spot in the summer, and it's in a higher price point than my neighborhood of Mirror Lake. There are two housing developments like mine there with twenty or so homes, complete with a cul-de-sac and community lake access.

There are also many homes and cottages scattered all around the lake, as there are in my town.

Some are waterfront and some are across the road from it. Some are worth hundreds of thousands, others are small cottages over a half century old that had never been improved.

His two properties fall into the brand-new-waterfront category.

They have extensive lake frontage, actually, and each of the two homes are over three thousand square feet, each assessed at well over a half million dollars.

The third property I find is a commercial property on Harrison Street in Stanton, near his office. I can't picture what building it might be.

The last property is on Mirror Lake. The parcel is a five acre lot with over a hundred feet of frontage on the lake. The property taxes are outrageous, even without a building on the land.

Welcome to New York.

There are vacant lots here and there all around Mirror Lake, between a few housing developments like mine, and others between the older cottages that have been around since the fifties. I'm trying to picture where his land might be when the intercom startles me.

"Morning! Jade McCall is holding for you on line one."

It's Claudia. I look at the clock. Wow, my ditzy receptionist is ten minutes early.

"Please take a message. Tell her I'm on another call."

"Sure thing, boss!" Somehow I don't even mind her cheer today.

I e-mailed Jade and Attorney Richardson first thing this morning while a detailed description of a direction for the committee was fresh in my mind. It was short and sweet, just noting the goals for our first meeting.

Richardson wrote back with one sentence confirming tomorrow.

Thursday at noon at the Sheridan.

Meanwhile Jade has been bombarding my in box with question after question.

I hit the send and receive button of my e-mail. My hunch is right. There is yet another e-mail from Jade.

To: Alexis M. Greene, Esq.
From: Jade McCall, Esq.

RE: PIERCE PHILANTHROPY GROUP PROJECT

Hello again Alexis,
Just wanted to know if Mr. Pierce is coming tomorrow? Perhaps it would be best for me to talk directly with him about the ideas for the first fundraiser. I'd like to get his input so I know what he's looking for.

Thank you,
Jade

Jade McCall, Esq.
Ballard & Lennon, LLP
4050 Jefferson Ave.
Stanton, NY 14077

I'm sure she'd like his input. And then some.

Keep your hands off him, plastic tits! He's all ours!

Now my horny alter-ego is getting jealous. Great. I say a prayer that she does not have access to any weapons.

I wait a few minutes and then reply, hoping to convince Jade I was unavailable when she called.

To: Jade McCall, Esq.
From: Alexis M. Greene, Esq.
RE: PIERCE PHILANTHROPY GROUP PROJECT

Hi Jade,

Unfortunately Mr. Pierce is unavailable to come to our Thursday meetings. Per his instructions, I am to meet with you and Attorney Richardson on Thursdays and report back to him on Tuesday evenings.

Whatever your ideas, I'm sure I can convey them to Mr. Pierce. I met with him last night and have a lot of information to go over with you tomorrow, as I referenced in my first email.

See you at noon.

Best regards,
Alexis

Alexis M. Greene, Esq.
Greene Law Office
423 Harrison Street
Stanton, NY 14077

Ha! That oughta do it. I bury myself in work, hoping I've been successful at my attempt to deflate Jade McCall's interest in setting eyes on Aidan in person.

By noon I've heard no response from Jade. It's a small victory for me and my everyday, unenhanced boobs. I may not be firmed by the hands of a skilled doctor, but I can out-compete with my words every time.

Gloria and I are sipping iced teas in the elegant dining room of the Lake County Country Club. Neither of us are the country club type, but the membership is reasonable and Gloria likes to network with other attorneys and professionals to drum up clients. Her husband loves the golf course in the summer and I love coming as her guest for the fantastic food.

We've both ordered the chicken Caesar salad and have devoured half a loaf of fresh bread while we wait. We trade comments about what an unbelievable few days I've had, while hers have been more same old, same old.

"Didn't I tell you this was what you needed, Lex? Since I opened my mouth at that meeting you've landed the biggest real estate deal of your career, never mind any transaction your father had ever have seen. And you've spent the night in the penthouse of a *freaking* billionaire."

I can't give her specific details about Eli Myers' sale, but she can put two and two together that Aidan is involved. Beyond the business stuff though, Gloria's most interested in my alone time with Aidan – until I convinced her nothing happened.

"You should be kissing my feet in honor of my gracious nomination." She stops the waiter for another iced tea.

"Or at least buying your lunch," I say smiling. "That much I can handle."

"As long as it's not a two thousand dollar dress or some fancy panties, right?" she teases me. Our lunch is served, hopefully ending this tangent of conversation.

"So," she asks between bites, "when do you meet with the committee? Tomorrow?"

"Yes, at noon. Jade's already pestering me, sniffing out Aidan's whereabouts tomorrow and whether he'll be in attendance. I've happily informed her that he will be unavailable."

"Huh," she says, wrapped up in her meal. I can't blame her – it's just a salad but it's amazing.

"I made it clear that I had spent time with him last night. That probably wasn't very nice of me."

"Well, don't lose any sleep over that. Pierce obviously wants to spend time with you. He's going to be a hot commodity. You should stake your claim as soon as you can."

"I don't think that's quite the direction this relationship is headed, my friend. But thanks for the 'atta girl."

"Just beware of that Jade McCall. She's always trying to get her hooks into rich men. To that gold digger a guy like Pierce would be like," she pauses, sipping more tea.

"Like what?"

"Like the jackpot of ten state lotteries all rolled into one."

"What, her life as a successful plastic surgeon's wife isn't satisfying enough for her?" I shake my head in disgust. Some people are just never happy with what they've got. At least her husband didn't die after only a couple years of marriage. Then again, maybe that's what she was hoping for.

"Apparently not satisfying enough." Gloria pushes her plate away. She never finishes a meal.

"I figured she was superficial, you know, about her looks and all. But does she really run around on Dr. McCall?"

"Well, you didn't hear it from me," Gloria qualifies, leaning in. Her tone has turned to a whisper. "But I'm pretty sure she's played golf with nearly every man here. If you know what I mean," she says with a wink.

"Yeah, I think I got it," I say, unable to help my look of slight disgust. "Her poor husband."

"Well, from what I've heard he's no saint either. But again, you didn't hear it from me."

"No ma'am," I say chuckling. "I never did."

Twenty-four hours later, I'm at the Sheridan Hotel where I first met Aidan. This time, I'm in the hotel's more intimate restaurant at a table set for three. I'm not distracted by Aidan Pierce's good looks today, but by Jade's well-enhanced chest as she leans across the white linen tablecloth rambling at me. She's carrying on about optional themes for the fundraising gala.

I'm trying hard to look away, to listen to what she's saying or focus on the few sheets of paper she's sprawled out in front of me, but it's like a train wreck. I can't take my eyes off her enormous bosom.

A fitted, red silk blouse with a plunging neckline highlights Dr. McCall's handiwork. The blouse is tucked into black pants so tight I'm surprised she can walk in them. I can tell she's dressed for the possibility that

Aidan might show up, completely ignoring the information I gave her yesterday. There's some comfort in the fact that she cannot possibly be comfortable in the pants or the six inch black heels she's got on. They make my fuck-me shoes seem appropriate footwear for church.

Attorney Richardson is late, but has e-mailed me that he's on his way from the courthouse a few blocks over. I'm not surprised. The schedule of a young attorney trying to balance assigned cases and a private office is always ridiculous and stressful. The Court dumps everything on you, especially the shitty cases no one else wants.

"So Alexis, what do you think of my ideas? Does anything fit into what Mr. Pierce may have suggested to you?"

I'm scanning the photos she's clipped to her notes which outline three possibilities. I can't really answer as once again, my attention has not been focused where it should be. I got through the selection of the gala date and time slot but then lost all concentration.

Somehow her excited babbling entered a distant place in my brain and I come up with a reply.

"You've obviously put some time in already, Jade. That's great. I can't really speak to exactly what he will or won't like, but I'd say that building the evening around a key speaker would bring in the most money. Someone that just about anyone would enjoy listening to."

She's smiling proudly. As obvious as it was, her idea does have the most merit. I decide not to burst her bubble.

"Great! Do you think formal is the way to go? Black tie?"

"Yes, I'd say. The auction idea is over-used already and his philanthropy organization is just getting off the ground. It's not prominent enough to do any type of awards-related fundraiser. The company is too new to community service."

"You have a good point there. And with all the people Mr. Pierce knows, I'll bet he can get someone phenomenal to headline. Like the Vice President or something."

I laugh at her wide-eyed, schoolgirl optimism, but she's probably right.

"I'll mention it when I see him, but it's probably a good idea for us to try and think of a few options too."

"Of course," she smiles. "So you think this will bring in enough donors?"

"Well, maybe not enough, but it's a simple idea, enough to excite Mirror Lake residents, and if we can get the right speaker it will be enough to attract larger donors from Falcon Lake and Stanton."

Attorney Richardson strolls in and apologizes for his tardiness. He looks like a young Republican on a tight budget, all department store blue suit and red tie. He could pass for cute, but his brown hair is unremarkable, cut short and parted on the side. His briefcase and shoes are both well worn.

"So what have I missed?" he asks, nearly out of breath. He sips his water as Jade hurriedly explains her few ideas and how we've narrowed it down to a keynote speaker with donors paying by the plate to hear the lecture. She seems on edge since his arrival just a moment ago.

"That's good," he says, calling over a waiter. "But I'd have to suggest we come up with something else to raise more money. These types of events can be losers if the entertainer or the speaker charges more than can be made selling tickets."

"I doubt that would be an issue for Mr. Pierce but I'd agree, Mr. Richardson." I stop while he orders his to-go lunch from the waiter, then continue. "I think we should do some direct action fundraising as well. We can set up a station to offer specific donation options for the new center. Five hundred for arts and crafts supplies, five thousand towards gym equipment. Larger amounts can be allocated towards student desks, computers and technology for use in the learning annex."

"Please, call me Allen," he says at me, then addresses both of us. "I think the direct action plan is a sound idea. Do you think so, Jade?"

There's a too-familiar tone in the way he addresses her.

"Sure, whatever." She seems irritated, putting paper away faster than it came out. She won't look in Richardson's direction at all.

Oh great, I've found myself in a spat between lovers. Or former lovers? Whatever the deal is, it's making me uncomfortable.

"Well, that should be enough to report to Mr. Pierce for now, Jade. If you need to be off, that's fine."

"Thank you, Alexis. I'll be in touch. I'll stop by the office here to secure the date with the staff on my way out. July second we said?"

"Yes, that should be fine. I will confirm it with Mr. Pierce, but I believe just over a month should be enough lead time, if we can get invitations out next week. Please come back to next week's meeting with the hotel's event details – two options for the dinner should do – and we can go from there. You'll have to squeeze in a meeting with the Sheridan's event staff before next Thursday."

She smiles at me. "Not a problem at all. And I'll think about keynote speakers and donors too."

"Very good. Please e-mail me if you have anything more."

She nods to us both and leaves, but for some reason I'm still uncomfortable. I guess having confirmation of Jade's cougar status is disconcerting whether or not she's sitting here.

I turn my attention to Richardson who has been scrolling through his phone.

"Allen? Should we discuss your direction in the project?"

"Oh, sure. Sorry. I just got called back to the office and I have to be back at the courthouse by one-thirty. What would you like me to do?"

"You can start by quitting this project if you and Jade cannot work together."

He's visibly taken aback, brown eyes darting from me to anywhere else in the room.

"I, er…no, I don't think that will be a problem. I'll…I can talk to her before we meet again. I think it's just a misunderstanding. Probably from a case we worked opposing sides for."

He's paddling, trying to keep his head above water. But I know Jade rarely runs in the same professional circles he does. She handles mostly estate law and divorce work. She wouldn't have any reason to be opposing counsel in a case of his.

"I don't need her distracted or upset. The fundraising is the most important part of the gala. I'm sure another attorney can step in for you on the approvals, if you're too busy." I recall Aidan's passion last night, the drive he has for this worthwhile cause. From somewhere in the depths of me, my backbone strengthens and gives my words a firm undertone. "This project is too important to Mr. Pierce to have any aspect of it fail."

"That's understood. Mr. Pierce has already selected land for the site in Mirror Lake, I understand?"

At least the idiot reads the paper.

"He has."

"And why is it he's using lawyers to facilitate this project? I haven't quite grasped that."

"I'm not at liberty to share details beyond what each of us has been assigned to do and my knowledge is a bit limited as well," I say. "But I think a significant aspect of the center he plans to construct focuses on law. How to share it with the youth of the community in a positive way, get them on the right side of it."

He nods in understanding. "I guess that makes sense. So would you like me to go ahead pursuing the county and Mirror Lake approvals?"

"That would be the next step. Let me know what you need. I presume you have the resources to track down the required applications? Reach out to the right authorities to get this moving?"

He smirks. "I'd like to think so."

"Great. If you have any questions, please let me know." I wish I could take over this aspect myself, already having a good sense of what needs to be done. But I have enough to contend with between Myers and overseeing the justice side of the Center and my regular clients. Eventually I will be pretty deeply involved, if Pierce's outline last night holds firm.

I have to hope Allen Richardson can stay on task, as something in my gut tells me he'd be the one to drop the ball out of the three of us. He looks around, likely wanting his lunch to appear so he's not late to court.

I stand and give him my typical firm handshake, looking him squarely in the eye when I say goodbye. I don't have a soft spot for Jade, but can empathize if she's been jilted by this prick. Everything about him just screams sleazeball.

I leave him alone and, just for fun (or maybe as payback for rejected women everywhere), on my way out I head for the kitchen and pull the waiter aside, paying him twenty bucks to secretly cancel Richardson's lunch order. He'll certainly be late getting back to court now.

Oh, how judges hate that.

18

Alexis

It's been a whirlwind of a week. The ups and downs since meeting Aidan leave me glad that it's now Friday. I'm expecting a proposal from his attorney to come in today, if he's true to his word. I have not heard from him since leaving his office on Tuesday night.

Anxiety rules my body at the thought.

I can't pinpoint whether it's a general sense of missing him that bothers me or just that I haven't heard anything from him at all.

So many things are hanging in the balance.

Like my career.

The weather is still cool today. A storm is expected later tonight with hot weather coming on its heels – just the opposite of earlier in the week. I recall a drunken me caught in the rain, draped over the broad shoulder of Aidan Pierce.

I banish the thought and keep working, knowing the only thing I can do is occupy my mind.

By one in the afternoon I still haven't heard from him or some phantom representative of him and anxiety is turning to dread at the unknown.

What if he doesn't keep his word?

What if he's trying to manipulate Myers behind my back?

What if he's trying to manipulate *me*?

I sent Claudia home at noon since she was going to visit her parents in Massachusetts for Memorial Day weekend and needed the extra drive time. Charlie has been in his windowless office, unaware of my mind's paranoid tangents.

I'm alone in my office contemplating my conceivable fates, when there's a knock on my partially closed door.

"Can a guy find a decent lawyer around here or what?" A smooth voice comes through the door with that hint of carnal tension followed by the scent I've gone weak at the knees for countless times already.

Holy shit!

It's him.

"Yes, come in," I say, mustering as much calm as possible. I hadn't planned on him just showing up.

Slick move sending your secretary away, dumbass – and with it any warning of someone coming through the front door, along with any sense of professional façade for this law firm.

Damn.

Do I look okay? I glance down at my outfit. Dark jeans, the stilettos, a deep plum colored blouse with a v-neck. My black business jacket is resting on the back of my chair and I contemplate putting it on, but I don't.

It's casual Friday after all and there's no time anyway. He's coming through the door, looking around my office with interest. I want to curl up in a ball, swooning at how amazing he is yet again.

I don't have the willpower to fight my attraction to him.

He just looks…

So. Damn. Good.

Another pair of expensive jeans (tight and tattered in all the right places), loafers, and another snug tee. This one is blue, setting off those sapphire eyes. He has a blazer on too, making him appear ready to get down to business.

But the jeans.

Fuck.

The way he fills them out is mind-blowing.

"Dressed down today, are we?" I ask, hoping I'm not being too casual. I stand up and gesture for him to sit.

"I was going to ask you the same." He takes a seat in one of the leather club chairs, placing a black folder in his lap. I hear footsteps headed for my office.

"Someone here, Lex?" Charlie calls. He peeks through the open door and, for the first time, is allowed to behold Mr. Pierce in person. "Oh, I – I'm sorry. I didn't realize you had an appointment."

Aidan gets up to turn and greet him and I can tell Charlie is as bowled over by him as I am.

In the split second Pierce still faces me Charlie mouths behind his back, *"Oh my freaking God!"* I have no doubt he would squeal if Pierce wouldn't hear him do it.

"Aidan, this is my assistant Charlie Young. Charlie, Aidan Pierce."

"Very good to meet you, sir."

"Likewise, Charlie. Good to know you. I believe we spoke by phone once before."

"Oh yes, didn't we though," Charlie confirms with a knowing smile.

They are almost the same height, Aidan with a slight advantage. But Aidan doesn't fill out his clothes linebacker-style like Charlie does. His muscular build is more inconspicuous.

Charlie is a master at this type of meeting. He breaks the ice with all of our clients or peers with an ease I've witnessed from few others. Uptight businessman or a master plumber, no one stood a chance. Charlie is a chameleon that blends into any situation, charismatic and friendly enough to make the other person comfortable no matter who they are.

I'd bet my convertible that Aidan possesses the same skill. I sit back to watch the two men size each other up, realizing that, put together, this team of male muscle could charm the pants off of just about anyone.

They both turn and give me a look like I'm some sort of situation they always have to handle. I want to smile too but I can't dignify their 'Poor Alexis Club' with a reaction.

They look at each other then, both grinning, and Charlie shakes his head in a what-can-you-do kind of way.

"All right you two, I get it. Thank you both for rescuing me the other night."

"So what's on the agenda tonight, Charlie?" Aidan asks. "Is Alexis taking you dancing again? Or maybe out for karaoke this time."

I shoot Charlie a *keep your mouth shut* look to no avail.

"Karaoke? Aww *hell* no," he says, beaming. "I don't *karaoke* with Lex. Didn't you know? She's got a killer voice. I don't compete when I can't win."

I try to smile graciously without throwing something at him. I don't need him to shower me with compliments in front of this guy. Somehow I feel like he'll use it to gain an advantage.

"Is that right?" Aidan asks. "I was not aware." His eyes haven't left mine, and I can tell he is relishing Charlie's information emissions. "Do you have proof?"

Time to put a stop to this train.

"No, he doesn't. Charlie, you'll excuse us please? I have some business to go over with Mr. Pierce."

He picks right up on my get-the-fuck-out-this-is-business tone and excuses himself, closing my door as Aidan retakes his seat in front of me.

"So, do you have something for me, Mr. Pierce?"

"I do. And I think we agreed you'd call me Aidan."

"Yes, sorry."

He pulls something out of his pocket and sets it in his lap, on top of the folder.

"Actually, I have two things."

"Mmm hmm," I say. Lord, I so want to bite that bottom lip of his. It's so perfect. Determined not to be further distracted, I continue. "Whenever you are ready to share, I'm listening. And I think we ought to discuss my meeting with the committee yesterday."

"Why don't we start off with that? How did it go?" His tone is so relaxed, and I'm grateful. It feels like we have overcome a big hurdle since Tuesday. There's less tension, less of an atmosphere of battling wills.

Unless I take into account the sexual visions I'm fighting off in my own head.

"It went well, I think. Mrs. McCall brought some general ideas and we expanded on them. Mr. Richardson was not much help at first, but he will get the job done once assigned tasks." I decide to leave out the questionable relationship between Jade and the sleazy, young Mr. Richardson.

"Very good, then. Did we decide on a date for the gala?"

"Yes. July second, if it fits your schedule. And with that secured we can roll everything out – media, invites, everything – five weeks ahead of the event. It's not a lot of time, but should be enough to get a great turnout here."

Typically an endeavor like this would be months or even a year in the making but, around here, Pierce himself would be enough of a draw. People would change plans to attend if they'd already made any.

He pulls out his cell, I assume scrolling through his calendar.

"Yes, that will be fine. The holiday weekend might be able to attract more people. The gala will be at the Sheridan as we discussed? I've chosen the venue specifically as it emboides revitalization of a former dilapidated property."

"I see the parallel. Clever."

Very clever Mr. Pierce.

To hold the first fundraiser in a relic of a hotel that had recently been transformed with major renovations was a nod to exactly the goals he'd set for the city and for Mirror Lake.

Transformation.

"As far as I know, the site is available. Mrs. McCall was going to secure the reservation on her way out, so details would be available prior to our next meeting. The invitations will need to go out by next week, I should think."

"Sooner is better. Also I have a website designed already and my assistant will handle the media campaign. We can get Richardson going as soon as we have the deal with Myers signed. Have you decided on a program?"

"A combination of a keynote address by someone who can bring in a substantial cost per plate, as well as a direct action donation table. It won't be enough to fund the entire project, obviously, but should be a great kick-start."

"Seems like you're on top of everything." He regards me with an appreciative smile, as though I've accomplished some elaborate task. Or maybe he didn't think I would able to hold a meeting and actually get anything done.

"I appreciate your confidence." I'm sincere, but he smiles at me as though I've said something sarcastic. He's so hard to read sometimes. "One other topic was mentioned. I was asked to inquire whether you'd have any ideas for a keynote speaker. With your connections…" *Crap.* I didn't realize how awkward and silly I'd feel asking this. "Um…Mrs. McCall thought you might be able to reach out to someone who would draw an even larger audience than we could."

Asking him to use his influence like this feels foolhardy.

But I promised I would ask, right? And part of me wants to see what – or who – he comes up with.

"Customarily I would say no," he begins. He pauses, watching me become increasingly uncomfortable. "But," he continues, "for this cause I will have no qualms about getting someone. Who might attract both Stanton residents and people from Mirror Lake or other suburbs?"

"Reaching both types of people was my thought too. It would have to be someone relatable to everyone."

"A Hollywood type? Someone from the art community? Or maybe a popular sports figure."

"Now you're talking. I was thinking maybe someone who graduated from Stanton University. There are some prominent alumni going pretty far back in their history."

"Great. I'll work in that vein and get you a list of names. If you come up with others, let me know."

"So, the offers for Myers. Do you have them?"

"Yes. I had my attorney prepare this."

He hands me the folder which has his company logo on it. I open it tentatively. It's a typical contract, several copies flagged for signature. The price is stated on the front page, the same as Myers said.

One point five million.

Somewhere inside my own head I hear a long, low whistle.

I flip through it and run my thumb over Aidan's signature. It's just as neat as the personal notes he signed to me, which I'm keeping in the nightstand next to my bed.

Shit, that has to mean something.

My therapist would probably have had a field day with that one, if I was still seeing her.

I push the thought aside so I can respond with some semblance of authority.

"I'll review it over the weekend and meet with Myers on Tuesday after the holiday. And the other thing?" I ask. I thought this was all I was expecting.

Have you learned nothing from spending time with this man? Expect the unexpected!

"Just this," he says, handing me a flash drive across the desk.

"And this would be...?"

"It's some voice files for you about the Center."

"And what would you like me to do with them?"

"Transcribe them, makes some notations with your thoughts and get a copy to me, if you would please."

He's got to be joking.

"You're kidding, right?"

"No. Why, is there a problem?"

Okay, so apparently he's dead serious.

If this guy thinks I'm going to play secretary on top of organizing his entire project, he's certifiable. He could easily have a computer program accomplish this task. I try to remain polite.

"No, not a problem necessarily. But I think it would be as efficient to have Charlie do that, for my review and then yours. He can get to it Tuesday, after..."

"No," he interrupts assertively. "It has to be you. I insist that you be the only one to hear these files. They're confidential."

What the fuck?

"Well, Aidan, that's all well and good, but I don't customarily do the work of a secretary. Take a look at the wall next to you. That's why I have the expensive law degree. I realize it's only from Stanton University and not as worldly as a degree from Yale, but it keeps me from having to fetch my own coffee or do my own filing."

I'm a complete liar now. I've done both of those things in the last two days alone.

"Alexis, I am not trying to insult you or force you to do this simple task. I can take the information back if you like." He looks disappointed, almost wounded.

Now I regret acting like a smart ass. How does he have an ability to turn me around so quickly?

"I just…don't you have someone else in your office that you trust to do this? To transcribe something confidential? They must do it all the time."

"No. There isn't anyone else. The files were meant for you. There isn't any speed required, really. You can take your time with them. If you can have it done for our Tuesday meeting, that would be fine."

"I can type a hundred words per minute, with a ninety-five percent accuracy rate. I'll have your transcribed files ready tonight, unless the drive is full of them. If so, I may need until tomorrow."

You idiot!

There goes my Friday night. Not that I had anything to do anyway. But he presented me with a challenge, backed me into a corner. I had to come out swinging.

He's trying not to smile, a mischievous look resting on his face coveying as '*gotcha*'.

"That is above and beyond, Greene. Above and beyond." He's smiling now, clearly happy he's gotten his way. "You have my phone number, as I think we established on Monday night."

I blush at that. Why does he have to keep reminding me of my momentary lapse in judgment?

"Go ahead and text or email me when you've gotten through them."

"Fine," I say, standing up. "Can't I just email them back to you?"

"No. Not secure enough."

"Very well," I say, giving in. "Anything else?"

"Just one more thing," he says, as he rises. He leans forward, his hands on my desk, coming close enough for me to inhale his scent. His eyes meet mine, and he's got that school boy look again. "Please make sure you use your home computer for the task."

"Why?" I blurt, unable to contain my curiosity. God, he is *so* close.

I am relishing it, not wanting our meeting to end.

"That's for me to know. For now. Let's just say there's some sensitive material that I would not want found at your place of business."

"I hope it's nothing relating to our real estate matter. It's completely unethical for me to consult with another attorney's client, and…"

He cuts me off. "It's nothing of that nature. I promise." He closes his eyes for a second, hiding their blue depths. I think he's going to kiss me, but he doesn't. He steps back and turns to leave. As he reaches for the door, he turns back to me.

"Your ears only. Home computer. Agreed?"

I nod. I don't understand the gravity of his instructions but I won't take them lightly.

"Agreed."

He leaves without another word, closing the door behind him. My heart sinks, knowing our time together is over and I won't see him again until Tuesday.

I email Jade to be sure she's secured the date with the Sheridan. She writes back within minutes saying she has and will be forwarding their requirements for payment and event details prior to our next Thursday meeting.

I buzz Charlie and ask him to set Myers up for a meeting on Tuesday morning. I decide not to mention the transcription Aidan has asked me to complete. I add that I'll be leaving early to get home and review the contracts so I can be prepared for Myers and tell him I'll call him over the weekend.

I pocket the flash drive in my jeans and throw the folder in my messenger bag to take home – which is exactly where I plan to go without delay.

By four o'clock, I've been through the contract three times. I'm sitting at home, curled up on the couch in the same clothes I put on this morning, too eager to have changed as I normally would.

The only thing I took time to do is let Huck out to do his business in the yard, then put on some music to read by.

I've searched for something highly objectionable in the contract, thinking there must be *something*.

But there isn't. Everything I wanted for Myers is in there.

A few questions linger about the timeline of the acquisition. Aidan wants to close the land purchase by the end of July. Considering the parcel is over two hundred acres that could be too soon. The property needs survey work completed which will take quite a bit of time.

The boundaries have been established for more years than I've been alive, but Aidan and his attorney are insisting on maps to ward off future objections by adjoining property owners.

I have to agree. Anyone seeing deep pockets could decide to sue Aidan over boundary line discrepancies. I'm doubtful anyone in Mirror Lake would want to do that, but there's always the possibility.

I can't believe I'm looking at it from his angle, looking to protect him too. In this particular instance it doesn't hurt my client so I guess there's no harm in that.

Yet I can hear my Dad's warning coming through.

Always think of your own client first. You have a big heart and morals, Alexis. Some people don't.

Reading through the rest of the contract though, Myers was right. He's getting one hell of a deal, resulting in everything he could ever have wanted. Money to retire on and share with his family, for one. Even though he has no children, he has a much younger sister – a widow – and some nieces he wants to help put through college.

He also gets to retain some land and barns to keep doing what he loves. Except now he can hire whomever he wants and buy whatever equipment may be necessary to make his smaller operation easier for him to run – if he wants to run it at all. The livestock and equipment he already has are his to sell or keep as he sees fit.

Aidan has also addressed the additional house on the property, the one that farmhands used to occupy when his operation was bigger. Mr. Myers has been renting it to the Hawthornes for a few years now and, apparently with this new deal, he will be able to keep doing so.

This had been a stumbling block with the R.E.E. negotiations. The home would have had to be bulldozed in order to make way for the housing development they had proposed. The Hawthornes are clients of mine and friends of Eli Myers and neither of us had been happy about that part, which R.E.E. had been insistent on.

The requirements about donating to the local soup kitchens and the new Center are stated, but half will belong to Myers to do with as he pleases.

The rest of the contract is typical with us to provide the usual documents. There is no realtor involved, so Myers is saved from listing the property and paying a huge commission. The down payment is sizable though. It's the largest I've ever seen at two-hundred and fifty thousand, held with Aidan's attorney until closing. I don't recognize the name of his Manhattan attorney.

I close the folder and set it next to me. I feel plenty confident in the deal, but decide I'll let it rest until Monday or Tuesday for a final review before meeting with Myers. Charlie's text from an hour ago indicates that meeting will take place at ten in the morning the day after Memorial Day.

I get up from the couch and the flash drive from Aidan falls out of my pocket.

I had forgotten all about it.

Your ears only. Home computer.

I realize then that transcribing these files will play his voice in my ears for as long as I want.

Maybe this will not be such a demeaning task after all.

In fact, I think I'll plug the earbuds in and let him completely take me over.

Yes, a fine idea! But first, a glass of wine!

Well, it is Friday night. Cocktail hour.

I put the flash drive on my desk on my way to the kitchen.

I've always loved this room, especially once Ben and I made some minor adjustments.

It faces west, gets beautiful afternoon light, and the décor makes it even cheerier. New white paint for the wood cabinets offset the soft yellow Ben picked for the walls. The pops of blue in the glass cabinet knobs are my favorite, bought from a replica antique catalogue.

The biggest change was the large banquette area we put in. Two maple benches are upholstered in blue gingham, replacing the small dining table the previous owners had. Modern stainless appliances, including my wine fridge in the pantry off the kitchen, were splurges that the previous owners had made, so they came with the house.

I'm barefoot and in search of a snack to go with the chilled wine I've opened. I plate a few crackers, some sliced parmesan and a small bunch of grapes and head for my office with a glass of Riesling in hand.

I plug the drive in and pull off five files in all. The first three have no titles and are just numbered one through three.

The last two are *"Alexis Greene Background"* and *"Open Last"*.

What the hell?

I'm intrigued beyond rational thought.

Of course I want to open the last one first!

You know what they say, Greene. Curiosity killed the cat.

I heed my own advice, and open the file labeled Number One first, then put in my earbuds.

Aidan's voice comes through smooth and clear, seducing my eardrums, not to mention everything below my waist.

"Alexis, the following should be transcribed in connection with the Center Project. Please save each of the three as separate documents."

Three files? I know I've pulled five off the drive.

I can hear papers shuffling in the background and the buzz of an intercom. He must have recorded this in his office.

The sound cuts out, then his voice comes back through with all background noise gone.

"Okay, first document will be a press release for the gala fundraiser, date to be determined."

Obviously he made this before our meeting, not yet knowing I'd proposed July second.

He carries on and I type away, my usual fast pace at work. The material is not out of the ordinary, a typical press release that will serve its purpose when the time comes. I finish it within minutes and am on to the second. It's a list of names of invitees to the gala that he requests, including many A-list celebrities from across the country and a few regionally famous business people. There are none I know personally.

202 · M.J. WOODS

His staff will send the invites out when they are ready, he says. Many may not come, but he goes on to talk about prospected donation amounts from certain guests on the list, including those who won't attend.

I can see why he wants this confidential. It is information only a trusted person should know, but I can't understand why he's chosen me and not a long time member of his staff.

There could be various reasons, I suppose. Maybe he's had an issue with an information breach in the past. The press would likely be persistent trying to obtain information from people close to him.

And, of course, no one knows little old me.

Apparently, I've earned his trust and suppose the test he gave me the other night about my intentions contributed to that.

The third document continues in the same all-business fashion. It's a draft of his speech for the gala fundraiser. Except for the liquid sex that is his voice, I'm starting to get anxious.

What the hell are the last two files about?

Before I can wonder further, he begins to get to the core of his speech. He talks about why he's getting so involved in the Lake County area at all.

By the end of it, I'm welling up. He speaks sincerely about helping the people of Stanton, Mirror Lake, and the surrounding communities.

He recalls happy childhood memories with his mother at an ice cream parlor in the same hometown as me.

He also references a not-so-happy event that took them to the West Coast when he was a small boy, but he never specifies what. Just that it was the turning point for his future when his mother met and married Reginald Pierce.

Wait a minute...

Met?

Married?

I thought Reginald Pierce *was* his father?

So does the rest of the world!

The speech concludes with his message reminding people to give of themselves before he thanks everyone for coming.

But I stopped typing several moments ago.

Aidan's voice abruptly terminates, then begins again, in a much more somber, injured tone.

"This speech is going to expose truths that have been long hidden, Alexis. And you're one of the few people that I've made aware. I've thought it over for some time and have decided to make you another memo. Please do not type it. Just listen."

I refill my wine glass then return to my computer, fumbling through the menus on the screen, seeking out the fourth file. The one made just for me. At first I thought it was about my background, maybe some profile he made about me. But now I realize *"Alexis Greene Background"* is *for* me, not *about* me.

He's going to talk about himself.

My curiosity is all-consuming.

I put the earbuds back in and listen as Aidan starts talking again. His smooth voice sounds a little more relaxed this time. I'm guessing maybe he took a break for a whiskey. But his speech is all the time perfectly delivered, under his usual control.

"I don't know why I'm doing this, Greene. I guess you've impressed me more than I thought possible. And there's nothing that says I have to give this to you, right?

It seemed like you were interested in my motivations for this project we're about to dive into. I said I wouldn't discuss that, but I think it's important for you to know what they are after all. I can't see any other way for you to realize how important it is to me, how important it was for me to work with someone with integrity and passion and an innate drive to help people. Someone who can help me change the future for the better.

Yes, I've read up on you. I know all about your service work throughout college. I've seen you in action, however briefly. I know you have the drive, and I know after pushing you tonight that you won't take shit from anyone.

You are the perfect fit to take this on with me."

I hit the pause button. Ok, so he made this after the evening we spent together in his office.

I think about how driven he was, how excited he'd been to talk to me about his philanthropy here. His excitement had been contagious and we'd worked through a lot of ideas together, like a team.

Fear and anxiety roll around in my belly, knowing some intense information must be coming my way.

Maybe he can't talk about this face-to-face. Maybe this is just his way.

But it doesn't matter how – or even *what* – he tells me. The point is he's telling me.

He is trusting me.

And that means he might expect me to open up in return.

This invokes sheer panic within me.

I don't want to scrape away at my own freshly healed scars. I don't want him to expect me to return the favor.

But then again, there's no way he knows *everything* about me. I don't care how much research he thinks he's done. I can keep my past buried, if that's what I choose to do.

I want to hear more, to trust him back. I want to help him with this project. He's right, it is exactly the sort of charitable work that I feel is worth any amount of time or effort.

And I want to make his pain go away, even if I don't know what caused it.

I've seen the depth of loss in his eyes, the way he struggles with something that is never voiced, never apparent just by looking at the surface.

Instinct tells me what lies beneath is something I know too well, a pain I recognize in myself maybe.

His charm and beautiful appearance distract the rest of the world from what is real. Whatever that reality is lies deeper.

So much deeper.

And maybe I identify with that too much.

I only see a glimpse of this when we're face-to-face and especially when he talks about helping people. The way he spoke in those moments – the sincerity of his tone, the emotion that came through even when he didn't intend it to – *that* is what is real.

When he revealed that part of himself to talk about his ambitions the other night he was so open. He seemed to be the truest version of himself then.

At least as far as I'd been witness to.

He never talked about the *why* of it all, and if he's about to share that with only me…

Maybe it's a side effect of the attraction I have to him, but I want to know more.

I can't define why. I just know I already *care*.

More than I have about much of anything in a long time.

I take a deep breath, then another.

I hit play again.

"Begin at the beginning, as they say. As I plan to mention at the gala, Reginald Pierce is not my biological father. Biology or not, he is and will always remain my one and only Dad.

My real father was an abusive alcoholic and recreational drug user. My mother was a nurse at Stanton Hospital. She put herself through school and made a decent enough living to keep us clothed and fed with the money she hid from my father.

Despite everything she faced living with that bastard, everything he took from her – and from my brother and I – she always managed to take care of us the best she could.

Then my mom met Reginald Pierce at the hospital while working a shift. He was recovering from kidney stones. Dad was humble, like my mother. He wasn't wealthy at that time and he wasn't a well-known businessman. Not like you might have seen him portrayed in the media now.

He and Mom had an instant connection. My mother always told me he was the sweetest patient she ever laid eyes or hands on. He was discharged only a few short days after she met him, but he started visiting the hospital the following week and even became a member of the board so that he could see her more often.

Within a few months, by both of their accounts, they were deeply in love. They planned for my mother to escape my father, which was made easier by the fact that she had never married him. The only wrinkle would have been me and my brother. But Reginald had some influence even then, and, as I understand it, eventually they got my father to sign over all rights to him as our adoptive father.

Reginald promised to take care of all three of us, but I never met him until the day we left New York. We moved to California and my mother never returned to New York. Neither did my brother.

I came back east to go to Yale, but for a long time the closest I could get to here was Manhattan. I wasn't ready to be here, to face my past.

But I have been planning this endeavor for years, since the sale of my first company.

I knew I had to come back here someday. To honor my mother and her courage. She knew that our life was horrible because of the circumstances, because of the man who conceived me – and she knew the best thing she could do was get us away from him.

That man ran the streets as a teenager because his parents were not there. His father was like him, always drinking or gambling, smoking something or shooting something. His mother was absent, always looking for her next drug-induced high by whatever means.

And he was no better.

Because he had no guidance, no options, no one that gave a shit whether he lived or died, my biological father became what he was. That one event set so many other terrible events into motion.

If it wasn't for Reginald Pierce, it would have been far, far worse. For me. For my mother. For all of us.

This is why I had to come back here. To do what I can to make sure this is prevented. No one should have to end up like my biological father or find themselves in a situation like my mother – without options and trapped. She was lucky she found Dad when she did, that they were able to build such a life together. Most women in her situation end up..."

The recording stops for a moment, then starts again, his thought left unfinished.

She had the courage to follow her heart when it was a risk. She didn't know how things would pan out, but she took that leap and trusted herself. Trusted Dad.

My mind is reeling from all of this information.

From the torture and fear in his voice when he talks about a man that was never his father, but an abusive bastard and a fucked-up mess in general.

I don't know the extent of what he went through. He's said nothing about that, but just the thought of Aidan as a small boy, being harmed or neglected (or worse) makes me ill.

The silence is broken by a more hopeful Aidan. I can see the cursor ticking down and know I've almost reached the end.

"I find myself wading deeper into a similar situation all the time. I want to take that risk too. I'm trusting you. But you have to let your guard down.

We are more alike than you know, Alexis. You have to trust me too. You need to know you can trust me."

This is not an easy ask. He must know this, be able to sense it about me.

But I'm in awe of him. Of his passion to help people, to not turn his back on an issue that he experienced in some far away life, a life that he could easily write off and never think about again with all the money and power he now has.

I'm shocked that he can open up like this, when so far I've pegged him as a firmly closed book. His actions had done nothing but confirm that thus far.

I suppose he's not opening up *to* me, really. It's *at* me, on a recording – but again I have to ask myself if that even matters. He didn't have to do this. He didn't have to tell me anything, doesn't owe me any explanations about his motivations.

He wants me to know enough about him to put my own faith in his ambitions.

He wants me to trust him.

I know after this Aidan deserves to know as much about me, about anything I'm willing to share. It's only fair after his confidence in me. But I don't know if I can. Keeping silent about myself is the easy way out. Why dwell on the past?

I can't tell him.

My secret-keeping days died with my husband. I should just let it be.

No. You just need to set it free. To someone like him.

My inner musings surface against my will.

I've longed for someone of my own again, someone I can confide in like Ben. Someone to fight the world with like Ben.

Someone I can physically touch in a way I've never had.

If that someone was Aidan Pierce, I had little doubt the result would be one intense experience.

19

Aidan

Samira must sense by now that something is off with me.

I'd been gone only a half hour to meet with Alexis two blocks away and deliver the contracts, but I'd also given her the voice files I'd made just for her.

The first few were the files I had intended to share with her from the beginning – details about the Center.

But the last two…

The last two I made on a whim and they were *personal.*

I've been second-guessing the decision since I got back to the office.

I wasn't sure how she would react once she heard them.

I wasn't sure I should have made them in the fucking first place.

For the last hour I've been continuously checking my phone for a text, my laptop for an email.

I'm supposed to be giving Samira details I've discussed with Alexis about the committee meeting and going over more particulars on that. I'm also supposed to be giving her instructions on all the other irons in the fire I've been avoiding all week – all of which should have been wrapped up two days ago.

But I can't concentrate and she knows it.

"Would you like to have me come back in an hour, sir?"

"No," I say. "That won't be necessary." It's already close to three o'clock on the Friday of a holiday weekend. I don't believe in keeping my employees from enjoying a long weekend break (when they're allowed to get one).

In this instance, I was letting Samira off until Monday evening – as long as she could be available by phone wherever she was.

"Really sir, it's no trouble. Perhaps you need a break."

"No, there's nothing here that cannot wait until tomorrow by phone or maybe even until you return on Tuesday. Why don't you take off?"

"I have no plans until this evening, sir. I can leave now and return in one hour."

"No, Samira. Please. Take off now and enjoy your weekend. It's well-deserved."

I have not spoken truer words all week. Every time I found myself distracted by thoughts of Ms. Greene, Samira saved my ass.

At one point I'd called a colleague the wrong name while we were phone conferencing and Samira had snapped me back to reality with her signature cold stare, coming up with a plausible excuse for the oversight.

Samira knew I was not at my best and she'd handled it as professionally as she always did. Sending her off for a holiday weekend a couple hours early was the least I could do.

"If you insist, Mr. Pierce. Please call me tomorrow as early as I'm needed."

"I will, Samira. Have a good holiday."

As soon as she leaves, I'm buzzing Byron's desk. He will only be as far away as Falcon Lake this weekend but he hasn't taken off yet.

"Do you still have that trace on Alexis Greene's phone?"

"Yes, sir. You did not instruct me to remove it."

Damn right I didn't.

"Please text me the details of where she is. You may head to the lake house, if you choose. We're done for the day. And I'd like to take out the bike tonight."

"Yes, sir. But a thunderstorm is predicted this evening. May I drive you in the Lincoln?"

"That won't be necessary. Thank you though, Byron."

No one looks out for me like this man. Not even my own mother. He's the most loyal employee I've ever had.

"I don't mind at all, sir."

"I'll be taking the bike. And both the bike and I will return safely," I insist.

Though I promise nothing as to when.

I shave and shower, hoping some sexual tension relieved (even if by my own hand) will clear my head of the thoughts of one Alexis Greene.

While I'm dressing for a ride, my cell chimes with a text from Byron telling me her exact whereabouts.

She's at home, in Mirror Lake.

Great.

Can I go there?

Do I even want to?

I'd been back once now, anxiety increasing with each passed mile until I'd confronted it.

But that was for business.

I'd been to the Town Hall to meet with the town's Supervisor and to see Eli at his farm.

The Town Hall was insignificant, never present in my childhood memories. And the farm was the setting for the few pleasant memories I did have.

Going back to the lake itself, near where it all happened…

I wasn't sure I should do it.

Or more to the point, whether I could. I'd tried before and struggled.

I decide to drive around awhile before I make up my mind.

Maybe by then she will have gone out, and I can find her somewhere else.

Anywhere else.

I drive to Falcon Lake again, this time taking the highway until I can exit to the county route that cuts through to the upscale lake town.

The town is busy as I pass through. I'm garnering looks from the elite that meander the walks of Main Street to shop or patronize the local restaurants. I'm not sure if it's the bike or me that's bringing the attention, but I ignore it.

It's Friday evening on a holiday weekend and everyone seems to be out and about, ready to kick things off. There's an energy in the air.

Or maybe it's just me, projecting my own anticipation.

Either way, this is not where I want to be.

I want to be with her, but I have no reason to call on her.

And if I did, I wasn't sure I could handle it.

I wanted her, more than I'd wanted any woman. I couldn't explain it, which I'd come to grips with.

Acting on it despite this was something else entirely.

Pursuing her could be dangerous for both of us.

Part of me said that was reason enough to avoid her, part of me said it didn't fucking matter. I'd have her anyway.

I'd already shared with her what I wanted to do to her, but the lingering anticipation stemmed from not knowing whether *she* knew I'd shared it.

If she had listened to those voice files, she knew exactly.

I turn down a side street, intending to head back to the highway.

Instead, I end up following the county route that will take me north into Mirror Lake.

If I can face my ghosts head-on without incident, I can definitely handle visiting the woman I want to bed.

I'd need to do one before I could move on to the next.

Slowly, but with intent purpose, I walk down the rocky dirt path, down the one lane road that leads downhill to the cabin.

As it comes into full view, I stop abruptly.

I'm motionless, able to feel the energy in everything else that moves around me.

The rustle of the green, freshly budded leaves in the light breeze. The movement of branches above me as a bird lands overhead. The dust kicked up from beneath my riding boots settling in an unnerving blanket of filth around me.

I'm the only thing on the planet that is not in some kind of forward motion.

My heart beats fast and, for a moment, I do not take another breath, another step.

Maybe this was a mistake.

I'm all for facing my past and chasing down the darkness head-on. I came here ready for a fight.

But maybe this is too much, too fast.

Therapy can only do so much to remedy each hurdle I jump while I'm here. In the last month, any time I'd wanted to dip a toe in these waters – to push the boundaires – I'd done so from across the lake, in the vacant lot I'd purchased just for that reason.

I'd become used to looking at the lakeshore I'd walked as a boy from a half mile away, standing on the opposite shore. But I'd yet to go down this path, to dive in head first.

I hear his voice in my head, and it angers me enough to move forward.

A man does not run.

The raspy voice is loud and clear in this setting, which should not be surprising.

This shoddy old cabin is where my memories of him are the clearest.

It looks so much smaller than I remember, yet the porch feels the same as I shrink back, feeling like a boy again.

I walk up the two rotten wood steps.

The bench is still here.

Without thinking, I run my hands along the surface of the seat. What's left of the white paint flakes off under my hands.

I can't believe it's still intact, practically in the same condition as when I was six years old, though the wood is a bit more faded and gray. The cover of the porch must have ensured the relic didn't deteriorate beyond recognition.

I had already confirmed no one lived here anymore.

I move to the front door but don't bother to turn the knob.

I already know I don't want to go in.

My phone pings in my pocket, startling me so much that I jump.

"You scared, boy?"

The bastard's voice reverberates through me and I have to shake my head to send it away.

I turn and leave the cabin behind me. I take off at a dead run, up the one lane drive that leads to the main road around the lake. When I get to the top, I'm breathless and hot. It's only sixty-five degrees outside, but my reaction to this setting (and my sprint uphill) has raised my body temperature.

I lean down, hands pressing above my knees as I catch my breath.

Once I recover, I pull out my phone to see who is trying to reach me.

A new kind of excitement floods me, chasing away the dark.

Alexis.

My heart continues to pound as I open the message.

> You asked that I let you know when I finished
> the transcription. I've completed it.

I can't help but wonder if she listened to all the files, but I don't want to ask either.

Either she did and she isn't acknowledging it, or she didn't – and she has no idea what she's in for. I don't want to address either scenario. Not at this moment. I type a response.

> Shall I collect the typed documents?

Her reply comes immediately.

> If you need them now, sure. Are you at your
> office? I can come there. Although maybe I
> shouldn't drive. I've had a couple glasses of wine.

I type back in haste.

> Do not drive. I'm nearby.
> I will be at your house in ten minutes.

I pocket my phone, replace my helmet, and hop on the bike, thankful that Alexis Greene has just saved me from myself.

20

Alexis

I'm not sure how much time has passed. I'm riveted, still sitting in front of my computer screen.

I've pulled the earbuds out and turned on some music through my computer. Sting's "Why Would I Cry For You" is relaxing me at a low volume.

Now two glasses of wine in, I decide I might as well text him that I've done what he asked me to do – but I won't let on that I've listened to the background file. I don't want to acknowledge his powerful words to me over this impersonal gadget.

I can't be dishonest. I won't lie if he asks me if I've heard it. It would go against everything he's said to me.

But I don't want to bring it up. Not until I can see him in person.

I text him that I've finished the transcription and his reply comes within minutes, asking if he should collect the typed documents.

Okay, so we're not going to acknowledge the rest. Good. I type back.

> *If you need them now, sure. Are you at your*
> *office? I can come there. Although maybe I*
> *shouldn't drive. I've had a couple glasses of wine.*

His reply comes quickly.

> *Do not drive. I'm nearby.*
> *I will be at your house in ten minutes.*

What the fuck?

Has he been lurking around here somewhere, waiting?

Then I remember his words about living in Mirror Lake.

Maybe he was visiting some old ghosts.

I text back that it's fine for him to come by, but I'm frazzled.

Everything is far from fine.

I don't know what I should do first with only ten short minutes.

Brush my teeth? Change clothes? Fix my hair? I decide it's better to have ten minutes than a lot more, as that's all the more time I would have to panic.

I run upstairs, thankful that Marta was just in. The house is spotless. There are no tufts of black dog hair in sight and I won't have to waste time running through the house to pick up dirty underwear stolen and discarded by Huck, who is bounding up the stairs after me. He's wondering what all the sudden hubbub is about.

I ditch my work clothes and throw on one of my favorite old shirts, a heather gray tee with a Stanton University logo on it. It's flattering yet comfortable, perfect for Friday night. I tuck it into a pair of more comfortable jeans and throw on some flip flops. I brush my teeth, comb out my hair and throw it up in a ponytail, then give myself a few sprays of a wildflower scent to freshen up.

My makeup is still in place from this morning, so a touch of lip gloss and I'm ready to face whoever is about to show up at my door.

Somber Aidan? Hopeful Aidan? All-business Aidan?

Whoever it is, I decide then and there that I'll take the leap and let him in.

It's been at least fifteen minutes since his text, and now I'm pacing the foyer. Huck is safely secured in the basement. He sensed my anticipation and was too hyper to remain with me to greet a stranger. I don't need Aidan being knocked over, though I'm pretty certain he could handle my handsome boy (or even bench press him if it was required).

It's after seven and dusk it starting to set in. I head for the kitchen, deciding to set about making something for us to eat. Maybe he won't join me, but after the minimal snack I've had and the two glasses of wine and my restless mood, I need sustenance.

As expected, Marta left some home-cooked meals for me. I'm trying to decide between a pan of macaroni and cheese, ready to heat and eat, and a pasta salad to go with grilled meats or fish, which I would prep myself.

I select the macaroni pan and throw it in the oven. It's still cool outside as the storm hasn't come through yet. It's a perfect evening for a hot dish.

I pull out some ingredients for a salad, set them on the butcher block island, then retrieve my favorite knife from a magnetic holder next to the sink.

The doorbell rings and I blow out a breath trying to calm my nerves. Huck is barking from the basement, as he always does at the sound of the doorbell.

I move hastily through the kitchen, heading for the door, knife still in hand. In my office, the list of Aidan's voice files is still open on the screen of my computer which is visible from the foyer.

Shit.

I don't want it to seem as though I've been sitting there, obsessing about it all this time. I run over and click the menu closed, then move to open the front door before he can ring the bell and alarm the dog again.

"Expecting a serial killer were you?"

I'm confused by his greeting, then follow his gaze to the large knife still in my hand.

"Oh, this – sorry, no, I – I was just getting ready to put a salad together."

He's standing on the other side of the well-worn screen door, still dressed down like he was in my office this afternoon. He's traded his Blazer for a lightweight motorcycle jacket though. Black boots have replaced the loafers he wore earlier. He holds a sleek helmet under his arm.

"Great, I'm starving."

"Please, come in." I push open the door to make way for him, but he stays on the porch laying his helmet down, then removes his boots.

"Okay if I leave these out here? Is your dog a shoe thief?"

"Sometimes, but he's secured tonight," I say with a half laugh. "The boots are safe."

He leaves them and makes his way in while removing his jacket.

It's all I can do not to drool. Of course he smells wonderful, with an added hint of fresh spring air and masculinity after his ride.

In my flip flops, I'm a couple inches shorter than I've previously been while near him. My gaze now lands eye-level with his chest. His t-shirt highlights his muscular build and the sleeves are tight enough to draw attention to his biceps. He's not off putting though, like some steroid-ridden body builder.

He's just a healthy, well-made, and incredibly toned man.

I take a step back, not sure what to say next.

Offer him a drink, you idiot. Have you completely forgotten your manners?

"Can I, uh…offer you something to drink?"

"Sure. Whatever you're having is fine."

"I've got some dinner in the oven too, if you'd like to join me."

"Thanks, I'd love to."

He's preoccupied, looking around the foyer, up at the stairway where family pictures grace the walls. Ben and me, Ben and his family, some of Huck with each of us. It doesn't feel like he's intruding, but I feel at odds being so attracted to him while photos of my dead husband are staring back at him.

"Please, come into the kitchen. We can sit and relax a minute while dinner heats up."

"Sounds great," he says, turning to follow me.

I gesture to the banquette for him to sit, but he lays his coat there, then selects a stool at the island counter.

"Can I help?"

"Sure, if you'd like." I hand over the knife and slide some tomatoes and cucumbers his way. "Let's see your knife skills, Mr. Pierce," I say without a hint of formality.

"Oh, I've got mad skills, Ms. Greene," he says mimicking my tone. His smile lights up the whole kitchen, outshining even the sunny walls.

I make my way to the pantry, select a new bottle of white from the wine fridge, and head back to the kitchen. He's already got the cucumbers sliced and has moved on to chopping the tomatoes. It's apparent he isn't a stranger to basic food prep.

"I'm impressed," I say. "Did you study with a master chef?" With his wealth, I wouldn't be surprised if he took lessons from some Food Network star on a regular basis.

"Not hardly," he says with a half laugh that lights up his eyes. "Just learned from watching my mother when I was a kid, then volunteering at shelters when I was in college. It was one of the few things they'd trust a college student to do when it came to food."

"Well, I'll agree with your assessment. You do have mad skills, Aidan."

The horny widow returns, straddling a chair in a naughty Catholic school girl outfit.

Let's find out what other skills he's got!

She's popping gum and blows a big bubble. I smack it over her face and she heads for a dark corner, pouting.

I can't have her here now. I need to have a conversation with him and a serious one. After he recorded those words spoken just for me, I know it's mandatory.

I pull a new wine glass from the cupboard and pour from the most expensive bottle I had stashed away, but I'm confident it will be the cheapest wine that has graced Aidan's lips in years, if not ever.

"Mmm," he says, taking a sip. "Love it."

"I'm sure it's not what you're used to," I say.

"Alexis, things don't have to be expensive or haughty to impress me." He looks at me pointedly. "Didn't we already establish that?"

"I guess," I say as I blush. I know he means me. "What I'm not sure has been established is why you are sitting in my kitchen, helping me chop vegetables, and trusting me with sensitive information."

He's finished the chopping and sits with forearms resting on the counter, a hand clasped around his wine glass. He looks contemplative or unsure how to respond.

I stop what I'm doing. Have I upset him? *Shit!* I didn't mean to. I just didn't know how to get the ball rolling. I had to say something.

"I'm sorry," I stammer. "I didn't mean…" I'm just going to drop it. Let sleeping dogs lie. "Maybe you can check the dish in the oven for me?"

He holds a hand up, gesturing me to stop. "No, it's a perfectly reasonable question, Alexis. Don't apologize." He gets up to move to the oven behind him, peeks in and inhales. "Mmm. Smells amazing. Did you make this?"

"No, Marta did. She comes in for me a couple times a month. Makes a few meals, does some cleaning. She's no Mrs. Schmidt, though." I say, not hiding my envy.

He gives me a smirk, taking a spoon off the counter to stir the contents of the dish in the oven. I relax, feeling the mood lighten. I throw the veggies over a bowl of greens while he goes on.

"I can't really explain it, why trust is coming easy with you. It's a feeling I get when I'm with you." He sits back down, sips some more wine and looks at me in wonder. "It's new to me. Do you get that, or is it odd?"

This man has taken over all my senses since the moment we met. Skepticism about his intentions has evaporated as quickly as it came, every time – always leaving me feeling like I can put my faith in whatever he says.

I just haven't been brave enough to tell him so.

"It's not odd to me at all. I get it. Sometimes our instincts are the best indicators of what we should or should not do. I've always believed that."

He's visibly relieved, his posture relaxing. "That needs a few more minutes," he says, nodding back in the direction of the stove.

I couldn't care less about dinner.

"Shall we move to the deck?" I grab my wine glass and gesture outside.

"Sure," he says, beating me to the door and holding it open for me.

We move out into the evening, a slight chill around us. The atmosphere holds an anticipation of the impending weather front. Something heavy is in the air. Or maybe it's just the unspoken subject that hangs between us. I sit in one of the cushioned black wicker chairs. He moves to the railing and leans on it, overlooking the backyard.

"So, I understand that part of it," I say. "The instinct part." Whether or not he's looking for an ego boost, he's about to get one.

"But you are the most good looking, available bachelor that's currently breathing on the East Coast, if not the entire country. Yet here you are in my house, cutting vegetables in my kitchen and about to break bread with someone who clearly does not run in the same circles as you." I take a breath. I don't know how I got all that out. I'm just glad I did. "So the question is, Mr. Pierce, what gives?"

He flashes me his knee-weakening smile in a what-can-I-say fashion, all shrugging shoulders and sparkling blue eyes.

I may not know why he's here, but as I look at him with that expression, butterflies are circling my stomach and a chill climbs up my back. The breeze picks up and the sensation extends through my whole being.

He's adorable. And sexy. And on my deck.

"Maybe you ought to go on that dating show," I tease. "The one where you kick off the women one at a time until that one special lady is left."

"No thanks," he says. "They already asked anyway. I turned it down." He says it matter-of-factly, like everyone gets such a request every day of the week.

I give him a blank, holy-shit look.

He was asked to star on a reality show?

Again I think it.

What the fuck is he doing here?

"What?" he asks.

All I can do is shake my head.

"What do I want with a bunch of cash crazy, elementary females, flaunting their fake laughs and cat-fighting over who gets to talk to me next." He leaves the railing and comes over to sit in the chair next to me. "Not my style, Alex."

It's the first time he's shortened my name, and his familiar tone makes me melt.

"Well, it's nice to know you draw the line somewhere," I say. "And what about Miss Ireland? Did she fit into that category?"

His mood immediately changes when I mention her. I'm not sure if it's to anger or just irritation, but the playfulness is gone. He thinks a moment, then softens.

"You mean Stella. Of course you would have questions about her. I sometimes block out the fact that my private life is not very private."

I lean back in my seat, waiting for him to reveal what he will.

"No, she was not fond of lavishing me with constant attention. She has plenty of her own money now that her business is successful. And," he hesitates for a brief second, "our relationship was not romantic in nature."

What?

"I thought the two of you were…" I pause, somewhat unsure of what to say. "I thought you were in love."

He scoffs out loud at my words. He's not looking at me. He's lost in thought, recalling her.

"No. It was quite the opposite."

I'm not sure how to continue. I can sense he doesn't want me to ask more, but I can't resist.

"And that would mean what?" I ask. "You were enemies?"

"No, not enemies. We were just not close. Our relationship developed out of expectations, out of mutual need. We attended functions together, traveled together sometimes. We each had spaces in the other's homes. But we didn't sleep together or live together permanently."

"I had no idea. The press has always made out like you were lovers."

"Well, we were." He looks at me as though I'm being naïve. "Just like anyone else, we had needs and used each other to fill them."

I shoot him a scolding look. "I didn't mean it that way," I insist. "I just meant it always looked as though you were *in* love."

"We knew each other sexually, yes. As far as being in love, Alexis," he looks away from me again, this time off in the distance. "I've never been there."

"But all the photos of the two of you," I go on, thinking about some of the ones Charlie and I had come across the other day. "She always looked happy, looked enamored with you."

He sputters a half-laugh.

"Most of that was acting. She always wanted to be an actress, and those photo ops were always a favorite of hers. She loved making other women jealous, making damn sure everyone knew we were together, when, in reality, we weren't. And the few times she expressed an interest in our being together, it was never out of what you would consider love."

This woman sounds like a straight up bitch.

"So she wanted to be with you, be more than some sort of arrangement and you refused?"

"Sort of. Stella is a complicated creature. Her perception of reality is skewed and that's putting it mildly. And our relationship became complicated because of it."

"So what then, the intimacy between you occurred just because she was there? A warm body?" I'm repulsed at the thought.

"Sex occurred, yes. Intimacy? No. We never kissed, unless it was for a camera."

"Never?" I can't hide my disbelief. I never would have guessed that was the nature of their relationship. Or that someone pinging such magnetism would live like that. *Could* live like that.

"No. Pecks on the cheek here and there at events or as a form of greeting but never intimately."

I swallow, finding some courage to ask more.

"Did you want to?"

"No." His answer is hasty, honest. "I didn't have romantic feelings for her, so I never saw the point."

"Have you ever been kissed?" Maybe kissing isn't something he prefers to do with anyone. Maybe he's one of those eccentric billionaire weirdos that's only into God knows what.

But he gives me a don't-be-ridiculous look. "Really?" He asks it with obvious sarcasm.

"Just checking," I say smiling. "And the last time would have been…?"

"Does it really matter?"

"No, I guess not."

I let it go, realizing I wouldn't want to answer that question either. My answer would be somewhere between months and years.

Holy embarrassing.

"Still, the whole thing seems kind of sad. I mean, the way it was with the two of you."

"It was, I guess. I didn't really think about it at the time. Our arrangement was to my advantage, so I guess I used the situation as much as she did."

"And how's that?"

"With her at my side, I didn't have to fend off other women as much and I could concentrate on my work. Everyone that knew us thought we seemed a good enough match. Our parents, our families and friends – it took some of the social pressure off."

"I guess that's a good reason to play along."

"I suppose, but it was selfish. And it only led to complications that could have been avoided if I'd just been alone."

"When you say arrangement, with the two of you, did that mean legal arrangement?"

He looks at me and I'm pretty certain this isn't open for discussion, judging by his expression. The timer on the oven dings repeatedly through the kitchen window.

"Saved by the dinner bell. Shall we go inside and eat?" I stand and move towards him, offering him a hand up from the low deck chair.

"I could definitely eat."

He takes my hand but instead of getting up, pulls me down into his lap. I'm facing the yard, sitting upright, not sure what his intentions might be. His grip and his lap are somehow strong and comfortable simultaneously.

"It seems like you know an awful lot about me now," he says quietly. "When will it be your turn?" His hand moves up my back to my neck and again I'm chills all over. "When were you kissed last?"

Ahhh, dammit! I should have kept my mouth shut. It takes all of my being to stifle a moan as he trails his hand back down, then firmly rests it on my back.

"Umm…it's been a long time," I say.

"I'd like to know more."

I turn and lean towards him, staying just far enough away as I did in his office, preventing myself from taking his bottom lip between my teeth as I've been aching to.

"Not now, I'm afraid." I look him right in those cobalt eyes lit with anticipation, then see disappointment at my answer. "I'd hate for dinner to burn."

But he smiles in acceptance.

"By all means, Ms. Greene. Let's eat."

He lifts me up with ease and sets me on my feet. I'm able to maintain balance, but I'm also feeling a bit dizzy. I'm not sure if it's from him or the wine. We head into the kitchen and Huck barks. I tell him to keep quiet as I pull dinner out of the oven and turn it off.

"Do you want him to be let out?" Aidan asks.

I consider it a moment. "If you don't mind hundred pound beggars at your feet while you eat, by all means." I'm pulling salad dressing out of the fridge and silverware out of the drawer in the island.

He smiles. "Not in the slightest. Where can I find him?"

"Past the pantry, the door to the left. Here," I say, handing him a dog biscuit from the jar on the counter. "Better take one of these if you don't want to be bowled over. And grab a loaf of Italian bread out of the pantry, if you wouldn't mind?"

He nods, takes the biscuit and heads for the basement door. I heave a sigh and slug the rest of my wine, wondering what the hell I'm going to do with this situation. I'm still reeling from his touch.

Huck comes bounding at me before I can have another thought, and I'm grateful I'm leaning against the island for support. He skids on the tile floor and stops abruptly, then leans in. I'm giving him some love when Aidan comes back with a loaf of bread in one hand, the other hand in the air. It's covered with dog drool.

"Oh shit," I laugh. "I should have warned you he gets greedy taking biscuits."

I take the bread and Aidan gives Huck a good head rub.

"It's no problem," he says grinning. "I'm just glad he didn't tackle me. Right, pup? Who's a good boy? Sit nice."

Huck does as he's told and Aidan grabs another dog biscuit out of the jar.

He even likes my wooly, slobbering dog. This guy has to be too good to be real.

But don't fucking pinch me if I'm dreaming!

Aidan washes up at the kitchen sink and the dog clamors to get outside. I let him out the back door.

"Plates?" he asks.

"Yeah, I'll get them. You could give us each a refill, I guess."

He moves back to a seat at the island and pours. "This truly is a good wine, Greene. Maybe not expensive, but impressive."

"It's from a local vineyard. And I'm surprised," I quip. "I thought you'd have better taste."

I move to the cabinet to pull out plates, the nice ones I save for company. I'm on tip-toes trying to reach and can't quite make it. He abandons his seat at the island to help me and moves in close behind.

Very close.

He reaches over my head for the plates, but doesn't look up. He's taking me in, his lips close enough to nuzzle my neck.

"I have exquisite taste, Greene." He tilts his head back some, looking at the contents of the cupboard and taking some of the tension away. "Are these the plates you're after?"

I tilt my head to the ceiling, holding my breath, eyes closed. Somehow I manage to verbalize a yes. My mouth is about the only thing that hasn't gone numb with anticipation, hoping to hear more words whispered, longing for him to be closer.

He sets the plates on the counter with one hand and leans into me from behind.

He is intoxicating.

He puts one hand on the counter to my left, with his other still to my right, closing me in between his very solid arms. I turn around to face him, and he's the perfect distance away for me to take in his face up close.

He's clean shaven again and looking at me with a hunger I haven't seen from him before. Or from any man for that matter, at least not that I can remember. I'm overtaken by it, with more longing and hoping...

My thoughts are interrupted by action.

He pulls me against him, his hand on my back. I can feel his heart pounding up against me, seeming to keep in time with mine. Electricity pulses between us wherever our bodies are touching.

I'm glad for him holding me. My knees feel like they might buckle.

His hand rests gently on my cheek and I close my eyes, leaning back. His touch is feather soft, his hand moving to my hair, pulling out my ponytail, roaming behind my head to tug at my hair.

His lips land on mine, softly at first, until the moment is lost to appetite.

His advance is fierce. Everything below my waist is aching for him, hoping he won't stop. All I can feel is the sensation of his hand twisted up in my hair and his lips and tongue assailing me with that hunger.

I open to his advance willingly, craving him desperately. Fear that I'll rip his shirt off and let things move full speed ahead quickly overwhelms me.

Yet just as I have the thought, he pulls back some. He takes my lower lip between his teeth gently, briefly – just as I've been longing to do to him – then leans back.

He's assessing me, waiting for a reaction.

I'm too astounded to give one.

His arm is still around my waist, the other leaning on the counter for support. I've gone completely limp, lazed back and looking into his eyes, searching for words and wondering what his will be.

Finally I just give up, giving him a holy-shit look.

He nods in agreement, steps back, and swigs some wine. He shakes his head, and I think I hear him say *wow* under his breath as he turns away from me.

Wow indeed, Mr. Pierce.

Fucking wow.

21

Aidan

An hour later we've finished eating, and somehow (though I have no fucking idea how), I have resisted kissing her again.

The way she fits snugly in her jeans, the way her chest fills out her Stanton U t-shirt...doesn't matter that her clothes are not skimpy in the slightest. She's sexy as hell, even completely covered up.

And that kiss. I was left unable to think, to breathe. It was like nothing I'd ever experienced. It was all I could do to put it out of my mind through dinner – which I noticed she barely touched.

Our conversation flowed easily from talk about her deceased father (whom I can tell she loved and respected very much just by the wistful way she speaks of him), to her mother (whom she clearly and without apology feels quite the opposite about). She's asked me about my parents, but has not brought up my brother. I don't know whether it was intentional but, either way, I'm grateful.

We'd also talked about music, which we both agree we cannot live without. Her taste is as varied as mine, which I appreciate – especially after Stella, who really had no preferences whatsoever. She didn't care much about it at all.

I suppose that fact about Stella was inescapable and should have been a red flag for me from the beginning. If you were near soulless, it was easy to be unaffected by something as powerful as music.

I clear the dishes to the sink while she puts leftovers away. It feels so domestic, something I'm honestly not used to but at the same time easy.

Like this isn't the first time we've been together this way.

"Would you like a tour? It won't take long," she says. She shares a sarcastic smile.

I push the thought away of my reaction when Byron had talked about coming here to take care of her dog…how I'd thought of nothing but seeing her bedroom, her shower…

Get it together, Pierce.

"Yeah, that'd be great."

She shows me her office, which is immaculate, as is the rest of the downstairs. Thankfully she passes by the staircase without going up. I'm sure that's where she sleeps, and I don't think I could resist her if a bed was within spitting distance. I'd insist on having her until morning.

I'm not sure she's ready for that, especially in a home she shared with her husband.

We walk past a closed door on our way to the living room.

"What's this room?"

"Uh, that's Ben's. I'd rather not," she says.

I raise my eyebrows in question.

"I never cleared out his things," she offers by way of explanation.

I shrug and continue to the living room. I'm certainly not going to push the issue.

"Do you want some coffee?" she asks. "I know you have to drive."

"That'd be great, please. I'll wait in here." I take a seat in the leather recliner next to the couch and I notice her expression change. She winces, then recovers her casual demeanor.

What was that about?

"How do you take it?"

"Black. One sugar." I feel like her mood needs lightening. "Like I like my women," I add, "hot and sweet."

"Oh, *good* one," she laughs. "Not obvious at *all*."

She's mocking me, but I don't care.

She returns a few minutes later with a couple of mugs, Huck following behind. She sets them down then remotes her home stereo on with some mellow, bluesy roots music. I'm not familiar with it, but it's catchy.

"Who is this?"

"Tedeschi Trucks Band," she says. "Your first time hearing them?"

"Yeah," I say, a bit absentminded. "I like it." I'm standing at the fireplace, looking at the objects on the mantle.

"They're amazing," she says. "One of my faves. This song is called 'Midnight in Harlem'."

I pick up one of the only photographs there, a picture of her and her husband on their wedding day. "You are stunning in this picture."

"Oh," she blushes. "Thank you."

I set the photo down and watch her as she settles onto the couch. I can tell she's uncomfortable about something. Is it me? Or the fact that I'm looking at her wedding photo?

Maybe that was a crossed line.

I take a seat at the opposite end of the couch, a space open between us just as there was in my office a few nights before. Huck crashes on the floor in front of the unlit fireplace, sprawled out and looking ready to sleep.

"I get the sense you're not comfortable having me here."

"No," she insists. "It isn't that. I mean, not in the way you think. It's just..."

I lean back with my coffee in hand, letting her get her bearings so she can explain.

"I'm just not used to this. Having someone like you in my home, I mean. In a place I shared with Ben. That was his chair you sat in."

Before I can apologize she puts a hand up.

"Please don't. It's not that big a deal. But yes, it is odd to me. It's uncharted territory and I just have to get used to it." She looks at me intently. "I *want* to get used to it."

Fuck me, do I want to kiss her again.

But I refrain.

"Alexis, you don't have to hold back about Ben. For God sakes, he was your husband. You don't have to hide him from me." I set the coffee mug down, trying to ignore those tantalizing lips that were on me just an hour ago. "It isn't like we're having an affair."

She isn't able to hold back a look of frustration. Clearly there's something she thinks I don't know.

"I appreciate your saying so," she begins. "But it wasn't that simple. Our relationship, I mean."

"I know you think you're keeping things from me, but you really aren't." I turn to face her. "I know everything there is to know about you, save the intimate details." I can't help my smile as I look at her. It pays to have resources, even if I have to pay to use them.

"And just what is it you think you know?"

"When I get involved with someone, whether it's on a personal or professional level, there are certain things I need to know ahead of time to protect myself. And them," I say. She gives me a look that begs more. "I have looked into your background. I know about your father's long and exemplary career as an attorney, your half-sister in Arizona, and your mother's, uh…questionable choices, let's say."

"That's putting it politely," she mumbles. "More than she deserves."

I'm relieved not to have offended her.

"And I know about Ben's citizenship interests."

By her expression it doesn't seem like she's relieved, like a weight has been lifted off her for good.

But then it isn't a look of dread on her face, either, like she's fearing an anvil in a Road Runner cartoon lurking overhead.

It's more a look of skeptical irritation.

"Is that right," she finally says, "and those interests would be?"

"I know you were married so that he could get citizenship here. He was born in Canada, right?"

"He was. And it was never declared to anyone or questioned by any authority – or even by my own father, for hell's sake – that we married for anything other than love for each other. Ever." She says the last word with some extra weight. "So why do you question it?"

So that's it. She's pissed I've figured it out without ever knowing her husband. Really, without ever knowing her.

I'm more certain than ever I've pegged her marriage correctly, but obviously I need to tread lightly here.

"I can put two and two together. I know you met in college, and I know he had ambitions to work in media here in the States. I do not question that you loved him, but, as I said, I also rely on my instincts. And my gut tells me that the two of you were just very close friends."

She looks stunned. I know it for sure then and for some reason it pleases me to have confirmation that she and Ben weren't intimately connected.

My instincts were right on the money.

I go on, hoping to ease her into opening up.

"I've already told you I know something about such an arrangement. And knowing you as I'm getting to, I can see that you'd sacrifice finding love to support a friend. Even if it meant marrying him solely to keep him in the country."

She draws her legs up beneath her, pulling a soft throw off the back of the couch to cover herself as she grabs for her coffee.

"There's more," she says. "There's more to it than any background check will ever find." Her tone is soft, sad.

"Okay," I say, my full attention on her beautiful, wounded eyes. "If you've listened to me, to what I said in those…" I drift off, looking down, then regain myself. "Whatever it is Alexis, I want to know."

Just say it. Please. Nothing that comes out of your mouth can make you anywhere near as fucked up as I am.

"All right," she says. She takes a breath, swallows hard and sets her coffee down as she sits up. Her baby blues are boring into mine. "Ben was gay."

Ummmm….what?

I stare blankly over her shoulder, then turn my gaze to the fireplace.

"What?" she prods.

"Nothing, it's just…I…"

I'm looking down, trying to get my shit together. She cuts me off before I can go on, her tone adversarial.

"Look, I had no problems living with my best friend who happened to be gay. If there's something about that you can't bear to hear about or even think about, perhaps you should see yourself out now."

"No, it's not that," I insist. What kind of asshole does she think I am? "Alexis, please. I'm not at all put off by someone's sexual preferences."

Some of the tension in the air evaporates, but I can tell she's still leery.

"I'm not creeped out by your admission. I'm just surprised is all. I had no idea. Truth is, I was trying to stifle a laugh."

"A laugh?" Oh shit. Now she's definitely pissed. "Well, I'm glad I can amuse you yet again."

"No, that's not what I meant. It's not that your disclosure was amusing. What was going through my head was amusing. I thought you were going to come out with something crazy, something outrageous. And that I'd have to make an excuse to get the hell out of here."

She's trying not to smile. "Such as?"

I need to lesson the tension.

"Like, like you thought Ben was from another planet. Or that you were into some sort of cult, or underground S&M club or something."

She lets out a laugh and then I'm laughing. I can't believe the direction our conversation has taken.

"Really," she finally says. "That's what you thought you'd missed?"

"What else could have been left out by a very invasive background check? Let me tell you, there aren't many things I don't uncover with the research I put into these things. But I must admit that's something I didn't find. And," I add as I look in her eyes. "It doesn't bother me in the slightest."

"Well, I'm glad I didn't shock you into running for the door." She's still smiling, at last seeming relieved. "But I guess we'll skip the tour of the basement where I keep the dominatrix toys."

I smile at her joke, attempting to void my thoughts of her wielding a riding crop, completely naked.

God, I'm a sick bastard.

"I will say it's an unusual lifestyle choice for someone like you to live with a gay man, let alone marry one."

Her face changes again, and I wish I could reel the words back into my mouth.

Dammit, why did I say that?

"What I meant to say, and, perhaps I could have said it with more tact, is that you were so young to get married and you are such a beautiful young woman still. To do what you did..." I trail off, then begin again. "Unselfishness is not a quality I encounter often. You gave up your own happiness in order to put Ben's dreams in his lap. It's refreshing."

"Who says I wasn't happy?"

My face sours against my will. I've missed my mark again. I'm trying to compliment her, not offend her.

"I'm sorry, again – poor choice of words." I trace my thumb over the handle of the coffee mug in frustration.

"It's okay," she says, moving closer and laying a hand on my wrist. "I think I know what you meant."

I look up at her. She smiles. This is better.

"I wasn't trying to offend you. I didn't mean to insinuate that you weren't happy with Ben."

"I know," she says. "And I need you to know, Aidan – I was happy. We met in college, and we had similar interests, like music. Our career choices were completely different, but it was okay that I needed more time devoted to mine because we were friends, not lovers. We didn't have to spend all of our time together. We didn't plan on having a family that needed our attention."

I want her to go on, but she seems pained, a guilty expression coming over her.

I think I can pinpoint why. If this was a secret she shared with her husband, she probably feels like she is betraying him. Who would have known about this? If her own father didn't, that would have been a huge weight to carry. If the secret was shared only with her husband, who was now gone, her feelings are warranted.

"Ben's work, trying to advance himself in television journalism – he needed to be at the station a lot or travel doing the pieces that no one else would take. So it was better that way. We had our careers, and when we were together we had fun, had each other. His sex life was private – we never really discussed it."

"Did you always know?"

"No," she says, lost in thought a moment. "We were already engaged, had known each other for a year. We were just friends, but for some reason everyone thought we were deeply in love, and we just let them believe it.

It was better for his citizenship that our relationship was as real as it could be. I suspected, at times. But it didn't matter much to me. I found out for sure before the wedding, when I saw him with someone."

"That must have been devastating."

"Well, no. I mean it was a bit of a revelation. It wasn't that I caught him, you know, doing anything." She flushes with embarrassment. "I just saw him with a guy, talking to him on a bench on campus, in plain sight of the world. But I saw it, saw how he was looking at that person across from him. It was a look he'd obviously never given me or any other woman."

I'm not sure what to say and given my track record of fucking things up the last few minutes, I keep my mouth shut.

"We were about to graduate from college and I was going on to law school. I knew that he would have to go back to Ontario if we didn't go through with the wedding, at least for awhile. I couldn't do that to him. I didn't know any other way to keep him here. I'm sure there would have been other options for him, but I just didn't want to put him through that."

"So Ben wasn't out with his family or yours?"

"No. He chose to keep his sexual preferences a secret, and I let that be his choice. I don't know if it was for his career or whether he just felt he'd be disappointing his parents. But it didn't matter. It was his choice and I respected it. I didn't push him to discuss it."

"That must have been difficult for both of you."

"I guess. I mean, I didn't know for sure until that moment, that day, and then I asked him and he confirmed it. But I never pined for him at all, wishing he wasn't gay. He was just a close friend like he always was."

"And that's why you weren't angry by it?" I ask. "It seems like a pretty huge betrayal, him never volunteering to tell you outright."

"I suppose, but it didn't matter. I never made the best choices when it came to guys anyway. And he knew I didn't have an interest in chasing after anyone. I was career-minded, wanting to prove myself to my father, to make him proud. Ben knew I was even more driven after my father died. And he always told me that he would understand if I ever… you know, found someone."

"You didn't want your father to know about Ben?"

"God, no," she says. Her expression turns to one of fear. "Most people didn't know. And still don't know."

I lay a hand on hers, reassuring her. "I would never repeat something you asked me not to."

"Dad was…we never told him. Unfortunate as it is, he would not have been comfortable with it. My sister Jill knows, but only because Ben asked me to tell her, thought it would help bring us closer for some ridiculous reason," she scoffs. "It didn't."

"How did she react?"

"She didn't think much of it. That's just it, she didn't really react at all. Said she'd support me no matter what, but we never talked about it again. We're just not that close."

"That's too bad." I wished every day to have my brother back. I couldn't imagine having him living and breathing somewhere, even if it was thousands of miles away, and never be in contact with him.

But I can't bear to bring that up. I take another approach.

"I know, to a degree, how it is not being able to reveal who you truly are to anyone but a select few. It's confining."

"Yes, it was," she agrees. "But I knew things would change if Dad, or other people, knew about Ben. No one openly speaks about it around here, but the men are different, from a different generation. You've seen our local Bar Association. It's a good ole' boys club, all the men joking about chasing skirts and keeping their wives in the kitchen."

"You don't feel things are changing?"

"Maybe some. But not at a very quick pace. If you want to make it around here, you have to play along. Once I prove I'm capable of more than doing the dishes, I can ignore that mentality."

"Don't you want to see women taking more active roles?"

"Of course. And I feel like I'm contributing to that. But I also don't want to be the one to undertake the overthrow of the establishment. I can't get much accomplished if I'm constantly going against the grain, defying what's expected."

I nod in understanding. "Is it too prying to ask how you handled your private life? I mean, did Ben ever see anyone else?"

"He always kept that part of his life private, even from me. I only really knew about one relationship he had. And it was while we were married. The only one, as far as I know."

"Oh?"

"It was only because I was introduced to the guy and spent time with him."

"Did you like him? I mean, was he a good person?"

"The best."

"I'd like to meet him sometime. Give me a perspective on who Ben was." I don't know why that's important to me, but it is. I want to know everything about her.

"You did," she says. "You met him today."

My light goes on.

"Charlie," I say quietly.

"Yes."

"I figured Charlie was," I don't say it out loud. "I just didn't add it up, I guess."

She giggles.

"You can say it. Charlie is gay. And he doesn't care who knows it."

I smile and shake my head. "Sorry, yes. I gathered that."

"No one knew about the two of them. Even though Charlie is openly gay, he isn't from here and didn't spend a lot of time around people Ben and I knew as a couple. Their relationship ended six months before Ben passed and they saw each other only occasionally."

"How did they meet?"

"Charlie was living in Manhattan. Ben met him on a trip down there for Channel Eight. They kept in touch but their relationship was difficult. Between the distance and Ben's desire to maintain the reality of our marriage to others, you can imagine."

"So Charlie moved up here after Ben passed?"

"Yes. I met Charlie when I went down to the city with Ben a few times. The three of us would do things together. Like shop."

"Sounds great," I tease. "We strapping male heteros just love to shop."

"Very funny," she laughs before turning wistful. "It was after Ben died that I got back in touch with Charlie. He came to the funeral and said to call him for anything. I knew he meant it. He saved me, picked up the pieces, came to help me open the firm. He stayed on as my assistant when I offered to pay him far more than anyone in his position would typically make."

"Well thank God for Charlie," I say. I move to the floor and kneel in front of her, looking into her eyes. "Because whatever he did to help you, it's done wonders."

"I don't know what I would have done without him."

Her hands are folded in her lap, and I cover them with mine. "I'm not sure how to say this without sounding trite. But I'm going to say it anyway. You are one of the most beautiful people I have ever met, Alexis."

She flushes and looks away.

"Look at me. Please."

She turns to me and I look for information in her expression. I don't want her to think I'm playing her. She needs to see I'm sincere.

"I just feel guilty," she admits. She's suddenly sad, regretful. It tugs at me, but it also fires me up.

"What the hell do you have to feel guilty about? He's gone, Alexis. I'm sure that was devastating to you. But you were friends, not lovers. Don't you think he'd want more for you, especially now? Don't you want that for yourself?"

"I just feel like I'm betraying him, letting someone else in. And because of whatever this…" she stops, backpedaling. "Because I made a promise to him, Aidan. And because…"

Tears are behind her eyes. I didn't want to force her to open up old wounds. But she goes on anyway, her voice breaking.

"Because I often wished for more. I wondered if I'd made a mistake, marrying Ben. And every day that he's been gone, all I've done is wish for my best friend to come back. Every day I apologize to a ghost for thinking, even for a second, that the way we lived our life together was a mistake."

She's voicing this revelation to herself for the first time as much as to me.

I can see it in the way her posture changes in release, the way her eyes close as she mutters a curse aloud at the fact she's sharing this pent up emotion with a practical stranger.

"You think you wished him away, don't you? That because you second guessed sacrificing one kind of life for another, God or whatever all-powerful being you believe in took him out of your life."

She looks at me in disbelief, as though I've read her thoughts. She mutters a yes and tears come. She's not sobbing, but she looks so sad. Tired. My heart is breaking for her, but I'm also elated.

She trusts me with something big in her world. It might not be as ugly as my past, but she is putting her confidence in me.

For some inexplicable reason, this leaves me feeling like I can fly.

I rise up to sit next to her, pulling her close. I search for a tissue and pluck one from the box on the coffee table, handing it to her so she can dry her eyes. She may be overflowing with emotion, but she's still beautiful. I smile at her, watching her come down from her admission.

"I hate to tell you this Alexis, but none of this is out of the ordinary." She looks up at me, her eyes softening. "You're just human."

"Yeah, thanks" she smiles with sarcasm, her voice calmed. "I appreciate that. Well, that and the fact that you've probably just saved me thousands of dollars in therapy."

22

Alexis

It's nine o'clock and Aidan's checking his phone for the weather report. "I should go," he says.

I'm disappointed, but concerned for his safety. We're in the driveway, my outdoor lights blazing in the dark. A storm is definitely coming, and I don't want him caught in the rain on a motorcycle.

"Yes, you should," I say. "I wouldn't want you to get caught in the rain, especially without Byron here to hold an umbrella for you."

He smiles at my wisecrack.

"Yes, I'm so delicate." I'm thankful for his playful tone. We haven't delved much into the revelations he made to me, but we both seem to be okay with that. We've certainly had enough serious conversation for one night with my mini-meltdown.

"Shit, your notes." I had forgotten the original intention of his visit. "Do you want me to print them off quick? I have the press release and your lists transcribed. But I haven't made my notes yet."

"No," he laughs. "Tell you what. I'll come by for them tomorrow. Early." He's standing there, boots and jacket on, looking as handsome yet bad ass as I've ever seen a man. "Did you have time to get to the last two, the ones that I asked you just to listen to?"

"Yes, I – no, wait." I realize I only listened to one of them, the one about his background. That was enough to digest. I had been eager to tell him I had the other three done, then when he showed up I forgot there was another file.

Holy shit, what does that one say?

"No, I – I guess just one. I didn't get to the one that said '*Open Last*'."

He's about to put on his helmet. It's resting in front of him on the seat, the lights from over the garage reflecting off the shiny black surface. As he pockets his phone, it occurs to me that if he puts on the helmet I won't be able to kiss him again tonight.

"You might have a bedtime story waiting for you then," he nods in the direction of the house.

Oh Lord. I'm not sure I can take it after tonight.

Who are you kidding? You're going to sprint for that computer as soon as he leaves!

He must be able to sense my anticipation because he adds further instruction.

"Bed is the best place for the last file, Alexis. Take it to bed with you on your phone."

"Yes, sir," I say, saluting. That gets a genuine, whole-hearted laugh – a first in my presence. It's a beautiful release from him and it fills me up to hear it.

I stride over close to the bike pretending to admire it, but I don't know the first thing about motorcycles beyond the Harley that Gloria's husband has in their garage.

But this one is black, as fierce as if it came out of a Batman movie, and he looks incredible sitting on it in my driveway.

"Tell me about this bike," I say. "What kind is it?" I place my hands over the helmet, ensuring that he can't put it on yet.

"It's a motorcycle. Do you really want to know more?"

"Sure," I say, not quitting with my flirtatious attempt. "Is it dangerous?" Now I'm batting my eyelashes, hoping I don't look foolish. His sexy smirk tells me I must not look too bad.

"Maybe," he says. "To some." He pulls me to him. My legs press against metal, my chest against his.

He kisses me insatiably this time, not as tenderly as before. He tastes like sweet coffee and a breeze swells around us making for a dream-like combination. My own urge takes over, until he stops abruptly, leaning his forehead on mine. He's breathless until he finally finds words.

"To some," he repeats. "It's *very* dangerous."

"Take me for a ride," I whisper, completely serious. My chest rises and falls too fast. I'm as out of breath as he was.

"Tempting," he says. "But not tonight. The storm." He puts space between us, then grabs his helmet.

"Not in the mood to take any more risks, Mr. Pierce? I thought you liked danger." I truly don't want him to go.

"Occasionally, yes," he says. "But I could certainly think of far more dangerous things to put between your legs."

Fuck me. Did he really just say that?

I stand there in awe as he puts on his helmet. I'm trying to hide that my entire being is restless, stirred (and okay, soaking wet) from his comment.

"Don't worry, you're quite safe tonight, Greene," he says, fastening the helmet. "For now."

"You never cease to shock me, Pierce. I'm in awe."

"Right back 'atcha." This time it's the school boy grin, the one that takes me out at the knees.

"You still haven't told me what kind of bike it is," I tease, speaking up a bit so he can hear me.

He starts the engine and the bike roars to life as he shouts back his answer.

"It's a Ducati. Google it."

He zooms down the street, presumably taking off for 250 Harrison. I can still hear the bike's whine when he's a mile away. I'm standing in my flip flops in the driveway, wishing the sound was coming closer instead of getting farther away.

My only comfort is the last file I have waiting in the house, knowing his sensual voice will accompany me to bed even if his body doesn't.

It's a bit early for a Friday night, so I deposit the coffee mugs to the sink and pour myself one last glass of wine. I'm worn out from dumping everything on Aidan. Once I'd let it out, it really didn't seem like such a weight. And it didn't seem to bother him at all. He had been a comfort but not too clingy. And he'd opened my eyes to see things in a different way.

The more I thought about it, the more he had a point.

What was I saving myself for? Why should I feel guilty about my attraction to him?

Perhaps I wasn't doomed to walk the earth alone forever.

Huck is laying on the kitchen floor beside me. I pick up my phone, deciding to text Gloria.

> *Aidan was here. He came to pick up some files I transcribed.*

Moments later, my phone is pinging relentlessly as I finish the kitchen clean up. I'm up to my elbows in dish water and can't answer right away.

> *OMG! And?????*

> *What happened?*

> *Hellooooo? If I don't hear from you in two minutes, I'm calling!*

I laugh out loud at the last one and write her back. I don't feel like talking.

> *He showed up on an amazing- looking motorcycle. (Harry would die!) Stayed for dinner. Never gave him the file- forgot. He knows about Ben and me.*

I can't tell her about his revelations to me from the voice file, but she's one of the only people that knows about Ben. I feel better just confiding in her about what I've shared with Aidan.

> *Holy shit!!! And?*

> *And he kissed me.*

My phone rings. Apparently the last bit of information was too much.

"Yes?" I answer coolly.

"You are shitting me," Gloria says matter of factly.

"No, not hardly."

"Where?"

"Where did he kiss me? On the lips, stupid."

"Yes, I gathered that. In what room?"

"Kitchen. While he was pulling plates out of the cupboard."

"How very domestic. Let's have breakfast tomorrow. We must discuss. Eight o'clock at the diner?"

"Sure. See you then."

"Good night, Lex. Way to go, girl."

I laugh at her congratulatory tone. This woman is the super-cool-yet-grounded mother or aunt I never had.

"Night, Gloria."

I disconnect and try to force myself to remain calm as I head for my computer. I transfer the *Open Last* voice file to my iPhone, grab my earbuds, and head upstairs with Huck following.

I've probably broken some sort of record getting ready for bed. Teeth brushed, face washed, tank top and sleep shorts on in under three minutes.

The rain has held out, but it's humid and I can see flashes of lightning in the distance as I draw the curtains closed in my bedroom. I open the window and take a deep breath in. The fresh air trumps air conditioning any day.

The promise of summer is palpable as humidity increases, the wind swirling branches in anticipation of rain. The breeze feels alive, too heady to ignore. It matches my mood and I inhale a few more times before climbing into bed, grabbing my phone off the nightstand.

The forecasters promise this storm will be a doozy. I'm grateful more than enough time has passed for Aidan to get home, knowing he won't be caught out in it. I put my earbuds in and turn out the bedside lamp. Huck is already snoring on the floor at the foot of the bed which I no longer hear as Aidan's voice fills my ears.

I lean back on my pillow, unable to contain my curiosity about what the hell could possibly be coming at me next. All I know for sure is that I'm following his directions, listening to it on my phone.

In bed.

Gah.

"Alexis, this does not need to be transcribed either. And it's just for you. Please find a comfortable spot and listen to this on a portable device if you can. We're going to do a little..." he pauses, and I can tell he's sipping something. "A little experiment," he concludes, sounding a bit mischievous, a bit buzzed.

I don't know for sure, but I picture him on the couch in front of the enormous flat screen in his office, lying back with a whiskey and recording his message to me in that haunting, sensual voice.

"Okay, I'm comfortable, are you?"

I am. Relaxed beneath my soft sheets and a lightweight blanket, I purposefully slow my breathing down, calming the anticipation.

"Good. Now, I need you to think back to that night at Mac's, when I came upon you, very drunk and looking…" he pauses, takes another sip. "Quite amazing."

Me? Amazing?

And here I pictured myself a disheveled mess that night.

"I'm going to tell you what might have happened, had we not been so preoccupied with other topics that night and had you had maybe one or two drinks less. Okay?"

For some reason, I nod.

"If you prefer not to know, well you can just delete this file then. I suppose there is a chance I've read you wrong after all."

I roll my eyes because, as usual, he was right from the start. He knows I want him. Knows I crave him as if I was lost in the desert longing for water, dying from thirst until he came along offering one cool sip of liquid.

"So, if I'm not mistaken, there was a point in time I was standing very close to you, face-to-face, asking you why in the hell you were calling me. In my head, I've changed your answer…"

I hear another slow sip and he starts again.

"You can use your imagination but if you answer the way I imagine, I'd have teased those pouty lips of yours, the ones that speak daringly at me all the time. No one has ever given me such lip so boldly, Alexis. It's so sensual, so challenging. And I can't resist a challenge, or an opportunity to break some rules.

Damn that we are working together, that I have to use that as an excuse to see you. Last night, I wanted to pick you up, wrap your legs around me, and fuck you. Crash your backside into that dusty bookcase and give you what I think you need. Fuck, maybe what we both need."

Holy heaven and hell, I can't believe what I'm hearing and how excited I am to hear it.

I can hear his breath catch and I realize I am gasping for air. There's a loud crack of thunder just as his voice stops.

And just like that night at Mac's, the storm is rolling in.

"If I had tried that, tried to lift you up and carry you away, would you have objected? If I had kissed you as shamelessly as I wanted to, would you have ended up in my bed the next morning instead of my guest room?"

Shut the front door!

He knows that's how it would have been. *I* know. He doesn't need to ask. I pause the recording so I can get up to shut the window. The wind has picked up enough to blow the curtains around wildly.

I'm not sure whether I wish I'd listened to this before he arrived tonight. I know if I had, the night might have gone much differently.

I'm back in bed, about to press play when my phone buzzes in my hand indicating a new message from Aidan.

> *Arrived at 250 Harrison safe and sound.*
> *Where are you?*

I'm flipping out, touched that he let me know he got home safely. So lame, but I can't help it. I'm swooning.

> *In bed. With my phone and earbuds like someone told me. Awaiting another storm.*

> *Thank you for that image.*
> *Are you playing the last file?*

> *Yes. Taking a break to...regroup.*

> *Wish I was there...what if I was?*

He wants to play?
Gah!
But I'm out of my element here.
I decide to be honest without saying too much.

*If you were here, I think it'd be a hell of a lot more dangerous than
a motorcycle ride. In a dark thunderstorm. Without a helmet.*

*It would indeed. I must sleep now. As should
you. Go to bed. I will be there early.*

Oh, great. Bossy Aidan is back.

*How early? I'm having breakfast with a friend
at 8. And thanks for your concern, Mr. Pierce.
But don't tell me what to do. Besides, I have
a bedtime story to finish.*

*Breakfast with who?
I can come by at ten instead.*

Hmmm. Interesting that he would ask with who. I decide not to be
coy and reply with the truth.

A friend. Gloria Stearns.

*Ahh, yes. The redhead who served you up on
a platter to me. Be sure to thank her. Where
did you leave off in your story?*

*She did no such thing. And I'm currently up
against the bookshelf at Mac's ;-O*

*Interesting...is that the kind
of face I think it is?*

*It's an emoji. What kind of face
did you think it was?*

An "O" face... lol

I can't believe this immeasurably wealthy man is texting me. In the
middle of the night.

About orgasms.

And that he actually typed l-o-l.

*No, no "O"...yet.
More shock and awe, that's all.*

*Keep listening, there isn't much more
but perhaps you'll get the 'O' anyway.*

Very well, Mr. Pierce.
I'll follow your instructions. Good night

Until tomorrow, Alexis

I set my alarm for six a.m., glad that it's only eleven now. I press play again and listen to the rest of Aidan's thoughts.

Thoughts that he could have kept to himself but chose not to.

"I guess you might be wondering what I'm doing, wherever you are, listening to this. I'm in my office, lying on the couch where we sat together earlier tonight. You just left an hour ago, and I've been babbling at this stupid thing for awhile now.

Admittedly I've had a couple pours of Jameson since then. My judgment might not be...spot on."

That may well be, but his speech is still clear as crystal, still smooth as silk, with no lisps or stumbles over his words. He's calculated, determined. And I'm completely wet underneath my silly pink shorts.

"I'm lying here, with only the light of the fireplace wondering why the hell I'm not in bed one floor above, why I need to stay close to someplace you recently were, where we were together.

"Why am I using this time to think about you, rather than thinking about other important things I usually contemplate at this hour?

You won't leave my mind, Alexis...your striking eyes, the smell of your hair, that incredibly tiny skirt you wore the first time we met...and those shoes. Entirely inappropriate, Ms. Greene.

Inappropriate yet a damn welcome sight in that batch of nameless executives, all with their professional composures, masks firmly in place and dressed the way etiquette tells them to.

Except for you."

I hear him take another slow, purposeful sip, then a sigh in hesitation or could it be yearning? I can't believe he is having the same indecent thoughts that have crossed my mind since meeting him.

"Close your eyes Alexis and think of us. Suspended in time at Mac's, about to make different choices than we did, about to find ourselves in the throes of something neither of us can ignore. Think of those gorgeous stems of yours wrapped around me while I'm buried in you. If you do that, you'll find me. Because in my mind that's where I've been since last night."

Then there's only silence and the fast rhythm of my heart doing backflips in my chest.

Every muscle in me is tense with *want*.

Wanting to hear more, wanting him here instead of thirty miles away.

I stop the player and hear the pitter patter of a few raindrops. Lightning flashes outside and I count.

One one-thousand, two one-thousand.

Crack!

A downpour hits the roof above me, loud and soaking.

I hit repeat on *Open Last,* lie down and close my eyes to block out the storm. I drift off to sleep, Aidan's erotic words spilling into my ears and my dreams.

I'm at Mac's, imagining exactly what he said.

I find him there, waiting for me, not hiding his want this time. He brings me more than close to my release in the dream, takes me all the way over the edge.

I wake up hours later wet with sweat, wet with my yearning satisfied, and wondering *how*.

How am I ever going to fight off the growing hunger I have for this man, and why the hell I would even want to?

23

Alexis

I'm awake in anticipation of my alarm at ten before six and, in the same moment, my phone buzzes next to my head indicating a new text message.

It's from Aidan, letting me know something has come up and that he'll come by later than expected.

Bummer.

Somehow I find the strength to play it cool, responding with "Okay". After last night, if I don't see him again soon, I anticipate a physical reaction from withdrawals.

But I certainly can't tell him so.

By seven-thirty, I've managed to get out of my own head, ready to meet Gloria in town at the diner. It's one of only three places to eat in Mirror Lake. We could only brag so much about a fast food joint and a pizza shop that people patronized because there wasn't much other choice. But the diner is typical home cooking and always good, especially for weekend breakfasts.

I'm walking through the front door of the restaurant, joining the rest of the town at the place to be on Saturday mornings. Gloria's Jeep isn't in the lot yet, so I take my place in line about four deep to put our name in for a table.

My phone buzzes in the pocket of my cut-off Levi's and I glance at it, expecting a status message from Gloria.

My heart momentarily loses its place, rhythm interrupted, and breath caught in my throat.

It's from Aidan.

> *Just okay? Was hoping for a dramatic plea*
> *for my presence this morning.*

It's my turn in line, so I pocket the phone and give my name to the gum-popping teenager at the hostess stand. She writes down Alexis, and I watch her draw a big circle over the 'I', instead of a regular dot.

I roll my eyes and take a seat on a bench along the wall, getting myself as alone as I can be.

Being flustered by Aidan in public (while he's not even in the room with me) is a new thing. I need to be as far away from people as possible, away from the hostess and the other waiting patrons. I attempt to steer the conversation to the point.

> *It's no problem. I understand.*
> *You gotta do what you gotta do.*

> *Appreciate your understanding, Greene.*
> *Will you be available at noon?*

> *Yes, will be home. Yard work awaits.*

> *I can send a landscaper to do it for you.*
> *Free up some of your time?*

> *Not necessary, Mr. Pierce. It's my time to*
> *contemplate handsome, wealthy men that*
> *keep me up late and exhaust me.*

> *As you wish, Greene. I'll come by at noon.*
> *Unless you have something else in mind?*

Whoa…not here!

The place is filling up and people are crowding around me, talking loudly over the hum of the air conditioner and the clanking of dirty dishes being cleared from tables. My face flushes. I feel like everyone in the restaurant can read the thoughts in my head like I'm a living newspaper cartoon.

> *Stop that now. I'm in public. Not a good time!*

Just the opposite, I'd think. Perfect timing.
I bet you're blushing.

Not hardly.

Now I'm flat out lying.

Really? What if I reminded you
of what you heard last night?
Did you ever... come to Mac's?

He doesn't play fair. I decide to fight fire with fire and try some shock and awe of my own.

As a matter of fact I did.
Came @ Mac's, more like. Twice. ;)

Ha! So there.

But his response is delayed, unlike the others, and in the meantime Gloria comes in. She fights her way through the other patrons to sit next to me.

"Morning!" She says over the din, leaning in for a quick hug. "And don't you have a mischievous look about you this morning." She's straight up beaming at me.

I smile and stow my phone away, trying to fight off a rush of longing after my naughty text to Aidan and the resulting heat that wants to take over my cheeks again.

"Is that a compliment?" I ask.

"I'd say you're glowing with after-sex-aura, except I know Mr. Money Bags went home last night. Yet somehow you're still looking different."

"Shut up, woman. You're full of shit." Another lie. I know I'm describing myself. I'm the one that's in denial here. She's likely right. Aidan has started to affect me in every way possible.

"I am *not* full of shit. You look great. Even blushing and sporting the Aunt Jemima scarf and a wife-beater, you manage to look pretty, Lex."

I laugh at that. I'm wearing a red bandana over my hair and one of Ben's white tank tops with my cut-off jeans. The tank is tight fitting on me and still smells like him, though it looks brand new. It's become a favorite, probably my usual attire to work in the yard this summer.

"We can't all be as perfect as you in the mornings. You probably rolled out of bed like that," I gesture to Gloria's flawless appearance.

She's in a melon and purple flowered ruffle dress, the straps perfectly fitted over her shoulders, the low neckline highlighting her ample chest. Her red wavy locks bounce around her neck where a silver chain and locket dangles. I know it holds a picture of her twin girls.

"Oh, this old dress?" She teases. "Well, thanks dear, but I hate to admit it, I didn't dress up for you. I've got a bridal shower to go to at eleven for my cousin Sherrie." She rolls her eyes. "Why a woman has to have a shower for marriage number three, I have no idea."

"Maybe she needs a new toaster."

"Her new husband will be the one needing that," she laughs. "He'll want to jump in the bathtub with it before long."

"Maybe it isn't a total loss. Won't they have liquor at the brunch?"

"Now that you mention it, my aunt did say something about mimosas," she says, looking over the specials listed on the chalkboard next to her. "Thanks, Lex. You always know how to look on the bright side."

"It's a gift."

"Drinks at eleven a.m. That'll be a nice primer for Harry's gig tonight at O'Reilly's. Are you coming?"

"Maybe. I might just ride along with you and drink way too much."

"Sounds good to me. Just text me by six. I'm riding out early with Harry and the guys to help with load-in and grab a bite. Tom and his new girlfriend are coming, so we'll have the bongos covered."

This means Gloria is hoping I'll come to do the Indigo Girls song. I don't say yes or no.

She turns her attention to her purse where her phone is ringing. "One sec," she says, holding up a finger as she reads the caller's identity. "It's Kate." Twin number one.

I'm preoccupied by my own phone buzzing in my pocket. It sends tingles from my waist downward, knowing it's from him. I'm dying to check it, but don't want to be rude or turn my face the color of a beet again.

The hostess calls my name to let us know our table is ready. Gloria's hung up from her distress call, letting twin number one know that her favorite bikini is hanging dry in the laundry room. We follow the hostess to a booth, and Gloria speaks up from behind me.

"These shoes are going to kill me before noon." As we're seated I look down at her sandaled feet. The braided wedges are a coral color to match the dress. They look amazing, but pain would be an understandable side effect.

"All I can say is, never mind how sore your feet might get. Hot shoes can get you in a *lot* of trouble."

We laugh as we're given menus and the hostess thankfully leaves us.

"Yeah, well – not for us old, married ladies. Did you get an honorable mention from Mr. Pierce on your stilettos?"

"Actually, I did."

"And? Don't keep me in suspense! What did he say?"

"Nothing, really." I can't help my cat-who-ate-the-canary grin, thinking about everything else he said. "Just that…that they were inappropriate."

She looks puzzled. "He insulted you?"

"No," I say, waving off her comment. "Inappropriate as in…in a *good* way."

Now she's smiling a mischievous grin of her own. "I told you it was time for something, girl. I knew it as soon as I saw you show up in those shoes that day. He's got the hots for you, doesn't he?"

"Based on last night, I'd have to say a definitive maybe."

The waitress comes over, takes our order, then brings coffee before disappearing again. She could be a twin to the hostess. Same blonde ponytail, same *duh* attitude. I expect our order will be utterly screwed up as she wrote nothing down. I'll probably end up with corned beef hash intended for one of my clients.

"So when will you see him again?" she asks.

"He texted me this morning. He's coming by at noon, I guess."

Gloria is sipping her coffee and snorts, a classic spit-take nearly playing out right in front of me. She regains her composure and lowers her voice. "Get the fuck out. What is the pretense of his visit this time?"

"He's going to pick up the notes I transcribed for some of the fundraising stuff. He forgot them last night."

"How convenient," she says, smiling. "And speaking of fundraising, how did it go with Enhanced Barbie?"

"Oh, fine. She was prepared and had some good generic ideas. She's not so bad, I guess. We have a solid plan, no thanks to that Richardson idiot. Did you ever hear anything..." I'm about to ask for dirt, then hesitate. I can trust Gloria, but I don't want to ask about an affair based solely on my presumptions.

"About what?" She senses my hesitation. "You can ask me anything, Lex. You know that."

"I know, I just don't want to start rumors that have no basis. I wondered if there was ever any public knowledge about Jade and Allen Richardson. Have they ever had an affair?"

"I haven't heard anything specific, no. But I wouldn't be surprised."

Gloria talks about some of the guys she's quite certain Jade has been with until our coffee and meals arrive. Thankfully the waitress got it right, since I feel like I could eat ten stacks of pancakes. We're left alone again and I pursue the topic.

"Have you ever heard of Richardson being on the opposite side of a case with her?"

"No, definitely not. Why? Did Jade claim they were?"

"No," I say. "He did."

She considers it. "I can't see how. She never has any dealings with criminal matters that he usually gets saddled with, and his private practice isn't really doing much yet. Her clients are private, mostly wealthy people looking to protect their money or divorce their spouse outside of court, without a long, drawn out battle. I don't think she even goes to court much."

"Well, I sensed something strange between them, and Jade just packed up her shit and left when he arrived. Once she was gone, that's the explanation he offered up."

I go on to tell her about the sleazy vibes I got from him and about canceling his lunch order when I left.

"Get out!" she laughs. "He had a one-thirty case in front of Judge Cramer that afternoon. I represented the petitioner. The judge had some not too kind words for him when he showed up fifteen minutes late."

"Mission accomplished," I say, grinning.

"I never knew you had it in you," she says. Her eyes widen as she changes the topic. "And speaking of that," she teases, "tell me about this kiss."

An hour later Gloria and I have parted ways and I've chatted with a few clients on my way out the door. I'm in the diner parking lot sifting through texts from Aidan. My phone buzzed a couple times during breakfast and I had to take it out of my pocket, worried the arousing effect would be visible.

There are five messages in all.

So glad I could help – I think. Did I help?

Ms. Greene, are you being defiant?
Very rude to keep me waiting.

You know how I hate waiting.

Where are you?

Perhaps you're a visual learner. I'll have to
show you how much I dislike being ignored.

Oh boy. I hadn't realized he could be *that* impatient. I'm debating whether to write him back now or keep him guessing longer just to make a point. The last text came in an hour ago.

I decide to mull it over some more and make a decision when I get home. I turn on some John Mellencamp for the short drive, put the top down, and cruise to Peaceful Drive, soaking up the sun and digesting a short stack of pancakes.

I arrive at what should be my house, but it doesn't look like I have the right address. There are two pick-ups with empty trailers parked at the end of the driveway, both advertising Green Thumb Landscaping. The Lincoln is parked in front of the garage.

One guy is on a commercial size mower in my yard and three other guys are tending to flowers beds, whacking weeds and pruning trees. All of them are wearing fluorescent yellow shirts sporting the Green Thumb Landscaping logo which is (of course) a giant forest-green thumb.

I park in the turn-around of my driveway and get out, half expecting Aidan to approach me from the Lincoln. Instead Byron steps out of the driver's seat and comes over to hand me a note. It's on the same monogrammed stationery as the ones that are tucked safely away in my nightstand.

"Ma'am," Byron says as I take the note.

I shoot him a disapproving look. "It's Alexis," I say, not hiding my irritation with his greeting. "I insist."

"Good day, Alexis," he says, all serious. He gets back into the Town Car and starts the engine. I'm left to assume he does so for the comfort of air conditioning because he doesn't leave. I'm standing in the driveway alone, once again dumbfounded by the actions of his employer.

I open the handwritten note and see it's the shortest one yet.

Are you free now, Ms. Greene?
Yours truly,
Aidan

Underneath his signature is his phone number, with the instructions TEXT ME BACK.

This man is maddening.

I'm livid that he went against my instructions and hired these strangers to invade my yard. It's embarrassing and over reaching.

But at least he's signed off Yours Truly, rather than with Kind Regards!

My horny alter-go is all doofy smiles, thinking we've been promoted somehow.

I pull out my phone. I'll text him back, all right.

> I SAID NO THANKS TO THE HELP WITH MY
> YARD, MR. PIERCE. WTF?!

His response is almost instant. I wonder if Byron already notified him that I've returned home. I suppose it's possible he's even giving him a play-by-play of what I'm doing from the comfort of the car.

> Seemed you needed some free time so you
> could write me back. Can you answer me
> now? And please stop hollering. It's rude.

I type back, defying his request.

ANSWER YOU ABOUT WHAT?

*I asked if I helped you reach your goal last night. I can't wait
any longer for an answer. I asked nicely that you stop the LOUD
CAPITALS. Can't you do anything I ask without SHOUTING AT ME?*

Oh, unbelievable. *That* is what this is all about? He wants to know if he helped me have an orgasm without even being there?

I'm exasperated, but also tempted to chase him down and show him exactly how right he is about his effect on me.

*Yes, okay? Yes, it was all your fault that I
woke up in the middle of the night finally
satisfied. Now will you call these goons off?*

*They are hardly goons at their prices and on
such short notice. Byron is there to oversee
and to protect you should anyone attempt to
hit on you.*

A moment passes, then another message comes in.

*And are you completely fulfilled now,
Ms. Greene?*

Not even close.

But I'll never admit it now.

I'm embarrassed by my thoughts and from his attention.

And now I'm sweaty from the increasing humidity.

I head for the house via the garage, let Huck up from downstairs and grab his leash. We exit through the front door and my canine is misbehaving, barking at the chaos throughout the yard, at the strange vehicles in and around the driveway. I give a tug on the leash and he finally sits. I use my extra-loud whistle and wave to signal Byron over. He exits the car and comes immediately.

Hmm. Maybe I could get used to this. He behaves better than the dog.

Huck is a happy ball of fur, his tail wagging excitedly as Byron approaches. But as soon as Byron is in front of me the dog sits, then lies down at my feet, still as a statue.

Wow.

This guy is like the Dog Whisperer without the whispering.

"Could you walk this beast for me? I need to tend to a few things," I exaggerate. All I really need to attend to is his pushy, incredibly alluring yet infuriating employer. But I leave that part out.

Byron nods and affectionately rubs the dog's head. At the change in his demeanor from stiff to adoring, I'm waiting for him to revert to baby talk. Instead he just gives Huck a simple heel command and they're off. I'm not sure which of them is happier.

My phone pings again as a reminder that I have a text I haven't responded to. I'm surprised that Aidan hasn't peeled into the driveway, racing in on his bike and screaming at me that I haven't answered him yet. I hit a button to reply to the last message.

> *Fulfilled, Mr. Pierce? HARDLY. And I don't even know this company, what if they try to take advantage of me?*

> *You're quite safe, Alexis. The work is paid for. Consider it a gift. But only if you'll agree to see me later. I'd hate the thought of you being unfulfilled.*

Holy shit. Did he just ask me on a date?

Reluctantly in my head (yet excitedly with every one of my girl parts), I reply.

> *Fine. You get your way Mr. Pierce. THIS TIME. Where shall I meet you?*

If we're going to do this, it has to be on equal ground. I can't have him here again so soon, especially if it's not under the pretense of his project. It's too tempting, and yet uncomfortable at the same time. Memories of Ben surround me here.

> *I've got something in mind. Be ready at six, I'll be by to pick you up then.*

I want to write back and insist that I have a say in where we're going, that I drive myself. Yet I know it's pointless.

> *I'll be ready. Dress code?*

> *Dress-casual. Something with skirt, perhaps? INAPPROPRIATE FOOTWEAR OPTIONAL.*

At that comment, my willpower dwindles to a flicker. I know I don't stand a chance against him.

Duly noted. And for the record,
I don't like to be kept waiting either.

I've taken Huck back inside for favor of air-conditioned space and offered water to him and Byron. Byron takes his bottled water and returns to the Lincoln without saying a word and Huck sprawls out on the kitchen floor, panting after his exercise.

I've surveyed the yard and the group of men in it. They're doing an excellent job and are almost done already. My little plot of earth could almost be called grounds as manicured as everything looks now. Not all the flowers are in bloom yet, but there are a few spring arrivals with the early heat we've had.

I'm grateful not to have to be out there today as hot as it is. Mowing my two acres takes me almost two hours. This crew has been here less than that and they have accomplished a lot more than mowing.

Some of these guys might have been enough to cause my horny alterego to emerge just a week ago, searching for inspiration. Now all I can do is compare them to Aidan.

He is all I can think about.

As the crew packs up and leaves, I step out onto the front porch. I wave to Byron as he drives away, then grab my phone up from where I left it on the porch, resting in the wicker swing.

Aidan is taking me out.

In a matter of hours.

Fuck.

I need to call in the cavalry.

I text Charlie.

Aidan asked me out. Any tips?

His response is almost instant.

WHAT???? CALL ME!

I call him and consider scolding him for shouting via text, just as Aidan did to me. The thought makes me smile as Charlie answers.

"What the hell, Lex? What happened?"

"Aidan asked me out. I guess on a date." Charlie is practically squealing on the other end of the phone. "Is that good shrieking or bad shrieking?"

"Alexis Marie – you have a date with Aidan *Fucking* Pierce. You know it's *more* than good! What are you doing right now?"

"Standing here looking at my lawn, which now looks like the golf course at Lake County Country Club. He had some people come and take care of the yardwork for me." I can't help my smile as I tell him about it, even if it does tick me off that he did it.

"Holy shit, Lex. Have you hit the jackpot or what? What are you going to wear?"

"I haven't a clue," I say. "He said dress-casual, something with a skirt." I leave out the part about the shoes.

"Oh Lord, woman. You so need my help." He pauses a minute. "What time are you going out?"

"He's picking me up at six."

"Okay, good. I'm at the Farmer's Market in the city. I'll pick you up in fifteen minutes," he says, then continues. "No, twenty. I need five minutes to call Pierre and set up some emergency treatments."

My subconscious is hovering in the corner, teeth chattering, and hiding underneath a blanket.

Treatments?

I end up giving in, knowing a man like Aidan would expect perfection or at least someone enhanced by "treatments".

"Okay," I say. "But nothing too drastic."

"Bitch, please. You're gorgeous! You don't need anything drastic, just some primping. It'll be fun. See you in twenty." And he disconnects.

24

Alexis

Charlie and I spend the afternoon at the small day spa in Falcon Lake called Pierre's. His good friend is the owner, who in reality is not French but a very regular, openly gay American whose real name is Peter Hamilton. The two of them have talked at me, over me, and about me while I've been poked, primped and prodded.

By one o'clock, I'm relaxing in a massage chair having a divine pedicure. I've succumbed to an eyebrow wax, some layers cut into my hair to give it some *oomph*, and highlights to lighten the mouse brown to a sexier dirty blonde. I like it thankfully, as I didn't have much of a choice in the matter.

My pedicure is nearly done, my toes beautified with a lilac color that reminds me of the dress from Aidan. As much as the boys have insisted, I've drawn the line at a waxing *down there*.

"If you insist, honey," Peter had said, leaning in to whisper. "But just make sure you clean that up. We don't need a virtual forest to get in the way of any..." he thinks a moment. "Log rolling?"

He winked at me while I sat there mortified, praying for a towel to drop over my head and hide my crimson cheeks.

When I was over my flush, I promised to make him proud and take care of things *down there*.

Peter is as charming and as handsome as Charlie, but in a completely different way. Jet black hair full of expensive product, with a flashy smile and over-the-top style. He's extremely likable, even though he really doesn't have to be.

Most of the women that live or work in Falcon Lake are beating down his door for appointments because he's just that good. It wouldn't matter if he decided to treat his clients like honorees at the Friar's Club, appointing himself as their personal roastmaster. They'd still come in droves.

The few other salon owners in town are too haughty to strike up a conversation with. Rumor has it their skills are just as lacking as their personalities. I've never found that with Peter on the few occasions I've visited here with Charlie.

I sit with my feet under a nail dryer and text Gloria to let her know I won't be able to make Harold's gig, unless Aidan cancels our date.

As usual it's too much for her and she's calling me immediately.

"Date? What date?"

"When I got home, Aidan had hired landscapers to take care of my yardwork. And then he asked me out."

"Did he call you?"

"No, he asked over text."

"Oh," she sighs wistfully. "Modern romance. It certainly seems to miss something. Where's he taking you?"

"I don't know. He just said he had something in mind."

"How very mysterious," she says, but she sounds distracted. I can hear a lot of commotion in the background and the twins are hollering at each other.

"Everything all right there?"

"Yes, I just got home. The girls are fighting over a pair of jeans. They have dates to the movies tonight." She covers the phone and hollers back at them, then returns. "Oh and by the way, my cousin got not one, but two toasters."

"Well, well," I chuckle. "Lucky husband number three."

"If you get loose come on over to O'Reilly's. We'll be there till closing. I'll have Harold run through "Galileo" with the guys for sound check," she adds, "just in case."

"All right, but don't count on me. If I don't see you, have a blast. And no driving!"

"Yes, Mom," she teases. "And you better call me tomorrow. I want to hear all about this mystery date."

I promise and we disconnect.

Charlie and I are having a snack in my kitchen, staring at the two outfits he has selected from my closet.

"I can't believe you only had three skirts to choose from," he says. He munches on a carrot stick. We eliminated the short black one that Aidan saw me in the first time we met leaving the Sheridan.

"I'm sorry, but I've lost weight. I got rid of all my fat clothes."

"Thank God for that. But I wish we had time to go shopping," he says, seating himself back on the stool. "Can you try them both on for me again?"

"No. Please. Not again." I look at the gauzy, floor length skirt in a bright bubble-gum pink and the tight white tank he's picked to complement it. "I think this outfit's too casual," I say, holding it up. "Doesn't it look more like a day at the beach? What if we're going to a nice restaurant?"

Charlie considers it a moment, then nods in agreement. "Yeah, you're right. It's going to be dinner hour, so I'm sure he'll feed you. You need to look a bit more classy. Go with this one."

He hands me his selection and takes the other outfit from me. I'm now holding a black silk tank-top with a niched neckline in the back and an extremely low-cut front. Gloria bought it for me when we were planning a cruise for last winter, which we never ended up going on. I've worn it once on a blind date that went horribly wrong when we ran into the guy's ex-wife.

The fit and flare skirt Charlie's picked still has the tags on it. It was purchased the same day as the stilettos. At just under two hundred bucks, it's the most expensive item of clothing I own, except for the dress Aidan gifted me. The skirt has splashes of color in purple and black on a white background and is far shorter than anything I would have picked.

"I don't know," I say, hesitating. "Maybe I should just dress up a pair of jeans with some heels and a flashy top."

"No, Lex," he insists. "This skirt and the black tank with the heels. It'll be killer! The skirt has such a great bell shape and with the heels – just think how much taller and more powerful you'll seem."

I give him a look. "Why do I need clothes for that? Aren't I fierce enough?" But inside I appreciate having all the help I can get, even if just from an outfit.

I'll probably be in a puddle on the floor just at the sight of my date.

"You will be more than fierce once you're all put together. So, the only question that remains is – are you going to?"

"Going to what?" I'm distracted, fighting to get the tags off of my skirt. I give up and reach for a pair of scissors out of the drawer in the kitchen island.

"Don't play dumb, Lex. Are you going to do the deed? The horizontal tango?"

"*Charlie.*" I say in a scolding tone. He knows I'm not comfortable talking about this stuff. I've always been glad I've never had to, unless it's in fun, speculating about celebrities we wished we could have a crazy night with.

"Well c'mon, Lex! It's been forever! You need to get laid more than *anyone* I know."

I sigh. That is a pathetic fact and a huge understatement.

"I think I forgot how," I say, scrunching up my face.

"You never forget how, babe. If it feels right, just go with it. Get caught up in the moment. Mount up and hold on."

I'm trying not to laugh. "So, pretend I'm on the mechanical bull? Is that the best advice you can give me?"

"Now you're talkin'!" he says smiling. "And actually yes, it is the best advice I can give you. Do you want me to help you finish getting ready?"

"No." I insist. "You've done enough and I need to have some breathing room before he gets here. Or maybe a shot of tequila or something."

"I can have Carter get you some weed," he says smiling.

I laugh out loud, though I'm sure he could follow through.

"No thanks. I want to be awake for this experience and without a bad case of the munchies."

"Good point," he says, finishing a glass of chardonnay. "I'm out like a boner in sweatpants."

"You did not just say that." I shoot him a sarcastic grin.

"Have a blast and call me tomorrow. Or text me if you want. Shall I take Huck with me?"

Undersexed Lex is doing cartwheels at the idea that our responsibilities might be taken care of clear through tomorrow morning.

"You know what? That would be awesome. Are you sure?"

Charlie's already whistling for Huck, who was passed out on the cool tile floor in the foyer. The temperature has reached ninety again today.

I gather up some food for the dog, his leash, and blanket. I clip him to a lead and walk him out to Charlie's big blue Cadillac, the one that used to be Ben's. He's taken excellent care of it, probably better than Ben would have. I throw the blanket over the leather seats in the back. Huck leaps up with his front legs and stands at the open car door, waiting for me to heft up the rest of him.

"Feed him just tomorrow morning and no people food!" I scold. I step out of the way and Charlie's giving my canine a ferocious but loving head rub.

"Yes, Mama," he says in a goofy voice. "I'll take good care of your boy, don't you worry."

"If you say so."

Charlie hugs me, then gets into the front seat and fires up the engine as Huck makes himself comfortable in the back. Charlie's apartment is just outside the city. He rents the entire first floor of an old Victorian and has full access to a backyard that's got plenty of room for Huck, at least for one night.

I wave at them as they drive off, my two gentle giants leaving me to contemplate how the next few hours of my life are going to go as my first date with a billionaire grows closer.

I've scrubbed every inch of me, and shaved as close as I can get (*all over, as promised!*) without hurting myself.

I'm dressed in Charlie's pick of outfits, and I have to admit the result is pretty va-va-voom. Dressy but comfortable and the colors in the skirt scream spring. The 'girls' are hefted up in my freshly laundered Zora's Closet bra, standing at attention underneath the low-cut silk top.

I touch up my hair with some mousse, scrunching until my fingers hurt. I look different than usual. Stylish, yet a bit racy.

Definitely not my typical all-business self.

My makeup looks like I've done something but is understated. My cheeks and lips are dotted with a soft pink. I line my eyes with a black pencil and wonder why I don't do it more often. They stand out this way. Ben always said they were one of my best features, a shade of blue he'd never seen before.

Undersexed Lex pipes up as I look in the closet mirror.

Wow. That ought to get us laid.

I slam the door on my horny subconscious.

Heightened suspense hangs in the air just knowing I'm waiting for him.

I indulge in a gin and ginger ale, ice cubes rattling around in my favorite old fashioned glass. I'm growing more comfortable in the heels as I whirl around the house, Dave Matthews doing his thing through a bluetooth speaker in the kitchen. I'm just getting into a groove, finally letting go of some of the anticipation.

I'm twirling in the foyer and the doorbell rings loudly, startling me out of my skin. I stop dead in my tracks.

The front door is open, and the rickety screen door behind me is the only thing between Aidan and me.

I can feel his gaze. My nerves are partying rave-style in my stomach, chills chasing down my skin.

I take a deep breath as discreetly as I can, hoping he can't tell. When I turn to face him, he's leaning in the doorway looking as though he's thoroughly enjoying himself.

"I see you started without me," he says nodding at my glass.

I take the opportunity to look him up and down.

There are *no* words. Every crazy bitch of my subconscious girl tribe is on a head trip and drooling.

This guy is sex walking.

Tailored charcoal-grey suit, no doubt Armani. Or, okay I really have no idea, it could be any eye-poppingly-priced designer. Charlie would know, but who cares?

It's so far beyond the suit.

It's the crisp white shirt unbuttoned at the collar to expose his skin. The one-day stubble that just looks crazy-good on him. His hair looks a bit darker, slicked back at the sides, but the customary chestnut brown is teasing through at the top.

And his eyes. Ohh, his eyes. They are my undoing, especially when they stare back at me so intently.

Like now.

"Sorry," I mutter, literally shaking him out of my head. I smile as I start for the kitchen. "I'll make you one," I call back over my shoulder.

The screen door squeaks as it opens and closes and I can feel the atmosphere shift, humming with an electric charge. He grabs me from behind and spins me around before I can get anywhere.

"Don't apologize, Alexis." He leans down to whisper in my ear, emphasizing each word. *"You. Look. Incredible."*

He runs his fingertips along my cheek, trails them to my earlobe, then stops. I look up at him, lost in how blue his eyes are. His hand is at the base of my neck, a look of gentle admiration on his face.

I expect him to let go then, but he pulls me to him roughly, his lips crushing on mine as though he has been waiting to do this for decades, never mind the three minutes he's been in the door. What I mistook for admiration was more like the appreciation a hunter has for his captured prey.

This kiss is nothing short of hunger being satisfied.

I love the taste of him. Mint and cinnamon. And the way his unshaven face feels as I grab him back.

Fuck me.

Sensation radiates up from my ankles, noticeable heat dwelling between my thighs. Everything is tingling.

Between the music and the hint of gin in me and his kiss, nevermind how I look. I *feel* amazing.

He pulls back gently, biting his lip. His hand hasn't left the base of my neck and his forehead touches mine.

"Thank you," I manage in a whisper. "Now how about that drink?"

"No," he says, releasing me. He steps back, breaking the bubble around us. "I'd love one, trust me," he says, forming a sly grin. "But we have somewhere to be."

"And that would be…?"

"For me to know, Greene. You ready? Is the dog taken care of?"

He's worrying about the dog? Sigh. My heart is tugged, thankful he would even think to ask.

"Yes, Charlie's taken him for the night."

His smile widens and I know a light bulb goes on the same way it did for me.

"For the night?" he repeats.

"For the night," I say back.

"As in, won't be back until tomorrow?"

"Probably," I say. "Unless Charlie decides to keep him forever."

He laughs at that.

"I see. So, it would seem there's no reason for you to return home tonight?"

Oh gawd! He's said it out loud. I have no idea what to think, what to do, what to say. I'm just thankful that I'm pretty sure I saw Charlie stuff some condoms in my little black going-out-on-the-town clutch.

"Guess not," I say with a purposeful lack of meaning. I do a quick check around, turn off the music, turn on the outdoor lights (just in case) and toss my spare key into my tiny purse along with my phone.

What if you have nothing in common and he's a total bore?

I dismiss the thought and lock the door behind me. I'm thankful no one happens to be out in the neighborhood this evening, seeing me all kinds of decked out with this guy next to me. It's an embarrassment of riches.

Byron is waiting for us in the driveway, standing next to the shined up Lincoln, which is running to keep the interior cool. It's still hot, and the air is thick and heavy.

270 · M.J. WOODS

We head for the back and I step in and right myself, taking my seat with as much tact as I can in such a short skirt. Aidan follows and Byron shuts us in. For the brief moment we're alone in the car, I lean back and close my eyes, feeling him next to me, his eyes on me. I can't believe how used to this I am becoming, how much I am starting to relish it.

Byron takes his seat behind the wheel and off we go to somewhere unknown to me. It's all I can do not to ask again.

"Dying to know where we're going, aren't you?" he asks, reading my thoughts.

"Nope. Couldn't care less."

"Don't be cute," he says. "It's killing you."

"How is it you always know what I'm thinking?"

"I can't reveal that," he teases. "But in this particular instance, I know you like to have a plan. You like to know what's going on at all times, in case you need the upper hand. You're conservative, careful."

"You mean boring."

"No, not boring at all. There's nothing wrong with being careful. It's a quality I admire."

"Well, I guess I'm throwing caution to the wind then because I am letting you take me wherever you want tonight," I say. And I mean it. For once, conservative Alexis Marie is bound and gagged, not coming back until absolutely necessary and damn the consequences.

"Good. And I promise to have you home before the dog comes back." He winks and I lean back again. Byron has put on some light jazz and it fills the car with a mellow mood. I can tell Aidan is not willing to have an in-depth conversation with Byron present, which I'm thankful for. I trust him but definitely don't want to speak about anything personal with him in earshot.

Aidan's phone rings, and I'm surprised when he answers it. It sounds like a business call and for the remainder of the ride he takes turns listening intently, responding sternly.

I pretend not to listen but can't help but overhear him talking about something in California. I move closer to the window and watch the scenery go by so I can more convincingly block out what he's saying.

I take out my phone and check it, reading a text from Charlie.

*Let me know how it goes! And text me the
stud's number, just in case I can't get you on
your cell.*

He's also sent a picture of him and the dog sprawled out on his couch.

Okay, I'll forward his info.

Have fun girl! You deserve it!

I smile at his reply as I text him Aidan's contact information. Charlie is right, it's probably a good idea for someone close to me to know how to reach him.

We're about thirty miles west of my house, driving around Pine Lake. It's much larger than Mirror Lake. I'm guessing we're headed to a winery or one of the fancy restaurants nearby. The entire east shore is dotted with them. Some are close to the water, some high up on the hill boasting gorgeous views of the lake and countryside far below. All of them are common stops for bachelorette outings, tourists, or popular wedding venues.

There are also a few restaurants the elite frequent, ones the everyday Joe either can't afford or isn't even aware of. I have to presume a place like that would be Aidan's choice. Privacy and luxury seem to be his thing and why wouldn't they be?

The car turns off a side road from the main route that circles the lake and my hunch is confirmed as we arrive at The Virginia Wright House. We pull around the circular drive and stop under the largest portico I've ever seen. A mansion sprawls to my right. A plaque outside my car door indicates the property used to be the summer estate of the Wright family. Their rise to influence is common knowledge, the family name infamous in Lake County since the twenties. The Wright moniker has graced everything from wings in local hospitals to the County Courthouse over the years.

The lake is out of sight from here, but I imagine the views from inside must be breathtaking.

Aidan's hung up from his call and apologized for the interruption, but I wave him off. I'm too excited to get a glimpse of this place.

He insists Byron stay put while he exits so he can be chivalrous and come around to open my door. As he closes his door Byron speaks up, startling me.

"Have a wonderful evening, Alexis," he says. I smile in the rearview mirror at him, and scoot forward in my seat.

"Thank you, sir," I say, teasing him with my formality after insisting he do the opposite. He smiles back, and I take the opportunity I'd been hoping for.

"Is there anything I need to know with Aidan? I don't know him well at all, and…" I trail off. I don't want to sound like a distrusting asshole, but I've done nothing *but* trust Byron and his boss without a lot to go on. I hope I can get a shred of confirmation that my instincts of feeling safe are right. And this person probably spends more time with Aidan than anyone else.

He looks puzzled for a minute, then thoughtful. He answers before Aidan can open my door.

"I am quite sure you are in safer hands now than you have ever been. Mr. Pierce is a high quality individual."

I smile and thank him as Aidan opens my door. Guess a guy can't get a more solid nod than that.

I step out into the evening warmth, immediately humbled by the opulence of our surroundings.

The driveway and walks are white brick. The mansion is European style, its grand facade looming over us. Hand-carved double doors are flanked by giant urns, their overflowing greenery and pink blooms welcoming us.

Aidan guides me into the foyer, his hand at the small of my back. We pass by a jaw-dropping staircase to end up in a small library. It's cozy, a full mahogany bar on one side and matching bookshelves opposite it on the far wall. A fireplace sets a warm ambiance even unlit.

The room is empty except for the elder gentleman tending bar.

Straight ahead are several large windows overlooking the lake. The view draws me in and I move toward it as Aidan says a familiar hello to the bartender.

"What would you like, Alex?"

"Gin and ginger with lemon. Please," I say over my shoulder.

He orders the same for himself. He joins me by the window while the bartender does his thing.

"Beautiful, isn't it?"

"Indeed." I can't take my eyes off the view. First of the vista in front of me, then of him. "Do you always surround yourself with beautiful things?" I ask it absent-mindedly as I turn my attention back to the window. I'm surprised when he takes a moment to actually consider his answer.

"I guess I do." He moves closer, stroking my shoulder with just the touch of his fingertip. Chills radiate, stopping where his touch ends. My head involuntarily tilts to one side and my hair falls away, leaving my neck exposed. He traces an imaginary line behind my ear, down to my shoulder, then leans in. "I've been waiting to surround myself with you for too long already."

I hold my breath. I don't want to resist anymore either. I'm all mixed up, half wanting to tackle him right here, the other half feeling astonished that his attention is lavished on me.

"Anticipation is one of the best forms of seduction," I say. "Down, boy."

He smiles that charming smile then nods in agreement.

He steps away, completely in command again, stone-faced even. I can't get over the control he has. He retrieves our drinks from the bar.

"Is our table ready, Sam?"

Sam is decidedly handsome, though a bit up there in years. His lean build is complemented by a tux. He's just short of Aidan's six-foot-something and his head is completely bald. It's shiny and sun-kissed and normally not a look I consider flattering. But on him, it works.

"Not quite, sir. You may enjoy your drinks on the veranda if you'd like some privacy. The dining room is currently full. I'll come out for you when we're ready, if you'd like."

"I think we will. Thanks, Sam." He drops some cash on the bar and gestures back to the door we entered from.

We make a left and head out to the covered porch that overlooks the lake, sitting at a small iron patio table. I'm grateful we are alone.

Stately grounds separate us from the edge of a cliff above the lake. The lawn is a brilliant green. Surrounding trees are trimmed to perfection. I can smell lilacs on the breeze that gently blows around us.

"So, if the dining room is full, are we waiting for people to leave? I'm starving."

"No, we don't have to wait. We will be dining alone. The rest is for me to know."

"Mmm. I see." I sip my courage in a glass.

He's taking in the view, clearly appreciating it as much as I have been. It's almost sunset, a brilliant orange reflecting off the lake below as the sun descends beneath the hills some miles away.

"Do you come here a lot?"

"A few times," he says, "since I've been in town. But never before moving here. Have you ever been?"

I give him a look that says *as if*.

"I thought maybe some previous date had tried to make you swoon with this view."

"Hardly," I say, taking another sip. I'm feeling braver with each one. "Shall we talk about what brought you to New York in the first place?"

"I'd rather not discuss it now."

"Why's that?"

"Because it leads to talking about work and I don't want to talk about work." He sends me the Prince Charming smile. "I want to talk about you."

"Well I'm sorry to disappoint you, but I'm not that interesting. I've already revealed all my secrets to you as of last night when you sat on my couch, so I think it's your turn. I'd like to discuss the bombshell you dropped on me."

I would?

I'm shocked at my forward statement. Shit, the beverage bravery has kicked in already. I slide my drink away.

"And would that be the bombshell about Mac's?" he asks, referencing his erotic message.

"No. The one about your father."

He lets out a brief sigh. "Yes, that is a conversation we need to have. But not here."

I nod, respecting his answer. I change the subject.

"How many dates have you brought here?"

"I don't date. You're the first I've been here with, unless you count Byron."

"Not Stella?"

"No. She's never been north of New York City."

"So that wasn't her room I slept in?" I try not to cringe, waiting for his answer. I don't mean to overstep, but my curiosity is on overload.

"Intended for her to use, yes – initially. But not hers, as it turned out. She's never been up here. And she won't be." He seems irritated at the thought of her or at my questions. I'm not sure which.

"I didn't mean to pry."

"No, it's fine. I'm just – it's hard to talk about her."

"Do you miss her?"

"Not really, not in the way you think. But she was one of the few people I've trusted in this life. When you have so few, it does pain to lose one."

"Why is it you have such a problem trusting anyone?"

"Experience." He leans back, takes a sip of his drink. "Trust isn't something I hand out to just anyone, as easily as you might lend them a pen. It isn't something I give without restriction or considerable thought."

"If you've been careful to surround yourself with people you can trust, why me?"

"I told you that already. I'm going with my gut. Plus, I'm fairly certain you aren't a tabloid reporter after me for my secrets."

"You never know, Mr. Pierce," I say mysteriously.

But he's not playful.

"Yes, I do." His voice is matter-of-fact, sending a clear message.

Oh. I get it. I know the ease at which he accesses information. He already knows everything about me he feels he has to know, just to be comfortable talking to me. It's disconcerting, yet fascinating and flattering all at once.

"What does the intriguing Mr. Pierce do while he's here?" I ask, gesturing around us. "Contemplate the crisis in the Middle East? Plan his next vacation to parts unknown?"

"Usually just try to relax and get happy, which means not thinking about much of anything."

"Get happy?" I try not to laugh. "You're kidding, right? With everything you have?"

"Everything I have?"

"Yeah, you know. Money. Knowledge. Power. Looks. Couldn't anyone be happy with that laundry list of awesome?"

He does not look as amused as I'd hoped, but he answers my question anyway.

"Just because a person has money, some common sense, and good looks doesn't make them happy. Don't you agree?"

"I suppose." I smile to lighten the mood. "Still, I wouldn't mind trying it."

"You already have the brain and the looks," he flatters. "But imagine having money and the resulting power. Great, right?"

"Like I said, most people wouldn't mind trying it."

"Sure. Unless all of that sends you to a bad place, surrounded by your own delusional head trip."

"Delusional?"

"No one can control everything. Power is fluid. It shifts. And money cannot buy everything."

"Still…"

"Then you realize you are surrounded by people who are either in fear of disagreeing with you, thinking you'll end their career, or hoping to take advantage of you so they can get themselves further ahead."

I nod in acknowledgement.

"Either way, it's never honesty you get. It's whatever they think you want to hear so you'll keep them close. It's taken me years to build the team of people I have around me. Now add to that the interest of the media in most everything you or your family does."

He shakes his head, visibly disgusted.

"People can be paid off to talk or leak some ridiculous detail about your private life, even if it's fabricated. To those people – the ones paid to be closest to you – you have to be sure what you offer is more attractive than what someone else will, to keep them from seceding from your camp. Or worse, joining up with your enemies. As for the rest…" he trails off for a moment, pondering.

"For those closest to you either by blood or," he says pointedly at me, "or by choice? Those are the people you have to protect from all the rest. It's exhausting always having to be one step ahead."

"I'd never thought of it like that. You're right, it does sound tiring and less than happy."

"It is. And it's a never-ending task, keeping everything in check, making sure old decisions are still good ones. Making sure new decisions are the right ones."

"That makes sense." I sip my drink again slowly, a thought coming to mind I can't ignore. "So what do you do to the detractors? The ones you think may jump ship?"

"Do to them? How do you mean?"

"Do you threaten them? Rain down consequences? What?"

"If I can't trust them, I don't need to threaten. I don't have any interest in hurting people if they choose to betray me. I make sure damage is minimized as much as possible and eliminate the threat, but only as it pertains to me or my family."

"So you don't use intimidation tactics the likes of trillion dollar oil and gas companies?"

"No. Never." He says it without hesitation and I believe him.

"You're right, Aidan. An existence like that does not sound rich with happiness. It sounds lonely."

He says nothing, but his expression is telling. As much as I don't want to be, I'm right. I've never seen him look pained like this. It isn't enjoyable.

"I can sympathize," I add. "I know exactly where you're coming from."

He drinks, then looks at me intently. Sam heads in our direction, putting an end to our discussion.

"We're ready for you, Mr. Pierce."

He seems slightly irritated at the timing of the interruption, but is outwardly gracious.

"Very good, thanks Sam." We stand and Aidan gestures for me to go ahead of him. Instead of heading for the dining room, we're following Sam to the second floor, where the hotel accommodations are.

He stops at the end of a long corridor, standing at the door to a room at the back of the grand house. A waitress in all-black, except for her fancy white apron, waits at the open doorway. She's probably my mother's age, mid-fifties or so. Her hair is dyed blonde, pulled up into a tight bun.

"Welcome sir," she says, taking Aidan in. I can tell by the long glance that she's never seen him before and appreciates what she's laid eyes on. She recovers her professionalism and addresses me.

"Ma'am," she says, nodding to me.

Grr.

"Please just ring down when you're ready, sir, and we'll bring the main course."

"Thank you," he says, dismissing her. She and Sam leave us for their duties.

We walk into a grand suite decorated in a Mediterranean style, all golds and reds and muted browns. A king size brass bed is diagonal in one corner, an elaborate bathroom suite opposite it. I'm completely confused, wondering if he's already presumed we're going to be spending the night together. There isn't a dining table in sight.

Suddenly faced with the possibility of what I've been fantasizing about, I feel nervous.

And faint.

"Alex, you're turning white," he says in my ear. "Relax, it's just dinner. Look out there, on the patio. It has the best view."

I let go of a held breath and turn to see a balcony door open up to a table set for two. White linens. A crystal vase filled with spring blooms. I walk to the outside to satisfy my curiosity but, more than that, in need of some air.

The view from here is exactly as he promised.

Stunning.

The air is sweet. Cut bunches of lilacs hang playfully from a large wrought iron arbor intertwined with climbing vines. The arbor stretches over the table, a gazillion twinkle lights dancing through it, reflecting on the silver flatware and casting a warm glow everywhere. It reminds me of the rooftop at the loft.

"You couldn't have known this, but lilacs are one of my favorites." I inhale the table arrangement, then take my seat.

"I may have noticed you had a few specimens in your yard. It's such a shame they don't last long. You like?"

"Yes, I love it. Are you trying to pursue me, Mr. Pierce?"

"I don't know, *Mizz* Greene" he jokes as he takes the seat opposite me. "I suppose I am, but I'm trying not to be terribly bad at it. I've never – well, let's just say this is a first for me."

"What, candlelight? Flowers? Dating?"

"Sort of, yeah."

I'm shocked. But choose not to say so.

"I'm truly flattered. It's beautiful. All of it."

"And I've never asked out a widow before," he says, teasing me.

"Jeez I never thought of it like that. You make it sound like I'm ninety."

"On the contrary. You are the most beautiful young widow I've ever asked out," he laughs.

I bow my head in acceptance of his backhanded compliment.

"I think I need another drink, as long as I know I won't need to drive."

"We're in Byron's capable hands for the evening. I'll call down for another round if you like."

"That would be great. Or maybe wine to go with dinner?"

"As ever a solid plan, Greene."

He leaves me to go back into the suite and use the house phone, and I take in everything around me. In the distance, the sun has gone down into the opposite shoreline. The homes and restaurants around the lake begin to come alive with lights, the candles and soft outdoor lights glowing brightly. The air has stayed warm, and I'm still comfortable in my sleeveless shirt.

"A bottle of Chardonnay is on the way. They left this for us to start with," he says, laying a cheese and fruit plate on the table. "I planned on the special for dinner. Do you like seafood?"

"Yes, typically. I'm not picky."

"So you're not vegan or one of those girls that can't ever eat bread?"

"No," I say, smiling. I can imagine he's dated his share of models who would order a glass of water for dinner. "Gluten is a major food group for me. If someone tried to remove bagels or pasta from my diet that someone would most definitely get hurt."

He laughs at that.

"But I appreciate places like this," I say. "I just don't have the occasion to do it myself. The single life of a working attorney is pretty boring, I guess."

"Why? You get to meet new people all the time. Help them, guide them. You have regular friends." He doles out the tray of fruit, some crackers and cheese. "You can come and go as you please. Who couldn't be happy with that?"

I smirk at my words being tossed back to me. "Being happy with it and having it be exciting are two different things."

"So you are happy that your life is boring?"

I let out an unreserved laugh. "No, that's not what I meant."

"Well then, what's not to like about having a predictable life?"

"I guess I don't think of it like that. I do have stability, but I never think of myself as lucky for having it. As though it was something someone would seek out. I guess I should think of it that way – you know, as a good thing. But I never really have."

"It's natural to dwell on the loss of someone before you can shift focus to what you do have."

"Yeah," I say, munching on the fattest purple grape I've ever seen. "Why is that?" I smile, trying to lighten the topic. I don't want to talk about Ben.

"It's just life, I guess. It's easier. It takes an effort to rise above pain, turn it into something positive. Don't you think?"

"Absolutely," I say in agreement. "And it seems like you speak from experience. Would you mind elaborating?"

"What was that you said about anticipation?"

I give him a wry smile. "Fine, have it your way. What's left to talk about then? You've eliminated work as a topic, and your past, and there's no music. I'm not a big fan of silence. Maybe you could tell me about all your celebrity friends. Does George Clooney really put his pants on one leg at a time just like the rest of us mere mortals?"

He's amused by my question, but ignores it. "We could always talk about *your* past. But first," he holds up a finger, pulls his phone out of his breast pocket and heads back into the suite. Moments later I can hear some music playing softly, probably through a docking station at the bedside. It's just enough, some soothing white noise in the background that won't drown out conversation.

"Nice," I say looking up at him as he returns.

"Dance?" he asks, offering his hand.

"No, thanks," I say, waving his hand away. "I'm a klutz. My medium is song, not dance."

"Really? I can teach you," he says, still standing. I notice again how even his hands are impeccable.

"No, you really can't. Please sit."

"You wouldn't let me?" He takes his seat, seeming hurt at my comment.

"No, I just know it isn't possible. Many have tried and failed. I lived with a gay man, remember?"

He lets out a full, contagious laugh. We're both more at ease then and the brave me opens up the floor to more probing. I lean closer to him, resting on my elbows.

"So, what is it you want to know about me? I thought you already knew everything from your extensive research."

"Not quite," he says, still smiling. "Tell me about these suitors before me, the ones you said were not good choices."

"That should take about five minutes," I say, taking the last sip of my drink.

"Lucky for you I've got that kind of time."

I sigh, reluctant to begin, but knowing the topic isn't going away.

"Let's see. When I was sixteen, I dated a guy that was ten years older than me. He was a motor head, into tattoos and motorcycles and trucks and fixing whatever broken down vehicle he could get his hands on, when they weren't on me. He eventually dumped me for my then best friend, but not before my dad found out and put a restraining order on the guy."

"Can't blame him there."

"Yeah, I suppose. At seventeen, the summer before my freshman year at state college I dated a musician. He wrote a few songs about me and we had mediocre sex twice in the back of his parents' minivan."

I give him a sideways glance before rambling on, wanting to make sure I'm not boring him. To my surprise, he looks riveted.

"I couldn't see myself with him long-term. I broke it off before I left for school. He could never sit still, was always having to go from one activity to the next, and I couldn't keep up. I don't think we ever just sat down and had a real conversation."

"Sounds like you had quite varied taste as a young woman. And then?"

282 • M.J. WOODS

"Then I went to school, concentrated on my work mostly. I had a few random dates, but then there was Ben. And that was that."

"Wait, so, two lovers? That's all you've *ever* had?"

I flush at his question. "Well, obviously, Ben and I never..." I trail off, avoiding eye contact.

"Yes, we've covered that. But I wasn't aware your romantic past was so," he hesitates, "so short." His gaze is slight disbelief, but also burning curiosity.

This sets me on fire below the waist. I know there's a bed a stone's throw away, and I can't help wondering if he wants to take me there as much as I want to be there with him.

"Sorry to disappoint you," I say. "Would you rather I was a slut?"

He nearly chokes on his drink.

"No," he finally sputters. "That isn't what I meant. I just...I'm surprised someone as smart and beautiful didn't have more guys chasing after her, that's all."

"You didn't ask me that. You asked me about who I dated. I'm no innocent, Aidan. I'm just picky about who I choose to spend my time with."

"Understood," he says, but he's smiling a mischievous smile.

"What?"

"Nothing."

"Bullshit, nothing. What?"

"Such crass talk, Ms. Greene. But then I suppose someone not so innocent would talk like that."

"Knock it off and tell me what you're grinning about, Pierce. Or Byron will take me home."

"I was just thinking there might be a few things I could teach you, that's all." He's still smiling so wide I'm sure his cheeks will soon hurt.

"Such as?"

"Most of it I can't do here, but there is one thing." He pushes his chair back, stands and holds out his hand again. "Dance with me."

I sigh in exasperation, giving in. "If you insist, but I make no promises that my clumsy feet don't take us both to the floor."

We move in time to some classical music, attempting a pretty basic waltz. After only one misstep (on my part), we are gliding around the tile patio. By some miracle I'm not falling down or worrying about what to do. He is leading me and my body is following, as though I'm his shadow. He pulls me closer and spins me around effortlessly.

I close my eyes, overwhelmed in the moment.

The warm air. The music. Him.

There's a brief moment of silence as the music ceases, and he takes a step back. I think he's about to say something, but the music is interrupted by a call coming through his phone, the speaker inside the room amplifying its ringtone.

He curses under his breath. "I'm sorry, Alex. I have to take this. It must be urgent. I told Lionel no calls unless it was."

I have no idea who Lionel is, but I bow and step away. "It's no problem." I smile graciously and take my seat back at the table, thankful my legs get a rest. Dancing with him has left them feeling a little wobbly.

He picks up the call in the suite, mumbling in a very irritated, stern voice. It's a brief conversation. Moments later he's standing behind me, resting his hands on my shoulders. It's a touch I'm unfamiliar with even as a formerly married woman.

Yet it feels so natural with him.

Natural. Comfortable. Craved, even.

"I hate having to say this again, but I'm sorry Alex. I'm going to have to leave. Would you like to stay?"

I turn to look at him and can tell any sting I feel that our date must end abruptly should be kept to myself. His demeanor is one of frustration and genuine disappointment. I can't make him feel bad for that.

"No, thank you. Do you have time to drop me off at home? Or do you have to be somewhere immediately?"

"Not immediately. We will take you home first. Again, I'm-"

I cut him off.

"Aidan, please. I understand. Work for someone like you doesn't just happen from nine to five."

He looks relieved at my understanding. Truthfully I'm relieved, too. The day has been a whirlwind, surreal and overwhelming. I need to digest it all.

Maybe confide in someone.

"I'll be fine. In fact, I think I'll have you drop me off at O'Reilly's."

"The Irish bar in Falcon Lake?"

"Yeah."

"Any particular reason?"

"I'd like to meet Gloria there. Her husband's band is playing tonight and I promised I'd try to come."

"I can do that on two conditions. No wait, three conditions."

Conditions? Oh boy. I'm hoping this isn't the part where he turns into overbearing-asshole-Aidan.

"One – that you won't drive yourself home afterwards."

Oh. Well that's easy enough. I won't have a car anyway and will have to hitch a ride home with Gloria.

"Done," I say. "And the second?"

"You must get something to eat."

"Agreed. And the last?"

"Promise you won't hold this against me. I need to know you won't be resentful not if, but when this happens. Because it will happen."

"I'm no stranger to running a business, Aidan. I'm perfectly capable of having a nice evening without you. And I don't mean that in a resentful, petty way. Whatever demands there might be on your time, I certainly don't expect to be one of them at this stage of the game."

He shakes his head, seeming dumbfounded.

"Alexis, you are truly something."

"But I have a condition, too," I say.

"What's that?"

"That we'll get back here. Sometime," I say wistfully as I take a last look around. "This place is *ah-mazing.*"

"I insist on it."

25

Aidan

The captivating scent of my date lingers in the car as we head back to Stanton, and I'm coming to a disturbing conclusion. We dropped her off at O'Reilly's not fifteen minutes ago. I have pressing business to tend to, but I know one thing for damn sure.

I miss her already.

I can't dwell on it though because Lionel is talking away at me on my cell. The three thousand miles between us unnoticeable as he goes on about the most recent developments with Stella.

We'd been over this countless times today in one form or another, ever since Ivan lost track of her late last night.

"Where did he find her?" I ask once there is a pause in his ramblings.

"At Shane Armstrong's beach house. Ivan assures me the scene is clear."

That bastard. Armstrong is a known cokehead, a washed up surfer that traded his board for the club scene in L.A. after an injury a few years ago.

He was the last person Stella needed to be hanging around with.

"She's at a facility now?"

"No, sir. At the hospital."

Shit.

"Under what pretense? The press will be all over that."

"I'm told her father is taking care of that end. It will be under the pretense of dehydration. A long day at the beach. Too much sun and champagne."

"I don't like it, but I guess we don't have much choice at this point. Instruct Ivan to stay with her round the clock. Or he can call on Curtis to share shifts if needed."

"Very good, sir. You're coming out?"

"If it's necessary. And *only* then," I stress. I don't want to leave New York.

"I believe Mr. Ireland is insisting on it. Perhaps I can persuade him otherwise."

"Just keep me informed. Have Ivan call you in an hour with an update, then get back to me."

"Yes, sir." He disconnects as we're pulling up to my building and Byron angles the car into the lot.

After we arrive, I spend ten minutes in the office. I call Samira to give her the update, apologizing for having to make her work on a Saturday night. As usual, she is unfazed. I ask her to watch all media outlets to see if anything is reported and stay in touch with Lionel, who acts as her counterpart in California.

Byron knocks on my office door.

"Sir?"

"Come," I say.

"How can I help, sir?"

"Ms. Rossi. I need to talk to her. Now."

"Yes, sir. I believe she is in Manhattan. Her people said she would be available to you by tomorrow morning."

"Get me her cell number, please. I only have her office line. It can't wait."

He exits to go to his desk, then returns in under three minutes. "I've emailed it to you, sir. What else can I do?"

"Nothing at the moment. I'm headed upstairs. I'll need you to stay in the office at least another hour until we get a handle on this."

"Of course."

I check my phone and, seeing the email from Byron is there, head upstairs to the loft. I'm impatient for the elevator and distracted thinking about the last time Alexis was here riding in it with me.

I am livid at having to cut this evening short with her. It was so good to laugh again, to relax, to just be in her presence. In the presence of her lean legs, her tousled hair that she clearly did something different with tonight, just for me. The way her tits lifted underneath that sexy black silk.

Now I'm livid *and* sexually frustrated.

Fuck.

I head for the kitchen in search of something to eat. There's a left-over plate of something in the fridge, something healthy with quinoa and greens and a southwest flair that Mrs. Schmidt threw together. I devour it, barely tasting it, and pull up Alanna's cell number that Byron emailed.

I wait for her to pick up as I slug a bottle of water.

"Hello?"

"Good evening, Alanna."

"Aidan," she says sweetly. "How are you?"

"I'm fine. And you?" My tone is clipped.

"All is well. Just returned from Miami. I understand you needed to reach me. Is there something you need to discuss about your portfolio this late on a Saturday night?"

"No," I say. Might as well get right to the fucking point. "It's about Stella."

She goes quiet on the other end. We never discuss her daughter. It's an unspoken rule between us. Alanna Rossi (formerly Ireland) is a financial wizard, a master at a man's game. She oversees a lot of my assets and I trust her implicitly.

The soundest reason for the trust I had in her was that she has nothing to do with her ex-husband, John Ireland.

"I don't know if you've heard, but she's been getting into some trouble."

"You left her, Aidan. How did you think she'd react?"

"Let's not go there."

"Look, I appreciate your situation. But there is nothing I can do. John would sooner kill me than let me meddle in her life. Especially now."

I assume she's referring to the fact that she married one of John's sworn enemies last year, Gianni Rossi. He and John had fought over properties from New Jersey to New York for years, each trying to advance his real estate portfolio. The difference was that Rossi never played dirty to get what he wanted.

And Ireland always did.

"I know you can't reach out to her directly. But you can use me. There must be something you, as her mother, can communicate to her to make her quit this bullshit. Or some string you can pull to help her."

"I wish there was, Aidan. But I don't even know my daughter anymore."

"Alanna, please. John wants her institutionalized. I am doing everything I can, but it may not be enough."

She heaves a sigh. "I'm not surprised. His answer is always to make the problem go away rather than face it. She needs help?"

"Yes. That's why I'm calling you. I know he excluded you from her life. Maybe there is a way you can help her without his knowledge. If you even want to help her."

"Don't try to manipulate my maternal instincts, Aidan. You're better than that."

I rub my temples in frustration. She's right. I'm grasping at straws.

"I love you both," she says. "But it could be dangerous for everyone if I get involved."

"I am at a crossroads, Alanna. I don't know how to help her without being sucked into her drama. And I can't have that right now."

"Perhaps you're overestimating the impact this will have on you. Can't you just ignore her? And her father too?"

"You know nothing good would come of that."

She's silent a moment. "No. You're right."

"Please. Anything. I'm concerned with the company she's keeping and she's getting involved in drugs. Is there someplace we can send her? Somewhere discreet?"

She sighs again in exasperation, giving in. She knows this is the last kind of dilemma I need to be dealing with given my past. "Maybe. Let me make some calls. I have some contacts on the West Coast."

"Thank you. I just…I don't want to leave here right now. If there's anything you could help me arrange from here, I'd be eternally grateful."

"You're really driven by this cause, aren't you? I don't know why else you'd want to hide out up there in no man's land."

I leave out that not wanting to be away from Alexis is part of my reason. It's too soon. "Yes. It is going to be a lot of work but things are moving forward. I don't want to abandon it when I'm just getting started."

"I'm proud of you, Aidan. Let me make some calls and get back with you. Is the morning soon enough?"

"It will have to be."

"We'll talk then."

"Thank you, Alanna."

"Only for you, kid. I'm doing it for you."

I dispose of my suit in the closet, then head for the bathroom. I turn on the shower, needing a release. I can't get Alexis out of my head. Damn this shit with Stella interfering.

I send her a text, then get into the hot water, letting the jets soak me.

I'm sorry, again. Wish I was with you instead.

I imagine her here with me, naked and wet, letting me do as I wish to her. As with every time my thoughts travel here, my release comes quickly and my distraction is satisfied. I towel off as my phone pings with a response from her.

*Don't apologize. It's all good. Gonna sing
with Gloria and Harry, they'll drop me home
after the gig. We'll talk tomorrow.*

Good. She's not driving.

But she's going to sing and I'm missing it. Fuck.

What are you singing?

*Aren't you supposed to be in a meeting? Or
ruling the world or something?*

I'm impatient, not waiting a moment to respond.

Just answer me.

Indigo Girls. "Galileo"

My heart all but stops.

Memories of Thaddeus flood me, thinking about the good days, about our high school years in Cali when we had no worries, fending off a slew of fast girls and chasing faster cars, or playing music and shutting out the world whenever we needed to.

She couldn't possibly realize that song would conjure up these thoughts within me (it certainly isn't my pick of songs), but facts are facts.

I type back.

You're kidding.

Nope. Why?

I call downstairs to Byron.

"Sir?"

"Meet me downstairs at the Lincoln. Now, please."

"Very good, sir. And the destination?"

"We're going back to Falcon Lake."

26

Alexis

Within a half hour I've been left off at O'Reilly's, along with the promise that Aidan will call me tomorrow.

In my little town it might be noticeable to arrive in a fancy car but here in Falcon Lake my departure from the Lincoln fits right in. The upwardly mobile are prevalent here, especially on the holiday weekend that unofficially kicks off summer. There are some bikers and middle class people too. Everyone mingles without incident but the wealthy are the majority.

I'm sitting on a bar stool next to Gloria, telling her everything about my non-date. I haven't been able to order a drink yet, but thankfully she has a big plate of food in front of her, and I'm cleaning up her untouched fish and chips as I babble on.

"Help yourself," she says. "Harold got it. The band eats free tonight. I wasn't hungry."

"You never eat," I scold.

"We shared pizza with the girls before we left. I'm good."

"I'm ravenous," I say. "So thank you. He had to leave before we could eat anything more than some grapes and cheese."

"Oh Lex, I'm sorry. That's such a bummer. But you said what there was of it was fantastic. And at least you're here!" She's beaming at me, and I feel happy just to be here with her. She knows everything there is to know about me and loves me regardless. No questions, no expectations. No explanations necessary.

I've finished eating and look around the barroom as I search my purse for some gum. The place has a true pub feel, all dark wood and low lights shielded by emerald glass shades. The air conditioning is cranked but it still feels stuffy with wall-to-wall people.

The band is set up towards the back of the building on an elevated platform that acts as a stage. An open area of hardwood below serves as a dance floor.

"I see Harry has the bongos set up. Please don't tell me I have to cap this deflated evening by singing for these shitfaced rich pricks," I say changing the topic. "And I'm clearly overdressed."

"Oh *come on*," she chides. "You look fabulous. And it'll be fun." She tosses back the last of her rum and Coke and jabs me in the side with her elbow. "Besides, it will take your mind off Mr. Big Bucks when we feed you this crowd's attention. The place is hopping tonight!"

She excuses herself to the bathroom and I watch her sashay past her husband, who is singing a Steve Miller tune. Gloria's wearing heels, flattering jeans, and a simple black shirt that highlights her *ba-zooms*, as Harry would say. She blows him a kiss and disappears down the hall to the ladies' toilet.

I've stayed behind to hold our seats. She was right, the place is busy. Everyone seems in great disposition, the warm weather a huge mood booster around here.

People in booths are eating late meals and chatting, some dressed nicely with designer handbags resting on hooks nearby, some sporting their finest rocker t-shirts and motorcycle boots.

Other patrons are bellied up to the bar or standing on the dance floor grooving to Harry's band, The Rebels. Gloria once told me they came up with that by picking a name from a hat. As it happened, The Rebels was the suggestion she had thrown in.

Left alone, I realize how disappointed I am that my date with Aidan had to end so fast.

Before we could finish our conversation.

Before we could ride him like a bike!

"Oh shut up, bitch," I mutter out loud.

No one hears me shouting at my crazy inner-sex-goddess over the din. I order a drink, pull out my phone, and text Charlie about my half-date. I check his reply when my phone pings, but the message isn't from him.

It's from Aidan.

I'm sorry, again. Wish I was with you instead.

My insides involuntarily flutter. He's somewhere putting out a fire that has to be dealt with now and he's thinking of me? Instant swoon.

Don't apologize. It's all good. Gonna sing with Gloria and Harry, they'll drop me home after the gig. We'll talk tomorrow.

There. That doesn't seem too desperate or disappointed, right?

What are you singing?

Aren't you supposed to be in a meeting? Or ruling the world or something??

Just answer me.

Indigo Girls. "Galileo"

You're kidding.

Nope. Why?

What, does he not like them? Hates that song? Loves that song? Hangs out with those kick ass ladies every other weekend? What?!

I'm waiting for his response for what seems like forever. It's a good five minutes before Gloria returns as his reply finally comes through.

Nothing, just hate that I will miss that. Be safe. And watch out for the men in there. I hear that bar can get rowdy.

I look around at the men in the crowd. Most look like they're thirty or older, and just stepped out of a yachting magazine. There are a few bikers and young guys, but they are definitely outnumbered. Most of the ladies are either well made up or specially enhanced. I half expect to see Jade and Dr. McCall here but don't see them in the sea of faces.

Rowdy? LOL! I think I'm safe with these yuppies. Goodnight, Aidan

Goodnight, Alexis

Gloria returns, shouting that we should dance. In five minutes, my drink is emptied and I'm feeling in a fan-*fucking*-tastic mood again after hearing from Aidan. I tell Gloria I'm ready to kill it on this song and she picks up on my mood change. She glances at my phone and gives me a knowing smile.

The band will break for fifteen minutes after the next song. When they return she and Harry will cover a Stevie Nicks tune, then we'll be on deck.

I open my tiny purse to drop in my phone, securing it on my shoulder as we head for the dance floor. Harry winks, nodding at me as I pass. He and The Rebels jam out on the Doobies' "Long Train Runnin'" and I move in time to their groove.

The bass player, whom I only know as Rob, does back-up vocals too. The harmonies are spot-on, as always. All four guys are professional musicians that have been at it longer than they care to admit, probably longer than I've been alive.

Harry is jamming on the harmonica as I feel some people watching me get down with Gloria. Guys perhaps in approval, but some of their dates not so much.

Oh well! I'm reminded of Aidan's compliments on my appearance and choose confidence over insecurity.

The band breaks into a Zeppelin tune next, their last before the break. Gloria and I are into it, dancing to "Ramble On" with a couple of the other band wives. They are all older than I am, but we have the music in common, all of us mouthing the words. These ladies have been there, done that – and have the tattoos to prove it. They are so much fun, especially when they're out.

As the song ends I'm fanning myself, definitely in need of freshening up before standing in front of a crowd to sing. The band breaks, pop music suddenly piped through the sound system. Some people stay on the dance floor, some head to the bar. I leave Gloria with the other wives and let her know I'm going to say hi to her hubby before I hit the ladies room.

Harry is going on to his bandmates about his appreciation for the new sound guy and what a good crowd it is. As he chugs a bottle of water, he catches sight of me.

"Well, ain't you something to see!" He gives me a best-friend's-husband side squeeze. "Been awhile since you've been all dolled up. I hear there's quite a guy after you, young lady."

I shrug. "You know me, Harry. Where there's a billionaire, I'll find him."

He laughs genuinely and, despite his bad ass look of leather boots, Harley t-shirt and worn jeans, everything about him is jovial. His grayed moustache and beard make him look like Sam Elliott, albeit with a few extra pounds.

Ten minutes pass as we chat about the weather, my lost deal, and finally about his twin girls and how teenagers are such a pain in the ass.

"So we'll get ya up there just as soon as I sing with my lady," he nods at Gloria as she saunters up.

"This lady bothering you, mister?" She smiles, cocking her hip with a what-gives stare.

"Nah. She looks a bit too fancy for me," he says, planting a kiss on her.

It's no kiss like Aidan laid on me tonight, but dang. The two of them are still enamored with each other, even after umpteen married years and two girls that put them through the wringer from premature birth to teen angst bullshit.

I often wonder how they do it. They make it look easy.

"Oh *gawd*. Get a room, guys," I kid.

"Aright," she says after their lip lock. "The bartender says O'Reilly wants us to get back into it before we lose the crowd."

"Dammit," he says. "A man's work is never done."

"Yeah, well. The sooner we wrap up this gig, the sooner we can get home." She winks at him suggestively.

"Tell him five more minutes. I just gotta hit the men's room and I'll be right back."

"Thanks for the warning," she says, shooing him off.

I feel my phone buzzing in my clutch. I snag a close seat at the end of the bar while Gloria flags down the bartender.

It's a text from Charlie, as I expected. His only response is a sad face and a photo of Huck sleeping. Before I can respond, Harry is gathering the guys back up. He invites Gloria to the mic, telling everyone about this amazing woman who has put up with his shit for thirty years and still sings like an angel.

"Oh he definitely wants some nookie tonight," she teases me. "He's laying it on thick."

"Go get 'em, woman," I say.

She steps away to join him, the crowd encouraging her, the band wives and I whistling and cheering in anticipation.

The band starts in on Stevie Nicks' "Stop Draggin' My Heart Around", getting the crowd paying attention again. Gloria is awesome, her raspy voice unique and always in tune, and Harry is a seasoned performer. All eyes are on them.

I'm distracted by some commotion behind me, towards the front door by the pool tables. Hopefully not a brawl over a lost bet, I think. You never know once you add alcohol. Maybe Aidan was right and some perfectly level-headed yuppies were getting rowdy.

I can't put off the unavoidable call of nature to find out. I leave my seat to beeline for the bathroom. The line is short, but I'm practically dancing in place waiting for one of the three stalls to open up.

I finish the necessary, wash my hands, and take a quick glance at the full length mirror on the back of the door.

I'm clearly flushed from dancing (and drinking?) but everything seems to be in place. My hair hasn't suffered too much from the heat and my outfit is still intact.

I exit to the hallway and pull out my phone, typing back to Charlie as fast as I can. I can hear Gloria's song wrapping up.

It's all good! He's been texting me. Gonna get
my performance of the month in with Gloria
then head home. I'll see you tomorrow!
Thanks for looking after my beast. xo

Texting...or sexting?! ;-) Amen girl!
See you in the AM!

Gloria's three minute song has ended with the crowd clapping and hollering their appreciation.

I unexpectedly feel butterflies, their wings obnoxiously batting around in my stomach. I head back to the corner of the bar and the bartender asks what I need.

"Shot of Patron. Lemon and salt."

He gives me a look of surprise, impressed.

"For courage," I add as I hear Harry mention my name. He says something about stellar attorney by day and songstress by night.

I look for Gloria, expecting her to be urging me over, but she doesn't see me through the crowd. The guys are huddled around her and Harry, shuffling around. Typically, Harry calls up his buddy Tom to the bongos on this one while I sing lead and Gloria is on harmony next to me.

I spin around, grateful to see my shot waiting for me. I set my purse on the bar and ask the bartender to keep an eye on it while I sing.

I'm normally not nervous performing, but something in the energy of the room feels different tonight. It's exhilarating, raw somehow.

I shake a dash of salt on the crook of my thumb. Drink-lick-suck.

Wahoo! My brain is doing backflips and getting ready to wow the masses.

That's better. Ready to crush it!

Dave, the drummer, has taken Tom's usual place at the bongos. Tom and his date are at the front of the crowd, standing on the dance floor. He gives me a thumbs up and I smile back tentatively, unsure why he isn't joining us.

Gloria has a grin plastered on her face as Harry moves closer to her, guitar in hand. She shrugs when she catches my eye, like she isn't sure what's going on.

Then I get a view of who is sitting behind the drumkit and nearly fall to my knees.

Holy fuck.

It's not just anybody sitting in for Dave.

It's Aidan.

He's *here*. And not dressed up all fancy like he was earlier. He's in tattered jeans and a tight gray tee, with a Yale logo on it – the same shirt I slept in the other night.

He's also wearing a ball cap and his flip flops are next to the drum kit. Apparently he's ready to tackle this (not so easy) song drumming with naked feet.

He looks like he belongs back there.

I'm able to size all this up in seconds, realizing it was him that caused the commotion up front before I headed for the ladies room.

And everyone here wants to see what he's gonna do next.

Screw it. Here we go. And he better be good.

I suppose if he sucks, I can live with that embarrassment through a four minute song. But then I'd have to ditch him forever. Because I really can't handle a show off that can't hack it behind the drum set.

Harry hasn't mentioned his newest band member to the crowd (likely a condition of Aidan playing at all). He urges me to come on up to the mic, getting the crowd cheering in anticipation. I take my place on the stage, glancing at Aidan only briefly. He smiles ear to ear and flips his ball cap backwards.

Fuck me, I could just eat him up.

"Don't worry," he mouths.

I'm so grateful my subconscious is passed out from the shot of tequila while it's given 'regular me' all the courage I need. I face the crowd as Harry cues everyone. Dave taps the bongos, Harry starts strumming away, and I come in on cue.

As Gloria chimes in with harmony, the drums kick in behind me, along with Rob on the bass, both sounds thump-thumping right through me.

I want to hold my breath in anticipation of what Aidan will do.

Will he totally flop? Does he have *any* idea what the hell he's doing?! But I have to keep singing.

Before I can work myself into a frenzy of worry, I realize he's killing it right out of the gate.

He *knows* this song.

We get to the bridge and I'm completely high on the music, the crowd and their random whistles of appreciation, and the comradery of the moment with Gloria and the band.

I turn around to him as he keeps the beat during the instrumental. He's not looking up, totally engrossed in the song and concentrating on what he's doing.

And he looks rock-fucking-star amazing doing it.

I glance at Harry and his bandmates and they, like Aidan, are lost in the music and enjoying every second of the jam. Gloria and I finish out the song in harmony with Harry, spot-on as we have rehearsed it to be since we met, the band closing out together with precision.

The room erupts with clapping and hollering.

I take a conservative curtsy, and Gloria and I move off the platform so the band can re-take their positions and keep on with the music.

From surprise, from excitement, from sheer adrenaline, I'm trembling, unsteady like a leaf in a thunderstorm.

Harry and the guys confer with Aidan in a quick huddle, and then Harry gets to the mic. Dave makes his way to the keyboard, a bit further back on the stage.

It's then I notice Byron standing at the rear exit, just at the other side of the platform. He sees me and gives a nod, but, as usual, no smile. I smile anyway, still high from performing.

"Okay, folks, we've got our guest drummer for one more song, then he's gotta jet." The crowd whines and Harry stifles their boos. "Trust me folks, this will be worth it. Here we go!"

He turns back to the band, guitar poised. "A one, two, one, two, three, four!"

The band breaks into "Glory Days" and the crowd goes ape-shit.

The Boss is one of Harry's favorites. Gloria and I just stand there looking at each other, rolling our eyes in shared sarcasm, but both stupid-happy. Harry is having a blast, we've kicked ass, and it's just one of those nights.

The guys even have the song's banter down. Their performance is almost as good as seeing the real thing. I know this is just what great musicians are capable of, their natural talent combined with years of practice.

But I certainly didn't realize Aidan had this up his sleeve.

The song ends and as the bar roars in appreciation again, Harry bows down to Aidan, who makes his way out from behind the drums. The women in the crowd are falling all over themselves, audibly appreciating him.

I catch sight of Byron again. He's waving me over.

As much as I'd love to hang out here, riding this high with the band and Gloria all night long, I am aching for Aidan.

He's talking with the rest of the guys while Harry says on the mic that they will take a quick break to reset. Aidan and Harry exchange words and a handshake, and I see Harry lean in to Aidan and say something more, seemingly serious. They're smiling as they part ways.

As Aidan makes his way off the stage, he tosses his hat into the crowd and a few people clamor for it as he heads in Byron's direction.

"Lex, you are going to Aidan, yes?" Gloria asks. She is trying to get my attention, waving in my peripheral vision. "You didn't tell me he was a drummer!"

I'm trying to process what has just transpired and now that the band has stopped, I can hear enough to converse with her.

I turn to her abruptly.

"Did you have something to do with this?"

"No! He just showed up while you were in the bathroom. He said he knew the song backwards and forwards, something about a band he had once. Trust me, I'm as shocked as you are."

I recall the text I'd sent him, telling him what Gloria and I were going to perform. He must have rushed to get here as soon as he read it. There's no other way he would have made it in time.

"Gloria, I love you, but I have to go." I kiss her on the cheek and grab my purse off the bar.

"You bet your ass you do!" She squeezes me in bear hug and I take a step back.

"Thank you," I say sincerely, "for everything."

She slaps me on the ass as I head away from her, towards the back corner of the building where Byron had been. The crowd is on the dance floor moving to the beat of a song featuring Rihanna's sexy vocals. A handful of young ladies are trying to get a peek at the guest drummer, pushing their way through the crowd to find him. He seems to have disappeared.

Reaching the back door, I can't see Byron anywhere and I'm deflated. Maybe they left in a hurry out of necessity.

I turn to scan the crowd and Aidan is smack in front of me.

He smiles, not saying a word, then spins me around, backing me up into him. We're at the edge of the dance floor.

"That was incredible," he says in my ear. "Alexis, your voice…can you feel this?"

He wraps his arms around me, grinding into me from behind, and I can definitely feel what he's referring to.

He's hard as granite.

My breath catches, a moan escaping as my head rolls back into his chest. Even with the loud music, I can feel his heart pound.

"You did this," he says. "Just listening to you sing, getting this close to you…"

I turn around to face him, clasp my hands around the back of his neck and pull him close.

"I would have to say the same about you. I had no idea you could play. Mad skills, Aidan. Mad skills."

He pulls me closer, the bass pumping through us. His lips trace my behind my ear before he speaks again.

"You want to get out of here?"

I nod, probably a bit too eager, but I'm *so* past putting up a fight at this point.

I can read his lips as he says *thank God*, letting out a noticeable exhale.

He moves us away from the crowd before anyone can stop us. We head out the back door with no one following and come upon a couple smoking cigarettes outside.

I can't see Byron or the car anywhere as I search the alley and assume he must be around the corner, parked somewhere along the street.

Aidan hands the smoking gentleman a twenty, telling him his date looks like she might need a fresh drink. By some unspoken bro-code, the guy gets it and takes his lady inside. We're left alone behind the building with the glow of a street lamp twenty feet away the only source of light.

The door slams behind them, closing the loud music inside. As fast as they are gone, Aidan is backing me up in the darkness.

The chill of brick touches the backs of my shoulders, then my arms as he grasps my wrists gently, pinning them above my head with one hand.

He leans in and I lose all patience, laying a kiss on him, letting the intangible zing take hold. He responds with equal greed, grabbing the back of my thigh, lifting my leg around his waist, grinding into me.

I'm about to object to the roughness of the brick behind me, but he saves me from it by spinning me around, so I can lay my hands flat against the building.

He presses into my backside from behind again, his breathing quick and needy.

I can feel exactly what's in those jeans now, still firm and almost frighteningly large.

He's nuzzling my neck, licking as he makes his way up, until his tongue finds its way inside my ear, making me curse in appreciation and need.

Apparently *that's* a hot button I never knew I had.

All the blood rushes out of my head and my clit is throbbing. He reaches beneath my skirt, expertly moving my thong out of the way.

Oh. Holy. Fuck.

"Aidan," I breathe his name, unable to think. Everything feels so good, yet so inappropriate.

"Shhhh," he says. "Just hold on, baby. I've got you."

This is so insane.

I'm drunk, soaking wet, and horny as a convict on his first day out of the joint.

His fingers are having their way with me from stem to stern while hidden under my skirt. It has been so long since this touch has been a reality for me. In the excitement of the moment I am completely open to him, letting him work me out of rational thought.

"Yes," I mumble. *"Don't stop."*

He complies, licks my ear and then sucks on my earlobe. Without warning I'm coming fast, a freight train derailing.

Fuck.

I unravel, right there behind O'Reilly's, breath heaving, my fingertips digging into mortar. I can feel him smiling, his head resting on my neck, his breathing matching mine as he lets me slowly come down from my orgasm, which I can't believe he's just given me.

In a dark alley.

Behind a bar.

"Alexis," he whispers, "that was so worth the wait."

Exactly what I was thinking.

In any other time or any other place prior to this moment, I would be completely mortified at what has just unfolded.

Somehow, the current Alexis is definitely far from it.

She is satiated, still leaning against a brick wall with a sexy as hell man holding up the rest of her and wondering how she is going to satisfy *him* now.

He asks in a whisper if I'm all right.

"Better than," I say, "I can't... Aidan, it's been so long."

He's kissing my neck, my shoulders.

"I know, baby. You needed that more than air to breathe."

"But *you*, I want... you... to..." I stammer, protesting the one-sided nature of our encounter.

"No," he says decisively. "Let me take you home."

I'm not sure if he means take me to my home or to his. I don't answer at first.

"Alexis, will you come home with me?" He's impatient, but there he goes, reading my thoughts again and putting my doubts at ease. "If you feel ready, there isn't any other place I want you than in my bed." His head is still resting on my shoulder, still trailing lips along my slick skin. "Please," he says, in a true plea.

"Yes, Aidan." I turn around to face him, finally able to get my bearings. "Yes. Take me with you."

27

Alexis

Byron drives us to 250 Harrison in under twenty-five minutes. It's the fastest I've ever made it to the city from Falcon Lake.

We ride in silence for awhile but our bodies are inseparable, my legs draped across his lap, his arms around me. My head lazes against him, listening to his heartbeat as he strokes my hair.

Midway through our ride, he adjusts himself to pull his phone out of his pocket and, seconds later, whoever he's summoning answers.

"You'll need to take care of California without me."

I can't discern the response, but the voice is distinctly female.

"No." His answer is firm. "I'm unavailable."

He listens intently.

"No. Call Lionel and let him know to check in with you. You'll hear from me tomorrow."

He disconnects.

I don't have any desire to ask what that was all about, though I can't help wonder who the woman was. Maybe the blonde from his entourage the first time we met? I know it's really none of my business so I open up another topic instead.

"I can't believe you know how to play the motherfucking drums."

He breaks into laughter, evidently not expecting that to come out of my mouth.

"You should have seen the look on your face," he says, "and I didn't know you could sing like *that*. I mean Charlie said you had pipes but damn, baby. You had the guys in that crowd adjusting themselves in their khakis."

I smile, looking up at him. I love that he's started calling me baby. Warmth floods me every time I hear it.

"How did you ever learn that song though? Of all the songs ever made, how in the hell did you know that one?"

"My brother and I had a band in high school. We learned it to impress a girl he was after," he says. "She used to sing it with us."

"That wasn't recent," I say. "You still remembered it? Do you practice?"

"No, not regularly. As soon as I saw your text, I downloaded it and listened to it like ten times on the way there. I guess that was enough recall."

"And "Glory Days"?"

"Gloria's husband, Harry, is it?"

I nod.

"He asked if I knew any Springsteen songs. I indulged him hoping not to disappoint, but I haven't played that song in years."

"Harry loves performing that one with The Rebels. And you killed it. Seriously."

"I try," he says with artificial modesty.

"So, for the girl your brother was after, did it work?"

"Actually, it backfired. She ended up chasing after our bass player instead."

"Inconceivable," I say. "And why didn't she want the drummer?"

"I was dating her friend at the time."

I think about Aidan as a younger man, making his way through high school, then college life. He must have gotten laid more than an eighties rock star.

"I didn't realize you had a brother until you told me about it in that file."

He's quiet for a moment. "I did, yes. He passed."

I sit up, surprised. The look on his face is heart-wrenching.

"I'm so sorry." I don't say more. It's obvious the topic is difficult.

Thankfully, Byron is pulling up to 250 Harrison, relieving us from the pressure of speech.

"Until tomorrow, sir," Byron says.

I thank him as I exit the car, heading for the lobby in case there's anything Aidan wants to discuss with him privately. The wind kicks up, cooling me off but also reminding me that underneath my skirt, I'm a hot mess. I'm hoping for a shower when we get upstairs.

Aidan joins me a moment later and unlocks the door, then leads me to the elevator. The building is empty and even more quiet than usual with both first floor storefronts closed this late at night.

"Do you want to get out of those clothes?" He's eyeing me from my neck down to my heels, a fierce intensity in his eye as I back up into the elevator.

"I think that's a good idea," I say. I lean against the back wall looking to see if the bulge in his jeans is still prevalent, but I can't tell. I'm hoping he'll come at me so I can find out but we've already arrived at the third floor. He says nothing more, taking my hand to pull me off the elevator.

He leads the way to the door, types a code into the security keypad, and lets us in. The scent of him is in the air, filling my senses as we move through the foyer and into the dark kitchen. He pulls out his phone and taps until a few dim lights come on.

He grabs two bottles of water from the fridge, gives me one and takes my hand again.

"Come," he says. "This way."

We're headed to his master suite, I can only assume. I have no idea where I'm going. I'm hoping I don't stub my toe as we make our way through the shadows.

Aidan is clearly on a mission.

We enter the bedroom, which is a mirror image of the guest suite I woke up in the other day. It's a bit larger and definitely more masculine. There's a door open to reveal a huge closet and another to an ensuite bathroom, just like on the guest side.

He calls out a name I don't recognize to some mysterious music God and an erotic pop song streams through speakers somewhere within the walls. I don't know the song, but the music is thrumming with heavy bass underneath a beautiful melody. The guy singing has a voice smooth as satin.

A few more dim lights are on in here; one on the bedside table and some recessed overhead. A neatly made, king size bed is the focal point. It's covered in a white duvet and more pillows than I've ever owned. He isn't moving in that direction, though. He goes to the bathroom and, seconds later, I can hear the shower start.

"Alexis," he speaks up over the volume of running water and music, but I can't see him. "Come."

I kick off my shoes, set down my purse, and remove my jewelry to a nightstand, then do as I'm told. I'm responding to his commands like a lap-dog, I'm fully aware. But I don't care. Being in his command is exhilarating.

From what I can see the bathroom is Carrera marble like the other one, but there are no feminine touches. The room's bright white is accented only by some black or dark blue. It's hard to tell. The lights in here are very dim, too.

I notice he's removed his shirt and all my surroundings are blurred.

All I can see is him.

I can't. Even. Handle it.

Every inch of him is carved and chiseled, yet his skin is so smooth it almost glows in the soft light. Hair is non-existent on his chest, which rises and falls quickly as he stares me down.

He looks like living, breathing art.

Two lines border his abs, which are (of course) perfectly defined. The lines disappear beneath the jeans that are now hanging a bit low off his hips. He's removed his belt and tossed it aside next to his shirt.

I notice the same symbol from his business card is tattooed just above his belly button. It's prominent, but small enough to fall well between his hips, with room to spare. His eyes are burning, waiting, distracting me from taking in further details. He motions his head towards the shower.

"All yours," he says.

"You're not getting in with me?"

"Actually I had a shower as soon as I got back here earlier," he says, a sheepish grin forming. "It was necessary, thanks to you."

I can decipher what he means, realizing he must have filled his own needs when he left me. The fact that he felt that a necessity intensifies my own libido.

"Come in with me anyway."

I take off my top and toss it aside to reveal the bra he technically owns. He closes the distance between us quickly.

"I thought you'd never ask." He kisses me heatedly, even as he speaks to me. "As much as I love this investment," he says unclasping the bra, "it needs to go."

It lands on the floor below as he takes over its job, holding up my breasts and doing what he will. His hands are so soft, gliding up my back as he buries his face in me. I moan as his hand travels back down my spine to the zipper at the back of my skirt, undoing it just enough that it will slip off over my hips.

He bends to slide the skirt down slowly. I step out of it as he's lowered in front of me, and he tosses it aside in the growing pile of clothing. He kneels in front of me, his hands slowly gliding up every inch of my legs until they rest on my hips as he looks up at me.

Without the buzz of alcohol, I'd probably be feeling insecure at the moment. I'm completely exposed to him with the exception of the black lace thong that doesn't leave anything to the imagination.

His eyes are seemingly full of approval and appreciation and I can't help turning my head in humility.

"Baby, stop being modest. You're gorgeous. Look at you." He rises, then turns me around to face the vanity.

I look at my reflection, seeing nipples erect on full breasts heaving in anticipation, his hands cupping them. He removes his hands only to slide them back to my hips and remove my one remaining piece of clothing. He rises, encircles me from behind with his arms, nuzzling my neck like he did back at the bar.

"See?" he says, lifting his gaze to my reflection. "*Bellissima.*"

Oh Lord, not compliments in Italian. The way it rolls off his lips makes me throb again. I have no defense to this. It's an Achilles heel I rarely have exposed. Men like this don't cross my path often or, now that I think of it, ever.

Even without the sexy utterances, he makes me *feel* beautiful. I close my eyes, leaning back into him.

"I've wanted to see you like this since we met," he says. "Some days it was all I could think about."

Somewhere in my depths I want to cry, never being complimented this way in my years as a grown woman.

"Your turn," I whisper aloud, suppressing insecure emotions.

I open my eyes again, watching his expression in the mirror, his lips curving to a smile.

He unzips his jeans and they drop to the floor with no effort, revealing absolutely nothing underneath.

Oh holy hell.

If maleness was determined on a zero to ten scale, he'd be in the double digits.

"Shower," he says. "Come."

"Yes, I'd like you to do just that," I tease. "This time with me here."

He laughs and guides me into the shower, shutting the glass door behind us. The entire surround is tiled in marble, which I would appreciate immensely if I wasn't instead wishing Aidan to hurry up and get inside me already.

There's a bench along one wall. Showerheads gently spray from all over, but the rain showerhead above is off. Steam rises around us as he grabs a bottle of soap. I have no idea what it is but it smells amazing, part of that scent that has become his signature to me.

He's lathering me from shoulders to shins and I'm just relishing every moment. As relaxed as I feel, I don't know how I'm standing up.

I manage to shampoo my hair quickly, removing the hairspray that had held it in place. He steps back watching me, biting his lip and visibly forcing himself not to come at me.

I step into one of the sprays of water, letting the soap wash off. I feel much better, having cleaned things up *down there* after my unexpected orgasm an hour ago. I spot some towels tucked into the niche at the back of the shower and formulate my plan for an attack of gratitude.

I back him up, kissing him as I go. He finds my tongue with his own and I'm blazing, despite the water cascading over me. I break the kiss and pull him down to sitting on the bench, as far as we can away from the sprays of water, then grab a towel to kneel on.

"Ohhh...," he moans in acceptance. "*Yeah*."

Apparently he knows exactly what I'm up to.

I can't recall the last time I did this and really have no idea if I'll be good at it. Instinct and yearning drive me. I've never felt a desire to go down on a guy like this, feeling like I will enjoy it as much as he might.

I'm pretty certain from his moans that I'm succeeding as I take in as much as I can handle. There's just so *much* of him. I change pace, slowing down enough to enjoy every salty inch, one hand holding him firmly in place. I'm about to speed up again when he stops me, tugging at my wet hair. I pull off, but slowly enough to have an effect as he lets out another groan.

"Not like this," he says. "I want you in my bed."

"Are you sure?" I ask, returning my attention to him, licking like a lollipop all the way to his tip.

"Yes..." he says. I'm not sure if he means keep going or stop, until he tugs at my hair again and makes me look up. "Yes, I'm sure."

I smile through hooded eyes and stand, stepping away so he can get up.

He turns off the water, towels me off with one towel, then himself with another. He wraps himself around the waist, as best he can with a raging hard on. I've draped mine over me, lost in thought and hoping my skills were not poor enough to cause his change in direction.

As always, he reads my thoughts.

"That, what you just did," he closes his eyes, smiles and inhales before returning his eyes to mine. "I can't even describe to you how good that felt."

Whether or not it's a silly reaction, relief floods me. Because who wants to be bad at that?

He pulls me close again, looking down at me with the same greed I felt from him last night in my kitchen.

"Are you sure you're ready, Alexis? I need to know you want this."

Am I *ready*? My subconscious is doing gymnastics, setting off fireworks and getting ready for the sex of epic proportions the all-girl tribe has been waiting for since this man stepped into my life.

"Yes, Aidan. I'm more than ready. Can't you sense that? I can't get close enough to you."

He kisses me softly, speaking at me while his lips press to mine. "You're on the pill?"

"Yes. And I can be more ready, if I can get to my purse," I say, hopeful that Charlie did stash some condoms in it after all.

"I've got it covered." He pulls me out of the shower and straight to the bedroom, now a man on a mission once again.

The low lights and the music are still on, both of us in towels standing next to the bed. He removes a few pillows on the closest side to us, then moves around to the other side leaving me standing there. I remove my towel and try to dry my damp hair a bit, securing it up in the towel like a turban, which leaves me completely naked.

A new song surrounds us as he commands "volume up". The song increases in intensity, and I realize it's ZAYN singing about battles between passion and pain, losing fears and finding paradise. The song might be a parody of itself, mainstream and overplayed on any other occasion hearing it.

But right now it feels like Aidan and I put to music. I fight him, then let him in only to be rewarded with pleasure. Even the conflict itself is a high I don't want to come down from.

He takes one look at me and comes at me from across the bed with urgency, naked and kneeling in front of me. His mouth takes mine over, then lips roam down to the cleavage he creates with his hands.

My legs want to buckle. I push on him, urging him to move back, so I can climb and kneel with him on the bed. Our lips seem melded together, tongues twisted, impatience building between us. Using his hands he urges my knees to part, then flips onto his back, having made space for his head. He disappears beneath me before I can get a breath.

I'm so close to losing it, but I don't want another release yet.

I'm frantic to feel him inside me, but I can't object to the job his tongue is doing. His fingers join the assault, and I can't hold back. I quake as sensation takes over, coming again, just as hard and fast as the first time.

He's moaning, licking me, taunting. He bites my inner thigh and a scream escapes me against my will, snapping me out of the high induced by Aidan's mouth.

He laughs, climbing over to reach into his nightstand. "Do you always come that fast?"

I blush in the darkness, not sure how to answer. It isn't like I have a lot of experiences to compare this to.

"Don't know," I comment softly, lazing back in the middle of his massive bed. I lay there with closed eyes, surprised at myself. I feel completely at peace, but still feel want for him, even after he's already satisfied me.

Twice.

I don't ever recall feeling this content and aroused all at once.

He tucks a condom under the pillow beneath me, then straddles me on his knees. "Are you sure?" he asks.

I nod fervently.

"If you want me to stop, you have to tell me," he says.

"Just what is it you want to do to me?" I wonder if I'm agreeing to something out of the ordinary.

"I told you already. You listened to it last night, remember?"

He lies next to me, fingertips tracing a trail from my neck, down the center of my stomach, then poised on my hip bone. I'm trying to think back to his "*Open Last*" recording.

I can't remember a word as he switches from hands to lips as his weapon.

From the indentation of my waist, over my hip, halfway down my outer thigh…every inch chases with chills from his lips gracing them. He shifts positions, rising over me, powerful arms surrounding me. He lowers himself to within an inch of me.

"I want to bury myself in you," he says. "Penetrate you, make love to you until I can't see straight."

I close my eyes, feeling insatiable, whispering *yes.*

Yes, yes, yes, over and over I repeat it.

He braces himself with the strength of one arm, using the other to remove the towel from my head. He fans my damp hair out around me, then resumes his position, hovering, kissing my closed eyelids, his tongue gliding over my neck, my breasts.

I take his face in my hands and bring him back to me, parting his lips to search for his tongue with my own. I bite his lower lip gently, as I've been aching to do for what seems like an eternity.

He gives me a heated look as he reaches under the pillow for the condom, dropping it in the center of my chest as he moves up, kneeling above me. I pick it up and tear it open while I hold it in my teeth, tossing the wrapper aside. As I unroll it over the length of him, I'm marveling at the sight.

He resumes his position of power, lowering himself until our bodies are unified, kissing me eagerly. I think he's going to enter, but instead he reaches inside me, fingers testing the waters.

"Mmm," he says. He removes himself and sucks on his finger. "*So good.*"

I kiss him in heated response, waiting for him to do as he promised.

"Hold on, baby" he says, positioning himself at my opening. He slowly enters, halting only to read me, obviously concerned for my comfort.

"Yes," I breathe. "*More.*"

He complies, and as he does gently bites my earlobe, effectively distracting me from a brief moment of painful ache he must have been predicting. His tongue finds my ear again, my newly discovered weakness eliciting greed. I open up beneath him completely, longing for him to be as deep as possible.

He fills me up, the intensity of this so unfamiliar. No cohesive thoughts can form in my brain. All I can do is *feel*.

How amazing his sculpted body feels over mine, how open I am for him as we fit together like a completed puzzle. I never want this to end.

"You feel so good. Oh my God, Alex…"

I want to talk back to him, but I can't get any words out. The pleasure is mind numbing. He splays a hand underneath me, lifting my hips up. He looks down at me, watching my reaction as he moves gently in, gently out.

My back arches in instinctive response, desire escaping me in a moan as my nipples harden to aching.

"You're so tight, baby. Are you all right?"

"Yes," I manage. "You're not going to break me, Aidan. This feels incredible."

I glide my hands over the muscles in his torso, trace his tattoo with my fingertips, his sculpted lines slick beneath my hands. I pull his face down to me, licking at his lips, moving hands through his hair, my hips gyrating in response to his quickening rhythm.

He lowers his mouth to close it around my nipple as he begins to drive faster, then faster still.

I can feel myself building to another climax, relinquishing all control to him as he whispers in my ear.

"Yes, baby. Let me in. I want to feel you come."

The next words he breathes send me spinning and doing exactly as he commands.

"Let go, Alexis."

My chest heaves as I scream out his name, clenching around him and lost in yet another orgasm.

I feel nothing but him, think nothing but him. I want nothing more than this, to be underneath him, having him buried inside me.

I've never been this high.

Not from anything.

He raises up on his arms, looking down at me, a prideful smile on his face. An involuntary wave of emotion comes over me, a tear escaping my eye.

It's unlike anything I've ever felt.

My breathing is fast and irregular, my face resting in an expression of complete euphoria.

He comes back down to me, whispering foreign words before and after my name, trailing kisses along my neck. My urge to please him overtakes me, and I wrap my legs around his waist. I watch him revel in the new sensation it creates as he leans back, all weight resting on his hands. He moves in and out of me, face skyward, muscles taught, *so* deep inside me.

Just as he says he's been aching to be.

It is an impressive sight.

My hands caress his chest again, my fingertips finding his nipples, and his expression changes. I can tell he's relishing it.

I've found his trigger.

"Come, Aidan," I implore. "Please. I want you to."

He does as I request almost instantly, as though he'd been waiting for permission. He groans in a low, sexy growl as he lowers himself around me and I can feel him releasing, pulsing into the shield between us.

When he slows his pace I unravel my legs, involuntarily leaving them splayed open. He relaxes, collapsed on me, wet with sweat and whispering questions about what am I doing to him, and how is he ever going to get enough of me.

I can't answer my own questions, let alone his.

Like how I can suddenly climax multiple times in an evening.

The third time in *missionary* position, no less.

I lay still, quiet and completely spent as he lays his lips on my hair, on my forehead.

"Please," he begs, lips still taunting me as he mutters. "Please tell me that was worth waiting for, Alex, because it sure as fuck was for me."

"What can I say, Mr. Pierce?" I tease. "You brought the shock and awe, as ever."

He moves off me, the sensation of his withdrawal taking over me like a forfeiture of pleasure. It feels almost tragic, making me want to plead for him not to leave the depths of me, but I say nothing.

I'm flat on my back, eyes closed, trying to process the moment and bring myself down.

He lies on his side, facing me. I can feel his eyes roam over me and I turn to peer at him.

"What?"

"Nothing. Just admiring."

"I'm not used to that."

"Get used to it," he says, moving towards me. "You have been interrupting my life for a week, lucky for me, and it's about time I got to appreciate the distraction up close."

He kisses me affectionately on the lips, then rolls away and heads for the bathroom. Moments later I hear the sink running. He returns with a warm cloth, washing me everywhere, paying special attention below my waist. The dampness floods me with warmth, then leaves chills when he takes the cloth away.

I rise and follow him to the bathroom on unsteady legs. He grabs a clean cloth, washes his face, brushes his teeth. I have to pee, but I'm not feeling inclined to do so in front of him. He wipes his face with a dry towel and smirks at me in the mirror, completely confident in his nudity – as he very well should be.

"I'll leave you be." He's perceptive as always. Before he exits he picks up his Yale t-shirt off the floor and pulls it over my head. It smells like him, and I close my eyes to drink in the scent. "I think this belongs to you now, baby."

He lays a kiss on me that leaves me seeing yellow fuzzy stars, smacking me on the bare ass as he leaves the room with the remaining bundle of clothing.

Holy Jesus in a manger.

Blown to smithereens are any grand plans of keeping my guard up with this creature.

I am beyond screwed, in every sense of the word.

28

Aidan

At one in the morning we are sitting in my kitchen trading stories about college days. Somehow we get on the topic of my time at Cal Tech, pranks my buddies and I played on classmates. At the last story I'm telling she's been laughing so hard it's soundless, looking completely amazing doing it with her still damp, just-fucked hair and flushed cheeks.

"So, apparently with your higher intelligence and the combined resources of a genius-mathematician-computer-geek, an engineer slash neuroscientist and you...wait, what were you majoring in again?"

"Applied mathematics. Computer science."

"And somewhere in there you fit in learning Italian. Or is *bellissima* the only word you know?"

"I paid very close attention in those classes, lived abroad for awhile. It's a romance language." I shrug my shoulders, "I figured it couldn't hurt."

She looks at me a moment, rolling her eyes as if this is a blow to her defenses. "It may not hurt *you*, but there's no doubt in my mind it's left a wake of weakened females lowering themselves at your feet."

I smile and let out a laugh. She might be right about that, but none of them compare to her. Not by a longshot.

"So between the three of you, the best prank you could come up with was to create a robot that was operated by remote control, to do some damage to school property?"

"Actually we programmed it to mow something onto South Field on campus during track season. My man Oates was trying to help another buddy get revenge on one of his academic rivals that happened to run track."

"That doesn't sound so bad."

"The school mascot is a Beaver. Let's just say what we designed the robot to mow was... not in the best of taste."

"Holy shit, Pierce," she says with a laugh. "Apparently you have a bit of bad-assery in you."

"In retrospect it was one of the more tame things I've ever done."

"Really?" Her interest is piqued as she caps her emptied water bottle and looks into my eyes. "Just what else is lurking in your past?"

I avoid her gaze.

I don't want to go there.

She grabs my knee under the counter playfully, but I jump unexpectedly at her touch, suddenly tense. Before she can ask, I pull myself out of my own head resting my gaze back on her beautiful eyes.

"To answer your question, my only defense is that we were sophomores trying to settle a grudge. My brother and I pulled off something equally juvenile in high school."

"Do tell," she says, heading to the fridge for another bottle of water. She ignores my lapse in composure a moment ago. "You want another?"

"No. I'm good, thanks."

I grab my phone off the counter and cue up some more music. Van Morrison's voice floats through the kitchen, echoing off the sleek surfaces of marble and stainless steel. She retakes a seat at the kitchen island next to me.

"So, senior year we hacked into the computer system and rigged the school bell, the one that goes off between classes."

"What'd you do, engineer a never ending lunch period?"

"No. We timed it to ring every five minutes. At the maximum volume. Then we locked the powers that be out of the controls, changing passwords to something crass. The administration canceled classes for the day."

"Clever," she says. "Did you get caught?"

"Eventually."

She hesitates before she asks more. "How long ago did you lose your brother?"

I fidget with the label on my empty water bottle.

"I'm sorry," she starts. "I didn't mean to pry. I still have a hard time talking about my dad, even though it was a few years ago. I shouldn't have brought it up."

I look over at her, still fiddling with the label.

"It was a long time ago," I manage. "But it's not something I open up about, Alexis. I'm not trying to be rude but there are some things I'm not... I just can't go there."

"It's okay," she reassures me with a hand on my arm. "I get it. So what did you and your brother do with your engineered day off?"

"He and a couple buddies drove to L.A. to see a concert." I let my expression soften. "I had other plans."

"A girl?"

"Yeah. A girl."

"I bet you've had lots of girls."

"My share, I guess."

"More than one at a time?"

"Never." This much is true. It's important she knows it.

"You never took advantage of women throwing themselves at you? All the traveling you've done, all the different women you meet, you never had one in every port?"

"My philosophy about women doesn't fit that lifestyle."

"Your philosophy, huh. What would that be?"

"Well I certainly can't reveal that," I tease. "But what you described, that isn't me."

"In general terms then, would you say exclusive? Monogamous?"

"I suppose."

"Is that why you stayed with Stella?"

I give her a stern look. I've already covered this with her. She lowers her head and apologizes.

"It just seems so odd that you're here with me after her. I see no similarities between us."

"That's not a bad thing."

She just looks at me. I can tell her curiosity lingers.

"Look, I will freely admit that getting laid can be easy for me, if I choose it to be. But that's not what interests me. It's not challenging."

"Oh, so I've provided some sort of challenge for you?"

"In some ways."

"And now that the challenge is over, because you've had me, what does that mean?"

"Is that what you think? That getting you into bed was my one and only goal?"

She shrugs. "Isn't that every guy's goal? Or maybe you're just using me to get to my client."

Fuck.

That is so far from the truth.

I wanted her from the moment I saw her.

But any man would.

Something else, something unfamliar lies underneath – like an inexplicable force that pulls me to her.

I couldn't give a fuck about who her clients are or how they relate to my business or charity. It could mean the end of me and it wouldn't matter. When she's near me all I want is her. Everything else seems to fall away.

I stand up and turn to her, wrapping her legs around my waist while she's still seated on the stool. I move her hair away from her face, my eyes fixed on hers. I trace the outline of her jaw, run my thumb across her bottom lip.

"I don't have a goal with you, Alexis. I told you. There is no playbook. There is no what comes next because I don't know. I saw you chewing gum and blowing hair out of your face at that meeting, and when you stared me down…how hot you looked standing in front of that camera in those fucking heels…"

My hands run up and down her naked thighs. I pull her closer, enough that she can feel she's gotten me worked up into another erection.

I want her again, need her again. Right now.

I kiss her softly, feeling her respond with yearning.

"I wanted you from that moment. You're like a magnet pulling me. Can't you feel that?"

She bites her bottom lip. *She knows.*

"Then the way you challenged me at Mac's that night, in my office the next day. You don't give in. You don't make me wonder what your intentions are, even if they conflict with mine. That test is new to me," I say. "I get high on it. On you."

She kisses me back, her tongue seeking mine, wrapping her legs tighter around me. I break our kiss, short of breath and resting my forehead on hers.

"All I want is you. I find myself not giving enough thought to anything else. Having you once was not the goal. I can't answer what this is, I just..." I tilt my head to the side, grinding into her, lifting her up off her seat.

I carry all of her weight with ease, her legs wrapped around my waist, her arms around my neck. I lay a kiss beneath her earlobe, melting my words into her ear in a whisper.

"*You* are the goal. Not having you isn't an option. *Per favore fatemi ti porti a letto, Alexis.*"

"I have no idea what you just said," she breathes. "But if you asked me a question, the answer is yes."

"I said," I whisper, "please let me take you to bed, Alexis. *Voglio assaggiare te, baby.*"

I want to taste you, baby.

My tongue is in her ear and she moans. I love setting her off like this. I stop only long enough to carry her off to my bed, setting her down on the edge, her feet dangling towards the floor. Van Morrison has followed us.

"Arms up, baby." I tug the t-shirt off over her head, the same one I put on her less than two hours ago.

She is a remarkable sight to drink in. Her breasts are so full (easily a C-cup), and they are perfection. Her skin tightens under my touch. I can't keep my mouth off her. I'm admiring her nudity, looking for any signs of markings, but she has none.

No tattoos, no piercings. Nothing. There isn't a single imperfection or alteration on her.

Yet there has never been another body beneath my gaze (or beneath my touch) that has altered me to this degree, and I'd never have predicted such an alteration could happen this quickly.

322 • M.J. WOODS

"You are completely unmarked. Not a single tattoo?"

"Nope."

"Can I ask why?"

"I could never make a decision about what I wanted. I'd seen some friends get them, thought about it myself. But nothing ever seemed important enough to get it inked on my skin permanently."

I'm thankful she doesn't ask about my ink. It isn't something I talk about. Every woman that was under me had to comment on it or try to figure it out so she could figure *me* out.

Alexis has done none of these things, beyond tracing the lines with her delicate fingers in a moment of passion – which had completely ignited me in the moment.

Then again she's a fucking unicorn. She's done nothing ordinary or expected, nothing any of the faceless women on parade had ever done to me before.

"You don't even have pierced ears," I comment.

"I kind of knew that." She smiles.

"Afraid of pain?"

"I don't know," she says. She's suddenly bashful. "I guess maybe. But I never had a mom around to do those kinds of things with me."

Just like that, she seems lost in sad thoughts.

"I think it's a facsinating fact about you, Alexis."

Hopefully a fact only I get the privilege of knowing.

"Ms. Greene, have you ever had multiple orgasms?" I ask it as plainly as I might ask if it's going to rain today.

That gets her out of her head, a soft laugh escaping her.

"Sadly, I consider myself lucky to have one in my dreams. Or..." she hesitates, then continues her admission, "or once a week flying solo."

I toss my pants aside. *Oh, this woman.* She has no idea how amazing she is and no idea what she's been missing out on. I can tell it won't be work getting her body to do what it's designed to, given how fast I can already make her come.

She's always ready, always willing. Her body betrays and contradicts her conservative nature, more in line with her sassy mouth than her cautious personality. She's got a wild side that's never been given room to breathe, let alone unleashed to its fullest potential.

The thought inspires me, and I excuse myself to grab my cell, seeing if I have the song I'm looking for. I cue up my choice, increasing the volume before I set the phone on the nightstand.

Billy Idol's "Rebel Yell" begins to play through my bedroom.

"Oh," she says grinning. "Good choice."

I laugh, a wicked smile forming as I gently push her back, kneeling on the floor in front of her beautiful thighs, which are open to me, inviting me with trust and softness like I've never known.

I revel in her, in the opportunity to taste her and show her what her body is capable of. Billy does his thing, surrounding us with his rebellious chorus about her crying for more.

I can guarantee I'll have her doing that in a matter of minutes.

I lick my lips before I set them on a path up her inner thigh, feeling her shudder beneath me. I peel off her thong in slow motion, then slide two fingers deep inside her as she arches off the bed, moaning in acceptance. She's already soaking, and my hard on strains inside my boxers.

"So wet for me, baby," I murmur into her damp flesh. "And you won't be flying solo anymore."

I devour her greedily, initiating her first climb of many.

I look at the bedside clock.

Four a.m.

Alexis is peacefully asleep next to me. I've watched her for over an hour. She's naked underneath my sheets, her beautiful frame rising and falling in fluid motion as I time my breathing with hers.

It's relaxed me for the last hour, but I can't seem to fall asleep. I don't know if I'm keeping myself from it, afraid I'll fall into a nightmare with her beside me – but it doesn't really matter.

The fact is I'm wide-the-fuck-awake.

I lay a kiss on her naked shoulder and she moans softly as she rolls over. I get up and throw on some pajama bottoms, heading for the kitchen. I pull out my phone and text Samira. I don't want to call and startle her this early. A text will still get her attention.

*What is the name of the boutique in
downtown Stanton where you got the
dress for Ms. Greene?*

Her reply comes under two minutes later.

*The Red Door. It's on the corner of 5th and
Main. Something you need?*

*Yes, Ms. Greene needs some clothes to keep
here at the loft. You know the owner there?*

*Yes. What specifically are you looking for?
I'll need sizes.*

Do they have a website?

Yes. www.reddoorstanton.com

I'll get back with you in five minutes.

I pull up the site on my laptop and pick and choose a few styles and colors. They seem to have everything I have in mind for her – casual to professional – and their sister site is a lingerie boutique that takes up the retail space next door where they carry *Zora's Closet*.

Perfect. Only the finest is acceptable for her.

And it's not Stella's line of lingerie.

I pad to my room and find her discarded laundry I'd tossed in the closet, noting the sizes on my phone. As I walk by the bed I see her heels discarded there. I note the size of them too and toss them back where she'd left them.

Those fucking heels. I have to adjust myself in my pants as I think about how she looks in them, making a mental note to fuck her with nothing on but those shoes and as soon as possible.

I put everything in an email, then text Samira back.

*I've emailed you a few ideas for colors and
styles, and her sizes. Include footwear too.
Have everything here by nine this morning.
Open an account at both shops, in her name.*

Very good, sir. And the limit?

Ten Thousand. Each.

*I'll have everything delivered to the loft
within a few hours.*

*Please contact Mrs. Schmidt and have her
come by this morning to make breakfast and
take care of the laundry.*

I'll do that. Will there be anything else?

No, thank you. As you were.

I keep my laptop open, deciding I might as well get some work done until Alexis rises and distracts me yet again. If I return to the bedroom, I won't sleep – and I wouldn't let her rest either.

By eight in the morning, Alexis still hasn't stirred. It's been agony not waking her, but if she needs rest, I refuse to keep her from it. I shower and dress and head back to the kitchen for my laptop as Mrs. Schmidt comes in, her usual cheerful but professional demeanor in place.

"Good morning, Mr. Pierce." She gives me a nod.

"Good morning."

"Shall I start about breakfast?"

"Actually breakfast is for two this morning." I can't keep the smile off my face as I say this.

What the fuck?

This is a first here in New York, but Mrs. Schmidt has been with me a long time. Before Stella, on occasion she'd be cooking up eggs for two and I never felt much about it one way or the other. Now I felt like a grinning idiot. "The other half of the two is still sleeping."

She smiles graciously back to me. "Laundry then, sir?"

"Yes. Let me get it from the bedroom for you so you don't wake her."

"Very well."

As I return to the kitchen with the dirty laundry Byron is coming through the door with a valet cart full of the clothing for Alexis. Samira has pulled off my last minute request, as always.

"Good morning, sir." His demeanor is standard Byron. If he's thinking anything about the fact that I've just dropped thousands on clothes for

Alexis, you'd never know it. Somehow I find it easier to stop grinning with him, unlike with Mrs. Schmidt. "Where would you like this?"

I think a moment, and decide putting it in my closet is too presumptive.

"Guest room closet. Mrs. Schmidt, would you mind setting everything up in there?"

"I'll do that right away." She takes the laundry from me and sets it aside as she follows Byron and half a wardrobe into the guest suite.

It's likely Alexis is going to be downright pissed at me for doing this, but I don't care. I won't have her walking out of here in the clothes she came in with, like some one night stand. She deserves far better than that.

And despite her misgivings, she's going to get it.

I want her with me as much as possible, and if that's going to happen she needs to be able to come and go without worrying about whether she is prepared to stay here at a moment's notice.

I suppose that will mean doing something to accommodate her dog too, but I have Byron for that. He would drop anything to take care of a canine in favor of a person he had to converse with.

My thoughts are interrupted as Byron comes out from the guest suite with an emptied cart and my phone rings on the counter.

Fuck.

It's Lionel. This can't be good.

"Yeah. What's happening?" I don't hide my anger. I did not want this to interfere with my morning.

"Everything is under control for now, sir. But she's asking for you."

"Are you there with her?"

"No, sir. I'm at the office. Ivan is stationed at the hospital. Curtis just ended his twelve-hour shift watch."

"What's John's status?" I feel tension mount, my jaw clenching just from mentioning Stella's father.

"He still wants to talk to you. I've told him you're unavailable, but he's insistent. Says if he has to track you down on his own, he will."

"He's still threatening to send her in-patient if I don't come out there?"

"Yes, sir. I've just told him you've been delayed with something there."

"Good. Keep him at bay for the next few hours. I'll fly out by tomorrow if we can't find a way out."

"Yes, sir."

He disconnects. I fill Byron in and send him downstairs to the office, telling him I'll join him soon.

I dial Alanna, hoping she's come up with a solution I haven't thought of.

"Aidan. Good morning." She sounds tired.

I dispense with formalities. "Your ex-husband really is a fucking bastard of epic proportions."

"Tell me something I don't know."

"Did you come up with anything? Because as of now it's looking like I'm on a plane tomorrow to deal with the both of them."

And I don't want to leave Alexis.

"I was able to come up with one option, but you're not going to like it."

"Try me."

"I've got a friend who's a director at The Meadows. It's away from L.A. It's exclusive. Most importantly discreet. They'll assess her, put her in their program for however long they deem necessary."

"What's not to like about that?"

"You'll have to go out there. My friend Jasmine is doing this as a favor to me. Stella will need you to go with her. The cost is beyond what she can afford and she needs someone to check her in," she pauses. "And someone to be released to. I think we can agree we don't want that to be her father."

Fuck. I collapse on a stool in defeat, running a hand over my face. There is no way to avoid this. I'm going to have to go out there and clean up her mess.

My schedule next week is filled with meetings with local organizations to discuss the center and its mission. I have a meeting scheduled for Tuesday that I'll definitely have to reschedule, not knowing how long it will take to corral Stella. This meeting is a lynchpin to my approval for forging ahead with the Center, once the purchase with Myers is inked.

This is not a good first impression on the Lake County officials who will ultimately approve the plans we'd be reviewing. Conflicting schedules of the architects and engineers, the Lake County reps, and myself had required three attempts just to secure the initial meeting for Tuesday after the holiday.

328 • M.J. WOODS

A trip to Manhattan was on my plate to follow up with ideas on the program for the gala, too. This will shoot those plans all to hell and keep me from Alexis in the interim.

Goddammit.

"I'll be on a plane tomorrow. Set it up."

"I will. I'll be in touch. And Aidan?"

"Yeah." I'm thoroughly displeased and don't hide it.

"Thank you for saving her from herself."

29

Alexis

For the second time in a week I wake up in Aidan's loft, unsure what time it is. Except this time I'm in his bed, not the guest suite. And I'm wearing nothing.

I'd fallen asleep wrapped up in him, quenched once again, but now I'm alone.

I can hear music coming from the kitchen and contemplate whether I should head straight for the shower or seek him out. I decide the shower would be better with him than without, so I toss on his Yale shirt and my underwear (the only clothing I can seem to find), and head for the kitchen.

To my surprise, he is not alone. Mrs. Schmidt is in the kitchen, preparing something for breakfast that smells heavenly. Sinatra is playing by the grace of the invisible music genie that seems to float throughout every room. Aidan is dressed casually in shorts and another chambray shirt, but he looks ready to tackle a day of whatever, as though he's been up and at 'em awhile.

"Hey, there she is." He's in front of a laptop at the island and abandons the screen to greet me with an unadulterated kiss. "Good morning."

"What time is it?"

"Ten. You slept well?"

"I guess I did. I'm sorry, I didn't realize you weren't alone or I would've dressed."

"Don't worry about it," he whispers. "She's seen you in this before, remember?"

I blush as Mrs. Schmidt comes across the kitchen to us and sets two plates on the counter.

"Good morning," she says with a smile. "Please enjoy, you two. Spinach omelets with cheddar. I hope you're hungry, Ms. Greene. Mr. Pierce insisted you would be."

He shoots me a knowing look beneath a smirk that melts my insides to goo.

Mrs. Schmidt seems happy to see me, and I wonder how many strange women she's had to make breakfast for in her years working for him.

"Good morning," I manage, still a bit uncomfortable with all this. "This is wonderful. Thank you."

As much as I want to retreat to the bedroom and put on pants, the omelets and fresh fruit she's laid out are making my mouth water.

And I don't have any pants here anyway.

I take a seat next to Aidan.

"If that's all for now, I'll see myself out," she says to him.

"Just one more thing," he says, eyes still fixed on his laptop. "Is everything all set in the guest closet?"

"Yes, sir. Samira chose some lovely things. Your dry cleaning is in there as well, Ms. Greene. It was due to be delivered to your home, but I suppose since you're here…"

"Thank you, Mrs. Schmidt. I'll be glad to take care of it from here." I smile at her, then bury my face back in my plate. "This is delicious."

She smiles.

"My pleasure, dear. I will see you tomorrow, Mr. Pierce."

She exits the kitchen and as much as I like her, I'm glad to be alone with Aidan again.

"What's in the guest closet?"

"Clothes for you."

"You bought me *more* clothes?"

"Yes."

"Aidan, I have my own clothes." *Does he think I'm some kind of penniless college student that can't dress herself?* Damn him and his overreaching.

"What's your point?"

"We already covered this. I don't need you to buy me anything."

"Do you have any clothes here? Did you really want to leave in the same clothes you arrived in? As much as I loved that skirt on you, it doesn't seem appropriate for a Sunday morning."

I think a minute. I guess he has a point. But damn if I will admit it.

"That isn't the point."

"What the hell is your point then?"

"I don't know," I say, resigning. "But I'd love a cup of coffee."

"You got it, baby," he says, ruffling my hair. He tends to a fancy look-ing piece of equipment built in the wall, then pulls a mug from a cabinet. "How do you take it?"

"Black," I say. "So who is Samira?"

"One of my employees."

"Is she the blonde that was at the meeting with you when we met?"

"Yes. And I called her last night when we were on our way back here."

"I can't help but feel weirded out that someone I've never met is pick-ing out clothes for me."

"Don't, Alexis. If it makes you feel any better, I picked most of them."

The fancy coffee machine is done whirring and sputtering and he sets a mug next to me as he retakes his seat.

I rest my elbows on the counter and cradle the coffee cup in my hand, closing my eyes. The warmth feels good, offsetting the chills I get when he uses my name. He taps away at his laptop for a moment, then closes the lid and pushes it aside, turning his attention to me.

"I know you aren't used to this, having access to people that can do things for you. But I hope you can accept it. I don't do it out of charity or because you can't take care of yourself. I do it because I can."

I take a sip, set the mug down and face him.

"I know," I begin. "I don't mean to sound ungrateful. I just don't want you to think I'm going to sit back and take advantage of you. Or of what-ever conveniences you have access to. Okay?"

"Fair enough. I promise *not* to presume you're using me to get a new wardrobe."

I can't help crack a smile.

"Now can we finish eating? I feel like sustenance is required after last night."

My mind fires on all cylinders thinking about last night, more chills overtaking me. He is far and away the most attentive and skilled lover I've ever been with. My head back, eyes closed, I let the memories flood me of every move, every whispered word of longing he spoke just hours ago.

My arousal must be visible.

"Come back down, Alex," he says. "Eat. Please. I have to leave soon and I'm not finished with you."

I do as I'm told, justifying my compliance by admitting to myself I do have quite an appetite this morning.

"Where are you going?" I ask between mouthfuls. "Don't you ever take a day off?" I know it's a stupid question as soon as it comes out.

"First, down to the office. I have to head back to California by tomorrow. And no, I don't."

I can't hide my disappointment.

"I won't be gone more than a week," he says in reassurance.

I nod in acceptance, hoping my thoughts aren't obvious. He has no obligation to tell me anything. I have no claim to him, but I can't help it. No part of my being wants to be away from him, and I'm fully realizing that in this moment.

The notion is terrifying, considering the man that is causing me this state of mind. Whether or not he makes a habit of dating exclusively, nothing has been spoken to assert that we are dating at all.

Tomorrow he could decide never to bed me again and what would I have to say about it?

Absolutely nothing.

From the corner of my eye, I see him pick up the paper napkin next to him. He plays with it a moment, twisting part of it, manipulating the paper into something. As he hands it to me I realize he's crafted it into the shape of a rose.

"Seriously?" I ask of his silly gesture. "Where did you learn this? Some origami master in Japan?"

"No," he says. "I learned it in ninth grade. You don't like it?"

"It's exquisite," I say. "The first paper rose I've ever received. Thank you."

"My pleasure. Is it enough to get me laid?"

I almost choke on the last bite of my breakfast, and now he's laughing. I take a sip of coffee, get up and take his hand, heading for his room once more.

"Let's find out."

By noon we've exhausted sexual appetite, showered (together) and now I'm back in the guest suite. Aidan is downstairs taking care of whatever important work wealthy people take care of on the Sunday of a holiday weekend.

I'm perusing the guest closet, uttering profane-ridden words of astonishment.

One wall of it is now full. This isn't a few things. This *is* a new wardrobe.

Undergarments, jeans and long sleeve tops in various colors, tank tops, capris. There are ten of everything. As promised, my dry cleaning hangs there as well. There's also a couple of casual sundresses and another professional dress similar to the one he presented me with the other day but instead of a soft purple, it's a sky blue.

Just another couple grand on the fancy dress alone. A drop in the bucket!

Footwear graces a long shelf above the racks of clothing. Flip flops, sneakers, sandals and heels that would go with any of the business attire. Everything appears to be in my size, though I suppose there's a chance something won't fit. Everything is high end, each item probably costing more than I'd spend on an entire outfit.

He must have arranged this while I was sleeping, making me wonder if he slept at all.

I dress in a new bra and panties, this set in a soft pink. I grab a pair of khaki shorts, a tank top and the flip flops. It's going to be warm again today. Though the day is half over…

I'm in my underwear heading for the guest bathroom to dry my hair, clothing in hand, when I hear Aidan burst through the front door, yelling for me.

"In here," I yell back.

I contemplate tackling him when he comes through the door, until I see him. The look on his face stuns me into stillness.

"What, Aidan? What is it?"

"It's your sister," he says. He's out of breath. "Get dressed. Something's happened."

"What's going on?"

"She's been trying to reach you," he begins. "Where is your cell?" His tone is bossy and critical.

"In your room. I guess I haven't checked it in a while," I defend. "I texted Charlie about the dog, but...wait, how...? Did she call you?"

"No," he says. "Charlie. She got a hold of Charlie and he called me."

I had forgotten sharing Aidan's number with Charlie last night. I never thought he'd actually need it.

"You need to call her," he insists. "*Now.*"

"Is she okay?"

He doesn't answer at first. I change my tone to demanding.

"Aidan. What the fuck is going on?"

"She's okay, it's not her," he assures me.

"What, then? Just tell me!"

"It's her husband," he says. "He's missing."

I'm dressed in under two minutes, not even taking time to dry my hair. I race back to Aidan's room and grab my phone, scrolling through messages from Jill and Charlie.

The first two from Jill are from an hour ago, asking me to call her. The third was ten minutes ago, telling me it's an emergency. There is a voicemail too. I don't listen to it and dial her back instead.

"Lex?"

"Yes, it's me. What's going on? Is Derek missing?"

"Yes," she chokes out through sobs. "He went camping with some friends Friday in Salt River Canyon Wilderness. The other wives haven't heard from their husbands either. We're afraid they're lost."

I'm relieved a bit, hoping this is just a lack of communication of some sort. Derek is an experienced outdoor guy. Rugged, tough, knowledgeable about the dangers of being out in the Arizona wilderness.

"Do you think they just lost signal or something?"

"No, they don't have a very good signal out there to start with. But they don't stay out of contact more than twenty-four hours at a time. If we don't hear from them, or one of us can't reach at least *one* of them…"

"Okay, okay," my brain is flailing, trying to figure out what to do. "Have you notified anyone? Were they at a campground?"

"No. Not their thing. They always go north to the mountains or to the desert. This was their first time in Tonto Forest. The wilderness has no maintained trails, Lex. It can be dangerous. I mean they know what they're doing, but anything could have happened."

I've never heard my sister this upset. She's usually the more composed of the two of us, especially in situations like this. Her concern must be warranted.

"They were supposed to be back within cell range by last night at the latest. It's been another twelve hours since then. This has never happened. My friend Jen is calling her brother, he used to be with the Ranger District here. But he says they won't send out a team until they are certain someone is in distress. It's too dangerous for their teams, too expensive. I'm scared, Lex. Something doesn't feel right, and I can't help him."

"There must be something they can do," I insist. "Aren't there tons of campers out there on a holiday weekend? Don't they have contingencies for this?"

"To a degree, but this area is at your own risk. A lot of places are. And because they didn't check in yesterday, we don't know where to look."

I sigh. I have no idea what to offer or how to help.

"Lex, can you come here? I don't know what to do. I can't leave the kids. My only reliable sitter is on vacation with her family. Please. I know it's a lot to ask."

When my father died she was here the same day, not batting an eye at being here with me for however briefly she could be.

Even though it wasn't her father. Even though she had a life, the same life she retreated to after Ben died. Jill wasn't the consoling type, yet she still made sure to be there for me the best way she knew how, the instant I needed someone.

It was true we weren't that close, but she must not know where else to turn if she's calling me. Our mother would be of no use in a situation like this, even if we knew where to find her.

"It's okay. I'm coming. Let me hang up and look into flights."

She lets out an audible sigh of relief. "Oh, Lex. Thank you. I can help with the expense to get out here," she says. "I have to go. Jen's calling in. I'll call you right back."

She disconnects as Aidan paces in, looking at me in anticipation of gathering more information. I feel shattered just trying to explain it, but manage to relay Jill's distress and the possible gravity of the situation.

"That area is not a place for the inexperienced," he says.

Of course he knows where my brother-in-law is likely lost. Whether it's because he lived nearby in California so long, or because he's just too fucking smart, I don't know. But I'm thankful I don't have to explain when I'm not a good source of information anyway.

"Jill's husband is very capable. But if it isn't normal for he and his friends to be out of contact this long…" I trail off. "My sister doesn't panic about anything. It isn't in her DNA."

"Well, that's a good thing."

"Yeah, except that right now, she's more than panicked. She's frantic. She wants me on a plane as soon as possible."

"And?" he asks, as though her request is not unreasonable in the slightest.

"And? And I'd have to book a flight. Get Huck to the kennel. I would definitely need to reschedule Myers and I can't do that. What about my office?" Now I'm as frantic as Jill as I go on, my mind racing. "Yet what the fuck am I going to do from here? I can't help her from two thousand miles away. I have no choice but to let someone down in this scenario. I hate this feeling."

He takes a step closer, rests his hands on my shoulders and looks down at me, centering me with his gaze.

"Breathe. And take a page from your sister's book. We don't have time for you to overanalyze and lose your shit. What airport do you need to get into? Phoenix?"

I look at him, stunned. Jill's predicament, his generosity, the events of the last few days…

"Don't play this game right now, Alexis. This is an emergency. If you need to get somewhere, I will make sure you get there."

"Phoenix," I repeat, backing up to sit on the bed. My head is spinning.

"I'll take care of it," he says. And he leaves the room as fast as he came in.

The next time I can be alone with my thoughts, it's Sunday evening and I'm sitting in Aidan's company plane, waiting to be cleared for take-off to Phoenix.

I have no idea how many phone calls had to be made or what Aidan had to do to get me here, but he got me here. Within six hours of my conversation with my sister, he had Byron drive me home to pack, let me make my necessary arrangements and collect anything I would need. He arranged for this fancy-ass plane to take me to Arizona and personally delivered me to the airport.

We said our goodbyes standing at the bottom of the steps on the tarmac. I was able to hold back any tears, but barely.

"I'm sorry I can't go with you."

It wasn't the first time he had apologized.

"Aidan, really. You've done too much already. It's fine."

"You won't have to drive to your sister's from the airport. I've arranged for a car for you. You'll have someone at your disposal for however long you need."

"Um….what?"

"Just think of it as your own personal Byron," he teases, nodding in the direction of the Lincoln twenty feet away.

"But at least I *know* Byron," I complain.

Er…kind of.

"I don't need some stranger to drive me around," I continue. "I have no idea what's going to happen when I get there. It isn't fair for your employees to be assigned to me when they could be doing something important. And it isn't especially noble of you to do it *without* my consent."

"I'm sorry, Alexis. I'm not budging on this. Ivan will pick you up in Phoenix and take you anywhere you want to go. He's a trusted member of my team and his training ensures your safety. And your sister's."

"I'm not in any danger, Aidan. Neither is she. I'm not the one lost in the middle of fucking nowhere. That would be my brother-in-law, remember?"

"Yes, I remember. And if Ivan does nothing more than drive you around the desert, he will have an easy few days and get to enjoy looking at you as much as I have the last twenty-four hours. Either way, he won't be bored."

I quit complaining at that point, knowing I wouldn't win. At least I won't have to drive around an unfamiliar city. I have no idea what the outcome of Derek's disappearance will be and if Jill is preoccupied, having a driver could prove to be more of a necessity than a convenience.

Aidan kissed me goodbye then, tenderly at first, then greedy, as though he didn't want to let me go.

"With any luck I'll be back in a few days," I muster.

"I'll be in California. I booked a commercial flight for tomorrow."

He says it conclusively, and I'm not sure if he's upset by this or unfazed that we will be passing like ships in the night. I have a pit in my stomach at the thought, realizing I don't know when I will see him again.

"You'll have me whenever you need me. Okay? I'm only a text or call away."

I nod in agreement, but can't face him. I don't want to give away that this departure is making me ache at my core.

"Alexis, please don't. It's killing me that I can't go with you."

His words relieved me enough in the moment to do what I had to do. I kissed him one last time, promised to text him when I arrived in Phoenix, and climbed the steps out of the reach of his gaze. I felt hollow as I watched Byron drive him away.

I'm buckled in my seat now, admiring the plush surroundings and trying to suppress my emotions.

The plane carries ten, but I'm the only passenger. The seats are supple leather. There's enough room for a team of people to move around if it was required. Two crew members are in the cabin with me, but they are in the front of the plane doing their prep, out of earshot and thankfully not paying any attention to me.

It's the first time I've ever traveled in such luxury. I freely admit to my-self this sure as hell beats cramming into a tight cabin with over a hundred sneezing strangers.

The female attendant brought my laptop on board and I grab it off the table in front of me, deciding on distraction. I won't have wi-fi for much longer and I'd promised Charlie an email with a checklist of responsi-bilities for the house and office for the next few days. He agreed to bring Huck home for me tonight and stay at the house with him for as long as I need. I'd left a couple hundred bucks on the kitchen counter for whatever incidentals he might need.

At Aidan's insistence that it could wait, I've pushed my meeting with Myers back to Thursday to go over the sale to Pierce Philanthropy Group in the hopes I'll be back by then. I've had a phone conversation with Gloria about what I know to this point, which is still not much.

Derek and his friends are still missing and within hours a team will be sent out to search. I'm hoping to arrive at my sister's and be with her kids so she can be with the other wives at the command post where the search will begin. I text Jill to let her know that I already have a ride from the airport but leave it at that.

I say a prayer when we take off that in a few days I'll be back home where I belong and so will Jill's husband.

Ivan has even less personality than Byron. He's spoken two words to me since we met at the airport. To add to the awkwardness, my time of the month arrived before we landed. I was completely unprepared and the first stop I require him to make is at the closest drug store.

On the bright side, I realize I have at least *seen* the guy before because he was one of Aidan's bodyguards at the bar meeting.

Before he completely rocked our world.

I shut my inner sex goddess up and send her on sabbatical. She obliges since Aidan is far, far away and I'm as bloated as roadkill on the side of a desert highway.

By the time we're pulling into my sister's development in Mesa, it's seven in the evening Arizona time, sunlight cascading between shadows. Homes are on top of each other here, but it's a safe area and off the main highway. Jill pays far less in property taxes than I do in New York for about the same square footage and (lucky her) she never has to shovel snow.

The Cadillac SUV pulls up to the one-story stucco she shares with Derek and their two daughters, Janie and June. I've only been here once when Janie was born five years ago.

I ask Ivan to wait in the car. He's dressed down in jeans and a black t-shirt, but he's still intimidating to look at. Broad shoulders, military haircut, biceps bigger than my head. I don't want the kids to be frightened by someone who might resemble bad guys from their nightmares.

The minute I open my door I hear squeals of delight, the girls' excitement for my arrival spilling out of the house.

"Auntie Lex! Auntie Lex!" June, who is only three, emerges from the open garage door sporting a chocolate stained sundress and matching ring around her mouth. Just the sight of her makes me emotional. She is adorable, resembling photos of her mother at that age.

I smile and refrain from scooping her up, respectful of the fact that we've never officially met. Most of our interaction has been on Skype or by phone in her short little life.

"Hi June Bug! Are you happy to see me?"

"Who's that?" she asks, pointing behind me. I turn to see Ivan unloading my bag and laptop. I do my best to reassure her that the guy with me is not dangerous.

"That's Ivan," I say. "He drove me here from the airport so we can have a slumber party. Isn't that cool?"

She shrinks back a bit, then calls out for her big sister.

"Janie! Come see Auntie Lex! She brought a boy!"

Oh, shit. That'll get Jill's attention for sure. Can't this goon follow directions?

It's then I notice he's holding a phone in his hand.

"Ma'am, it's for you," he says handing it to me.

Another guy with the ma'am, for hell's sake.

I take the phone as Jill and Janie appear in the open front door of the house. Ivan disappears into the driver's seat before they can see him. I wave to my sister and hold up a finger, telling them I'll be just a second.

"Hello?"

"You didn't text me." Aidan's voice comes through the phone smooth as ever, riling me, relieving me, making me want to lose it to tears. I hear him sip something.

"I'm sorry. I forgot. Unexpected detour," I say.

"You made it okay? Ivan said you asked to stop at a drug store."

"Yes, Mr. Interrogator. I needed tampons and Advil. That okay by you?"

He sputters, and I release a half laugh.

"What? Not the answer you expected?"

"No," he says. I can hear his smile through the phone. "I suppose that would be a necessity at some point."

"Yes, well, thank you for sending Ivan. It was nice not to have to navigate to get here. We just pulled in, though. I'm going to say hello to everyone and get Jill on her way."

"Yeah, sure. I should let you go. Let me know how the search goes."

"I promise," I say.

"Alexis?"

"Yeah," I say, preoccupied with June who is tugging on my shorts wanting me to come in the house.

"Nothing," he says.

"I'm sorry Aidan, I'm just distracted. Was there something else?"

"No, I…"

I can tell he wants to say something. I just don't know what. It's ten o'clock there and I imagine he must be out-and-out exhausted after our late night and all the craziness that unfolded today. I encourage him to complete his thought.

"Please say what you were going to say."

"I haven't stopped thinking about you since you got on that plane."

Emotion floods me. I know this is as close as I'll get to him saying he misses me.

And this after less than a day apart.

I'm trying like hell not to cry.

"Thank you," I muster. "Likewise."

"Call me as soon as you know something."

"I will. Good night, Aidan. Get some sleep."

"Yeah. Solid plan, Greene, as ever."

I smile in response, unable to talk for fear of my voice cracking. He utters three more words before disconnecting.

"Good night, baby."

I sent Ivan away without having to introduce him to my sister. I've got his cell number programmed into my phone for whenever I need him.

After an hour of countless games of Go Fish, a very hectic bath time, and reciting two princess stories, the kids are finally tucked into their beds. My luggage has found a home in the guest room and I've downed two ibuprofen and a bottle of water.

I'm polishing off a peanut butter and jelly sandwich at the kitchen table while Jill gives instructions about the kids. What to do if they wake up, where emergency numbers are, what they will and won't eat.

"I think I got it," I say. "Are you all right?"

We haven't even spoken Derek's name since I got here. I can sense the kids don't have any idea that something is amiss. They think I just came for a spontaneous visit and Daddy's away camping.

"Yeah. I'm okay. Steph is picking me up in ten minutes. That's Joe's wife," she explains. "Did I ever tell you about Joe and Steph? They're great…"

I interrupt her try at avoidance.

"It's okay to lose your shit now," I tell her. "The big sister is allowed to do that sometimes, you know. Especially in these circumstances." She's silent. "You don't have to hold it together for me, Jill. I'm not one of your girls."

She just looks at me a minute, almost through me. She is beyond tired, beyond frazzled. Her curly brown hair is tied back in a ponytail, her clothes disheveled from a long day of being mommy and adding worried wife to her job description. As she sucks in a breath, I can tell I've given her leave to do just as I've prescribed. She starts sobbing so much that she can't stop.

I go to her, my arms around her, letting her come undone. I can't imagine the weight on her shoulders at this moment. Beyond mere empathy, I'm glad.

Glad that she isn't here alone.

Glad that I can help.

Glad that whatever I went through with Ben might help me to help her.

"Oh Lex," she chokes out. "It's so fucking stupid why I'm crying."

"Your husband is M-I-A in the freaking wilderness, Jill. It's not stupid."

"No, it's not that. We had a fight before he left. I'm such a jerk."

I pull back and rest my hands on her shoulders. We are essentially the same height and I'm looking her square in her auburn eyes.

"A fight? So what, you mean before he left you were acting like a typical married couple?"

"I gave him hell for wanting to go this weekend. It's one of the few holidays my catering isn't in demand and I wanted us to do something as a family."

"You wanted to spend time with your husband and children. Last I checked, that's not a crime," I insist.

"I told him not to go, Lex. I threatened him, acted out. I behaved like a spoiled child who wasn't getting her way."

I grab a tissue and wipe her tears, then hand her another so she can blow her nose.

"You didn't do anything wrong, Jill. You couldn't have known this would happen. Couples fight. Couples make up. He's going to be okay. They will find him, and everything will be okay."

I cringe at the words I'm speaking, knowing how much I once hated hearing them. But that was different. There was nothing that could have been done for Ben at the time.

Derek had to be found. I could not watch my sister go through what I'd been through, especially with two daughters to care for.

Two daughters that adored their daddy.

"I didn't even say goodbye, Lex. Not a kiss, nothing. I just let him go." She's talking through tears, trying to get it out. "I called him a selfish asshole and I let him go."

"He'll be back, Jill," I say, comforting her as I embrace her again. "He's a tough bastard and he'll be back."

While we wait for her friend, I insist that my sister get a quick shower and try to pull herself together, reminding her to pack a bag of extra clothes for Derek and herself.

She emerges dressed in jeans, hiking boots, and a Mirror Lake sweatshirt, carrying a small duffel of clothes as her friend pulls into the driveway.

"Here," I say, handing her a brown baggie. "I packed you a sandwich and some chips. And two mini bottles of whiskey I stole from the plane."

"Thanks, Lex." She seems better. Determined, even. She hugs me and grabs for her purse. "What'd you do, steal them from the beverage cart while the flight attendant wasn't looking? Have you turned into a bad ass on me?"

"Not exactly," I say. Now is not the time to go into just what kind of plane got me here. I haven't even had a chance to disclose Aidan's existence yet and there's no time now.

"Do you have your phone?" I ask. "Oh, and a charger?"

"Yes, on the kitchen counter. Can you grab them?"

I run to the kitchen to retrieve Jill's phone and it startles me, ringing in my hand. The display reads Gila County Sheriff's Office. I race back to Jill, swiping the green button to answer the call before voicemail picks up. I hand her the phone and mouth 'sheriff'.

She answers, listening closely. She throws a hand over her mouth.

"Okay," she finally replies. "Yes, yes, we're on our way." She disconnects and I stand there waiting for her to speak for what seems like a full minute.

"Jill, what? They found them?"

She nods frantically.

"And?"

"I don't know. They aren't sure. They've been located. Someone stumbled on them and radioed it in, and my friend Jen's brother picked up on the call. There are injuries is all they'd say."

"Oh, Jill. Okay. Okay. But they found them. This is good news. You have to stay positive."

She nods in agreement, unable to speak.

"Go," I say. "You'll have to fill Steph in on the way."

She hugs me tight.

"Thank you, Lex. I love you."

"Love you, too. Now get going."

She promises to text me soon and runs out the door.

I shower and crawl into the guest bed in pajamas hoping to get some sleep, but I'm wide awake. It's been two hours since Jill left. I still haven't heard from her. I sent her a message half an hour ago to let her know I was going to get some sleep but to call me anyway, if there was news. I'm wondering if she's out of cell range.

It's one a.m. in New York. Too late to call Aidan. I'm afraid even a text will wake him. He must need rest too, if he's nearly as exhausted as I am.

It's then I remember I have his *Open Last* file still on my phone. I grab my earbuds and set the recording to play on repeat. I fall asleep at last, his voice in my ears, wishing he was lying next to me instead of thousands of miles away.

I wake with a start at my phone ringing, the headphones still implanted in my ears. With closed eyes, I feel around for the phone. I squint to look at the display and hit speaker when I see it's Jill.

"Lex? Did I wake you up?"

"No," I say in a fog. "It's fine. What time is it?"

"It's almost two a.m."

Less than two hours of sleep. Damn.

"Is Derek with you?"

"Not yet. They've been found, they should be arriving back here at the ranger station shortly. None of the injuries were serious enough for an evacuation, but we're headed to the hospital from here."

"Oh shit. Is he all right?"

"I don't know for sure. They think he may have broken a leg. Minor injuries beyond that. The other guys were banged up too, but we are hopeful everyone will be okay. They got lost and had a hard time making their way back. Derek fell along the way – I didn't get much more."

"I'm so glad they're safe, Jill. Take your time getting back. I'll be fine with the girls."

"I'm over two hours away, so by the time we get the guys back here and to the hospital to get checked out, I'm not sure what time I'll get back."

"It's fine. Just do what you need to do," I reassure her. "The girls and I will call you after breakfast to check in."

"Thanks, Lex. I don't know what I'd do without you."

30

Aidan

I haven't heard from her all night. It's nine in the morning on Memorial Day, and I'm packing to board a commercial flight to get to California and get Stella out of the hospital. Not my preferred method of flying, but I'd let Alexis leave in a hurry with the company plane and booked a first class ticket for myself. It had allowed me enough time to prepare for my trip last night – a trip that I hoped would be short.

I'd moved all my meetings for the Center planning back one week. Except for one engineer who had reminded me how inconvenienced she'd been to set up the first meeting, I'd done so without too much objection. I explained I'd had an emergency back in California and had only been met with understanding from everyone else.

I barely slept, subconsciously waiting for Alexis to call, wondering what was happening with her sister and lost brother-in-law. I'd finally passed out for a few hours of rest after midnight.

Ivan updated me on her whereabouts after I'd spoken with her by phone when she got to Arizona. She hadn't left her sister's house since she arrived. Whatever was happening I didn't want her facing it alone, but I couldn't get there.

I resent Stella and her constant drama all the more for keeping me from where I want to be, even if she doesn't realize it.

If she had known anything about Alexis or how badly I fucking miss her right now, I have no doubt she (and her asshole father) would go to far greater lengths to keep us apart, just to spite me.

I'm zipping my luggage when I hear the chime of my phone in the bedroom. It's a text from Alexis, letting me know they've found her brother-in-law. He's injured but otherwise intact at a local hospital. It's only six in the morning out there.

My body responds with uncontrolled relief, feeling a thousand-pound weight lift.

Her brother-in-law has been found alive.

Everything will be fine.

I text her back.

> *I'm relieved to hear that.*
> *I'll be out of touch while I head to California.*
> *I'll call you later about*

I type *'about coming home'* but rephrase it before I hit send.

> *about getting you back to New York.*

My feelings for her are strong, but I can't exactly define them either. I decide it better to stick to terms that won't be misleading.

She responds with an okay and a smiley face emoji. I laugh despite myself, my mood suddenly lifted. I turn my attention to my own hurdles, determined to put Stella and her bullshit behind me so I can move on here.

Here.

Where I'm starting to feel more at peace than I ever have, more at home than I've ever been.

"I don't care how pissed he is. Make him wait another ten minutes."

Lionel gives me a nod and heads back to the waiting room of my L.A. office where John Ireland is apparently fit to be tied. It's three o'clock in the afternoon on a Monday holiday and I'm sure he wants to be off to the nearest yacht party with as much hard liquor, tits, and ass as he can handle at his age.

I'm toweling myself off after a run on the treadmill. The fast five miles was just what I needed after the flight to bring my energy up and clear my head.

I could be a real asshole and make him wait longer while I grab something to eat – but decide I'll be better received if I only let him simmer in his own pissed off world while I shower and dress.

I put on a crisp white button down and black pants that Lionel has left out for me, leaving the tie and suit jacket on the hanger. I don't need a power suit with Ireland. It won't make a bit of difference with him how I dress. It's all in how I play his game.

I buzz the front office for Lionel.

"Yes, sir."

"Now."

"Very good." He disconnects.

I stand in front of my desk, glancing around the room a moment while Ireland is allowed in. The surroundings are so different from my small New York hub, which has apparently grown on me. This place already feels foreign.

The sleek chrome and black leather chairs scattered about, the clear glass partitions and stark white walls throughout the space. Even the artwork I'd commissioned just for this office five years ago doesn't feel like me anymore.

I've been away under two months but none of this is familiar. In this moment, I know my decision to go to New York was the right one.

Fuck what John Ireland wants.

I'm getting out of here as soon as possible and going back to where I belong.

I hold my straightened posture as the two-hundred-fifty pound lone threat to my preferred path comes through my door. He's shorter than me by a few inches, but still commands a room. He looks his usual self – half Italian mob, half miserable old Irish prick.

He's dressed in a black tailored suit with a white shirt and maroon tie. The expression of his wide face holds no approachability whatsoever, which has been the case the entire twenty plus years I've known him. His puffed cheeks are tanned from the California sun yet red from high blood pressure.

"John," I say, trying not to grit my teeth. "Have a seat. Can I offer you something to drink?"

"No. This won't take long."

Damn right.

I take my chair behind my desk and sit back in relaxed posture. "Good. I've got to be getting back anyway. What can I do for you?"

He's leans back in his chair, his thin lips in a tight hold until he releases them to speak. "You can take care of your obligations, Pierce. That's what."

"I have done everything we agreed, John."

"So allowing my daughter to trash my good name, flush her earnings down the toilet while she dabbles in coke was part of that agreement?" He gives me a sarcastic, bastardly smile. "I wasn't aware of that."

"Our arrangement never specified that I'd be Stella's babysitter for life. You wanted me to help her professionally, and I did that. It's never been a secret that I have no romantic interest in your daughter. We went our separate ways, and she lives a lifestyle far beyond her means thanks to me. You should be grateful."

"Her choices directly affect the both of us, Pierce. Now I can handle this, if you'd like to be hands off. But she'll be placed where I want her, and you won't have any say about it."

"I couldn't have known she would decide to become the stereotypical L.A. party girl the minute I left town." He considers me, still raging mad. I go on before he can interrupt. "I've got a handle on this, John. Her business hasn't been affected by any significant measure. And I've got people taking care of her, making sure her mistakes will be kept private."

At least the ones she's made so far.

"I don't care if you've got a fucking army at your disposal, Pierce. *You* are the only one she listens to. You will need to remain here in California, if she has any hope."

"Not going to happen."

"Then I'll be forced to commit her under the guise of a mental illness. I'm not having her ruin everything I've worked for."

Ironic how her childish behavior often mirrored her father's and even more so that this fact would escape his comprehension for the rest of his miserable days.

"That won't be necessary. I'm taking care of it."

"How do you intend to do that from New York?"

"I'm collecting her this afternoon. She'll be going to a treatment program for as long as necessary."

"What happens when she gets out?"

"That will be up to her."

Or dependent on her behavior, anyway.

He says nothing, obviously trying to figure out if this is a solution or a temporary fix that will cause him more problems down the line. I can see him resign as he takes a breath and responds.

"You better make good on your word. You'd never have gotten this far in Mirror Lake without me. And if you don't take care of Stella, I'll pull my funding." He leans forward over his round belly, regarding me with obvious loathing. "Not to mention certain information that might find its way to the light of day in the process. I doubt that would be very good for you, Pierce."

"Are you threatening me?" Let the fucker say it out loud. It would be all I needed to hear.

"I'm telling you that you better not fail my daughter. Without my backing, your frivolous charity for the damned will be compromised. Are you willing to risk that?"

I don't answer. I already know I don't need one red cent from him, but it's better I keep that to myself.

For now.

"You going to risk having to abandon that hellhole you crawled out of? That senseless cause you're so eager to fund to uplift the dregs of society?" He scoffs as he gets up to leave, then turns back to me. "It'd probably be the smart thing to do, kid. No point in dredging up the past. I can tell you from experience."

"I'm not interested in your life experience, John. I'm not looking to become you. That you can be certain of."

Apparently that little dig hit home. He leans forward on my desk, into my space. I can smell his aftershave. His breath reeks of liquor. "You don't have the sac to be me, Pierce."

I don't turn away from his smug stare. It's all I can do not to choke him. My fists are clenched tight, hidden from his view, but I'm sure he can hear the sound of my rapid pulse. My own ears are pounding, my heart beating out a rhythm to accompany my rage.

"Stick to your pathetic endeavor as a do-gooder, Pierce. You're too soft for this game. You always were."

I'm seething inside, but somehow keep my composure. I want to fucking kill him.

"Let's just say if you want my help and not my interference..." he trails off as he steps away from my desk as heads to the door. "The choice is yours, Pierce."

"Stella will be taken care of."

"You've got that right, Pierce. One way or the other, she will be."

"Don't concern yourself with it another moment, John." Sarcasm drips from my words, a crooked grin coming over me. He turns back to meet the glare of my eyes that betrays my false smile. "You should know this about me by now. Whatever it is I set my mind to, I do *not* fail."

The door closes behind him, and I jump up from my seat. I'm pacing the room, irate and frustrated.

He'd sooner commit his own daughter for no good reason than get her any help, sooner damn me in the process than actually give a shit about his own flesh and blood.

He's no better than the bastard of a father I was born to. John Ireland might not be physically abusive, but his ruthlessness was simply a different kind of evil. I feel sick at the thought, knowing I shouldn't have let myself get involved in his world in the first place.

I knew better.

And now I have Alexis to consider too. If he found out about her, there was a chance she wouldn't be safe.

The glass partition between my office and the small room that houses my gym equipment reveals my reflection. I see a fleeting glimpse of my father, my face in the same twisted expression he'd have when he was about to inflict his fury on me. Furrowed brows, cold eyes, arms held tensely away from my body, ready to brawl with whatever next got in my way.

I pick up a heavy, faceless statue off my desk and hurl it through the glass. The shattering of the wall stuns me, echoing loud enough to send Lionel running in.

"Sir?" He looks past me to the broken glass. There are small shards everywhere.

I rifle hands through my hair, then force them to my sides, clenching and unclenching my fists. "It's fine, Lionel. Get maintenance up here after I leave."

"Yes, sir. Should we move the meeting back?"

"No. Just redirect everyone to the conference room. I'll be there in ten minutes."

He leaves without a word as my promise to Ireland reverberates through my head.

I intend to follow through.

What I've set my mind to is getting the Irelands out of my life permanently. At this, I refuse to fail.

Stella's attending physician at the hospital is a slight Indian woman. She's probably not much older than I am, but thankfully she seems to know her profession as well as I know my own. She left to confirm with Stella that she agreed to be released to me and comes back into the shoebox size consultation room with a reserved smile.

"Mr. Pierce, Miss Ireland has agreed to be released to your care. You'll be taking her to The Meadows, you said?"

"That's correct." After a few phone calls to their facility and speaking with the woman her mother Alanna put me in contact with, Stella's place had been reserved – after a hefty deposit, of course, but at least they would be ready for her today.

"I am recommending four weeks in their program. I'll get in touch with the doctor on staff there. By the time you arrive there, her plan should be in place."

"Is four weeks enough time for her recovery?"

"I believe so. She doesn't present with long-term abuse, and their program is very good as I'm sure you know."

"That's my understanding, yes." It had better be, for the cost. Sure I could afford it, but only if it was going to make Stella see the error of her ways and get her the help she needed to be on her own.

Because I am fucking done.

"She will need a support system in place when she gets out, Mr. Pierce. Do you plan to be that support? Does she have any family?"

"She does have family. She will be taken care of, Doctor."

"She tells me you recently left the area. Do you plan to come back?"

"With all due respect, Doctor, I don't think that's any of your business." She sees I'm not going to divulge anymore and she isn't happy about it. If she only knew I was the better option, perhaps she'd shut the fuck up. But I'm not willing to get into it with her. "Is Stella free to go?"

She regards me with skepticism, but finally resigns. "She is. Would you like to use the exit at the back of the building? I understand there's some press outside."

"Not necessary, thank you."

"Please reach out to me if you have questions. I'll be in contact with The Meadows to check on her progress." Obviously this woman doesn't trust me. Who knows what bullshit Stella has been feeding the staff here for the last few days or what facts she's been leaving out. "Stella is in a precarious situation, Mr. Pierce. I don't want to see my patient's health in jeopardy."

"Trust me," I say. "Her health is my top priority."

It's the truth.

Once I know Stella is healthy, I can get her on her own two feet and out of the way of whatever I might have with Alexis.

I must say it convincingly enough because the good doctor leads me out of the room to where her patient is waiting.

Curtis is stationed outside Stella's room. I nod to him and follow the doctor in.

Stella is waiting impatiently, tapping the toe of her high heel as she leans up against the hospital gurney. She's primping herself, looking into a compact mirror. She's in one of her customary tight-fitting dresses, this one a melon color. She looks more like a visitor than a patient about to be discharged. I can't help but wonder how the doctor doesn't see her vain ways as an indication that her problems lie much deeper than an experiment with partying.

This woman is clearly an actress thriving on attention.

"Aidan!" She smacks her compact closed, tossing it into her large designer bag. She throws herself at me. I let her hug me and pat her back with one hand, then step back. I have no desire to play her games right now, but I can't let the doctor think I'm uncaring.

"Stella. You look well." She does look rested and, as always, she doesn't have a hair out of place.

"Oh," she shies away in a feign of humility. "You flatter me. I'm so ready to get *out* of this place. Can I go?" She bats her eyelashes the doctor's way.

"You are being released to Mr. Pierce, but you will be taken to a treatment facility. One that aids people with addiction."

Stella forms an immediate pout, letting her dark hair fall around her shoulders as she slumps her posture. "Treatment facility? Aidan, what is she talking about? I don't have any addiction."

"You didn't tell her?" I shoot a scolding look at the doctor.

Jesus Christ. This oughta be great.

I turn my attention to Stella. "It's just temporary. They will help you understand and assess your drug use. I'm sure you'll be out of there in no time. And the amenities at this place are amazing. Think of it as a vacation."

Now the doctor is shooting *me* a disapproving look, but she doesn't know Stella like I do. Telling her this will be work will only dissuade her.

"Mr. Pierce, this is not going to be a vacation." She regards Stella with concern. "You need to get a handle on this, Miss Ireland. Before it ruins your health long-term. Do you agree to go into treatment voluntarily?"

Shit. I hold my breath, waiting for her to flip out.

I'm surprised when she nods in agreement, becoming demure. "I'll go. But only if Aidan takes me there."

I release my held breath. "That's what I'm here for. And you'll be released to me, as soon as you've completed the necessary evaluation and treatment."

"Okay," she says, brightening. "As long as I can get out of this place, I'm happy. It's terrible here, Aidan. So many sick people," she grimaces, "and half the time my phone doesn't even work in here."

I give the doctor a look, hoping she's absorbing this glimpse at the real Stella. Superficial. Arrogant. Completely selfish. The doctor disregards us though, excusing herself to answer a page coming over the hospital intercom.

It's hard to believe I was able to ignore Stella's personality to the degree I once did. She was a big part of my life for two years, and now I can't stand to be in the same room with her. I can only defend my blindness with my pity for the situation she faced, having John Ireland and a parade of Hollywood starlets that passed through their house as her only role models growing up.

The girl never really had a chance with him as a father, and I was sympathetic to it.

Stella grabs up her bag and sashays out of the room ahead of me. Curtis follows behind us. Our elevator ride down allows me to give her some direction. "There are reporters outside," I tell her. Now out of the earshot of the doctor I switch to my commanding tone, which I know she responds best to. "You will say nothing. Curtis will get them off our backs and drive us to The Meadows. Do you understand?"

She stills, looking up at me with her brown eyes open wide. "You mean we're going there now?"

"Yes."

"I thought I could at least go home for some clothes," she whines. "Maybe you could take me out tonight. Can't I just go there tomorrow?" Her tone is suggestive as she wags her eyelashes at me.

"No. I've already taken care of your things. They'll be waiting there. Your bed is only available if I get you there today. Then I'm going back to New York."

She's crestfallen. "Aidan, please don't go. I want you nearby. What if I need you? Who's going to run the business while I'm gone? I'm behind on work already. There's things I need to..."

I cut her off. "You have a great team in place, Stella. Felicia will keep me updated about how things are going until you get out."

"*Felicia* just wants her hooks in you," she spits out at me.

"Jesus, Stella. Enough with the jealousy. Felicia is a business associate. One that we both agreed to hire because she's not only capable, but she has a high tolerance level for your bullshit. If she finds out about this recent escapade of yours, I'm not sure you'll be so lucky as to keep her."

She considers my words. She knows this is true.

We'd been through a rotation of staff in the two years that the boutiques and lingerie line had gotten off the ground. At the storefront level, Stella was hands off. But in the boardroom she always found a reason to get rid of any women that came through. One wasn't knowledgeable enough about the industry. One was too good looking. One wasn't good looking enough.

One had held my gaze a little bit too long at a meeting and, unbeknownst to me, Stella had fired her immediately after.

Somehow Felicia Grimes knew how to carry herself, never coming across as a threat but holding her ground with all things business. She was able to size Stella up at our very first meeting, and, after reviewing Felicia's background and her impressive resumé, I'd insisted that she oversee all operations with a set contract term so Stella couldn't fire her on a whim.

It had worked. Stella's businesses were thriving.

Felicia was the only other person that could put Stella in her place as quickly as I could. She knew how to manipulate Stella into doing what was best for herself – or the business – without Stella even realizing it. Yet I doubted she'd risk her reputation in the fashion industry with an irresponsible and unpredictable coke-head for a boss.

"Stella, this is the arrangement. Take it or leave it. If you don't want to go through this program, I can't make you. But I won't stand here and watch you destroy yourself. You'll be on your own with your father making decisions for you."

She sighs, finally pushing away her childish façade for her best attempt at being an adult. Apparently the thought of her father running her life scares her enough. "I'll go. I said I would. But why can't you stay? I want you to be here when I get out."

"New York is my home now. That isn't going to change. I'll come back for your release, but that's it."

Clearly she was hoping my return here was more permanent. I wait to see what she'll do, impatient with her and this whole fucking mess.

"I don't understand why you feel the need to move across the country. To some small town life that holds absolutely *nothing* interesting. Can't you run your charity from here?"

"No." I leave my one word answer to hang in the air as the elevator reaches the ground floor.

"What's so important back there?"

I bite my tongue. She has no idea about my past and she cannot know about Alexis. Especially not now.

"Whether I stayed here or not, Stella, you know we're done. I will support you, but it's going to be from a distance. You need to get used to that. If you can't, there will be nothing but problems." I level her with my stare. "For both of us."

A look of confusion on her face is quickly replaced with presumed realization. "Daddy is threatening you, isn't he? Did he make you abandon me?"

"I will not discuss your father. You need to know that my decisions are my own. Is that understood?" My tone is almost threatening. She needs to know who's calling the shots, that I refuse to answer to her father.

Finally, she nods with reluctant acceptance.

"Good." We leave the elevator car and start for the exit. "Let's go. And keep quiet."

We step out through the automatic doors, into the light from the snaps of camera bulbs and shouts from the few reporters gathered. I shield her, my arm at her back, and put her into the sleek SUV ahead of me as Curtis shuts us in.

She tries to come nearer to me, but I move away, pulling out my phone to check in with Ivan.

All I can think about is getting free of this and making my way back to Alexis.

31

Alexis

By eight a.m., I'm relying on five hours of sleep and dozing off watching cartoons with June and Janie. They've eaten breakfast twice since six a.m. We've talked to their mama, so she could assure them she'd be home later. When the girls retreat from chatting with her for the television, she explains to me that she and Derek are at the hospital.

By Jill's account it's fortunate he and his friends were found when they were. Derek's pretty banged up and unable to walk with a broken leg. They also think he may have broken ribs from his fall.

The other two guys were better off, with only minor injuries from pulling Derek up out of harm's way. Jill should be home by dinner time, but Derek is stuck there at least overnight to rule out any complications.

I've texted Aidan, Charlie, and Gloria to let them all know Derek's been found alive and mostly well. Aidan responded first, saying he was relieved and would be out of contact for part of the day while he flew to California but would be back in touch later to discuss my return to New York.

Charlie and Gloria are both relieved too, and I tell them I hope to have a more solid plan for my return once I talk to Jill face-to-face. In the meantime, I decide I better make the most of my visit with these adorable nieces of mine, not knowing when I'll get another chance.

"Girls!" I clap my hands together, trying to wake myself up and get their attention while I'm at it. They peel their eyes off the television.

"How would you like Auntie Lex to take you to see some wild animals? There must be a zoo or something around here, right?"

Their eyes light up, wide with anticipation.

"Can we see the tigers?" Janie asks. "Can we get cotton candy?"

"I think that sounds like a great plan, kid. June Bug what do you say?"

"Zoooo!" She's jumping up and down and, before long, both of them are dancing around the living room, roaring like tigers.

I text Ivan and tell him to pick us up in an hour. I can transfer the car seats from Jill's Nissan in the garage to the SUV and have him cart us around. If he thought he was getting off easy on this Memorial Day, he's so wrong. He's about to be my co-pilot for a day of adventure with two very loud, excitable little girls.

I would have bet I'd witness Ivan pop more ibuprofen than me, but he hasn't shown a single sign of being frazzled by our hectic day. He's never out of our sight, but his presence has not been intrusive either.

We've been to the zoo, thankfully early to avoid the blazing heat that settles in by noon. We stopped at a diner for lunch, then stopped briefly at a mini-golf course. The girls got soaking wet, running through the misters of water that cooled off hot patrons, and we had to make our way to a department store around the corner to get them dry clothes.

It made my day to ask Ivan to come in with us so he could help me navigate the store with the two of them. He was a sport about it, but I haven't laughed like that since sitting in Aidan's kitchen. Watching a burly Russian bad ass in steel-toed boots hold piles of pink girls' clothes was comical.

Our last stop is for an ice cream on the way home. The girls' eyes are drooping as they lick their mint chocolate chip cones, their sugar high not yet kicking in. As excited as they've been all day, they've also been the most well-mannered girls. But they are tired and definitely ready for some down time. It's going on four in the afternoon.

"Whatta ya say we go home, girls?"

"Is Mama gonna be there?" June is polishing off the last of her treat.

"I don't know," I say. "Maybe."

I clean the girls up as best I can with a few flimsy paper napkins and pile them back in the SUV, asking Ivan to head back to Jill's. My phone rings five minutes into the ride.

I'm as excited as the girls were for ice cream seeing that it's Aidan calling.

"Hey there," I answer coolly.

"Hey yourself. How's your sister?"

"I haven't seen her yet. She's due back sometime soon."

"Do you want to wait until you see her before we arrange to get you back to New York?"

"That's probably a good idea," I say, looking over at the girls. They're an endearing sight, both asleep with curly haired heads resting on each other.

"How are you doing?"

"Fine," I say. "Just exhausted. I didn't sleep much."

"Me either."

"When I did I had you to thank though."

"How's that?"

"I played your voice file on repeat. The one about Mac's."

"Ahh, I see. I wish I could talk about that now but unfortunately I have a room full of people staring at me."

I laugh, a bit embarrassed at first, then intrigued.

"Really? So if I said something profane, that wouldn't go over well right now?"

"I guess you could say that."

"What if I asked you to speak to me in Italian? Could you do that?"

"Stop it, Alexis. I'll call you later."

Oh boy. This might be a good time to take the upper hand. I think a minute, recalling a phrase I'd looked up on the plane yesterday before taking off.

"Okay. Hey Aidan," I nudge.

"Yes?"

"*Ti voglio dentro di me.*"

"Ohh," he says scolding. "That...that is definitely an unfair play, Greene." And he disconnects.

You gotta love Google.

I high five my sexy subconscious for the idea to look up some rather heated words in Italian. I was happily surprised that even a sample of the correct pronunciation was available at the click of a button. I'm laughing quietly to myself in the backseat, hoping Ivan isn't paying attention.

But my victory is short lived when he texts me not seconds after he's hung up. He's upped the game once again, leaving me hungry for him, defenseless.

> *I will be inside you as soon as possible,*
> *Alexis. And this time without the fear*
> *of breaking you.*

By evening, between the time change and lack of sleep, I'm a bit goofy. I've fed and bathed the girls, played dress up, had a tea party and forced them to brush their teeth, making them roar with laughter at silly Aunt Lex through it all.

I couldn't help but recall the few memories I have of Jill and me as I watched the girls play. We were farther apart in years, her seven years older. Whenever I hit my milestones she'd been there, done that, and was pretty far removed from it. Between the age gap and the fact that we both spent more time in our respective fathers' care than together with our mother, the lack of closeness between us isn't unusual.

The occasions we were together, we were each other's best company (especially when our mother was otherwise occupied).

But our memories are not as fond as June and Janie's will be.

I'm grateful Jill is on her way home. I can appreciate just how hard this parenting thing is. Entertaining these kids and tending to their every need has zapped me. Once I tuck them into bed, all I can think about is collapsing on the couch in front of some mindless television.

At nine o'clock the house is completely quiet, the television on at low volume. I'm dozing off when I get a text from Jill.

> *Lex, I hate to do this to you. Can you come*
> *pick me up? I don't want you to have to drag*
> *the girls out, but I don't have a choice. Steph*
> *had to get home this afternoon, and I don't*
> *have a car.*

This is so unlike Jill. She's as Type A as I am, if not more so. Her house is immaculate, the whim of her little girls the only out of control thing about her. I imagine it's killing her to not have a plan or a way to get her ass home on her own.

The girls are out cold.
But I might have another option.

I really don't want to leave Derek, but I don't
want the girls to see their Daddy yet.
If you come pick me up now they'll be
asleep in the car.

Do you have a place to get comfortable?
Is there an extra bed?

Yeah, they put us in a nice room with a cot
for me. But I can't ask you to keep the girls
overnight again.

We'll be fine. I'll send someone for
you in the morning.

Send someone?

I understand her confusion. I can't believe I have the capability to take care of her like this either.

Yes. I have someone here
that can pick you up.

My phone rings with my sister's number on the display.

"Lex? Are you drunk?"

"No."

"Well, what are you talking about? Is someone there with you?"

"No. I didn't mean here. I meant here, as in Arizona."

"Who is it? A boyfriend?"

"No. I don't want to get into it right now but I have a driver here with me. If you want to stay, I will have him pick you up in the morning. Problem solved. The girls can stay in bed and they won't have to see Derek until he's ready to come home."

"How the hell can you afford a driver? Are you blowing your inheritance from Ben on some crazy extravagant lifestyle?"

I can't help but chuckle at her. It shouldn't make any sense. But it's too late to get into it now.

"No, Jill. A friend of mine set me up with it so I wouldn't have to get around on my own while I'm here. The driver is trustworthy, don't worry. His name is Ivan. I'll have him pick you up tomorrow so you can be with Derek tonight. When's a good time in the morning?"

She sighs, reluctantly accepting my help.

"I don't know, how about ten? I'm a half hour from the house. Banner Gateway Hospital."

"Great. I'll set it up. Look for a black Cadillac SUV, the one that dropped me off here."

"Okay. Send him to the main entrance. I'll be down there at ten a.m. What does he look like?"

"Trust me, you'll know him when you see him."

That's an understatement.

"If you say so. Oh and the girls don't have anything going on tomorrow, so you'll have to be with them until I get home."

"That's fine," I say. "We had a great day today, but man did they exhaust me."

"Welcome to my world," she says. "Except for the fact that Derek is lying here in pain, this is like a vacation for me."

"Yeah well, your vacation ends tomorrow dear sister. See you in the morning."

She chuckles, says good night, and disconnects. I zap the television off and head to bed, hoping the girls won't rise before the sun tomorrow.

The girls sleep in, sufficiently tired out from their outing with me the day before. I'm enjoying a quiet cup of coffee in the kitchen while I wait for them to stir. Aidan woke me briefly with a text at six a.m. asking how I was. I waited until I rose at seven-thirty to fill him in that Jill got stranded at the hospital and I'll be needed here at least through today. I assume he already knows that I've put Ivan on a mission this morning, but I mention it anyway.

Apparently his attention is elsewhere as I haven't heard a reply since eight o'clock, and it's now going on nine-thirty. We're in the same time zone now. I can only assume he's just busy.

The girls wake up together, coming to find me in the kitchen and asking after their mama.

"She'll be home soon, guys. I promise. What's on the menu this morning," I prod. "Pancakes? Scrambled eggs?"

An argument ensues over which one is the better choice, and I'm only able to settle the battle with the promise of cartoons afterwards if they'll agree on bowls of Cheerios and a banana.

By ten-thirty when Jill comes through the door, they're zombies in front of the television. June runs for her mama, keeping her from taking another step as her legs are secured in June's arms.

"Hi, Mama," Janie says from across the room, not taking her eyes off the television.

I smile and shrug my shoulders.

"Sorry," I say. "My powers are weak in the mornings and cartoons seemed to be the one thing they could agree on. I think our trip to the zoo yesterday wiped them out."

She smiles, picking up her littlest daughter and holding her tight. "It's fine," she says. She sets June down, then stops at the couch to give Jane a peck on the head.

"Girls, Aunt Lex and I are going to have some coffee in the kitchen, okay? You stay put a minute. Maybe we'll take you out for lunch this afternoon."

Jill guides me into the kitchen, clearly wanting to discuss something out of earshot of the girls.

"What's up?" I ask.

"Um, who's the stud that brought me here, Lex? He had the personality of a dead bug, but he sure was easy on the eyes. What the hell is going on with you?"

I sigh, resigning myself to the fact I have to disclose Aidan. I pour a second cup of coffee, making myself comfortable at the kitchen table.

"It's kind of a long story," I say.

"Well, I've got about five minutes before the girls come in here asking for something."

I spill as much as I can in the allotted time limit, leaving out unimportant details but sufficiently conveying the fact that Aidan screwed up my biggest real estate deal, saved me from career suicide, and then screwed me – except I put it nicely.

"Lex, do you realize this guy is like, a *gajillionaire*?" She's joined me at the table with her own mug of coffee and a bagel.

I nod, not sure what else to say.

"He's on the news out here all the time," she continues. "His girlfriend owns a boutique on Rodeo Drive and one in Manhattan. She has her own line of clothing and lingerie for shit's sake."

"I don't know much about her other than what I could find online." Something occurs to me, disturbing me enough that I have to ask my sister, who has always been more into girlie fashion stuff than I have. "What is the name of her lingerie line? Is it Zora's Closet?"

"Hell no," she says. "Zora's Closet is in a league of its own. Princesses wear that shit. She probably wishes her line was as amazing as that."

Whew. I'm not wearing underwear his ex-girlfriend designed.

"Anyway," I say, "he says it's his ex-girlfriend."

"Just be careful," she says. "I don't want to see you hurt. Not after what you went through losing Ben."

"Thank you," I say. "But it's only been a week. I promise not to abandon my senses just yet."

Based on what my heart says, I'm lying through my teeth right now. But if Aidan doesn't even know this, then she doesn't need to worry about it either.

"Does he make you happy?"

I think about that for a second, realizing I haven't even considered the question myself. I'm overcome just thinking about him, a smile coming to me easily.

"Okay, then. I guess that's a big fat yes," she says, laughing.

"Yeah," I resolve.

Apparently I'm not hiding anything.

While I'm showering, Jill talks to the girls about Derek. She explains that Daddy had a bad time camping and won't be home today. He's well enough for them to call him at the hospital, and they've just hung up with him when I come out dressed for the day.

"How's he doing?"

"He's okay. They're thinking Thursday for his release. Would you want to head to the mall with us? It'll be a good distraction for the girls."

"Too hot to be outside today?"

"Yeah, definitely."

"All right, yeah. Let's do it."

We all pile in Jill's SUV and celebrate the start of summer vacation by lavishing the girls with new sunglasses, hats, and a new pair of sneakers for each of them. I spoil them both with a stop to build stuffed teddy bears while Jill fields a couple of client calls for her catering business.

I've kept in touch with Charlie throughout the day. For being the Tuesday after a holiday, things are quiet in the office. We've put everything off with Myers until whatever day I get back. He's been told I had a family emergency. Anyone else that needs my time has been scheduled for next week.

I plan to make arrangements this evening to head back before the weekend. I let Gloria know the developments via text.

After having dinner and one last ride on the indoor carousel at the mall, we arrive home with two tired little girls. I kiss them both goodnight before Jill whisks them off to ready them for bed and enjoy them by herself for a while. I'm glad for the quiet, the comfort of the sofa, and Aidan's voice playing in my ears as I listen to *Open Last* again.

I doze off until Jill comes out from her bedroom, quietly calling for me.

"Hey," I say in my lowest volume. "I'm in the living room."

She comes in and collapses on the other end of the couch, ready for bed in yoga pants and a t-shirt.

"I'm exhausted."

"Me too," I say. "Your girls are so good, Jill. But damn are they something to keep up with. I don't know how you do it."

"Me either," she admits, eyes closed. "Did it go okay yesterday? I'm sorry I wasn't in touch very much. It was a whirlwind."

"They were great, really. Our day was a bit crazy too, but they had fun. The zoo, lunch, mini golf, ice cream. I don't think they were awake more than a minute after their heads hit the pillow last night."

"It was the same tonight. That's the trick, Lex. Teach them manners, keep them fed, and tire 'em out. That's pretty much the secret to parenting."

"Good to know. So do you really think Derek's okay?"

"Yeah, he will be." She switches positions, sitting up and resting her feet on an ottoman. "I hated seeing him in such pain. But the doctors say he should be well enough to recuperate at home."

"You think he'll be well enough by Thursday?"

"I don't know for sure, but I think so. They just want to make sure he doesn't overdo it after his fall. He did hit his head pretty good, but his ribs didn't turn out to be broken. Just bruised."

"Jesus. And a broken leg too?"

"Yeah. He'll be on crutches when he gets out."

"Oh, that sucks. What about work?" Derek manages a sporting goods store nearby, and I can't imagine his job is going to be happy about him taking any extended time off.

"He'll need some time to get used to hobbling around, but he will be fine to go back eventually. They'll make sure he's comfortable. He's too valuable to the store. And he can do some of his work from home."

"Well that's a relief."

"Yeah. I, I need to say something to you, Lex." She sits up straight, eyes fixed on mine. "I'm sorry I wasn't there for you when you lost Ben."

"It's okay, Jill."

"No, it isn't." She makes her best attempt at being assertive through raw emotion.

"But it is. I understand. I've barely walked in your shoes a day, and I understand. Your business, juggling a marriage, and parenting besides. I get it."

"Still. I should have stayed with you. I should have helped. You've always been the more sensitive of us, Lex. I don't handle the emotional stuff well."

I know this much is true. She has always been the sensible, even *more* conservative of us. She doesn't ask for help or let people know when she's struggling. And she doesn't know how to offer help either, beyond the practical.

Now she's clearly emotional, remorseful of her perceived shortcomings. I move closer, laying a hand on her shoulder.

"You were there, Jill, in the way you could be at the time. You did enough. And I had support from Charlie. I can't imagine where I'd be without him. If you had tried to do more, you would have been stretching yourself too thin, and I might never have reached out to him. The way things worked out – it's the way things were meant to be."

She sniffles, nodding. "If I had realized the gravity of what you must have been going through, though. Just laying eyes on Derek, seeing that he was okay. All I could think was that you never got that chance. I wish I could have been better to you. Better *for* you."

"You're lucky, Jill. Just remember that. And don't dwell on the past. I know we aren't as close as a lot of sisters. But we are what we are. And I'm grateful I could be here."

"Well, I don't intend to keep you," she says, wiping her wet eyes. "When are you going back to New York?"

"I don't know. I wanted to talk to you first. Do you need me to stay?"

She leans back again closing her eyes, contemplating something.

"No. The girls are all done with school but I have care lined up for them for the three days a week I have to be out for work. I'll stay home with them the other days. The only thing I had to arrange for is someone to take care of Derek when he gets home, for the first couple days while I can't be here. But I have an option for that."

"You're sure? Is one of the other guys going to check in on him?"

"No, they're all back to work."

She doesn't say more. It seems like she's holding back.

"Jill, who is going to help you? Derek's family is in Oregon, and your dad isn't able to help out."

Her dad is over seventy and lives in a retirement community twenty minutes away. I know Grandpa Don isn't going to be any help in taking care of Derek or helping out with the kids.

"I really don't mind staying an extra couple days. I know you'd never ask it of me, but if I'm back by the weekend…"

"Lex, you don't want to know. Just trust me that I have it covered."

Now I'm definitely not giving in. She's withholding *something*, and obviously it affects me too.

"Spill it, Jill."

She sighs in exasperation, pushed into saying more when she doesn't want to.

"It's Mom, okay? In two days, our mother will be here to provide help, beat me over the head with suggestions and drive me bat shit crazy. And it's probably better if you're not here to watch."

My eyes pop wide open, my head shaking in an attempt to fix my hearing. I can't believe what just left her mouth.

"Are you fucking kidding me?"

"No," she says, still laid back, eyes closed. "I'm not."

I'm reeling. My chest feels weighted, an ache forming in my throat. I haven't spoken to our mother in years. It's been ten since I've sat in the same room with her.

"Where…" I start, trying not to lose my voice. "Where has she been?"

"Sedona. For the last two years."

"Is there a reason you didn't think I should know this?"

It's an unspoken rule between us that we keep our mother as distant from our lives as possible. We've never disagreed about this.

"Not really. I just didn't think you'd want to know."

"I need a drink." I'm on my feet in a hurry, heading for the kitchen and trying not to panic. I grab a bottle of red from the wine fridge as Jill follows me in. "Where are the glasses?"

"There," she says, pointing to a cupboard. "Get me one too, please."

I do as she asks and pour, then take a seat at her kitchen table.

"All right," I say. "Go on."

"Lex, there isn't much to say. I know you don't want Mom in your life. And she won't be. I haven't even told her you're here."

My mind eases at that, but my heart is still racing.

"And when did you decide you wanted her in yours? Has she had some sort of miracle transformation? Because last I checked she was still a pretty shitty human being. And a drunk."

She sits down with me, sighing. Clearly she has struggled with this topic in her own head.

"Not a transformation, but yeah, she's different." She sips some wine and goes on as I give her a skeptical glance. "Don't get me wrong. I wouldn't leave her alone with my children to go out for a pack of gum. But I can trust her to get me through a day or two of helping Derek while the rest of us are out of the house."

"How long has she been coming around? Do you see her all the time?"

"God no. She moved to Arizona a couple years ago. She claims she was 'called to Sedona', and went there to heal herself," she says, shaking her head. "You know I don't believe in that hippy bullshit. But she found out I was living here and she called me."

"You can probably thank the fucking internet for that."

"Yeah, really," she says in sarcastic agreement. "So we talked a few times and, finally, she wore me down. I agreed to meet her halfway, to have dinner with her at Christmas time. Since then I've only seen her once, but she calls regularly and talks to the girls."

"So what, she wants to be Grandma Connie now? Buy the kids some dollies and pretend she didn't royally fuck us up as kids?"

"No, Lex. You know I wouldn't allow that. I mean she is Grandma to them, yes. But I keep her at arms' length. She seems better than I ever remember her, but she's still our mother, which means it's possible she'll change as quickly as the direction of the wind."

I blow out a breath. I can't believe I'm within a car ride of our mother or that it's possible she'll be sitting in this room in under forty-eight hours.

"She asks about you all the time, Lex."

The thought makes my emotions twist inside my gut, like a cloth being wrung out. It wasn't that I'd never wanted for her to care or to be in my life. She just never was. The idea of her giving a shit about what I'm doing is at war with my resentment for her.

"Wait," I ask, counting back through time in my head. "Were you in contact with her when Ben died?"

"No. It was just after. The week I got back from his services, actually. She had been in Arizona about six months by then. But I didn't see her until the end of last year."

"Does she know about Ben?"

"Just that he passed. I didn't give her any details. I wouldn't do that without telling you. And I have been meaning to tell you about her. But she isn't a daily presence in our lives, and I thought I had more time. I wasn't expecting this to happen, obviously."

"I get it, Jill. I'm not angry with you. I'm just…this is a lot to take in. You know I've had a lot going on myself, just in the last couple weeks…" I'm starting to well up. "I just wasn't expecting this news. I don't even know how to process it."

"Listen," she interrupts. She lays a hand on mine. "I am not going to force our mother on you. She doesn't even have to know you were here. You got yourself out here, so I'll pay for your flight home as soon as tomorrow. If you want to revisit this topic, we can. But you don't have to be faced with it now."

I sit up and stretch, tilt my head back, and close my eyes. I'm utterly fatigued, drained beyond measure. I take another sip of wine and set my glass down, hoping I don't drop it with my trembling hands.

"Are you all right?" She looks at me with eyebrows raised, head tilted.

"Yeah," I manage. "I appreciate your offer, big sister. But I won't need you to get me home. I already have a way back."

Which is exactly where I intend to go without delay.

At ten o'clock, the wine is emptied and both of us drag ourselves to our respective beds, emotionally spent. From the comfort of bed I text Aidan that I'd like to leave tomorrow and, within five minutes, my phone is vibrating with a call.

I don't want to answer, but my unwillingness to stay here any longer forces me to. I have to get these arrangements made.

"Hey there," I say. It almost hurts to talk.

"Are you all right?"

"I'm fine."

"You sound exhausted, baby."

"I am."

"You really want to go back tomorrow? Maybe you need an extra day, just to relax."

"Trust me, if I stay here any longer, relaxing will be impossible beyond measure."

"What's going on, Alexis? Something with your sister?"

"No," I say. "I just need to go home. It has to be tomorrow."

"Please talk to me. I can't hang up worrying about you right now. I'm dealing with enough here."

"Well I'm sorry to add to your list of complications," I spout. "But you don't need to worry about me."

"Knock it off," he demands. "You know what I mean. I need to know that you're okay."

"I'm so tired, Aidan. I just can't right now. I need to get home before Friday. I can just book a flight from here if that's…"

"No," he asserts. "Consider it done. I'll text you with the details."

He doesn't offer any more and I can't bring myself to care. I thank him and disconnect, laying back in the bed and crying myself into a dreamless sleep.

32

Aidan

I hang up with Alexis, frustrated and edgy, screaming profanities to my empty hotel room.

I need to be with her.

Her voice tells me something is off. More than off, really. Something felt altogether wrong, but she won't tell me what.

I know she isn't aware of what I'm actually doing out here or that Stella is among my concerns. As much as I know that could trouble her, I know it isn't what she's upset about now. It would be impossible for her to know.

The leak to the press won't be news until Thursday's late day news cycle. I made sure of that. By then I'll be back in New York, able to tell Alexis about everything – or at least as much as I can without facing repercussions from John Ireland.

I'd gotten Stella through her check in at the treatment center last night. I spent two hours talking to her counselor, her doctor, and lastly her mother's friend Jasmine Hernandez. She pulled me into her private office, giving me a chance to express my gratitude that she had opened up the spot for Stella in the first place.

We agreed that information would be kept between the two of us. Stella had no warm fuzzies for her mother, thanks to the tarnished picture John Ireland had worked so hard to paint for Stella over the course of her life.

I was confident she was in good hands when I left. I would be under obligation to come back for her release in four weeks, if she fulfilled her requirements, but I had to put that aside to move forward.

The only break I had taken yesterday was to call Alexis, even while a room full of suits sat around me working, waiting for my direction.

She'd challenged me as always, drawing me in and giving me a semi-hard on just at the sound of her voice, then full-on with the Italian phrase she'd taught herself.

It required acute focus to shake her out of my head.

I spent all day today making the most of my time here, meeting with various teams on lingering projects that needed my attention.

I delegated the last of my responsibilities for everything here on the West Coast knowing I'd spent enough time over the last year planning my absence, at least for the day-to-day operations. Lionel would be running point and would keep me informed as needed.

The last order of business was a meeting scheduled with my college buddy Oates in the morning to talk about pursuing his new start-up which, if it worked out, would be profitable for both of us.

My head wasn't present to contemplate any of these things now. Not after hanging up with Alexis sounding so…

I don't know. Distressed? Scared?

Something was wrong in her world and it drove me mad that I wasn't privy to exactly what.

My mind is on her.

On what's going on and how I can make it better.

On her body, the softness of her curves, the sass of her mouth and how she tastes.

It's maddening and frightening all at once.

I have no idea how to fit her into my world and tuck her safely amidst all the chaos in it (or among the demons of my past) without damaging her. An insurmountable task, at least until I remove one very prominent threat.

John Ireland had to be out of the picture soon, before he could realize Alexis existed. I recognize she could easily become my Achilles heel.

And Ireland could not be allowed to know it.

I call Lionel and then Ivan, making the arrangements for her flight to-morrow. I scroll through my contacts for the one person that can help me.

Dimitri Floros answers on the second ring.

"Pierce, you crazy fucker. Are you back in town already?"

"Briefly," I say. I can tell I'm on speaker as my voice echoes back to me.

"My ass. Admit it, man." My brother's oldest friend talks with an obvi-ous obstruction in his speech, likely a cigarette hanging out of his mouth. "You hate New York."

"No, Dimitri." I laugh despite myself. "But I need a favor."

"Name it," he says.

"In person."

"Sounds serious."

"It is."

You have no idea how serious.

"I'm on a smoke break, then finishing up some art. I need forty-five minutes. An hour, tops."

I look at the display on my phone. It's going on ten-thirty now. I hadn't thought about the late hours he keeps, that I might actually be interrupting his work. An hour will have to do.

"Fine. Meet at the shop?" I can picture Dimitri about to grace some two hundred pound biker with ink. His tattoo parlor is smack between a Harley dealership and a barbecue-beer-and-blues joint called Eve's Ribs.

His shop has become a goldmine, even pulling the interest of some reality television producers (whom Dimitri promptly told to fuck off). But he never tired of thanking me for recommending the location. His busi-ness had been an investment when I helped him get it off the ground five years ago and I was still invested.

I know exactly how he's doing. His gratitude is warranted, even if this business yields me the smallest return in a long list of others.

"Nah, man. Meet me at Eve's. I'll buy. We need to celebrate."

Before I can ask what he's talking about, he disconnects.

I'm on a stool at Eve's an hour later. Blues music revs through the bar and bounces off the patrons around me. A plate emptied of all but rib bones sits in front of me next to a cold draft beer. I feel a slap on my right shoulder and, in my peripheral, see the source is Dimitri's strong arm.

I turn and rise off the stool as he greets me with a rough bro-hug and another firm smack on my back. He's a couple inches shorter, a couple years younger – but he has thirty pounds of muscle on me, easy.

From his arm sleeves extending beyond his black t-shirt to his mop of slicked back hair to his riding boots and jeans – everything about him is dark. His features shout out loud the Greek heritage passed down from his father.

"I knew you'd be back," he says with a shit-eating grin. He waves to the beautiful blonde behind the bar and avoids staring at her displayed cleavage when she comes over to ask what he'll have.

That's unusual.

Dimitri is the definitive high-scoring bachelor. He'd be the first to pay homage to this girl's tits and have her legs wrapped around him in a dark alley before she could have a chance to beg him for exactly that.

She clears my plate away and moves to get Dimitri his Guinness. I can't help but laugh to myself. Even his choice of beer is dark. "I'm out of here as soon as possible," I say. I empty the contents of my pint glass and nod for another.

"Pierce. You know you hate it back East. Why are you torturing yourself going back there?"

"You've got it backwards," I say flatly.

Before I can say anything, he lays down a Benjamin for my meal and our beers, which totaled under thirty bucks. The barmaid sets down our drinks and takes away the cash to make change.

"How's that?" he asks.

"I hate it *here*," I clarify. "Not there."

Blonde-with-tits is back with the change in a hurry and Dimitri leaves her a healthy tip before pocketing the rest. She smiles at the both of us in thanks, with obvious suggestion behind her eyes. Dimitri ignores her, but I can't tell if it's because he's preoccupied or honestly disinterested.

I haven't known him to pass that up on any occasion, but I have no intentions of acknowledging her signals either.

"Thank you," I tell her with finality. "Have a good night." I gesture to a table outside, away from the room full of dancing and drinking patrons. "Out here," I say. I nod in Curtis' direction, where he's parked with the SUV across the street.

"I see you brought your boyfriend," Dimitri jokes, also nodding to Curtis.

"Let him hear you say that."

"Nah," he says. "I wanna live."

We take a seat in some rickety metal chairs. He lays his smokes and a lighter on the table and I reference his earlier statement. "So what are we celebrating?"

"Nevermind that, asshole. What the fuck are you doing back here if you're so happy being a Yankee?"

"I need help with something."

"You know I'd do anything for Thad's big brother." He takes a long pull off his pint, then lights up a Marlboro red.

"It's Ireland. I need a way to…I need him out of my rearview."

"You know I'd do anything but *that*," he says, setting down his lighter. It clangs against the table as he blows out a smoke ring. "You've got the wrong guy."

"I know," I say. "It's a big ask." I sit back, crossing a leg over my opposite knee. I'm not sure how this is going to go, but he's my only option at this point. I'm as relaxed as I can be. If he says no, I'll have to find another angle.

"I'm not in it anymore, bro. I don't know if there's anything I could do for you, even if I wanted to risk losing my fucking balls."

Dimitri was the best hacker I'd ever known, and one of the few people I'd trust with anything – even my life.

His doubts about my request were the biggest hurdle I faced getting him on board. The skills he perceived to lack to get the job done were likely just the opposite, as honed as they always were. Dimitri was well read, and I knew he discreetly kept informed about his old field of interest, albeit legally now.

He had the expertise, he had the anonymity – especially now that he was established in his preferred life of Harley salesman by day and tattoo artist by night – and he had the genius mind that would be needed to get Ireland off my back.

But Dimitri knew Ireland's reputation as well as he knew the tattoos he'd inked into his own skin. Ireland was no one to fuck with.

Especially if there was a risk of being caught.

"I get it. I wouldn't ask if I had any other way. You're the only lifeline I've got, man."

He considers me a moment as he puts out his cigarette under the sole of his boot. "You realize you'd be sentencing me to death."

I hold a breath. That is the last thing I want. Dimitri had a rough childhood, worse than me and my brother. He'd survived it and thrived despite it. And he'd tried like hell to save Thad from the path he was on all those years ago. Dimitri Floros always walked on the side of good intentions, even if it had been on the wrong side of the law.

"I avoided jail by a cunt hair, Pierce. I don't want that risk. Never again. And my life is worth something to me now. More than it ever used to be."

"You'll be protected. I can guarantee it." I was confident in that. I wouldn't make the ask without that reassurance.

"You can't guarantee anything when it comes to that bastard."

"I can and I would. You know I'd never ask you to jump without a net. You're like a brother to me." Dimitri knows this is true. I can see he's honored at me voicing it, as cliché as my words may be. "Ireland deserves to go down. We both know it. And I'm not even asking for that. All I need is for someone to get creative, find a way to get him out of my life. Keep him at bay so he can't interfere."

"You're forgetting that it's a package deal with him, Pierce."

I twist my brows up, uncertain of what he means.

"Stella. You can't remove one without the other. It's ineffective."

"I've thought about that."

"And you're ready to cut her off, too?" I say nothing at first. He continues with a grimace. "Not that I'd blame you. It'd be about fucking time, honestly. She sucks the life out of you, man."

He has no idea how right he is. "She'll be taken care of, but I don't intend to have anything to do with her beyond that. I'm keeping thousands

380 · M.J. WOODS

of miles between us. She knows that. Ireland knows that. All I need to do is get her to come to her senses before she ends up…" I trail off.

"Like Thad," he says, finishing my thought.

I don't respond. I don't have to.

"Man. What a fucking predicament you put me in with this shit."

"I don't want to do that, Dimitri. You're where you're meant to be." I gesture to the Harley place two storefronts down, to his shop next door which is now dark inside, only the black and purple glow of the fluorescent *Inked* sign in the window lighting up the sidewalk. "I don't intend for any of this to be put in jeopardy. But where I'm meant to be is New York. And I can't get Ireland to wrap his head around it. It's going to take something more to remove him from my life."

"What do you have in mind?"

"I can't answer that until I have more information. At this point, that's what I need. Anything and everything on him. I can't go in myself. It's too risky. Too obvious."

"If I didn't have news of my own I'd jump all over this, man."

"Does this have something to do with what you wanted to celebrate?"

"It might." He grins slyly and lights another cigarette.

"Then out with it," I say. "Let's see if we can help each other."

Curtis slows up at the address I gave him. It's one in the morning, and I'm not sure exactly what the fuck I'm doing. My pulse throbs, my ears filling with the sound of my heart pounding, eliminating the silence in the vehicle.

I parted ways with Dimitri a half hour ago. We'd reached an understanding, but he'd also given me the scrap of information to lead me here. The address required nothing more than a free, completely legal Google search to obtain – but it could prove to be dangerous, nonetheless.

Just how dangerous – and for whom – I was about to find out.

I instruct Curtis to wait in the car. Shane Armstrong's beach house looms low across the road. A gate denies access to the driveway, but the surrounding tiled wall of the property is low enough for me to scale. I doubt there is much security here, as this guy is more known for having himself and his party habits as his number one enemy. The only one he needs protection from is himself.

Until he decided to start partying with Stella anyway.

The house is mid-century modern, one-story with walls of glass and angled roof lines. I'm sure Armstrong inherited it from his parents, who had died years ago. He didn't have enough taste to pick it out himself and all his money went up his nose. It wasn't likely he could afford to buy it.

Once on the grounds, I look for any signs of life. The landscaping is overgrown, the building in need of maintenance. Lights blaze out back while the front of the house is dark. I walk around to the courtyard, hoping I'm not on display for anyone. No alarms go off, no outdoor lights are thrown on me to reveal my intrusion.

I can hear giggling coming from the pool area, which is surrounded by the wings of the house that jut out towards the cliffside. The surf pounds beneath, but I can't see the ocean in the distance – only darkness. I can hear "Stay Useless" by Cloud Nothings playing from a tabletop speaker, the fitting lyrics amplified and carried to me over the surface of the pool.

The giggles are coming from Armstrong's date as he is about to snort a line off her exposed belly. The dark haired girl is completely naked, lying back on a chaise by the pool. I make a sound to indicate my presence and she darts up to sitting, then to standing – all before he can level the straw to the line above her navel. White powder disperses, some of it to the concrete pool deck, some of it into the breeze as I get a good look at the girl. She can't be more than eighteen or nineteen.

"The fuck, bitch!" Shane hollers as he stands. He smacks her with the back of his hand in punishment. She stumbles back and then cowers, holding her cheek with both hands as she starts sobbing.

My fists clench at my sides, my chest heaving. I hold myself back from knocking him out. I need to deal with the girl.

"You should call a cab," I say, moving towards her. She looks at me, wounded to the core and scared as hell. I hand her a fifty from my wallet. "*Now.*" She grabs her phone, then her skimpy dress off the back of the chaise before darting into the house, still sobbing.

"Who the fuck you think you are, bro? We were having a good time here." Armstrong moves to pick up a glass tumbler off a patio table, brown liquid swishing around inside as he sways backward a step.

He's wearing a collared white shirt and board shorts. He can't be more than five foot seven. His brown hair is twisted every which way into dreadlocks.

Once I can see the girl has disappeared from view through the house, I move forward and grab him by his collar. I yank him up to meet my gaze and he drops his drink, the shatter of glass breaking the quiet. "Stay the fuck away from Stella. This will be your only warning. Got it?"

He juts out his chin and sneers. "Ahh. So you don't want me playing with your toy while you're out of town? Stella told me about you." He can't move away under my grip, but he sways his head in mocking. "*Mistah fuckin' billionaire.*"

I loathe this asshat.

"She's not a toy, you piece of shit. And she's not mine. She's a friend. You come near her again, I will *end* you." My threat is severe and certain, and I pull his collar tighter, so much that it's almost choking him. "That would mean no more nose candy for you, *bro*. No more house. No more *anything*. Your choices will be limited to being carted away in a cruiser with the little red lights on top or having your ashes scattered out there." I nod to the ocean behind him. "You like this place enough to spend eternity here?"

He doesn't speak, doesn't move an inch. I set him down, figuring he's gotten the message.

He tries to throw a punch before I can walk away. I move to the side in reflexive response, but not before his knuckles graze my cheekbone.

Damn.

It's been a long time since I've ducked a punch.

Armstrong falls to the cement after his effort, not even sober enough to catch himself. He narrowly escapes falling into the pool.

Before I can channel my rage into a counterattack, the anger dissolves into disgust at the pitiable waste of human life at my feet.

"*Fuck you, bruh,*" he moans into the hard surface below him. "Stella told me about you. She said you won't fuck her anymore."

I give him a swift kick to the groin, and he groans in agony.

"What," he groans, continuing his taunting. "So she came to greener pastures. Get over it, man." He coughs and sputters, trying to roll up on all fours. "It's the law of the jungle, bruh." His speech is slurred, but I understand every word, even as he collapses back to the cement.

I squat down next to him and lift his face up by his hair. "You could have fucked that cunt as long as you wanted, you deluded asshole – but you screwed that up by pulling her into coke. Do you have any last words?"

His eyes go buggy at my threat, his paranoia finally getting the better of him as he realizes I could easily kill him and have every desire to do so.

"No, it wasn't me man. *I swear.*"

"Bullshit. You think your reputation isn't well known?"

"It wasn't me, man!" He's pleading now, an even more pathetic version of the punk that tried to punch me. "It wasn't me! She always had her own. *Her father.* She's running drugs for *her father.*"

No. That wasn't possible. John Ireland wasn't into drugs. Never had been. His heart condition couldn't take it. And I would've known if he was pushing it.

"You're lying to save your own skin. John Ireland doesn't run drugs, and he'd never tolerate his daughter doing it." I can't believe I'm sitting here defending these people.

I'm running through conversations in my mind. With him, with Stella. There's no way this kid's ramblings have any merit.

Do they?

"No shit, right? That fat bastard is at death's door with that heart condition. But he distributes. He got into it when he lost his ass on property out here." His eyes are closed, refusing to look at me as I have him by the scalp, but his resolve and his voice are strong with insistence. "Do you live under a fuckin' rock man? He had to make up for his losses. *Everyone* out here knows that."

Fuck. John did have some big losses in the real estate market here, just within the last year. Could this be possible? After the guy sat in my office and reprimanded me for the shit Stella was into, could he be at fault for dragging her into some underbelly of drug running to start with?

Everything in me screamed *yes.*

Yes, this was entirely possible.

This was John Ireland we were talking about. I put nothing past him. He'd not only auction his own soul to the devil if the profit margins were right, he'd offer his daughter's up too.

I have some digging to do and realize the character lying in front of me may actually be an asset. I couldn't get to Stella now to confirm any of this with her. Even if I was allowed to interrupt her one day progress at The Meadows, I couldn't discuss this topic there.

"Guess what," I say. "It's your lucky fucking day, Armstrong. I'm going to let you live tonight."

He cracks an eye open and looks up at me. "Ah man, I promise. I won't go near her. Ever again."

"No, you're right about that. But I have an assignment for you. Could you use a windfall of cash?"

He looks skeptical, then nods frantically.

"Stella is off limits for you. But I'll have a big payday for you soon, if you can accomplish a simple task to earn it," I say. My wheels turn as I think about just how useful he can be for me.

He nods more frantically than before. "Yeah. I'll do it. Whatever it is."

"If you don't pull it off, I'll make good on my threats. Understood?"

"Yeah, man. Yeah. Just let me up."

"Can't do that, *bruh*. In fact, you never saw me tonight. But I'll be in touch, so hopefully you won't forget our conversation."

I pick his head up again and throw it to the concrete deck hard enough to stun him. He moans, and I wait as his features fall into silence when he passes out cold. I pick through his shorts and find his phone, snapping pictures of all of his contacts with my phone and noting his cell number.

I head back to the street on a mission.

Curtis has his watchful eye on the cab that is pulling up for the young lady I'd found with Armstrong. I wait in the shadows for the cab to take off, then hurdle the wall and approach the SUV.

"I'm gonna need someone to babysit and make sure this guy gets up in the morning," I say. "It should be a woman. Have anyone in mind?"

"I'll make the call." I ask no further questions. The less I know about Curtis' associates, the better. If he trusts them, then I do. I climb in the backseat.

"Good. Take me back to the hotel first, then I'll leave you to it. And I'll need you to deliver some information to Dimitri in the morning while I'm meeting with Oates." I'll have to handwrite a note to him tomorrow morning. I can't risk sending it electronically in any form.

"Yes, sir."

I pull up Dimitri's number and send him a text.

> *May have found our in with that side project*
> *we discussed. Need to do some research.*
> *First set of facts delivered to you tomorrow.*
> *I'll be in touch.*

His reply comes before we reach the hotel.

> *Whatever you need, man. I'm in.*

I sit back in my seat, eyes closed, running a hand across my cheek. Armstrong's attempt will no doubt leave a mark but, hopefully, nothing lasting. I didn't intend to brawl with him. I just wanted to threaten him enough to scare him off.

Little did I know that would get me more than I bargained for, more than I could have wished for.

My lips curve into a smile realizing the key to removing the Irelands from my life may have just fallen in my lap.

33

Alexis

I wake the next morning in the same position I fell asleep. The house is quiet and still. I check my phone and see that Aidan sent me a text at six a.m. telling me to expect Ivan at noon. I'm told I'll be taking the same plane back to New York that I came out in. I depart at one o'clock Arizona time and arrive home around eight in the evening New York time.

And apparently Ivan is coming with me.

Oh, joy.

I respond with nothing more than 'okay'. As rude as I was to Aidan last night, I can't imagine he wants to hear much more from me. His text came in hours ago. It's already nine o'clock.

I pad to the kitchen to fire up the coffee brewer and make myself some toast. Jill's left a note telling me she took the girls to their babysitter and will be right back. My heart sinks that I won't get to kiss them goodbye.

I feel more rested but still jittery knowing my mother may be hours from coming here. Multiple scenarios play out in my head of us running into each other before I can leave. I call Charlie to distract myself.

"Lex, hey! How's the desert? How's Derek?"

"Not home yet. He's due back tomorrow."

"Is your sister holding up okay?"

"I guess. Pretty well, considering." I'm debating whether to mention my mother to him.

"When you coming home?"

"Soon. I should be home by nine tonight actually. Will you stay and wait for me? I…I don't want to be alone."

"You know I will. And hey, Huck really misses his mama."

"Have you been letting him sleep upstairs?"

He hesitates.

"No," he says. I can tell he's lying.

"Charles Young," I say, scolding. "Please tell me you did not let him sleep in my bed."

"No, I didn't. But…" he hesitates again. "I hope it's okay, Lex. I've been using Ben's room. I didn't want to disturb your stuff upstairs. And it was just sitting there, empty."

I don't say anything at first, only because I'm not sure how to feel. My instinct would be to get angry at Ben's memory being disturbed but, for some reason, I'm okay with it now. It's Charlie after all, and I know how much he and Ben cared for each other.

"Oh shit, I'm sorry Lex. I should've asked. I just…"

"It's okay, Charlie. Really. It's time. I really need to get his room cleaned out, maybe even move on from that house. It's…" I sigh, overcome. "I don't need to avoid that room anymore. I need to face it. And I don't need a house to keep his memory with me."

"Wow, Lex. Are you okay? That's some heavy shit for a Wednesday afternoon."

"Well, it's only nine a.m. here," I say, trying to lighten things up. He laughs softly. I love that he always gets me.

"Look, I'm sorry. I really should have asked. But I'm glad you're cool with it because it's been nice reminding myself of him. I miss him too, Lex."

"I know, Charlie. I know. I'll see you tonight. Text me if anything comes up at the office. Oh, and write out a check for the mortgage payment on the building."

I'd almost forgotten it's the first of June.

"You got it. See you later, babe. Fly safe."

We disconnect, and I'm glad I didn't mention my mother. It will be that much easier to put her out of my mind when I leave here. I can go home and forget that she's pushing her allegedly reformed self on Jill and she can go back to being nothing but a memory to me.

An hour later, I'm hugging my sister goodbye before she heads for the hospital. I haven't mentioned our mother at all and, thankfully, neither has she. She's going to let me know how Derek is the minute he gets home and she'll smooch the girls for me. We promise each other to keep in touch more often.

I haven't heard from Aidan, but with everything else I have to contemplate, I'm almost relieved. With my emotions on full throttle and my time of the month wrapping up, it's probably for the best. I'd likely bite his head off for no good reason.

I fire up my laptop after she leaves, intending to check work emails. There are a few flying back and forth between Jade and Allen Richardson that grab my attention. Jade has secured the gala date with the hotel and has three menu options and two options for invitations that she attaches to the email. She suggests I present them to Aidan and have a response by our meeting tomorrow.

In the meantime, Richardson replied that he wishes he could make it to the meeting but that he isn't able to.

Great.

He hasn't done a single thing he proposed. I fire off an email to both of them.

To: Jade McCall, Esq.; Allen Richardson, Esq.
From: Alexis Greene, Esq.

Re: Pierce Philanthropy Group Fundraiser Gala

Hello,

I am out of town but returning this evening. Mr. Richardson, if you are unable to attend and have not completed anything as discussed at our last meeting, I anticipate that Mr. Pierce will want to appoint someone else in your place. Someone will let you know.

Jade, this is great work, thank you. I'll run the menus and invites by Mr. Pierce and hope to have an answer for you tomorrow so we can get the hotel plenty of notice. I believe his office will have the head count tallied and his PA is going to send out the invites by Friday.

I hope to have more information as to the entertainment options as well. Jade, did you have any further ideas?

Thanks,
Alexis

Alexis M. Greene, Esq.
Greene Law Office
423 Harrison Street
Stanton, NY 14077

I fire off another quick e-mail to Aidan, forwarding him the ideas Jade presented and add that he should appoint someone else immediately to replace Richardson, either from the Bar or on his staff since Richardson has proven to be an epic fuck up.

I hate that I didn't trust my gut and get rid of him sooner.

Within forty-five minutes, I'm showered and dressed. I've chosen a tank top and shorts and thrown my damp hair up in a high ponytail to fight the desert heat. With the few minutes I have left, I check my laptop one last time for any more emails. There are none from Jade or Aidan, but Richardson replied with one sentence saying he understood and to keep him informed if he's needed.

Not likely, asshole.

I set my bag and laptop in the foyer as I hear Ivan arrive. It's noon on the dot. I'm starting to wonder if these men Aidan employs are robots. Ever punctual, ever threatening, ever emotionless. Ivan speeds off with me and my belongings in the Cadillac, heading for the airport. He's his usual charming self, not saying a word the whole ride.

When we arrive at the airport he hands off the SUV keys to a similar looking goon. Crew cut, jeans, black t-shirt, thug boots and dark sunglasses. He is the size of a small tank (Ivan is more of a medium tank), but they seem to have the zero personality trait in common. They nod in acknowledgement of one another and part ways saying nothing as goon number two climbs into the SUV.

Ivan grabs my bag and heads for the plane. I follow, carrying my purse and laptop, my mind wandering about what awaits me back home. He stops to hand my bag off to someone loading the belly of the aircraft, and I go up the steps to board ahead of him.

A wall of scent overtakes me as I enter the cabin.

Aidan.

I look around franticly, not seeing him anywhere. My senses are on overload.

I want nothing but him.

"Ivan," I ask, turning to him as he steps on board. "Is Aidan here?"

Ivan nods and disappears through the door in front of me, into the cockpit. I hear the bathroom door slam closed behind me at the back of the plane. His scent comes on stronger, willing me to turn around.

I feel like I'm dreaming at the sight of him, all tension releasing from me. He's in jeans and a white t-shirt. Sexy Aidan, as always. But he looks tired, as though he's been put through the wringer just as I have been since I left him. There's a mark on his right cheek. I can't tell from this distance, but it almost looks like a bruise.

Before I can say a word he's coming at me, as if pained and relieved at the same time. He folds me up in his arms, kissing the top of my head.

He takes my ponytail out, letting my damp hair drop around my shoulders, running his hands through it. He pulls me closer as he inhales, muttering words in Italian I don't yet know.

"I can't believe you're here," I manage. It feels foolish to say it, but it's the truth. I can't find any appropriate words to vocalize how much I needed him.

I'm set off as he kisses me in response. His relief at seeing me comes through in a torrent, mirroring my own. Everything in me is tingling with want, damn the fact that I'm coming off that unfortunate fate women are saddled with once a month.

I step back breathless, looking at him, trying to figure out what it could be that he's been facing in the days without me. Whatever it is, it couldn't have been good. He leads off before I can inquire.

"Are you all right? Since you hung up last night, all I could think about was getting to you."

"I was going to ask you the same," I say, ignoring the weight of my own drama. I want to find out what's eating him. I run a hand over his cheek. "What happened to you?"

"It's nothing, baby." He draws me back to him, but I pull back, not letting him distract me.

"You look exhausted, Aidan. Let's sit down."

"Yeah, I will. I will. You go ahead. I'll be right back. I have to check in with Ivan."

"What for? The guy barely speaks," I scoff.

He smiles at my remark. "Yes, but he's our pilot, so I probably ought to confirm with him where we're going."

Of course he is. I feel like an idiot.

"Great idea," I say, resigning to a seat. "I'll wait here."

I pull out my phone and text Charlie that Aidan has just shown up and I'll let him know when we land. The two-member crew is securing the door, prepping for flight when Aidan returns. I'm sitting on a long couch along the windows, as far back and away from them as I can.

"Do you want something before we take off? Water?"

"How about one of those mini whiskey bottles emptied over ice?" I'm starting to wonder if I have an issue, realizing I'm asking for a drink in the middle of the afternoon. Probably a rightful concern considering my mother's history. But right now I need something to chill out my nerves.

He glances at me, assessing.

"It's been a long three days, Aidan. I assure you, I don't make a habit of this."

"I didn't say a word."

"I know. But you were thinking it."

"Not actually. I was just wondering if you still have your period."

My eyes go wide, my mouth hanging slightly open.

"Not what you were expecting?"

"I guess not."

He moves to the bar, fills two short glasses with ice and whiskey and comes to sit beside me, leaving the drinks on a table next to us. The sofa is huge, big enough for him to stretch his legs out comfortably. I take a sip of my drink then set it back down and move closer, draping my legs across his lap and resting my head on him.

"Can you tell me what happened in California?"

He's lazed back, eyes closed, his hand moving up and down my back.

"I wish I could, but no. No need to worry. It's just business. I took care of it."

"Do your business dealings always result in having punches thrown at you?" He opens his eyes and looks down at me without responding. "What?" I say. "You didn't think I'd notice?"

His expression changes. With his complex stare somehow I feel assured not to worry, yet shut down from pushing the topic.

He leans back again, eyes closed. He isn't going to share. I'm not sure what more I can ask anyway. If it's business he's been concerned about, I can't expect him to open up about that. And there's probably not much I can do to help him.

"So," I begin, realizing there might be something he can offer me. "When you said you looked into my background, what exactly did you learn about my mother?"

He opens his eyes, fixing them on me. He was not expecting this topic. "Why?"

"Because it's my mother. I haven't seen her in almost ten years. And I'd like to at least be as informed about her as you are."

He accepts my answer and sits up a bit, wearily rubbing his forehead.

"A lot of the information I have is old. History about where she's lived, her known… friends."

"You mean the trail of men she's slept with along the way," I say flatly. "What else?"

"She's had several stints in rehab the last few years. I don't know much more, other than her last known address."

"And where was that?"

He looks at me for a moment, an expression of revelation coming over him.

"Oh God, Alexis. Did she…was she there?"

"No. Not yet, anyway. What else?"

"Her last known address was Sedona. I… I'd completely forgotten that. Did she try to see you?"

I sigh, wishing I could have just left all this behind like I wanted to. But as the plane ascends I'm opening up, telling him about my mother's supposed reform and inching her way into Jill's life.

"Baby, I'm so sorry. I should have thought of that. I've been so preoccupied…" his voice trails off, and I can tell he's struggling with his perceived oversight.

"You can't think of everything, Aidan. It's fine. *I'm* fine. I didn't have to see her, and I won't have to. Unless I decide to. That's the way I want it." I sigh in frustration. "I really just want to forget about it. At least for now."

He nods in agreement and we both sip from our glasses, comfortable in silence until there's nothing left in them but ice. He takes mine and sets it aside with his, pulling me closer.

"We are going back to New York, right?" I'm suddenly incredibly drowsy. His answer comes immediately.

"Yes," he says softly. "We're going home."

I lean in and close my eyes as the plane levels, reaching altitude. After three days of being overwhelmed with worry, exhaustion or anxiety, I finally relax, asleep in his solid arms within minutes.

I wake up stretched out on the couch by myself, a blanket tossed over me. Aidan is across from me in a chair, tapping away at his laptop.

"Did we land?" I ask.

"Almost." He responds without looking up.

"Should I have Charlie pick me up at the airport?" The question pulls his attention.

"Why?"

"I don't know, I didn't want you to expend resources to get me home."

"I was hoping you'd come back to the loft."

It relieves me to hear this, but I'm pulled in two directions, not wanting to ditch Charlie or further neglect my responsibilities.

"I should probably get back home," I say regretfully. "Charlie's been so good to take over for me, but I don't want to take advantage."

He abandons his seat, kneeling beside me where I lay stretched out on my side.

"There isn't anything pressing enough that it needs your attention at nine o'clock on a Wednesday night. You can get to work from my place tomorrow, if Charlie is okay with staying one more night."

He's waiting for me to reply, but I don't. Again I'm stuck disappointing someone I care about. He's not sure how to read me.

"Do you want to spend the night with me?"

"Yes, I do but…"

"Then what's the problem?"

"I'm not used to making choices like this. I asked Charlie to wait up for me, and I feel bad blowing him off. I've been neglecting my dog and my responsibilities for four days."

He stands, pulling his phone out of his pocket, tapping out something, then sits back down at his lap top. "You should buckle up," he orders.

"Yessir," I reply, rolling my eyes in contempt as I sit up. He doesn't take his eyes off the screen in front of him.

"I sent Charlie a text to let him know you're staying, if he's okay with it."

"You did what?"

He just looks at me, fingers still poised over the keys, then turns his attention back to the computer.

"I didn't ask you to do that," I protest. My tone doesn't hide that I'm unhappy with his typical overbearing bullshit.

"I know."

"Then why did you?"

"I'm taking the decision out of your hands. I made it for you."

"I can make my own decisions."

"Apparently not." His tone is irritable. I can feel anger building as I sit on the edge of my seat, body tensed, driven mad by his smugness.

"What the *hell*, Aidan? Can't it be enough that I want to be with you? Why do you have to be such a cocky bastard?"

He finally looks away from his screen to address me.

"I'm going to give you some unsolicited advice. If you want something, then take it. Quit worrying about what other people think when you make a decision and just decide."

"So you think what I want right now, in this scenario, is you?"

He gives me his charming *you can't fucking resist me* smile. I'm torn between frustration and craving. I'm still on the edge of my seat, panting and wanting to come at him for two very different, very conflicting reasons.

He's staring back at me, now ignoring whatever he was working on moments ago, and I can feel the familiar electric charge increasing between us. My teeth clench, pulse racing. His erratic breathing is visible.

"Don't move," he commands.

He gets up and heads for the cockpit. Moments later he's moving back through the cabin. He passes the forward seating area closest to the front of the plane, and as he does pushes a button on the wall. A glossy wood partition emerges and eases shut behind him, closing us off from the front of the plane.

I didn't even know that was there.

Between the lavish trim and technological amenities that are visible to me, this plane has all the features of a freaking spaceship.

His phone pings with a notification. He looks at it, then sets it down next to his computer.

"Charlie says no problem."

Thanks loads, Charlie. I have no idea what you've just resolved me to.

"I thought we were ready to land. Aren't we getting off?"

He's standing over me, his crotch almost level with my eyes. He looks down at me with a sinful smirk, and I realize the double entendre of what I've just uttered.

"If you're a good girl, maybe," he grins. "You didn't answer my question earlier."

"What question?"

"Your cycle. Is it done yet?"

Oh shit. I was not anticipating this.

"Almost. But..." I'm looking at the floor, leery of answering. I haven't checked things out 'down there' since we left a couple of hours ago. "Maybe we should wait."

"No," he says. "Use the bathroom if you need to."

I get up from the couch to stand and face him, looking into his eyes. They give nothing away, but standing in his gravity I can't do anything but want him. Anger for him diminishes, but now I'm pissed at myself, at my lack of willpower and inability to resist him.

"Go," he says, gesturing behind us to the facilities. "Whatever you need should be in there. Bring a towel out with you."

I head for the bathroom and do as he's asked, discarding what I need to. Washing is not as much of a requirement as I'd feared. I'm wet from yearning, and more ready for him than I thought. I take an extra moment to splash some water on my face, trying to relieve any lingering apprehension, then dry off and bring the towel with me.

He's back on the couch, silent and waiting, fully dressed except for his naked feet.

"What is it we're doing, Aidan?"

"I would bet the house you've never done this at thirty thousand feet," he says. "I wanted to take the opportunity."

I can feel my nipples harden under my shirt. Of course I've never done this. Anger has all but evaporated at the excitement of what he's proposing.

I straddle him, feeling he's already hard.

"What if I'm too mad at you?" I ask.

"I don't care," he says. "I'm going to fuck you anyway."

Whoa.

Everything in me tenses in anticipation.

He takes the towel from me and sets it next to him. In one smooth movement his hands glide up my front and remove my shirt over my head. On the way down he pulls the thin straps of my bra off my shoulders, caressing as he goes. He forces the cups down, pushing my breasts up underneath them. He's looking in my eyes, thumbs tweaking my nipples as he bites his lip. My head falls back, my breathing intensified.

"Looks like you're not too mad."

I groan in response. With a leg on each side of him I'm teased by the contents of his jeans, feeling him throb beneath me. I'm impatient to feel him inside me when I realize I'm unprepared.

"Wait...I'm not...did you bring anything?"

"I've got it covered, baby," he says grinning. He lifts his hips and I rise up with him as he pulls a condom out of his back pocket, then rests back to sitting.

I should have known.

I rip it from his hands, wanting to take control after his attempt at putting me in my place moments earlier. I have my bra off faster than he can, unwilling to wait. I'm unzipping him, pulling out his length and tossing the wrapper aside, readying him.

I step off him just long enough to remove what remains of my clothing, giving him time enough to remove his pants. He sits back down, placing the towel underneath him. Still standing I pull the bottom of his shirt up, then lift it off over his head. I stop, rejoicing at what my eyes are taking in.

Fuck me, did I miss this view.

I straddle him again, knees on the sofa, arms resting on his shoulders. I start moving down the length of him hesitantly, hands braced on the seatback behind him. I'm unsure of myself, knowing I was sore when we parted ways Sunday.

He pulls me close to him, hands moving along my back, whispering in my ear. "I missed you, baby. *Mi piace essere dentro di te.*" His tongue finds my new favorite trigger, my ear wet from him.

Just from this my inhibitions dissipate. My mouth goes slack, head back as I slide all the way down, letting him fill me up. The sensation is carnal, not the same as when he was last inside me. My need outweighs all thought.

Our upper bodies are pressed together, his arms surrounding me, hands roaming as I ride him. His hands move around to cup me as he teases my nipples with his tongue. He's watching my every reaction, a savored smile gracing him.

He leans up then, moving forward and lifting me with him to the edge of the seat. I'm overcome by him being so deep. His hand slides down from my chest, thumb tracing along the center of my stomach until it reaches my clit.

I moan, accepting his soft touch, starting to lose control. He is relentless. As much as I move in avoidance of the heightened sensation he doesn't let up, trying to drive me to climax and force me to give in.

"Yes, baby. Let go," he urges.

I slow my pace in defiance, moving up and down more deliberately. His breath catches and I let his craving build, continuing my slower speed. He moans, giving in and wrapping his arms around me, pulling me to him as I move up and down his shaft, lowering myself onto him in altering rhythms of descent.

Quick then slow, quick then slow.

I can tell he's close. He holds my hips still for a moment, breathing heavily, forcing me to stop. I lean my forehead into his, panting, and he kisses me with sweet appreciation.

"You feel so good, Alexis. All I want is to feel this, to be deep inside you." His lips trail along my breasts, his mouth overtaking me.

I moan as he moves his left arm behind me, left hand resting firmly in the middle of my back as he guides me backwards. His right hand moves up and down the center of my outstretched belly, then lands to rest between my breasts. I'm arched back, hair dangling to the floor as I let him hold me. His soft hand roams both mounds of flesh, molding over them in appreciation.

He traces a fingertip down the center of me, finding his way back to my clit.

I'm getting a head rush from being literally upside down, but somehow it's overshadowed by the sensation of him inside me, the expert way he circles my clit with the tip of his thumb. Again, he doesn't let up.

"I want to watch you. You are so beautiful when you come."

"*God... Aidan...*" I can feel a tremor building, ready to overtake me.

"That's it, come for me," he coaxes. "I'm right there with you, baby."

I pull myself back up, riding him faster, ready to release as he moans, calling out my name. I can feel him pulsating as I clench around him, giving him exactly what he wanted and coming at his whim, in harmony with him.

The same high I felt the first time with him overtakes me, intensified by our surroundings, by the exhaustion of the last few days. I'm heaving breaths, panting and completely overcome with the same euphoric rise.

My body goes limp. His arms circle me, hands moving through my hair as he breathes me in deeply.

When I regain myself, I lean back still astride him and a bit dazed. Our skin is slick from exertion. He pushes hair away from my face, my head resting in his palm as I close my eyes.

"*Bellissima,*" he says softly. He traces kisses all over my cheeks, my bare shoulders.

I can't speak. The plane is starting to bank and reduce altitude, and I lean forward into him again, letting him hold me. He rocks me in his arms, still inside me, swaying with me as we descend. I'm enraptured at the combination of sensations. The high from him, the sinking of the aircraft.

The ability to think leaves me.

"Alexis," he whispers.

"*Hmm*," I moan into his neck. Even wet with sweat, he smells incredible.

"I think I like it when you're mad at me."

34

Alexis

We've landed in a haze of fog and rain. It's cooler here than it was in Arizona, probably by thirty degrees. I'm chilled in my sleeveless shirt and shorts as we exit the plane and walk to the Lincoln. Byron is packing the trunk with our belongings and we climb into the backseat.

"I forgot to ask you if you saw my e-mail about Richardson," I say as we're shut into the car.

"I did."

"You need to replace him."

"I'd like you to be his replacement. Samira will help wherever you need her."

"You want me to...I thought..."

"You'll be handling the approvals needed to subdivide the Myers farm. It makes more sense for you to handle all the red tape on the approvals we'll need for the Center."

"I've never been closely involved in a project this big."

"Alexis." He shoots me a look of impatience. "You will be fine. You're more than capable."

As irritated as I am that this topic is closed, I'm humbled by his compliment. "I'm sorry I didn't bring this to your attention sooner. I was hoping Richardson would handle it. I should've trusted my gut."

"It's fine. I'm happier having you do it anyway."

"I...I think he and Mrs. McCall have a history," I say. I hate spreading suspected rumor, but if this is a possibility he should probably be told about it.

"I'm aware," he says.

Of course he is.

"Richardson is out of the picture," he says with certainty. "I'll be sure he understands that. He has a conflict anyway."

"What conflict?"

"Let's go over it later." He's closed his eyes, head resting back on the seat. Even in the darkness, I can see he's more drained than when we got on the plane. "I have a lot to talk to you about, but I just can't now. Tomorrow morning, before you head to the office."

"I really need to get home tonight."

That gets his attention.

"I thought we already covered this," he says. "Charlie is fine with it."

"I know. But I want to go home. I'm tired, I need a shower. And I miss my dog."

I'm flattered that he still wants me to come home with him, even after my initiation into the Mile High Club. If it was only sex he was after, he wouldn't necessarily want me with him tonight. We've already scratched that itch.

Yet, even now, I can tell he doesn't want to resign to my request.

"Aidan, you're exhausted too. I can see it. I don't know what you've been dealing with, but clearly you're in need of sleep as much as I am. I can have Charlie pick me up at your place."

"No," he says. "I'll take you home right now, if you insist that's where you want to go."

It wouldn't take much convincing for me to stay with him, but I don't disclose that. I know I need some distance. And it's the right thing by Charlie.

"Please understand," I say. "We can see each other tomorrow."

"You get your way, Alexis," he concedes, resting his head back again, "this time."

The driver door opens and Byron is instructed to head to Peaceful Drive. As he closes the door the cool air reaches us in the back, chilling me to the bone. Aidan must sense me shiver.

"You're cold? Why didn't you say something?"

He turns on the heat with the controls nearest him, then pulls me close, warming me with his body. I'm getting more and more comfortable with him, relishing every time we can be this close. I smile as goosebumps rise, then ease with the caress of his hands over my bare limbs.

I soak him up in the moment, knowing soon I'll be wishing I hadn't insisted on going home.

When we arrive at my house a half hour later, Aidan is sound asleep. I take the opportunity to stare at him. He looks so content and it warms me to see his godlike features finally relaxed. I don't want to wake him, but all wrapped up in him I know there's no other way if I want to get out. Byron exits the car, presumably to get my things and still Aidan does not stir.

I glide the back of my hand down his sore cheek, attempting to wake him gently. He's startled, waking brusquely. Maybe he forgot where he was? There's a fear behind his eyes I've never seen before.

"We're here," I say quietly.

He pulls me into him tighter, his chin resting on the top of my head.

I'm full of regret at my choice to leave him, the feeling flooding me sooner than I anticipated.

"Don't go."

"It's okay," I urge, pulling back to look him in the eyes. "I will see you tomorrow."

"Yes," he finally agrees, shaking himself as though he's coming back to his senses. "Tomorrow."

I kiss him gently, lingering for a moment, then untangling myself from him. He opens his door and gets out, adjusting himself in his pants as he does. The gesture draws a laugh from me, and he smiles in response.

"Do you want to come in?" I ask.

"Wish I could, baby. I've got a lot to get through tonight. Do you want to meet me after work? You could come by the loft when you're done for the day."

"Yes," I say. "I will."

He pulls me close as Byron returns to the vehicle after depositing my things on my front porch. I'm so cold. It's still drizzling a light rain. I can't wait to get inside but wish he was coming in with me.

"Good night, Aidan," I manage.

He kisses me with fervor. "Good night, baby." He disappears into the back of the Lincoln and the car pulls away. I'm left standing in the driveway freezing and full of sadness that, once again, he's gone.

Charlie is watching television when I come through the door, Huck sleeping at his feet.

"Hey girl," he says not looking up from his sitcom. "I thought you were staying with Mr. Money Bags tonight?"

"Change of plans," I say. "Is there anything to eat?" Huck hears my voice and stretches, then runs for me. I set down my stuff and brace myself, letting him lean in so I can love him up. He still smells good after his grooming last week.

Charlie turns from the television to look at me. My body is chilled, wet from the rain, my shoulders stooped in exhaustion.

"Lex, you look like shit," he says. "And you must be freezing. It's hardly above fifty degrees outside. Go get in the tub," he orders. "I'll make you something. What do you feel like?"

"I don't know," I resign. "Anything."

"How about some soup? I made a batch of chicken noodle Monday night when the weather turned cool."

"Sounds wonderful," I say. He comes over and hugs me, and I can't contain a few tears.

"Whoa, what's this? Are you okay?"

"I'm just...I'm overwhelmed. I'll elaborate when I get out of the tub," I promise. "Why don't you stay tonight anyway? It's already going on ten. You don't need to waste time driving home."

"Yeah, sure. I'll get some soup heated up for you. Go unpack, get yourself a bath. You'll feel better," he assures.

I nod and grab my duffel, heading upstairs with Huck following. Half an hour later, I'm warm from a bath and come down dressed in comfy pants and a light sweatshirt. Charlie's at the island with a bowl of hot soup for me and a glass of red for himself. Huck joined him long before I did, having smelled food in the kitchen.

"Do you want anything to drink?" he asks.

"Just water would be fine."

He fills a cup with ice and water from the dispenser on the refrigerator, then sits down next to me.

"Okay," he says. "Dish."

Between slurps I fill him in about the ups and downs of my days away. He is as shocked as I am that I was so close to my mother while I was out there.

"Did you want to see her?" he asks.

I consider, taking a sip of water.

"No. I panicked at the thought of running into her before I could get home. Is that terrible of me?"

He gives me a look.

"Lex. I know what you went through. It's not terrible. In fact I'd say it's expected. She wasn't a mother to you. Why would you suddenly want to see her just because your sister did?"

I know he's right, but I'm still at war with myself. Maybe I should get back in to see Dr. Flint soon. She'd make room for me. I should email her office tomorrow.

"Anyway it doesn't matter now. She won't know I was ever there, and I don't have to see her. Unless it's on my terms."

"I'm glad. I think you made the right call."

I push my empty bowl away, full and content and exhausted. Charlie perks up his tone, changing topic on me.

"How are things with Aidan? We haven't even had time to discuss. Did you guys get busy or what?"

A smile takes over me against my will.

"Ohhhh yeah," he hoots, his eyes sparkling. "Get it, girl! No wonder you're exhausted!"

"Yeah," I say, rolling my eyes. "No wonder."

"Here's to the end of your sex drought," he says, clinking his glass with mine. "Hallelujah!"

I sleep through until eight o'clock the next morning. I wake up to Huck licking my face and Charlie calling to me from downstairs. I have to think for a minute to figure out what day it is.

Thursday.

I'm meeting with Jade today.

"Get up sleepyhead," Charlie shouts. "Time for work!"

I throw my feet to the floor and shake myself awake, then pad downstairs. He's all dressed and ready to head out the door, looking handsome in dark dress pants and a blue shirt.

"I'm headed in to open up with Claudia," he says. "There's fresh fruit in the fridge and I stocked up on coffee pods while you were gone. Oh and Huck's been fed and done his business already. Take your time getting in. There's nothing scheduled today."

He's amazing.

"Thank you, Charlie." I hug him tightly, then lay a hand on his flawless cheek. "You have no idea how much it means to me, to have you looking out for me."

"Please," he teases. "I know exactly what it means. If it weren't for me you'd be well on your way to fat and not dating a sexy-as-sin mother-fucking-billionaire." He air kisses me on both cheeks. "See you soon, babe."

He heads out the door, and I'm left to my own devices. I feel much better after a good night's sleep in my own bed but decide a workout on the treadmill might help clear my head from any remaining fog. I'd sooner run outside, but it's still damp and rainy and not expected to get warm again until later.

I grab my phone from the charger in my office and glance at it. There are only a couple of emails for work, nothing that can't wait until I get to the office. There's a text from Jill saying that Derek comes home today.

She's excited and promises to call me soon. Gloria's text asks if I'm home yet. I respond that I am and suggest we get together this weekend.

Aidan sent a text at midnight, saying he wished I was there. I'm glad I hadn't seen it, or I might have driven straight there to accommodate him. I text him back with a good morning and ask if he slept well, but he doesn't respond right away.

I head for the basement to get my workout in, bringing my phone and earbuds for my running playlist. Huck follows me, and I fire up the small flat screen tv as he climbs up onto his old sofa. I mute the sound, plug in my earbuds and fire up the machine.

I'm about two miles in, panting and slowing my pace to a fast walk before I pick up speed again. Aerosmith's "Walk This Way" is loud in my ears encouraging me to keep going until I catch a glimpse of the television. I'd left it tuned to Channel Eight's late morning news, just for something to look at while I logged my usual five miles.

Melanie Adams is reporting from outside Aidan's building in Stanton. She's dressed in the requisite Channel Eight royal blue windbreaker and holding a large umbrella over her head as she carries on about something.

The station cuts to video footage, which (thankfully) takes the place of Melanie's image on the screen.

It's an amateur video, likely a cell phone recording and shows two figures walking away from a hospital. The video is shot from behind the couple. There's a well-dressed man hustling away from the building. He's escorting a woman in a dress.

What the hell does this have to do with Aidan's building?

The woman has long black hair, which is partly covered by the man's arm draped around her, shielding her in a protective posture. The couple moves to an SUV and after the lady is tucked safely inside, Aidan's face becomes visible.

He's shooing away a couple of photographers as the video pans over to show a few paparazzi lurking around the vehicle.

And then he's disappearing into the SUV too, and I catch a glimpse of Goon Number Two giving the photo-snapping vultures hell before he climbs into the driver's seat. He's the same guy that Ivan barely acknowledged yesterday when we got to the airport. Mr. Small Tank, the one who took the SUV keys from him.

What in the flying fuck?

I cancel my program on the treadmill, rip out my earbuds and grab for the cable remote, unmuting the volume. I hit the back button that rewinds live television and wait in agony to get slugged with whatever punch in the gut Melanie Asshole Adams is about to deliver. I hit play when I get to the opening shot of her standing outside his building.

"This is Melanie Adams reporting live from the Pierce Philanthropy Group Building on Harrison Street. What's hot in local news today? Well, definitely not the weather, but let's just say things *might* be heating up for a certain celebrity that now has prominent ties to our city."

The video comes on screen again as Melanie squawks through a voice over with her cheesy disposition.

"That's right Lake County ladies. Sorry to break your hearts this morning, but this video has just been released by *The Tattler Online.* The footage confirms that Aidan Pierce was seen in California with his former girlfriend, Stella Ireland, this week outside an L.A. hospital. Mr. Pierce has declined to comment, but we in Lake County wish to express our well-wishes for Miss Ireland. Fire up your online dating profiles, ladies. It looks like this eligible bachelor may be off the market once again. Reporting live from Harrison Street in Stanton, I'm Melanie Adams."

I turn off the television and sit next to Huck on the couch, speechless.

Fury, insecurities, and fear roil around in my belly coming to realizations about Aidan. Still sweaty from running, I deep-breathe myself into control.

It's just business. I took care of it.

My phone rings in my hand, but I silence it without even reading the display to see the caller's identity.

What he'd been dealing with the last few days, the thing that had made him so distraught that he almost didn't look like himself…

It didn't have anything to do with business.

And everything to do with her.

By the time I emerge from my shower with cheeks stained from crying, it's going on ten-thirty. I have five missed calls and two voicemails from Aidan. He had been the one calling me while I was downstairs. I can't bring myself to listen to the messages. No one else is trying to reach me, so I presume Gloria and Charlie haven't seen this tidbit of celebrity gossip yet. I pray neither of them does before I have a chance to tell them first.

I dress in a skirt and blouse, covering myself in make up to soften my ragged appearance.

Huck is secured in the basement and I head to the city with dry eyes. I have no more tears to give up. I'm still spent and recuperating from Arizona, and jet lag, and mind-blowing sex with Aidan.

All I want to do is forget about all of it and bury myself in everyday work.

I park in my lot, then enter the breakroom as my phone pings with a notification. It's a one-hour reminder for my meeting with Jade McCall at the Sheridan.

Shit.

I don't want to see her or give even one spare thought to Aidan or his project.

A crushing sense of foolishness overtakes me. Here I thought we were at the beginning of something and I was so completely off base. So out of my element with him and his realities.

What could I *possibly* have been thinking? I was not in my right mind. And I had not been since the minute I shook hands with him.

I bypass Charlie's office door and head for mine, closing the doors to the hall and conference room. I take a seat at my computer, sending an email request to Dr. Flint's office asking for the soonest available appointment.

There's no way I can deal with this alone, and I can't further burden anyone else in my personal life. Charlie, Gloria, my sister. They all have enough. They don't need to take on Alexis the Basket Case.

That crazy bitch needs professional help.

I remind myself I've been through far worse. I can move on from this.

It was just a fling. A way to get my sea legs back. If I ignore what was underneath, I can do this.

I'll be fine.

I have to find someone to take my place on Aidan's project. Maybe Gloria will do it. Aidan's already removed Richardson, so that's out of my hands. All I have to do is fill Gloria in on the details so far and have her agree to work with Jade. She'll go for it.

At least for me she will.

I fire off an email to Jade asking to reschedule. I tell her that her ideas were well received but I'm just returning from my trip out West for a family emergency, so Aidan or someone from his staff will be in touch with her about the event details soon.

I text Charlie that I'm here but that I don't want to be disturbed for a while and tell him I'm taking him to lunch. I can tell him about Aidan then.

My phone pings again, but this time it's a text from Ben's sister Pam asking if I'm coming up this weekend to celebrate his birthday.

Shit and double shit.

I write back furiously, holding back fresh tears. I ask her to extend my apologies to her parents but that I just can't this weekend, using the excuse that I've just returned from an unexpected trip to Arizona. She responds with a sad face, asking me if everything is okay. I assure her that it is and that I'll call her this coming week.

She'll be home from college for almost three months. There will be plenty of time to go visit them. I'm saddened that it won't be on Ben's actual birthday, which falls this Saturday. But it can't be helped.

This version of Alexis is no company for her former in-laws.

The next thing I need to check off is scheduling Myers. He has to get in my office to review and accept Aidan's purchase contract. As much as I don't want to be reminded of Aidan, it's what Myers wants and it's my job. I resolve to keep the two matters separate as I get Charlie on the intercom.

"Hey. Thought you wanted to be left alone?"

"I know. Sorry. Can you call Myers and set him up for tomorrow morning? Ten a.m.?"

"Already done," he says. "Except he's coming at nine-thirty."

"And that's why I pay you the big bucks," I quip.

"See you in forty-five for lunch."

"You got it," I reply. "Let's go to the pub across the street. It's on me."

As I'm disconnecting with Charlie my phone buzzes with two consecutive texts from Aidan.

> *Why haven't you called me back?*

> *I need to talk to you. Now.*

When I don't respond, a third comes through.

> *IF YOU DON'T CALL ME I'LL BE AT YOUR OFFICE IN TEN MINUTES.*

Jesus he can be a persistent asshole.
Clearly he thinks I've seen Melanie's news report.
Or wants to find out if I have.
I formulate my reply and text him back.

> *I'm sorry, I've been busy. I'll be out of the office the rest of the day. Something came up.*

There. Sufficiently answered and yet ignored.
His reply is immediate.

> *Alexis, what the fuck? I need to talk to you. It's important.*

> *Myers is coming in tomorrow on the purchase offer and I'll forward a signed copy to your attorney if he agrees. I'm headed out the door.*

I know he's only a couple of blocks away, but I can duck out before he can make it here if I have to.

> *I know you must have heard about Stella. I have to see you. Please.*

Stella? Oh you mean the *business* you had to take care of? *Pffft.* No thanks.

I deflect his persistence again. I refuse to acknowledge that my heart is rattling inside, ready to burst into pieces.

> *I'm going somewhere with Charlie now. Headed to Canada for the weekend to see Ben's family. They asked me a couple weeks ago. It's his birthday Saturday. I'll try to call you when I get back.*

At this he doesn't respond, and I'm confident he understands to just leave me alone.

I'm not going to allow further blows to my dignity by getting into this with him. He saw Stella and decided I didn't need to know about that which is his prerogative.

But I have rights too.

My trust in him is all but gone.

My gut is telling me to run.

The decision to forge ahead without him comes more painfully than I predicted, but I'm confident in it too.

I'm doing the right thing.

The right thing for me.

The best place for me to be is far away from Aidan Pierce.

Music Playlist for

Balance

The Amped Series: BOOK ONE

"You're So Vain" - Carly Simon
"Wake Me Up" - Avicii
"A Pirate Looks At Forty" - Jimmy Buffett
"Volare" - Dean Martin
"Cheap Thrills" - Sia
"Sunrise" - Norah Jones
"Polka Dots and Moonbeams" - Frank Sinatra
"Why Would I Cry For You" - Sting
"Midnight In Harlem" - Tedeschi Trucks Band
"Without Expression" - John Mellencamp
"#41" - Dave Matthews Band
"The Joker" - Steve Miller Band
"Long Train Runnin'" - The Doobie Brothers
"Ramble On" - Led Zeppelin
"Stop Draggin' My Heart Around" - Stevie Nicks
"Galileo" - The Indigo Girls
"Glory Days" - Bruce Springsteen
"We Found Love" - Calvin Harris featuring Rihanna
"Pillowtalk" - ZAYNE
"Caravan" - Van Morrison
"Rebel Yell" - Billy Idol
"Stay Useless" - Cloud Nothings
"Walk This Way" - Aerosmith

Author Biography

Author M.J. Woods lives in Central New York with her family and her beautiful but unclever Bernese Mountain Dog. She has worked in the legal field of a small town for over twenty years, and dreamt of becoming an author since the dawn of the home computer. She draws inspiration from the country landscape and the law, both of these woven through multiple generations of her immediate and extended family.

To find out more about the author including upcoming releases, giveaways and the latest Amped Series news, visit
www.mjwoodsbooks.com

M.J. loves hearing from readers! Please send an email through the website, or drop a line on Twitter, Instagram or Facebook.

CPSIA information can be obtained
at www.ICGtesting.com
Printed in the USA
BVOW03s1823131117
500309BV00001B/17/P